BLUE WATER

JOSEPH PARCELL

This is a work of fiction. Names, characters, organizations, places, events, and incidents are either products of the author's imagination or are used fictitiously.

Published by Inkshares, Inc., Oakland, California
www.inkshares.com

Cover design by Joseph Parcell
Interior design by Kevin G. Summers

ISBN: 9781947848566
eISBN: 9781947848573
LCCN: 2018930933

First edition

Printed in the United States of America

PART ONE

ONE

AEGRI SOMNIA

I'VE BEEN HERE before.

The old room is dark, but I know where I am. I know what the room looks like in the light. It's cold tonight; I don't ever remember feeling cold before.

The clock seems louder than usual too, almost as if I can feel every tick wash over me from behind. The old grandfather with a mocha finish watches over the room. The glass panel on the front is cracked, a single shard missing from the top left of the pane. A piece of masking tape covers the glass around the edge of the hole, a temporary attempt to make it safer.

I can't see it in the dark, but I know exactly what it looks like.

A radio plays some beautiful classical music from behind me. I couldn't name the piece, but I know I've heard it somewhere. It sounds like perfect sadness and beauty.

I'm sitting comfortably alone in an oversized, elegant-looking antique chair. The fabric is an olive-green felt. The chair itself smells like it's sat in a grandmother's house for decades, but it's worn in all the right spots to make it feel like it was made for me. The floor under my bare feet is covered by a red-and-black shag carpet, worn on all the common footpaths and poking through the spaces between my toes. I know all the details of this old house: the dirty windows, the china cabinet with less china than is necessary for a cabinet, the softball-sized, scratched rock on the mantle over the fireplace that has never been lit. I remember it all, but I can't remember how. Every time I've been here, it's been dark.

The body lies on the floor to my right. I've always assumed it was a woman because of the pastel-blue nightgown and the long fingernails with the remnants of a red nail polish, long-ago applied but never cared for. She's old too; the blue varicose veins crawling up the outside of her legs, like a parasite just under the surface of her skin, are enough to guess she's over seventy. I couldn't tell from her face because all that's left above her shoulders is a blood-soaked carpet, cracked skull, and the inside of her head spilled outside, like an egg dropped on the kitchen floor. Whoever she is, she didn't die well.

I'm sad that she's dead, no matter how right it feels.

And here's the weirdest part: the beautiful music, the comfortable chair, the rhythmic pounding of the clock, the corpse—I feel at peace, like I could be on vacation. But inevitably, my relaxed heartbeat starts to awaken. I can hear my breathing. My mouth is drying out.

I know what's coming.

Outside the house is nothing. I know that. This is all there is. The air in here is all that's left, and it's stale. It hasn't been breathed since the last time I was here. I wonder if on one of these visits it will run out. I doubt it. This always goes the same.

My skin awakens, as if listening in the silent dark, and I feel the movement of every little hair on my arms that twitches in the shifting air. My heart begins pounding harder and harder, and now the sound waves from my chest have overpowered the clock. I can hear it in my ears, along with the music and the clock, both seemingly louder than before. Now I want to leave. I want to get out of the chair and run through the kitchen, make a right at the oven, over the bad step to the patio, and out the front door. But I know I can't. There's nothing out there. Nowhere to go. And I'm terrified to move because as soon as I do, it will begin.

Static starts coming over the music, like the station is starting to go out of range and another program is intruding on the frequency. I hear voices speaking very matter of fact to each other. And even though I'm making the effort this time to understand them, I can't. I never can. Then the pulsing sound starts, quiet at first but always powerful, always somehow gigantic. There's no point in stalling anymore, it won't stop.

Boom . . . boom . . . boom . . .

I turn around to look at the radio, thinking maybe if I see it, I might be able to decipher the people speaking. It doesn't work. It never does.

And when I turn back, she's there.

The voices on the radio sound more frantic now. Something is going wrong.

In an olive-green felt chair directly in front of me sits me. It looks like a giant mirror was placed in the room, but I know she's real. She mimics every slight move I make, until she doesn't.

"What time is it?" she asks me.

I take a moment. Maybe this time I won't answer her. Maybe this time something different will happen. I sit still, and as I do a feeling of dread overcomes me. An urge rises up, like suppressing a yawn. I have to answer her. I can't do this wrong. Even if I tried.

I turn slowly to the grandfather clock behind me, now ticking louder but being drowned out by the almost painful pulsing drumbeat lying under every noise in the room. She makes the same movement, looking behind her at nothing. The people on the radio are going into a full panic now. People yelling at each other, blaming each other. I still can't make out what they're saying. All I can do is see the clock, now lit by a single light coming from the floor. A light that no electrician would ever install.

It's not a grandfather clock anymore. Now it's a gold pocket watch. The hands are both pointed at twelve. Only there's no twelve. Every number has been replaced with a Roman X. And, somehow, now it's louder than ever.

I turn back slowly and give her the same answer I always do. I know this is when it all goes to shit.

"Three o'clock."

When I turn back, she doesn't.

Boom. Boom. Boom.

She starts convulsing, like she's trying to turn back to me but her face is stuck to some invisible flypaper. This is wrong. We need to be in sync or else . . . something. I don't know what. But I know it's bad.

Then comes the gunshot. Through the static, over the music, over the arguing, barely over the ear-splitting pulsing, a single shot rings out. The arguing stops, the music stops. The static is louder than ever. I am terrified.

I don't want to look, but I know I'm supposed to. I have to. This is how it plays out.

My reflection continues to struggle desperately to get away as I look at my hands, now covered in blood. The pulsing speeds up.

BoomBoomBoomBoomBoom.

She's starting to scream. Something is holding her there. Something is hurting her. It needs to let her go or everything will break. The static and the pulsing. The pulsing and the static.

BOOMBOOMBOOMBOOMBOOM.

"Emily?" a man's voice asks somewhere in the room.

And everything stops.

The squirming reflection of myself, the pulsing, the static, the terror, all stopped. I take a deep, slow breath. It's almost over. But the worst part is starting.

The little girl is here.

A young girl, maybe seven or eight, stands in the kitchen door. She's in purple pajamas, and she's carrying a large stuffed bunny. Her long hair is tangled, like she just got out of bed, like I was making too much noise and woke her up. Her eyes are closed. As long as I've known her, and it's been most of my life, her eyes have always been closed.

"Hey kid, go back to sleep," I hear myself say.

She turns around slowly, yawns and walks back into the kitchen. There's only one bedroom in this house and it's not hers, so I'm still not sure where she goes. It's so calm, so quiet. And inside I beg for it to stay this way. But it won't. It never does. The sound is coming. I hold my breath waiting for it.

I hear her door close.

And, like an explosion, everything happens at once.

The static comes back at full blast, the pulsing shakes the house, and my reflection breaks free. She swings her face back to me, and I don't want to see it. It's going to be horrible, it's going to be painful. It's going to be death.

And every time before I see it, I wake up.

"I saw her again."

The office smells like bleach. I imagine Dr. Harper wiping down every inch of the office after one of us psychos sits on this couch. Like crazy is contagious. Her degrees, plaques, and photos of her family are all over the walls. Bookshelves full of all the same psych doctor books. I wonder if they read them all or just buy them so they look legitimate.

"You mean Carrot?" Dr. Harper replies looking up from her notebook. It's the first thing I've said in ten minutes.

"I hate your office." I say, for no real good reason at all.

"I'm sorry you feel that way, Emily. What do you think I should change?" she replies in an annoying and transparent attempt to engage me in conversation.

"I don't know." And I don't. I don't want to talk about the stupid office.

"Sure you do."

So rather than get into an interior decoration discussion, I go with, "I mean I hate coming here."

"Therapy is difficult. Anything worth doing is. Your insight into your feelings is important work."

"I miss Dr. Parker. . . No offense." It looks like I'm trying to make this personal now. Honestly, I have no idea where I'm going with this. I just don't want to talk about the dream. I don't want to talk about anything. I just want to run out the clock.

"His decision to transfer your case to me wasn't a slight against you, Emily. You do know that, right?" She waits. She wants me to make eye contact. She won't speak again until I do. I sigh to myself and look up, letting her win. She smiles and continues.

"There comes a time when we need a fresh perspective, when we've tried everything we can think of."

"You mean I was too fucked up for him," I reply sharply. So now I'm making it personal about me. A pity party. Not sure why I made this turn, it never works.

She doesn't take the bait, of course. She's too smart to try.

"So let's talk about Carrot again."

I roll my eyes. Eight minutes to go. "Fine."

"Were you awake or asleep?"

"Asleep."

"Any idea who she is?"

I don't answer.

"Were her eyes still closed? What do you think that means?" Dr. Harper asks with that tone, the one that says she knows but wants me to answer. The truth is neither of us has a fucking clue, regardless of her patronizing half smirk. I don't answer. Instead, I just look around her office, pretending I don't care. I'd love to know why Carrot never opens her eyes. It's been bothering me since I first met her, back when we were the same age. For the last twenty-five years I haven't figured it out.

"Are you still convinced she's real?"

Honestly, at this point, I don't know. If I say no, then all the time I spent trying to convince her, and Dr. Parker before her, and the orderlies and my case manager before him, and my parents before that, would be an embarrassing waste. If I say yes, I'm lying. Dr. Harper seems to understand exactly what's going through my head. She is infuriating.

"Well that's progress," says Dr. Harper smugly, like she did something with her leather chair and her notebook and her DSM-5.

"Does that mean I can stop the meds?"

"No. It means they're working. In fact, I'm going to recommend we increase your clonazepam to 2 mg."

Terrific. "I hate the way they make me feel. I can't concentrate. I feel drunk all the time."

"Then don't drive," she says, tearing off the script from her pad.

I hear the buzz, and I know without looking. Without moving my head from the pillow, I reach out and find my phone. This is my post-therapy check-in from Beverly. I manage to groan out a hello before she starts in.

"Hello, sweetie."

"Hi, Mom."

"Did I wake you up? It's 8:15 at night."

Shit, is it? I overslept again. "I work at the store at nine," I say, getting up as quickly as I can manage.

"You're still working nights? Honey, you know I don't like that. It's not safe. You're there all alone . . ." Her speech goes on while I get dressed. I've heard it all before. My name tag, where is my name tag? My apartment isn't big enough to lose anything. Most of my stuff is still in boxes, which is embarrassing because I've lived in this shit apartment for almost five years. I spent the previous half decade in a small, eight-by-ten-foot room at Sandy Shores Psychiatric Care. If it didn't fit in that room, I learned to live without it. When mom dropped off all my old things from home on move-in day, I couldn't believe how much crap I had that I used to think I couldn't live without. None of it has moved since that day, and all the boxes have just assimilated into makeshift furniture. I'm pretty sure it's all here to make space for Beverly's new sewing room.

"Honey?"

"Yeah, Mom?"

"Are you even listening?"

"No, not really." No point in lying.

She sighs. Beverly and I haven't seen eye to eye in a long time. She got a court to declare her my legal guardian long after I was eighteen, and she had me placed at Sandy Shores. Part of my work with my case manager was to try to prove to me that my mother had no choice. I agree, I probably didn't leave her many options—but, say, believing me.

"So how was your appointment with Dr. Harper?" This, of course, is the only reason she's calling me. It feels like gossip, like she wants to know but not to be helpful. Harper would say that's me being defensive, and she's probably right—although Beverly hasn't cared enough about the beginning of this conversation to even turn down the TV blaring in the background. It sounds like some medical drama. She loves those.

"It's confidential," I say, knowing that won't be enough to stop the inquisition.

"Ha ha. You know what I mean. Do you still feel like you're getting better?"

This is something my mom will never understand. She thinks schizophrenia is like a cold. With enough therapy and orange juice, one day I'll be her daughter again. I've done my best not to jump over a table at her when she flippantly just assumes I could stop if I really tried. I haven't always been successful.

"She prescribed more pills."

"More?" Now it sounds like mom is sitting in the living room directly in front of her hospital show. The worst part is, she called me.

"Well a higher dosage."

"And is that helping?"

"I guess so." Where is that name tag?

"Sounds like she knows what she's talking about," she passive-aggressively rubs in my face.

"I guess. So how's work?" I ask, trying to change the subject to anything else.

"Fine," Beverly counters, not giving me an out. She sits there waiting for me to continue about therapy. Or she's really into her show.

"Hey, Mom, can you turn down the TV? It's hard to hear you." My mom doesn't respond. And instantly my stomach drops because I know why.

"I'm not watching TV, honey. I'm on the dock."

I still hear them. Something has gone wrong.

"Honey? Are you hearing things again?"

Yes.

"No, I think it's just a bad connection. I dropped my phone in the toilet a week ago, and it's been messed up ever since. The guy at the store said my warranty didn't cover it, but he could cut me a deal on a new one when my contract is up in three weeks, so I'm trying to tough it out." That's the key: lie with lots of boring detail.

"That happened to your father once. They told us to put it in a bag of rice." My mom doesn't remember telling me that story before. I knew my mom would jump at a chance to help out with something she didn't think I'd know. I've gotten pretty good at lying to my mom over time. I tell myself I'm saving her the grief of worrying about something she couldn't understand. That may have been true years ago. Now I'm saving myself.

"Hey, Mom, I have to get ready for work. Can I call you later?" That last bit is just me being polite. I'm not going to call her later. We both know that.

"Sure, Em. Love you."

"Love you too, Mom." It's not a lie, but I still have to force it out.

Hanging up, I finally find my name tag sitting in my purse, the most sensible place to put it and also the last place I look.

Sitting beside it, a white paper bag stapled shut on the top, stamped blue with the title "St. Mark's Pharmacy." I tear open the bag and grab the small orange bottle. EMILY HUNTER CLOZARIL (CLOZAPINE) 500 MG. REFILLS 03. I wonder how many orange bottles I've had my name on in my life. I'll bet you could build a palace out of them.

Do not drive until you understand how this medication affects you. Do not operate heavy machinery.

I put the bottle back down. I can barely handle an overnight shift on half this dosage. We're rolling the dice tonight.

Fucking Jenny.

I get it, I'm late. I'd be pissed too. But when it's Jenny, I don't seem to feel as guilty. Jenny is obnoxiously nineteen and has always been on my case. She doesn't know about me, at least officially. Gil, the store manager, has been discrete. Maybe she feels something is up, maybe she's jealous that there might be something interesting about me. Maybe she hates this job too and takes it out on me. I don't really care.

She taps her watch while staring at me wide-eyed, asking without speaking if I'd ever heard of a clock before. I give her a glance back as if to say, "You have no idea what I've been through, but I'm lucky to be alive and only fifteen minutes late to work."

She rolls her eyes and plucks off her name tag. She grabs her purse and pulls a cigarette, menthol, to her perfect little ex-prom queen face, not bothering to get outside before lighting it. She obviously has somewhere important to be and has to get started giving herself cancer as soon as possible.

I can't stand the smell of cigarettes. At Sandy Shores, everyone smoked. I'm not sure if mental illness comes with a nicotine addiction or if everyone did it because it was one of the only things they had that was their own. Our rooms had to pass inspection every day at 11:00 a.m., our food was all prepared, the TV was scheduled, our money was held in the main office, the rides into the community were scheduled and supervised, and the orderlies—sorry—"residential technicians" were on permanent power trips. They learned pretty quickly that they couldn't bully me, which made them bully the more vulnerable of us even more. Honestly, it made me feel worse. That's how they got to me.

Otherwise, we had nothing but time to fill. Mental health patients don't always make for the best conversation, so I spent the majority of my time alone, trying to distract myself from everything going on in my head and in my home. I learned to crochet, made jewelry, I even tried to teach myself Latin just to alleviate the boredom that would drive the most neuro-typical person into sharing a bunk bed with me at the nuthouse.

The only thing most of us had a choice in is when we could go out to the courtyard and smoke. We were all on fixed SSI payments and given an allowance of thirty-eight dollars a month, so some people bought bulk bags of tobacco and rolled their own, often selling them to the other residents. Other people bought dollar-store cigarettes, which I imagine are the only consumer product on Earth that are less healthy than a Marlboro. The smell always brings all of it back. I feel my shoulders sink every time I breathe it in.

Maybe that's why I hate Jenny. Or maybe it's because to her a bad day is no Wi-Fi on her newest bedazzled iPhone, the one with the screen she carelessly shattered but cannot remember how. She'll never know how bad a day can really be. And I hate her because she'll never know that she'll never know. Her problems are the problems I dream of having but never will.

It's not really her fault. Fuck her anyway.

The door chime rings as Jenny scuttles off, and I am alone. Gil's Corner Grocery is in an old, worn building complete with creaky wood floors and bricks that are falling off the back of the south wall. Most of our customers have been coming here for the last fifty years, back when Gil Sr. bought the building. Now that Gil III is running it, it's been outpaced by the Walmarts and Meijers of the world. Old people's fear of change is really the only thing keeping this small market afloat. Gil III knows that. The truth is, he doesn't want the store, he never did. He's counting the minutes until our customers die out and the store goes under, then he's free. His light at the end of the tunnel is literally the light at the end of other people's tunnels.

I wonder what that feels like. Hope.

I know I'm never going to escape. No medication or therapy is ever going to get rid of this. Best-case scenario is I live with it and function as a member of society. Currently, I'm at best-case scenario. And I'm miserable.

When I was a kid, I thought it was fun. I thought I had a vivid imagination and could see things grown-ups couldn't. Then when my friends at school started to think I was the weird kid, it wasn't so fun anymore. Now my parents didn't understand me and my classmates ostracized me. I was alone.

Well, almost. There was always Carrot.

The night I met her, I was eight, asleep in my room under the brand new *Jem and the Holograms* bed sheets I had gotten for my birthday. Around 2:00 a.m., I woke up to someone screaming. I opened my eyes and jumped like I was on fire, and there she was, lying in bed with me. Her eyes were closed like she was asleep, but she was squirming and crying like she was in the middle of some horrible night terror. She was wearing her purple pajamas and cuddling with a dirty-looking stuffed rabbit, which was obviously offering her no comfort. What happened next I've never understood. I never screamed, I never panicked, I never even questioned who this random little girl in my bed was. I just put my arm over her and hugged her tight, shushing in her ear. I protected her, comforted her. And almost instantly I could feel her muscles loosen, and her screaming stopped. She relaxed, and I cuddled her the rest of the night. When I woke up, she wasn't there.

My mom was making cinnamon rolls, so it must have been a Saturday. I could smell them baking from my room. I got up and found I had wet my bed. I hadn't done that since I was just out of diapers. I remember pulling all the sheets off the bed and getting dressed, then throwing all of it down the clothes chute. I went downstairs, and my mom asked why I was already dressed. I don't remember what my excuse was. I asked my mom who the little girl was. My mom asked me what little girl I was talking about, and I told her that the girl's name was Carrot. I could tell my mom thought it was cute that I had an imaginary friend—that is, until I mentioned that I couldn't believe she slept through all the screaming. Our troubled relationship began that Saturday morning over cinnamon rolls.

"Just this."

I look up to see his face. Kyle. I'd been working on a crossword book for God knows how long. I couldn't afford an iPhone like everyone else who works the overnights here. I check the time to see it's 3:16 a.m. I hope he hasn't been standing here long while I was a million miles away.

Kyle is a regular here, the youngest customer we have by at least thirty years. He's wearing the dark-blue scrubs again before heading into work at the hospital. I love the dark-blue scrubs, especially when he's got the little bit of stubble going on.

"Hey. Another late night, eh?" I say, trying to keep it cool.

"Wouldn't miss it," he says with a smile. That smile, the stubble, and the dark-blue scrubs. My lucky night.

"I hear those things aren't good for you," I say, pointing out the five-hour energy supplement he's set on my counter. I hadn't really heard that.

"Really? Something that's supposed to give you five hours of unnatural energy that comes in a little bottle isn't good for you?"

I laugh. Maybe too hard. He doesn't care.

"I've got fifteen minutes until I start shift number two. I guess the risk of damage to me is better than falling asleep and giving a catheter to the wrong patient." And there's something in his eyes after he says it. Regret? Like he wishes he hadn't mentioned catheters. Is . . . is he flirting back? I smirk and tilt my head down slightly, like I've seen in the movies over and over. I realize immediately it felt forced and awkward, and now I wish I hadn't done it.

"Well, good luck with the rest of your shift," says Kyle as he picks up the small bottle and heads for the door.

"Yeah, you too," I say, completely out of ideas for anything else. I want to ask him out, I want to grab his ears and kiss him, I want him to take me out of this store and this life and build us a hut in Fiji and live out our lives eating coconuts and fish together. I'm pretty sure I'm going to have to be satisfied just dreaming of those dark-blue scrubs, the stubble, and the smile.

I don't want to stare as he leaves because he could see me in the reflection of the dirty storefront window, so I look back at my book, hoping he reconsiders and asks me out.

Fifteen down: *One Flew Over the Cuckoo's Nest* nurse.

"Emily?"

"Yeah?" I say, looking up over-enthusiastically. The sound of him saying my name is breathtaking.

Only it wasn't him. It wasn't anyone. I'm all alone.

No no no no no.

My ears begin ringing painfully as my eyes begin to water and burn. It's like looking into a dust storm. My vision starts to close to a single point, and I can hear my heartbeat, I can feel it in my neck. Everything gets really cold, but I can feel myself sweating.

This is going to be a bad one.

I close my eyes, try to control it, try to calm down, try to breathe, try to . . .

Breathe. Breathe . . .

The ringing is so intense I cover my ears. I know it's useless, I know it's already inside. I can't help it, it's like fishhooks pulling my eardrums.

And then it stops.

All I can hear is my breathing, and it sounds like I'm breathing into a bucket, the sound reverberating all around me. My vision is still blurry from my tears, but not blurry enough to miss what's directly in front of me.

Me.

Like another reflection, except this time it's facing away from me, like I'm watching a TV screen projecting from a camera behind me. And she's stuck again, shaking, convulsing violently. I move my right arm, she twitches hers to the same position. This isn't right, this is all wrong.

This has never happened while I was awake before.

Sure, I've seen things, I've heard things. Carrot I almost exclusively saw while I was awake most of my life. But this reflection thing is new, usually contained in a recurring nightmare. Never like this. Never backwards. Never outside of the dream.

I want to scream, but I'm too afraid to try. Instead, I tell myself to calm down because I know it isn't real. It's in my head. It has to be, right?

Right?

The reflection shakes harder now. She's trying to turn around to face me. I know somehow that I really don't want her to. I don't want to see her face, not after she shakes. How I know this, I couldn't say. I feel it, like it's some psychotic instinct.

"Emily," I say to myself, though my words sound like I'm underwater, "wake up."

She's torn her arm free of whatever held it. She's close now. I'm going to see it. I'm going to see it.

"Emily!" I say again, "Wake up!"

Her leg swoops around unnaturally, as if there were no bones in it restricting how far it could go. Or as if she broke them to get loose.

"Emily! Wake up!"

But that time it wasn't my voice. And as I blink, it's over, and Gil III is standing in front of me with two other employees.

The sun is out. It's 7:32 a.m. I've lost four hours. I haven't lost time since before Sandy Shores.

"Honey, are you OK?" he asks, genuinely concerned, while Becky the assistant manager and Dan the morning shift try not to laugh. I'd normally give him shit for calling me "honey," but I can't stop shaking. I feel cold, like all the blood has left my body. And my stomach starts to churn. I notice a small pile of cash and paper notes on the desk.

"Yeah . . . yeah, I'm fine," I say in a manner no human should ever believe.

It's obvious he doesn't. Gil is aware of my situation. At least a little bit. I told him when I got hired that it wouldn't be a problem, so now I'm a liar to Gil too.

"Why don't you take the rest of the morning off. We can do the receipts," he says, and I nod in acceptance. I grab my purse and my crossword book.

The crossword book. It's destroyed. It looks like I took the pen and carved a single word into it:

CONIR.

I wish this was the first time this had happened. It's not shock I feel or even confusion. Just disappointment.

I walk out the front door and pitch the crossword book in the trash can right outside the door, and as I do, the smell of the cigarette butts in the ashtray on top of the can wafts up to my face. I take two steps away pretending it wasn't enough to put me over. Two steps is all I can manage before I rush back to the can and promptly vomit what little I ate last night into the front flap. The cigarette smell is overpowering at this distance, and I start dry heaving.

I collect myself and walk slowly and steadily toward the bus stop. I definitely rolled the dice last night. Looks like I lost.

TWO

QUEM DEUS VUIT PERDERE PRIUS DEMANTAT

"I THINK I'M going to lose my job."

Dr. Harper seems unfazed. "Why do you say that?" she asks, as if it's a preconditioned response.

"I lost time again," I say, and now she's interested. I wasn't her client last time this happened, but it's detailed heavily in my case history. I'm sure she's feeling a little excited now that she gets to have a shot at it. My theory is that psych doctors are more collectors of insane experiences than helpers. Everyone I've seen has been thrilled to get a real nutjob like me to add to their repertoire. No one actually ever cared, except Dr. Parker.

"Have you been taking your medication?"

"Yes."

"Did you see or hear anything this time?"

I don't answer. I don't make eye contact either. I just play with the Rubik's Cube I got off her desk. That's a mistake.

"Did you take your new dosage?"

I don't answer again. Doesn't matter. She's going to blame it on the meds.

"So, you didn't take your medication last night, which resulted in a major break in reality—the result of which is that you might lose your job. Am I interpreting your silence correctly?" Smug bitch.

I don't want to talk anymore. I just want to run out the clock again.

"Emily?"

"I can't go to work all doped up. They make me feel horrible, and I already was low on sleep and had to work a double."

And silence. She's waiting for me to look up, so I do.

"Take your meds."

My eyes fall back down at the Rubik's Cube in my hands. Turning it, twisting it, knowing I'll never solve it. I'll never make it right again.

"Emily."

I look back up, sighing incredulously.

"Say it," she says.

"I'll take the fucking meds."

"Thank you."

"So that's it?" I say, tossing the puzzle aside. "For the rest of my life I have to take these goddamn pills that make me feel like shit because I can't go fifteen minutes without flipping out?"

"I do agree it's odd that an episode occurred so quickly after a missed dose. How long did it take last time?"

Magic Marker. The smell is the first thing I remember. I had fallen down the stairs somehow, and my face was sticky with blood that was staining my mom's carpet. There were police in the living room. My mom came running up to me at the landing and took the marker out of my hand. She had been crying before I fell, her eyes stained red. The cops were already making their way to me, flashing lights in my eyes. I didn't know what was happening, I didn't know what day it was. I asked my mom why the police were here, but she was too busy looking at the upstairs hallway I had just fallen from. I had written in black permanent marker all over the walls one single nonsense word over and over:

CONIR.

"Five days." I reply.

"Breaks like this occur usually around times of stress or anxiety. Emotionally charged situations. Do you recall what happened before you lost time?"

"Kyle came in," I say. Harper smiles knowingly. "No, bullshit. He's cute, but I wasn't in an 'emotionally charged situation.'"

"It's OK if you have feelings for him."

"I don't," I lie.

"Attachment is a sign of improvement."

"I don't," I lie again.

"I'd encourage it."

"Oh, hi Kyle. I'm Emily. I'm an Aries, I like movies, and I'm a diagnosed schizophrenic with full-on auditory and visual hallucinations, as well as not one but two major mood disorders. Would you like to carry my baggage?"

Dr. Harper isn't impressed, but she has no retort. She knows I'm never going to date anyone. Hell, I hate hanging out with myself; why would anyone else enjoy it?

Harper looks at the clock. Time is mercifully up. She makes me promise to take my medication one more time, gives me some "recovery takes responsibility" horseshit, and sends me on my way.

My meeting with Gil the next day goes just like I predicted. He calls me into his office and shuts the door, speaking to me in hushed tones. It's sweet, him being this protective of my little secret. I guess it's not so secret anymore. Still, he's trying.

"How are you feeling, Emily?" The first thing he asks is about me, not about what happened, although I know that's foremost on his mind.

"Better," I answer, looking at the floor. It's a move I learned a while back, looking ashamed, like you're the victim of your own mind but it's too shameful to say anything about it. I use it on my mom all the time. This time, though, it's legitimate. I hate letting Gil down. He's been nothing but nice to me since he hired me. He never made me feel weird or different. I guess that's over now. I've left him no choice.

He doesn't say anything. He just turns to our closed-circuit monitor with the tape of last night's shift. He pops in an old VHS tape, and there's the back of my head on the bottom of the screen. It's the register camera. The date and time are stamped on the video feed. He begins fast-forwarding the tape, and I move out from behind the counter and mop the floor in about thirty seconds, restock the beer fridge in about a minute, and dust the shelves in twelve seconds flat. Then I sit behind the counter working on my crossword puzzle book at around 2:39 a.m.

He stops fast-forwarding at the 3:14 a.m. mark. I get to see Kyle come in, and from this perspective I can see his face. We have a conversation at the counter that's over far quicker than it felt last night. He walks to the door, we say goodbye, and he turns back and starts talking to me again. If I was angry with myself before, I'm furious now. Not only did he actually turn back like I was dreaming he would, but I never answered him. I've stopped moving. This is completely humiliating. And, of course, there's no audio on the tape, so I can't hear what he's saying. He gives up after a second and leaves, I'm sure believing I'm purposefully ignoring him. He walks out with a hop in his step like he's embarrassed. Now I'm sure he was asking me out. I'm so sure this couldn't get worse.

Then, of course, it does.

I don't move. For the next four hours, I don't move. Gil fast-forwards the tape and I don't move, I don't twitch, nothing. I thought I moved my arm when I saw the reflection of myself, but I guess that was in my head too. I never covered my ears, I never winced in pain. I just stopped.

Customers come in throughout the night. Some try in vain to buy groceries from me, others just take what they want and walk out. Some leave cash and notes about what they took. No one bothers to call an ambulance about the catatonic woman in the store. One scumbag waves his hand in front of my face for a couple minutes, and when I don't respond, he squeezes my tits. Then, laughing, he walks out with a case of beer and a handful of the cash that had accumulated to that point. Gil is very purposefully not making eye contact with me after that.

Then on the tape, I see Gil walk in. He's talking to me but not looking at me, probably asking how the night went. I don't answer. He comes over to me and starts talking, and I jolt awake. The rest I remember. And, lucky me, after I leave the tape clearly shows me throwing up in the trash outside. I walk away and, on the tape, Gil shakes his head in shock and disgust. He stops the tape at once; he probably didn't want me to see that part. I don't blame his reaction.

"So let me start," I say, trying to cut off whatever speech he's got planned. "My psychiatrist put me on some new medication recently. Apparently I didn't take it correctly, and this was the result. I just came from her office before I got here, and she told me what I did wrong." All not technically a lie so far. "So this shouldn't happen again." Almost made it.

"Does she know what happened?"

"I didn't take the right dosage. She says I was lucky it wasn't worse."

As he wrinkles his kind and worried face, I can see he's buying it. I can't tell if what I'm feeling is relief or shame, but I'm sure it's some perfect combination of both.

"Emily, what happened . . . it can't happen again."

"I understand." Still employed.

"This is a first and final warning." I can tell that pained him to say. I don't know why; I'd have fired me.

"Thank you. And thank you for understanding."

"See you tonight, darling." And again, I'd call him out on being so familiar, but now just doesn't seem like the time.

My bathroom mirror steams up almost instantly, the price of a small bathroom with no ventilation. I consider turning the radio on after taking off my clothes but decide against it. No more radios for a little while.

The little orange bottle is still there, sitting on the counter, staring at me as if to say, "You promised."

Here's the thing about psychotropic medication: it's good for your mind but horrible for your body. When I was at Sandy Shores, we'd have to get all our meds at the office window after standing in line. I started getting there first because the amount of time it took to pop everyone's meds was obnoxiously long. Usually there were one or two pills designed to treat whatever mental disorder the resident had and about nine or ten others to treat the side effects from those pills. Something to treat weight gain, something to treat insomnia, something to treat loss of appetite, something to treat depression, something to treat acne, something to treat cramping, something to treat nausea, something to treat incontinence. . . The cure was worse than the malady.

Which is why I'm not taking these pills tonight.

I step into the shower, and it's too hot. It's always too hot, but my shower has two temperatures: too hot or North Atlantic iceberg. I've gotten used to taking fast showers that involve a lot of wiggling to keep the water off of one part of my body for too long. I begin to wash my face at the end of the hot shower dance, and I notice the water stinks. Terrific. Who knows what pipe is leaking into what now. This apartment complex should be condemned, but the landlord is on the city council. I'm not sure how that's not a conflict of interest.

It smells like burnt meat. What would make the water smell like burnt meat? I wipe the soap off my eyes hoping not to see a brown tint to the water.

There is a face directly in front of me, a pale, featureless, motionless face, like a death mask, floating unattached to anything. And in an instant I've jumped through the shower curtain, tearing it off the rod. My leg hits the toilet, and I stumble crashing to the floor surrounded in nothing but a moldy curtain. The water is spraying out of the shower, spilling onto the floor as I had hit the nozzle on the way out. I look up at the shower, vaguely aware that I may have sprained my wrist.

There's nothing there.

I take some deep breaths as I untangle myself from the curtain and shut the water off. I am now totally aware that I have definitely sprained my wrist. With my other hand, I reach up, grab the bottle, pop the lid, and swallow four pills without water.

THREE

IN SOMNIS VERITAS

BIRDS ARE CHIRPING. Kids are playing outside. The sun is going down. I used to play outside when I was a kid. When the streetlights come on, go home. Remember? There's a sign in front of me as I sit on a bench. I wonder if Kyle is going to the store tonight to get his energy drink. I wish I didn't have to work tonight because I sprained my wrist, but it doesn't hurt anymore. Nothing hurts right now. The sign says STOP.

Just stop, Emily. Just stop.

I feel thoughts running through my head like water down a hill. I can't stop them. I can't catch them. This new dosage is too high.

Just stop.

"Are you coming or what?"

"Yeah, I'm coming," I say to the bus driver. I get on the bus on my way to Gil III's store.

By the time I get there and get my name tag on and get behind the register, I can convince myself I'm OK, but I know I'm not, like being drunk and convincing yourself you can still

drive home. But I feel like I'm handling it
breathing and staring too hard at objects in

"It's OK, I got it," says the customer
knocked over a donation can in front of the
giving her the change for whatever she just
enough to grab it for me, which is good bec
could bend over to grab it right now.

"You OK, sweetie? You don't look so
everyone call me "honey" or "darling" or "sw
pens in this building.

"Yeah, cold medicine," is all I say. Hopef
a full excuse. She smiles and walks to the do
just sold her.

"Orange juice," says the next customer.
and I'm acting like I'm stoned out of my mi

"Orange juice to you too," I say. He sm
Emily.

"Cold medicine will just make it easie
cold. Your body needs vitamin C."

"My body needs a lot of things," I reply
before the filter between my mind and my m
to stop me. I can still feel the words in the air
that felt like hours it takes him to smile and

"Just that? No energy drinks?" I say, poi
he's buying and desperately trying to change

"Yeah, I'm off tonight."

"So . . . you just needed eggs at 3:00 a.m

He looks sheepish. That's when it dawn
to see me. I'm not even nervous, and inside
I'm completely keeping my cool. Maybe thes
after all.

THREE

IN SOMNIS VERITAS

BIRDS ARE CHIRPING. Kids are playing outside. The sun is going down. I used to play outside when I was a kid. When the streetlights come on, go home. Remember? There's a sign in front of me as I sit on a bench. I wonder if Kyle is going to the store tonight to get his energy drink. I wish I didn't have to work tonight because I sprained my wrist, but it doesn't hurt anymore. Nothing hurts right now. The sign says STOP.

Just stop, Emily. Just stop.

I feel thoughts running through my head like water down a hill. I can't stop them. I can't catch them. This new dosage is too high.

Just stop.

"Are you coming or what?"

"Yeah, I'm coming," I say to the bus driver. I get on the bus on my way to Gil III's store.

By the time I get there and get my name tag on and get behind the register, I can convince myself I'm OK, but I know I'm not, like being drunk and convincing yourself you can still drive home. But I feel like I'm handling it by focusing on my breathing and staring too hard at objects in the room.

"It's OK, I got it," says the customer in front of me. I knocked over a donation can in front of the register when I was giving her the change for whatever she just bought. She's nice enough to grab it for me, which is good because I don't think I could bend over to grab it right now.

"You OK, sweetie? You don't look so good." Why does everyone call me "honey" or "darling" or "sweetie?" It only happens in this building.

"Yeah, cold medicine," is all I say. Hopefully that counts as a full excuse. She smiles and walks to the door with whatever I just sold her.

"Orange juice," says the next customer. Of course it's Kyle, and I'm acting like I'm stoned out of my mind.

"Orange juice to you too," I say. He smiles. Score one for Emily.

"Cold medicine will just make it easier to live with the cold. Your body needs vitamin C."

"My body needs a lot of things," I reply with a smirk, right before the filter between my mind and my mouth has a chance to stop me. I can still feel the words in the air during the second that felt like hours it takes him to smile and laugh it off.

"Just that? No energy drinks?" I say, pointing out the eggs he's buying and desperately trying to change the subject.

"Yeah, I'm off tonight."

"So . . . you just needed eggs at 3:00 a.m.?"

He looks sheepish. That's when it dawns on me: he's here to see me. I'm not even nervous, and inside I'm shocked that I'm completely keeping my cool. Maybe these meds are alright after all.

"So when is your next night off?" I ask, holding eye contact with him instead of shyly dropping my gaze as I've done every other time. Who is this confident woman all of a sudden?

"Um, Wednesday," he replies.

"I'm off Wednesday too."

He gives me a strange look. "Don't you work Wednesdays?" How sweet, he knows my schedule.

"I can be off Wednesday," I say, still looking into his beautiful green eyes. He's trying to keep a calm exterior, but those eyes are betraying him. "I can also be at Giovanni's at eight o'clock." I don't know who this girl talking is, but I think she's my new best friend.

"Yeah? So can I."

"It's a date then." Holy shit, it's a date?!

"OK . . . well, I'll see you then," he says as he starts toward the door.

"Don't forget your eggs," I say. He realizes he left them on the counter and comes back.

"Goodnight," I say with a smile that would have turned me on if I had seen it.

"'Night," he says fetching the eggs.

Flawless.

And then it was Wednesday.

I never go out, so I have nothing that looks appropriate for a date. There's a skirt-and-blouse combo that my mom bought me for job interviews, but it was only ever worn once when I got the job at Gil's, and it's been slowly decaying, wrinkled and neglected on a hanger in the back of my closet ever since. I was heavier when I left Sandy Shores because all they ever served us was cheap and loaded with sodium and sugar. I'm pretty sure if it weren't already out of style and business casual, it would be at least two sizes too big. I don't even think I've ever washed it.

I settle on my nicest jeans and an old *Momentary Lapse of Reason* tour T-shirt my mom got in Cleveland and passed down to me. Maybe it will make me look edgy. It seemed apropos. This whole idea of a date seems against my better judgement.

There isn't a "what if" I fuck this up. I'm terrified of what happens "when."

Part of me wants it to go wrong, so I can tell Harper I was right all along, that I'm too loony to even attempt to be human. Part of me wants to sabotage my entire life and any chance I have at happiness just to prove a point. It would be easier that way. Nothing changes.

The downside is, of course, nothing changes.

The Clozaril is staring me in the face on my bathroom counter. I was on this when I crushed it at the store two days ago, but I don't want to come off drunk. Take it? Don't take it?

I pour two pills into my hand, which is technically half my nighttime dose. Then I swallow one of them.

Giovanni's is the nicest restaurant I've ever been to, and I am severely underdressed. I'm twenty minutes late as well because I didn't know the bus schedule to get here. Also, I'm pretty sure I forgot deodorant.

Kyle stands up when I finally arrive and pulls out my chair. He shaved the scruff. I appreciate the effort, but he looks better with it. He's traded in the scrubs for a black suit jacket and a bright-blue button-down. It balances out.

"I'm sorry I'm late," I say, sheepishly.

"Were you late? I hadn't noticed. I just got here too," he lies. The bread plate is almost empty. He's trying to be nice.

"Thanks for inviting me out," I say awkwardly.

"Me?" he feigns offense. "This was all you. All I wanted was some eggs."

I smile, not just with my lips, but I feel my eyes light up as well. It's too early to have any hope this won't be a nightmare. That's not stopping me.

"I think we're the youngest people in here," I say, observing the plethora of white hair and bad toupees, and speaking just to avoid silence. "I feel like this is somewhere my parents would go. Well, if they . . . weren't . . ." And there's our first overshare of the night.

Thankfully, he smirks at me. "Divorced or dead?" he asks bluntly.

"Divorced."

"Me too. Twice, actually for my dad. How old were you?"

"Twelve," I respond.

"Ah, the perfect age to blame yourself for it."

"Yeah, well, I did," I say.

"Most kids do. They're usually not right."

"Usually," I reply with a bit of levity. "I was . . . troubled as a kid. Well . . . not just as a kid." And there's our next overshare. Jesus Christ, Emily. Stop talking.

"Oh no, you're not a psycho, are you?" he asks jokingly. I don't laugh.

The sweat starts around my temples.

"So how's the bread?" I ask, deflecting.

"Oh. Uh . . . Did you want some?" he moves a small plate with some yellow liquid and green flecks of something toward me.

"No, no, I'm good." I'm not sure what that stuff is, but I'd rather not look more stupid than I already do. I notice I'm grinding my teeth, and I wiggle my jaw from left to right to try to ease the tension in my face.

I hear Harper's voice in my head. *Breaks like this occur usually around times of stress or anxiety. Emotionally charged situations.*

Keep it together.

He regrets this already, she says.

"So what's good here?" I ask, my voice quivering slightly as I try to open the menu, not realizing immediately that it's only one-sided and doesn't open. None of the prices end in *.99* and instead are just very large whole numbers in a fancy-looking font. *You showed up to this restaurant in a Pink Floyd T-shirt and are asking this man who probably only wants you for what's in your pants to pay more than you make in a week for you to eat. If you don't at least blow him, he's going to hate you.*

"I don't know, I've never been here before," he answers. *You trapped him. He's looking for the exits.* I look down over the menu, searching desperately for something I recognize that is also less than ridiculously expensive. The house salad is seventeen dollars.

My stomach is less butterflies, more jellyfish. Everything inside me feels like it's being lightly electrocuted. I'm holding my breath, and I don't even realize it.

Harper's voice is berating me now. *You're right, Emily. This was a terrible idea. Who are you trying to kid? He's judging you. He knows. You're a lunatic, and he knows, and he wants to run away from you and laugh at you and tell his friends about the time he went to an expensive restaurant with a cheap idiot psychopath who couldn't even dress herself and didn't know how to eat bread, and they'll laugh at you too. He knows. He knows.*

The waiter walks up to take my drink order, and I just go with water "for now." Water is most likely going to be my main course.

"So," he says, looking up with that smile of his, "Emily—I know that from your name tag. What's your last name?"

"Hunter," I say, and I realize my eyes are starting to water.

"Emily Hunter," he says, as if judging the resonance of my name. "So my next question is: who are you?"

So my next question is: who are you? That wasn't Harper. That was a man's voice.

My hand is moving on my lap, back and forth in swift little strokes. If there were a pen in it, it would be tattooing a single word into my thigh.

"Not much to tell really," I say back. I feel my face flush. He smirks at me, thinking I'm getting embarrassed, not realizing I'm desperately clinging to sanity.

"Come on," he prods. "There's something special about you."

I manage a little chuckle. "'Special.' That's the nice way people say it."

Boom. Boom. Boom.

"Say what?" he asks with a cute little curious twitch to his face.

Breathe, Emily. *Die, Emily.* Breathe. I can smell every plate of food in the restaurant. I feel the air move every time the waiter opens the door to the kitchen.

She's coming.

"You wouldn't believe me," I say. I look down to my lap to avoid eye contact, and I can see my veins bouncing with every pulse in my wrist.

"Oh, Ms. Hunter. You'd be surprised what I'd believe."

Oh, Ms. Hunter. You'd be surprised what I'd believe, the man's voice repeats.

My throat dries out, and the waiter hasn't brought my water yet. My eyes dart around the restaurant for him.

She's here.

In the back of the restaurant, near the bar trimmed with imitation ivy, a middle-aged couple sits at a table enjoying a meal and each other's company. He is wearing a wedding ring, she is not. They look hungrier for each other than they do for the hundred dollars worth of entrees in front of them. They don't see the little girl standing on their table, her eyes closed tight but somehow still staring me down.

Please, no.

"Emily?" asks Kyle.

Emily?

"Would you still love me if you knew I was insane?" I hear myself say out loud.

Kyle staggers, I'm sure both at the *l* word as the *i* word.

He doesn't love you.

I know that. How could he? I'm a fucking disaster.

Carrot is on the floor now. She's standing still but keeps getting closer. Her hand reaches out to me.

She needs you.

She needs me.

"Emily, I . . . I . . ." Kyle says as he searches for anything to say. "Are you OK? Are you . . .?" He looks behind me to see what I'm staring at. He can't see her either. No one can. No one but me.

I am special.

"Why do you think you're insane?" he asks, and somewhere in the fog that has enveloped my mind, I notice he didn't have a problem with the word *love*. I'm not sure if that's better or worse.

"I don't. They do. They all do. But they're wrong."

She has to show you something.

"She has to show me something." Maybe I said that out loud too.

Kyle leans in and whispers something to me. I don't know what. Carrot is directly behind him now.

"Leave." I hear myself say. Kyle looks around cautiously, then pushes his chair back.

"Not you," I say.

I stand up and leave the nicest restaurant I've ever been to.

I follow Carrot home. She leads me up the three flights of stairs to my creaky metal door. Now she's inside, so I unlock the door and join her. She's standing on my table, clutching her stuffed rabbit tightly. I'm so happy she's here. She's my oldest friend. Every time I see her, it's like no time has passed at all. We're back together, like we should be. Like we need to be.

I look at her standing there, and I finally ask after all these years, "Are you real?"

She turns her head to me and mouths the word "yes."

"What do you want?"

She mouths, "You know." And she's right.

I walk past my bedroom into the bathroom, where I know she's waiting for me. She stands in the bathtub, which is still missing a curtain. I had spread towels on the floor to catch the water when I take a shower. I grab the latest little orange bottle with my name on it and pop the cap. I lift the lid on the toilet and dump them all, flushing them out of my reach forever.

I look over to Carrot for approval. I know she's happy, and so I'm happy. Now we can be together without any interruption from the drugs. All the people who want to keep us apart don't realize how important it is that I can help her. I have to do what she needs me to do. I have to.

Carrot smiles at me from the tub. And, in a flash, for the first time ever, Carrot opens her eyes.

That's the last thing I remember.

FOUR

FIAT VOLUNTUS TUA

I HEAR KNOCKING. I don't know if it's my head pounding or the door.

Everything is blurry, but even with my limited vision I can see it looks like a bomb went off in my apartment. The table is flipped over, the cabinet doors are ripped off, one of the dining room chairs is actually implanted into the drywall by its legs. The carpet is soaked, there's debris and broken glass everywhere. My TV has a rolling pin sticking out of its screen and is somehow still on, blaring sound at full volume. I don't even remember owning a rolling pin. Destroying my TV seems to be the first time I've ever used it.

My mouth tastes terrible, like a combination of morning breath and thirst, and I suddenly realize I'm starving. That's probably contributing to the headache.

Knock knock.

It's definitely the door. My first thought is that it's the landlord. Worse, the police. Even worse . . .

"Emily, are you in there?"

Mom.

She's frantically knocking now. I can't ignore her; she'll get the landlord to unlock the door. I know I've lost at least a day by how hungry I am. She's probably worried I killed myself.

"EMILY! Damn it, open this door!"

"Hold on, Mom!" I yell out, and instantly my mom's fear turns to rage.

"Open this door now, Emily Michelle!" Middle names haven't scared me since I was ten.

I try to minimize the major damage. I pull the chair out of the wall and flip the table right side up. I unplug the TV and set it on the floor behind the stand. And then I see it reflected in the broken mirror in front of me:

I've written all over the wall again.

This is going to bring back some unpleasant memories. Mom bangs on the door harder. This is probably the worst situation I could ever imagine. She's already worried I committed suicide, and I'm pairing it with this. It's that night all over again.

The largest wall in the apartment is covered from floor to ceiling with black magic marker. The writing is different this time. A few new words, some drawings, but still pretty indecipherable. *Conir* is written all over. Some *X*'s with dots on top of them—I've seen those somewhere before. Most prevalent however, and taking up most of the wall, are two brand new phrases that I must've gone over fifty times:

BLUE WATER

And even bigger:

HELP ME

There's no hiding this. Time to open the door and take my licks.

I undo the chain and twist the deadbolt, taking a deep breath and trying to brace myself for what is about to happen. I have to stay calm, I can't get emotional. I have to realize how this would feel from her point of view. Last time this happened, I almost died. I was twenty-two, and my mother had just made me switch doctors yet again, and he prescribed something new. It had been a while since I was on any drug because the doctor before him was more into holistic medicine and behavioralism. I didn't know my mom was counting my meds to make sure I was taking them, and she confronted me in my room when I had gone five days without. We had some big fight about it, like we always do. She wanted me to take my pills; I didn't want to. She won. I took my pills.

All of them.

In hindsight, it was a pretty stupid way to try to win an argument. I don't know to this day if I wanted to die or I wanted to show up my mother. More than likely, I wanted to do both. I wanted out. I felt miserable all the time, and in that moment, it was all my mom's fault. Police and EMTs showed up to the house and did an emergency stomach pump, as well as sedate me with a few painkillers afterward. They rushed me to the hospital, and I was there for six days before they let me go home. I stayed in my room for another three days. My mom would come up and feed me, check on me, but I was pretty out of it. On the afternoon of the third day, the police came to the house to talk to me about the suicide attempt. My mom was talking to them in the living room, letting them know I was asleep and in no place to talk—when all of a sudden, they heard me scream some gibberish from the top of the stairs. Moments later, I was at the bottom of the stairs, bleeding and confused.

That's the first part I can recall. I don't even remember taking the pills. Between the argument and that moment, nothing. No, not nothing. I remember the woods. Running through the woods. And the pulsing sound. That solid, deep drumbeat. That was the first time I heard it. They told me it was a dream, and of course it had to have been. It seemed so real.

That was the big one. That was "The Incident."

After that, the relationship between my mother and me became strained. She petitioned for guardianship, a court found me a danger to myself, and I was placed at Sandy Shores for the next six years.

And now I stand here in a demolished apartment, after who knows how long, with insane scribbling all over the wall. For the first time I acknowledge that I feel sorry for her. She didn't ask for this.

I open the door and see her face. The fear-turned-rage has now turned back to fear as she sees me. Of course I must look a mess. I didn't even bother to check. Her eyes leave me and survey the living room. Then the wall.

She doesn't speak. She doesn't yell. She hugs me and cries.

What have I done to this woman?

FIVE

CAUSA LATET, VIS EST NOTISSIMA

SHE HUGS ME tight, so tight that I know she thought she'd find me at the end of a rope.

"Are you OK?" she asks.

I'm not sure how to answer that, and it occurs to me she didn't know what she meant by it, so I just say yes.

She pulls her head back and looks at me, her eyes stained red again.

"Your boss called me. He said you didn't show up for work last night. He said he was worried."

"I got my shift covered," I tell her, and instantly my face drops. Kyle. Fuck me. He saw it all. He knows it all. And now I'll never see him again. Another good man gone. At least this time he only left me and not my mom too.

"He said you got your Wednesday shift covered."

"Yeah, I . . ." Then it hits me. "What's today?"

My mom sighs, and I can see the tears well up in her eyes again. "Em, it's Saturday."

Three days. I lost three days.

Mom takes another look around the room and comes back to me. She tries to force a comforting smile, but it comes across more like she's reached her limit and is doing everything not to crack.

"Have you eaten?" she asks in a spot-on motherly tone.

"I . . . don't know." Judging by the pain in my stomach, no. My head is still a bit foggy and in pain. It's hard to focus. The light poking through the cheap blinds covering the door is extremely bright.

"I'll make you a sandwich." Mom walks into the kitchen. If she can find anything in there to make a sandwich with, it'll be a miracle. I hear glass crunch under her feet as she steps over the cabinet doors lying on the floor. "I must've left you about fifty messages, Emily. Why didn't you answer your phone?"

I survey the destruction in my apartment. "I don't know where it is."

"My phone is in my purse. Call yours."

I find my name under contacts in my mom's much-cooler-than-mine phone. I hit send and listen. It rings once, but I don't hear it in the room. A second ring. If I broke my phone, I swear I'm . . .

"Hello?"

What the hell? Someone answered. Now I'm going through all kinds of scenarios in my head. Did I leave it somewhere? Did I leave the house and give it to someone?

"Hi, um . . . I seem to have lost my phone. Who is this?" I ask.

"This is Emily Hunter. Who is this?"

I feel the color leave my face. I'm still hallucinating. Suddenly there's a commotion on the line, like people arguing or fighting. My mom walks back into the room with a bagel. Apparently that's all she could find. I hang up the phone quickly.

"It must be dead. I never heard a ring."

Keep it together. Keep it together. I can't do this in front of mom. But I can feel myself slipping. Mom looks up at the wall as I wolf down the bagel. I could eat ten more.

"How long has it been since you took your meds?" she asks with a hint of frustration in her voice.

"I don't know," I reply. "You said it's Saturday?"

"Goddamn it, Emily, how hard is it to swallow a fucking pill?"

Good, let's fight. We've rehearsed this one over and over. Maybe I can focus on this and keep myself here.

"Here we go," I say, egging her on.

"Don't start with me, Emily. This is serious."

"Oh, no shit, mom. You mean it's not normal to black out for three days and write all over your walls?"

"I'm glad you think this is funny."

"I don't think it's funny! But you jumping down my throat isn't going to make this any better." I'm pretty sure I've used that exact line verbatim before.

"Why do you have to be so impulsive? Huh? Why do you have to be so stubborn? I swear to God, Emily, it's like you want to be sick!"

Huh. That's a new one. And it instantly sets me off. I'm no longer trying to fight to stay focused. This is going to happen whether I want it to or not.

"I don't want to be sick!"

"Then why do you do this?! Why is it every time you start to do better, you have to ruin it? You were doing better with Dr. Parker, and you ruined that. Remember when you were getting all your freedom back? I get a call at work telling me my eighteen-year-old daughter was in the hospital after getting hit by a car while chasing her imaginary friend across the street. I can't DO this anymore Emily! I can't get that call."

She collects herself. I don't notice immediately, but I'm crying. So is she. She sits on the only chair that somehow survived my blackout.

"Emily. I can't ride with you to the hospital again, wondering if I'm going to lose my baby girl. Watching you die in front of me. I can't drive over here wondering if you're going to be alive when I get here."

"It would be easier for you if I wasn't," I say, and as the words are still in my mouth I am regretting them. I know what I'm saying is way over the line, but I'm emotional and angry and starving and hating myself for what's just happened. The look on my mom's face is . . . I'll never forget it. I know that the instant I see it. This is one moment I can never take back.

"I'm sorry," I say as soon as I can. "That wasn't fair. I don't . . . I don't really think that."

She takes a breath. "I just want to help you."

"What makes you think I need your help?"

She looks at me as if to ask if that's a serious question. Her eyes then point to the mural I've marked on the wall. The one with the giant *HELP ME* splashed in the middle of it.

"OK, you're right," I say.

"I don't want to be right. I just want you to be safe."

"I get it. Look, I'll call Dr. Harper and see if I can get an emergency session."

My mom nods, still surveying the damage. She's heard it before. So I say something she's never heard before:

"Do you want to come too?"

She looks up to meet my eyes to make sure I'm not kidding. I've never offered to let her be in the room before. I know she's always wanted to come so she can talk to the doctor or see how it works. Mostly so she can feel protective, like she's doing more to help. She's never pressured me to let her in, and I'm sure she thought I'd never ask. She tries to remain calm.

"OK. Yes." My mom smiles.

"Good. I definitely need a shower first. Can you call? No phone," I remind her.

"How about we go to lunch first? That bagel wasn't enough for you."

"Sounds great," I say. And it does.

"I love you so much," she says, and she hugs me hard.

"I love you too," I say, hugging her back, looking over her shoulder at the mural.

"Promise me you'll be OK."

Carrot is standing at the mural. I'm pretty sure she's been there the whole time. Her eyes are beautiful now that I can see them: bright blue and stunning. She is holding the dirty rabbit with one arm and with the other pointing at the words *BLUE WATER*. She stands directly under the words *HELP ME*.

"I will," I say.

I'm not sure who I said it to.

SIX

CONTRA PRINCIPIA NEGANTEM NON EST DISPUTANDEM

DR. HARPER FITS me into a cancellation she has that day, and we're in her office within three hours. She's eating a sandwich at her desk when we open the door.

"Dr. Harper?" Beverly says, walking up with her arm extended. "Beverly Hunter."

"Very nice to meet you, Mrs. Hunter."

"Beverly, please," she says with a smile. These two are going to get along famously.

I smile too because I should.

We all sit down, and after a little explaining, my mom hands Dr. Harper her phone. Harper scrolls through the photos Beverly took with her phone. She looks at each one thoughtfully, like a guy trying to impress a girl by looking under the hood of her car when it breaks down, all while having no idea how cars work. This is a show for my mother.

"Tell me about 'blue water,'" she says, not bothering to look up from the phone.

"I don't know what to tell you," I say.

Mom chimes in with a disappointed "Emily . . ."

"I don't know what it means, Mom."

"Then why did you write it?" she comes back with.

Harper interjects. "It's OK, Beverly. It's quite possible she doesn't know."

"Then why would she write it?"

"That's what we're going to try to find out." Harper turns back to me. "So, you don't recall doing any of this? No memories of the last three days? Even if it's vague or fuzzy."

Running through the woods. Alone in a torn-down building. The room with the olive felt chair. Screaming.

"No, nothing," I say.

"That's not uncommon, Emily. Don't worry about it. What I do want to know, however, is how did our deal get broken? I recall you saying you'd take responsibility, that you wouldn't miss your meds again."

"Again?" Beverly says, shooting me an evil eye.

Harper hasn't broken eye contact with me. "Emily, I'm bound to keep our sessions confidential unless . . ."

"It's OK, you can tell her everything." It won't matter soon anyway.

Harper turns to Beverly. "Last week, Emily had a lapse in her medication and had a shorter blackout similar to this one." My mother's evil eye is becoming plain sinister now. Harper continues before Beverly has a chance to say anything. "It was one missed pill, and the blackout only lasted a few hours. We had just switched her medication, and they are known to produce a lethargic feeling similar to intoxication until the body fully acclimates to it. It's no excuse, but she had reported that's why she missed it."

Beverly turns to me, her eyes still angry. "Is that why you missed it?"

"No."

I feel Harper's silence. I almost want to smile, but I don't. Not yet.

"No? Then why didn't you take it?"

"Carrot told me not to."

Beverly closes her eyes. I know she never wanted to hear Carrot's name again. She shouldn't have come then. She sighs heavily, letting everyone in the room know how tired she is of this issue.

"Carrot is her imaginary friend," she says to Harper. "She's had her since she was about three."

Three? I don't remember her being there that long.

"We've talked about Carrot, Beverly. She's not imaginary." Now I smile. I can only imagine what's going through Beverly's head. "Carrot is an auditory and visual hallucination consistent with her current diagnosis."

"She's been hallucinating since she was three?"

"Likely not. Chances are she began the hallucinations later and just assigned that name to this new thing."

"Or she's real." I can't help it. This conversation between these two is a waste of time.

"I thought we talked about this, Emily," Harper says sternly, with a hint of patronizing undertone. I'd be annoyed if I cared. "We agreed Carrot wasn't real."

"I never said that."

She thinks it over. "No, I guess you didn't. You implied that."

"That was the medicine . . . 'implying.'"

I know that Harper is getting a little frustrated. She thinks she has to start over now. If she'd listen, this wouldn't be such a struggle.

"Why would Carrot want you to do something unsafe?"

There's no sense in not telling them. Lying again isn't worth the effort. "She needs my help. I can't hear her when I take those pills. I have to save her. I'm the only one who can. She's stuck, and she's in pain."

They're both silent and looking at each other, as if one is waiting to see what the other says. I break the silence.

"She's opened her eyes. They're beautiful."

"Didn't you hear your doctor, Emily? She's not real! She's in your head."

"It's OK, Mom. Really. I know what I have to do. I don't expect you to understand. I can hear myself. It sounds crazy." And it does. These two have got to be so lost.

"It is crazy, Emily!" she says.

"Let's take a break for a second," Harper says, stopping us before Beverly jumps out of her chair at me.

"No problem," I get out of my chair and head for the door. "Is your vending machine still broken?"

"Nope, all fixed."

"Great." I could smash a Twix bar right now.

The drive home is a long, quiet one. Beverly seems in shock, almost afraid to talk to me. When I left the room, she had stayed back and Dr. Harper told her an earful. I listened in from the door I had purposefully left open.

First, Harper had her sit back down, telling her she's glad she came in.

"It's important you see this," said Harper. "Emily is in the first stages of what we call complete decomposition. Her refusal to take

her meds, despite the negative consequences, is seemingly rewarding to her. What that indicates to me is that those negative consequences are not really registering with her. She seems to be rapidly detaching from reality."

I could hear Beverly sniffling. Harper pushed through.

"She seems to be developing delusions of grandeur, which isn't uncommon with patients diagnosed with schizophrenia. Her idea that Carrot is real, that we're wrong, that's always been there. But now she's claiming to have this ultimate purpose, to save her. That's something new."

It isn't. I know that now. Beverly turns a corner and comes to a red light. Cars start to pull in behind us.

"The speed at which a missed dose results in a blackout is, quite frankly, alarming," continued Harper. "Considering especially the severity of this last blackout, and I know this is hard, but I would highly recommend re-admittance to Sandy Shores immediately."

The light turns green, and as soon as Beverly lets off the brake, I jump out of the car. I'm at a full sprint in moments. Behind me, Beverly—my mom, screams for me to get back into the car over horns of the drivers being held up at the intersection. I can't. I have to find Carrot. I have a plan.

I wonder if I'll ever see her again.

"I know this won't be a popular decision with Emily, but as you are still her legal guardian, I implore you, for your daughter's safety, to make this move. I see no other alternative that isn't a major risk."

I burst through the door to my apartment, already starting to smell the mold in the carpet. I grab the red backpack I had filled with clothes, cash, and toiletries after I took my shower. On the way out, I take one last look at the mural, and I find my phone sitting on the dining room floor. I make a phone call and start running down the street. Mom will look for me here. Cannot linger.

"What's important is that she's monitored constantly. She's had too much freedom."

The taxi picks me up five blocks from my apartment. Noticing my frazzled appearance, my light luggage, and that I'm headed to the airport, the cabbie asks no questions.

My flight is in a small Cessna, and on takeoff and landing, my ears pop painfully. I feel it in my teeth, and I can tell the other three passengers feel the same way. I get out of the plane, and it's dark out. The stars are amazing out here. I've never been this far north the whole time I lived in Michigan. I'm in the fingertips. There's virtually no light pollution here, and I feel like I can see the entire galaxy. I see the car waiting for me and jump in the backseat.

"Where to?" asks the second cabbie of the day.

"Is there a motel in town?"

"Yes, ma'am," he says as he starts the meter and starts down the long, straight, featureless road.

"We know she has a history of self-harm, and she has the potential to be destructive when she believes these delusions are real. But now that we know she believes they are telling her to do something, something she believes is imperative to the safety of this imaginary little girl, I would say the situation has escalated, dangerously."

Nothing but farmland, the occasional tree, and at most three cars pass outside the cab on the fifteen-mile drive into town. And then, finally, I breathe a sigh of relief as the first sign of life, quite literally, is illuminated in the headlights of the cab. And for some reason, I know I'm right. I feel it, like everything is clicking into place.

WELCOME TO BLUE WATER. EST 1891.

SEVEN

NON DECOR, DUCO

I DON'T REMEMBER ever feeling this happy.

I wake up with no alarm clock, just to the flickering light of the sun peeking through the old flower curtains hanging over the small window, dropping almost low enough to hide the off-white cinder blocks beneath the sill. The bed was pretty uncomfortable, like sleeping on a slanted rock you had to fight from rolling off of, but I didn't care. It was a beautiful morning. It was going to be a beautiful day.

I step into the shower, and the water temperature is perfect. No more scalding or freezing water. I take my time, shave my legs, do my hair, put on makeup. I close my eyes, deep breath after deep breath, without ever stopping this stupid grin I have on my face. Rummaging through the backpack, I find one of my nicest-looking outfits.

I'm going out on the town today.

Blue Water is a small town, technically a village, in Northern Michigan, on the southern shore of Lake Huron near Hammond Bay, east of the Mackinac Bridge. The nautical theme plays heavily in what could generously be called a downtown area, as the village lies on one of the largest shipping routes in America, through the Great Lakes. All the bakeries, bars, and antique shops are littered with maps, models of lighthouses, and pictures of thousand-foot freighters as decorations. In front of the seemingly endless lake, an actual lighthouse towers over the main–and, honestly, only–street going through town, appropriately named Lake Road. Although beautifully maintained, the lighthouse appeared to be out of commission. A small plaque marked it as a historical site:

MILLEN LIGHTHOUSE. This lighthouse was donated to the city of Blue Water by the USMC in 1968, and it serves as a beacon of hope. Sailors on Lake Huron used it to navigate the Hammond Bay at night. The previous lighthouse, sorely in need of renovation, was completely torn down and replaced by the Morrow Lighthouse, which was renamed by unanimous city council decision in 1981 to the Millen Lighthouse after the passing of Blue Water resident, hospital curator, and humanitarian Dr. Gregory Millen.

"Nice day to look at the water," a man's voice called from behind me. I wait a second to hear if someone replies before concluding he was talking to me. Sitting on a bench near the sidewalk, a short, slightly older man, who looks like he just came in off one of the ships, smiles at me. I smile back, completely aware that I'm meeting someone who has no preconceived notions about me. He doesn't know about my condition, my medications, my history. To him, I could be anyone, some random stranger enjoying the view.

I'm human again. Just a person. I'm alive.

"Never seen anything like it. It's beautiful," I say. To be honest, it's the most beautiful thing I've ever seen.

"Not from around here then, I take it?"

"Just visiting," I say. "Maybe more."

"We don't get a lot of visitors," he says. "Most tourists stay closer to the island." He means Mackinac Island (somehow pronounced "Mack-in-awe" for non-Michiganders), a pretty popular tourist trap known for its fudge shops and the Grand Hotel, built in the 1880s. No cars are allowed on the island, so everyone travels by horse-drawn carriage. It's supposed to be amazing; everyone always talks about their magnificent trip to Mackinac. I went there once when I was ten. I just remember the smell: fudge and horse shit.

"You'd think you'd have plenty with this view," I reply. "What does oceanfront in Malibu have on this?"

"The weather," he says. "Starting in September it gets pretty damn cold up here. Huron's been known to freeze every now and again."

"Sounds like you've been here a while," I say, segueing pretty brilliantly, I must say, to the topic at hand.

"Born and raised. Got a house on Canal Street about three blocks south of here. Used to be my folks' house. Graduated from high school and got a job on the lake like my dad and his dad. The water just kind of . . . gets in your blood."

I nod and smile. "Maybe you can help me. I'm trying to find out about someone who lived here, probably twenty or thirty years ago. Would you be the guy to ask?"

He shuffles on the bench, like he's ready for a challenge. "I can sure try."

"I'm looking for information about a little girl who passed away in this town, somewhere between 1983 and 1989."

I've suspected this for a while. I've even done research on the subject of visitations by spirits. There's a woman named

Allison DuBois, who's become a personal hero of mine, who has written a few books on the subject. She began having visions when she was a child too, just six years old. She'd have strange dreams about dead people she couldn't possibly know, see visions, hear voices. Basically everything I'm going through I read about in her first book. She thought she was going crazy until she started listening to her dreams, following her visions. And by doing so, she began solving cold murder cases for the Glendale Police Department in Arizona. They made a TV show about her life, and she was played by Patricia Arquette.

I think this is why I'm here. Carrot needs me to help her move on. How I'm going to do that, I can't tell. But you can't take a journey without taking a first step. Possibly the most helpful thing Dr. Harper has ever told me.

The man on the bench sits thinking, and I can tell he's both trying to figure out the question and figure out why I'm asking it. In my rush to get to this part of the conversation, I now realize I've completely skipped over introducing myself or getting his name. It's probably not too important though, as it looks like he's drawing a blank.

"The only ones I can think of are Becky Johnson and Tyler Gordon. They were in my class. But it was a little bit before. Probably 1979, 1980. But Becky wasn't little, she was 16. Car accident. They said Tyler was driving drunk, Becky wasn't wearing her seatbelt. Found Tyler with his pants around his ankles, caught on the accelerator. They said his foot couldn't reach the brake and they hit a tree. I'll let you fill in why."

"I'm going to guess that's not what I'm looking for."

"Yeah, probably not," he says. "Don't remember a little girl dying, but who knows."

It's OK, I was prepared that it wouldn't be this easy. "Alright, thanks anyway. How about an easier one: where's a good place to get breakfast?"

His face lights up. "Ah, that I can help you with. Water Street Café. Get the pancakes. About a block or two up the street. Maybe someone there knows about your dead girl."

I thank him, still without introducing myself, and head down the road. The Water Street Café is exactly what I was picturing: a cozy little diner with a long counter on the west wall, booths on the east wall, and a single row of tables up the middle with a window overlooking the lake on the north end. The walls were decorated with the standard pictures of various freighters and vessels. More than one of the SS *Edmund Fitzgerald*. The diner has a moderate amount of customers eating a moderate amount of pancakes. Looks like bench guy steered me in the right direction.

I sit at the counter, next to the register, by a handmade donation jar made from an old Folgers can with the words *Save Riverview Hospital* emblazoned on the side in a combination of permanent marker writing and highlighter stars and sparkles. From the kitchen behind the half wall directly in front of me, I hear the sizzling of the grill cooking breakfast that smells more delicious than anything I've eaten in years. Everything about Blue Water is the best part.

"Coffee?" a young girl asks, holding a glass pot and flashing an adorable smile.

"Yes. Please." I say with a modest amount of desperation. I may not have gotten a nicotine addiction at Sandy Shores, but I sure as hell picked one up for caffeine.

As she's pouring, I notice her earrings. Nothing too special, but I'm in such a good mood, I spontaneously throw out a compliment. "I like your earrings. They're cute."

"Oh, thanks!" she says. "I like your watch."

I can't tell if she was really looking at it or if she's just uncomfortable getting compliments and had to return it.

"Thanks," I say back.

"My mom had one that looked like that. She used to let me borrow it so I'd know when to come home when I was out riding my bike in the woods," she says, and then her smile sinks a little. "Haven't thought about that in a while." Her eyes are lost in some distant memory, and I suddenly feel sad. My mom has left thirteen messages on my cell phone since I jumped out of her car. I didn't get any until last night when I threw my phone on the charger at the motel. I promised myself then I wasn't calling her back until I found Carrot and I could tell her I was right. She'd try to talk me into coming home, and I couldn't risk her succeeding.

Still.

The sadness is instantly gone when I notice the girl's name tag. My heart skips a beat. This has to be kismet.

"Your name's Allison?" I ask.

"Allison Jacoby, yeah. What's your name?"

"Emily Hunter." I reply, no longer anonymous in Blue Water.

"Nice to meet you," she answers. "What are you doing in Blue Water?"

"I'm trying to find out about this little girl from this town. She must have died here sometime in the eighties."

"Bit before my time," she says, and of course she's right. By the looks of her, she's twenty-two, tops. Pearl Jam was before her time. "How little was she?"

"Eight. Maybe ten."

"Do you have a picture of her? Maybe some of the folks here might know her. Plus my brother's a cop. He might be able to help."

"No, no picture." That would be too easy.

We sit in silence for a second, until Allison says four words that almost make me cry instantly.

"Is she haunting you?"

My breath stops in my chest, and I look at Allison with tears that hide in the bottoms of my eyelids. This is the first time in my life someone led with "You might not be crazy." The first time someone suggested what I believed, instead of the idea that my brain must be broken. Allison is now my new best friend. Sadly, I realized, it didn't take much. Also there wasn't any competition.

She sees from the look I give her–and the fact that I can feel my face getting flushed as I try to not jump on the counter screaming, "YES! THANK YOU! YES!"–that she's hit it on the head.

"She is, isn't she?!" Then she gets low, to the counter with me, and talks in hushed tones. "I totally believe in all that stuff, you know? Oh my God, OK . . ." It's apparent now that she doesn't know what to ask. I proceed cautiously. I don't want to freak her out too badly or make her think I'm insane.

"I've been seeing things. She . . . told me to come here."

"Oh my God! That's so crazy!" says Allison, a little less hushed than before. I know what she means, but I still flinch at the word *crazy*. She picked up on it. "Not crazy like *crazy*, just wild, you know? What did she look like? Was she all gross and gnarled, or like normal?"

"No, she looks like a normal eight-to-ten-year old in her pajamas with a stuffed rabbit."

"Wait, *looks*? Do you still see her? Is she here now?" she asks, really enthusiastically.

"No." And it dawns on me, I've felt great all day, but I've also not seen or felt Carrot since I got here—actually, since I got on the plane. A sinking happens in my stomach. Is that because I'm going the right way? Or the wrong way?

"Does she have a name?" she asks.

"I call her Carrot. I'm not sure why. I don't know if it was my idea because I didn't know what else to call her."

"Yeah, let's hope that not really her name," Allison says. "Hmm. That's really not much to go on." Allison looks down the counter to an older gentleman, who is less-than-patiently waiting for a warm-up on his coffee. "Tell you what, I'm off at seven. If you haven't found her by then, I'll see what I can do to help you out, OK?"

I can't believe how well this is going. Out for breakfast and already I have a partner. I'm not sure how much good she can do, but just having someone believe me without questions is invigorating enough. "Yeah, sure. I'll be here. Thank you."

Allison goes down the counter, and I drink the best cup of coffee I've ever tasted.

The rest of my morning into the afternoon isn't as fruitful. In fact, it's downright horrible. I walk around town, going into every business I can find, which takes only a couple hours, asking anyone I can find about Carrot, and getting absolutely nowhere. No one has heard of any little girl dying in town at any time, let alone the 1980s. If only I had anything else to go on beyond a vague description. This is about when doubt starts creeping in. I don't want it to, I fight it, I pretend I'm not thinking it until about 3:30 p.m., when I collapse into the park bench all of this started at.

What if they're right? What if I'm not like Allison DuBois? What if I'm fucking crazy?

I can feel my palms sweat with every "no" I get. My face muscles feel tight, like they do right before crying. They've felt this way for hours.

I reached the end of Lake Road an hour ago. There's nothing but houses inland. I think about going door to door, but the doubt is starting to weaken me. I'm starting to feel a new sensation: anger.

Harper's words have crept into my head. Just a whisper at first, now they're mocking me:

"Delusions of grandeur . . . She believes they are telling her to do something, something she believes is imperative to the safety of this imaginary little girl . . . I would say the situation has escalated, dangerously."

What am I doing here? How could I have been so wrong? I'd guess maybe I'm in the wrong place, but what else could Blue Water mean? *Blue Water could mean anything, idiot–not the least of all that you're bat-shit insane,* I hear in Harper's voice. Why would I see these things if I wasn't supposed to? *Why did the Son of Sam think the neighbor's dog told him to kill people? Because he was a nutcase like you, Emily.* The waitress believed me. *Oh, Allison? Your proof that you're supposed to be here is some young kid waitress who has the same name as some phony psychic they made a TV show about, and she believes your fucking delusions? Are you serious? You aren't worth the effort to fix, Emily. You're a piece of shit. Your mom wishes you were dead, your therapists all laugh at you to each other after you go home, you aren't human, Emily, you are less than human, you are useless, you are a burden, no one loves you because you are broken, you are sick, you are fucking insane, and you should drown yourself in the lake, tie a big rock around your neck and jump in the water—*

And I scream.

Two people across the street turn their heads toward me, see that I'm not being murdered, and go about their day. I feel the sweat dripping from my hairline and rolling over my temples. They were right. They were always right.

I feel something else now, something I didn't think I would feel. Calm. Relief. And a terrible smile crosses my lips. *It's OK, Emily, you're just insane. You're just Fruit Loops. You don't have to get them to listen anymore. You don't have to make them believe you. You were wrong. Of course you were wrong. There's nothing here. There never was.*

I spent so much time fighting, so much time swimming against the current, that I never realized it was easier to just stop and let it take me. I'd go back to Sandy Shores. I'd live there for the rest of my life. I'd get my meals on time, I'd get my clothes bought for me, I'd be driven wherever we were going. I'd take my thirty-eight dollars a month, and I'd hide it in an envelope I taped under the top drawer so the orderlies didn't steal it while I was sleeping. I knew where I was going. It was easier to know what the future held. It wasn't up to me. It never was.

And like she knew, that exact instant my phone rang. I look down to the caller ID and I exhale, knowing I can go home, knowing I can be safe. I don't have to try anymore, I can just let go.

Let go.

"Hi" is all I can muster. I'm so ashamed of everything I've put her through. I made Dad leave, and she stuck by me. I made her sit with me in an ambulance as I died in front of her, and she stuck by me. I made her life hell, and she stuck by me. I don't deserve her. She doesn't deserve me.

I look out at the water. The lake is probably pretty cold this far north.

"Oh my God, Emily." And she's weeping instantly. "Baby, are you OK?"

Baby. I imagine her holding me after I was born. A blank slate. I was like every other baby born: full of potential, full of possibility. I imagine the joy she must have felt holding me for the first time, the love she had for me in that moment, the dreams she had for my future and for our future together. That last thought puts me over, and I start crying too.

"Mommy, I'm so sorry." I'm not sure why I said "mommy," but I couldn't stop at this point. I just wept.

"Honey, no. It's OK." Saying "mommy" gets her too, and we're both complete wrecks. "Just please tell me if you're safe."

"Yeah, mom, I'm safe. I feel so stupid." I wonder how many people have drowned in the lake, probably in various shipwrecks, all of them scared, spending their last gasps of air hoping they were remembered and yet all forgotten. I'm sure I'd be forgotten too.

"You're not stupid. No one thinks you're stupid."

"You were right. Harper and Parker were right, the asshole orderlies at Sandy Shores were right. I'm fucking crazy."

"You just need help, Emily. And if you're ready and you don't want to fight it anymore, it will be so much easier."

"I'm so sorry, Mom. I'm so sorry you have me for a daughter."

"I'm not," she says with so much conviction that I believe her. It makes it worse. I'd be doing it for her. She's given so much, she deserves a break. She deserves to be free.

"Emily? Please, just come home. Are you far away? Can I pick you up?"

I laugh at how ridiculous this all is. "Mom, I got on a plane."

She doesn't sound mad. In fact, she kind of laughs too. "A plane? Honey, where are you?"

"I'm in this cute little town. Actually, I think you'd really like it. It's quaint and quiet. There's this little antique shop full of old crap that you could fill your house up with."

I can hear her smiling on the phone. "Just more stuff for you to clean out of my house when I'm dead. What's the name of the town? I can send you money to fly home."

But I'm not listening. I'm looking in the window of the antique store at a picture frame made from repurposed wood, probably from an old ship that sunk in Lake Huron a century ago. The frame is beautiful, and someone took a lot of time working on it because it's priced at more than I make in a month at Gil's. But that's not what I'm interested in.

I'm interested in the picture sitting in the frame, of a little girl with stunning blue eyes and purple pajamas holding a dirty stuffed rabbit.

"Mom . . . I gotta go. I'll call you back later." Once again, I think we both know that's a lie.

"Emily? No."

"I love you, and I'm safe," I say, and I hang up.

That was the last thing I ever said to my mother.

I believe the store owner has never seen someone so enthusiastic about antiques before. He's a short, elderly man with a kind face and a perfectly sculpted comb-over of thin, white hair. I imagine most of this stuff was probably his. I rush him with more energy than he's experienced in years.

"Sir?" I almost scream, making him jump and look up from his book, casting his eyes in every direction to make sure his store wasn't on fire. He sees me coming with the frame, takes off his glasses, sets them on the table, and gives me a puzzled look.

"Well, how can I help you, young lady? You like the frame?"

"No! I mean, yes, it's nice," I say. "I want to ask you, who is this little girl in the photo?"

He touches his shirt pocket, looking for the glasses he just took off. He checks the top of his head too. This would be adorable and comical if I wasn't holding life-changing proof of my sanity in my hands. I reach over to the table and grab his glasses, handing them to him. He smiles to me and awkwardly takes them, fumbling to put them on his head. Then he squints through them to study the little girl staring back at him in the frame.

"Ah, that's Carrot."

I feel my face get flush again, and my throat tightens. I don't want to move. For a second I can't breathe, and I start feeling dizzy. The store owner sees this and reaches over to me to touch my arm. "Miss, do you need to sit down?"

I nod, because as my vision is getting narrow, it's all I can do. I'm not about to black out, I'm about to pass out.

He sits me down in a beautifully made Adirondack chair and rushes as fast as he can, which is honestly quite fast for a man his age, to the back of his store. He comes back with a glass of ice water and starts pushing air over me with a make-shift fan made of a newspaper. I take a few deep breaths, and I feel my body calming down already. I thank him for his kindness before I start the line of questioning that is burning in my mind.

"Her name was actually Carrot?"

"Oh, heavens no. Carol. Carol Emerson. Kids used to call her Carrot. You know, playground nicknames and such. She used to be good friends with that Albert Forrester kid. I think she stayed with his family for a while. Odd duck, Albert. But they got married, so I guess she saw something in him."

"Married? But she's just a little girl!" I say. He looks at me oddly, as if I don't know how photographs work.

"Well, yes, in this picture she's a little girl, but she grew up. They got married right out of high school. Then, of course, there was the tragedy. So sad to see a life taken so young."

If she lived longer, why was she appearing to me as a little girl? Maybe that was a clue. Something happened when she was young? These answers were giving me more and more questions. But, for once, I at least had a lead.

"You may not believe me, but I think I'm being haunted by her ghost," I say. I'm not sure why I volunteered that information because he looks at me like I just told him I'm a martian. That's more the look I'm used to when I tell people. Not everyone will be as open-minded as Allison.

"I doubt that," he says.

"Like I said, you may not believe me," I reply.

"No, you misunderstand me," the store owner says.

I walk up the sidewalk quietly to the porch of a small, white ranch home. The metal railing going up the stairs to the front door wiggles in my hand as I touch it. If I applied a little pressure, I could pull the whole thing down. I stop on the stairs and wiggle it a few more times, fully aware that I'm stalling. I gather myself and take the last two steps to the door. I raise my arm to knock, but it feels heavier than it's ever been. My knuckles tap the door, but even standing here, I could barely hear it. I dare myself to knock again. I hear movement inside the house. No going back now.

The door opens. I ask, even though I don't need to. I know immediately, and now I know absolutely nothing but this.

"Carol Forrester?" I ask.

The sixty-year-old woman with fierce blue eyes gives me a pleasant smile as she leans onto the doorframe.

"Yes?" she says.

PART TWO

EIGHT

NON SUM QUALIS ERAM

WHAT FOLLOWS IS the most awkward silence possibly ever experienced by mankind. I sit in Carol's living room, sipping on a cup of coffee that has gotten cool, while she sits on a piano stool facing me, stunned I knocked on her door and told her that her eight-year-old ghost is haunting me.

"I'm not sure where to start," she admits. I definitely understand.

"I know it sounds crazy," I say, flinching again at that word. For too long, people told me it *was* crazy. There's something to it, I know that now. "I wouldn't even say it out loud, but it brought me here. I dreamt about a little girl who looks just like you did at her age, who went by the nickname Carrot, who lived in a town called Blue Water. She needed my help, I came, and here you are."

"I don't need your help," she says, rather quickly. I can tell she's getting defensive, probably because I'm still sitting in her house, and she's getting uncomfortable with me being here. I need to adjust.

"I'm not saying you do. In fact I think I need *your* help. I don't know why this is happening. All I know is that it *is* happening. I'm just following where it takes me."

"I'm not sure what to do with any of this," says Carol. She's still upset, still on edge. I don't blame her. "A stranger shows up on my doorstep saying she's been seeing my ghost since she was a little kid—only I'm not dead—and I'm supposed to know why?"

"I don't think you know why, Carol." Saying her name was supposed to sound comforting. Instead, as it came out, it sounded patronizing. She is already reacting to it in her face. I can tell I'm moments from getting kicked out. "Maybe there's something we're not thinking about, something that connects us."

"I don't believe in any of this stuff. Ghosts, psychics, any of it. It's not real." She's shutting me down.

"With all due respect . . ."

"It's not real," she says over me. It's clear this conversation is over. Although, it feels like she's hiding something. Maybe I just want to believe she is. I need to change the subject or else I'm done. I look around the house. It looks like it hasn't been updated in decades. The walls are all decorated with framed sketches of stylized glyphs and symbols.

"These pictures are really beautiful. Did you do them?"

Her eyes don't leave my face. "My husband drew them, God rest his soul."

Her husband. This must be the tragedy the store owner was talking about. "How did he pass?" I ask, and the daggers in her eyes indicate I have just officially overstayed my welcome.

"He was attacked. Hit on the head." She stands up and takes the unfinished coffee out of my hand. "Now, if there isn't anything else . . ."

Yeah, time to go. “I’m sorry to barge in on you like this. I know it’s a lot. If you think of anything . . .”

“You’ll be the first to know dear,” she says, of course, not meaning it at all, just trying to get me out the door. I smile. Being on this side of the polite lie is a different experience.

The Water Street Café is lit now by fluorescent lights and a single TV in the corner playing a Red Wings game that two people are watching intently. The rest of the diner is at about a third capacity. I guess the breakfast is the big seller. The clock is sitting at 6:50 p.m. when I step in and sit at the same stool I took that morning. Allison’s face lights up when she sees me, but dulls the moment she sees the expression on my face. She can tell something has changed.

“Hey, I’m almost finished, and I’ll be right with you. Can I get you anything?”

“Coffee,” I say. “I’m about a half-cup short.”

She walks the pot over to me and pours a fresh cup. “Any luck out there today?”

“I can’t tell,” I reply, and I honestly can’t. It’s hard to focus on anything except the swirling pool of questions in my mind. “I found out who the girl was–or is, anyway.”

“Is?”

“Do you know who Carol Forrester is?”

“Uh . . .” She squints, digging through her mind. “Yeah, older woman, lives on Clark, white house?”

“That’s her.”

“She’s not dead,” Allison says with a look that describes everything going on in my head.

"No, she's not."

"I'm confused."

"Join the club," I say. For the life of me, I'm stumped. Allison DuBois talked to ghosts who wanted their murders solved. I'm talking to a ghost that's not even dead. We sit quietly, and I can see Allison is just as puzzled as I am. I'm now wondering if she's going to stick with me or take this opportunity to bail. I know what I would do if I were her.

"Her husband died in the haunted hospital."

I purse my lips. The idea of a haunted hospital seems a little ridiculous, even for me.

"The what?"

"Riverview. It's an old mental institution that closed down thirty, thirty-five years ago." A mental institution. They haven't been called that in half a century. Names tend to stick like that. At any rate, I thought, of course, it had to be a psychiatric hospital. Why would it be anything else?

"There's a dispute about whether or not it's on Blue Water village property or on federal parkland, so no one's done anything with it since it shut down. It's just been sitting there, boarded-up for decades. I think they were going to turn it into a youth center at one point, but that fell through. Now they're petitioning to make it a historical site. I don't know why, I can't imagine pitching it to the tourism board."

"Because it's haunted," I say with less than subtle sarcasm.

"Says the woman who strolled into town looking for ghosts." I smile. Touché. Allison bought into my ghost story without question; the least I could do is hear her out. "All I know is that half the town has seen some strange stuff up there."

"That's because half the town used to live there," says a gruff voice from behind me. A short, fat middle-aged man sits at a table eating a steak, eavesdropping on our conversation. He gets up slowly, laboriously. I assume at first it's because of his weight, but then he reaches for a cane and limps over to us, making me feel a little guilty.

"Ma'am, I don't believe we've met," he says with a smile.

"Emily Hunter," I say with a nod. He makes eye contact and gives me a glare like he was trying to place my face.

"Ms. Hunter, I'm Mayor Henry Altman. And as mayor of this fine little town, I can safely say, you don't live here."

"Just visiting, Mr. Mayor."

"Chasing ghosts, I hear." He doesn't laugh, but he might as well. I turn to Allison, but she's staying quiet.

"Apparently not."

"Well, that's a shame. You certainly came to the right place for it. This is the site of the world famous Haunted Riverview Psychiatric Hospital." Allison looks at the countertop, fingering at a small smudge staining the surface. She's been made fun of before for this. I know exactly how she feels. "What Ms. Jacoby here has told you is true. The hospital got boarded up years ago. Major loss in funding, and the facility just shut down. What she isn't telling you, however, is that once the place shut down, the patients were just released. The most severe were transferred to prison; the rest, well, there was nowhere to put them, nowhere to ship them off to, so they just let an entire hospital full of patients go. And since none of them had any life skills or money, most of them just stayed here. Unfortunately, a scenario like Riverview isn't that uncommon when there's no funds left."

Altman is taking joy in telling this story, but he still can't keep his eyes off me. Maybe because I'm a stranger, maybe because he can tell I'm not charmed. He finally finishes up his big speech.

"Sadly, that's why so many people here in Blue Water have paranoid delusions about the hospital—half of them were institutionalized there. And if you knew the stuff that happens in state mental hospitals, you probably wouldn't blame them." He's not wrong.

"I wasn't," spits Allison. "I've seen things. Well," she dials back, "heard things."

He smiles at Allison. "Well, that I cannot speak to. But, ma'am," and he turns back to me, "the haunted hospital is nothing more than a local urban legend."

"What about Carol's husband, Albert? He died in that hospital. Do you really think it was a mugger?" asks Allison, although I'm sure she already knows the answer.

"He wasn't mugged. You talked to Carol?" he asks me. I nod. "She told you he had his skull caved in after a mugging?" Sort of, but I still nod. "She tell you he still had his wallet, with eighty dollars cash and a credit card on him when they found him?" I can't conceal the puzzled look my face immediately contorts to, and Altman knows she left that out. "Did she tell you Albert had a brain tumor? They found it in the autopsy. Big one. Did she tell you about the dementia it caused? How she'd call the police because he kept wandering off in the middle of the night, not knowing who he was? She left that out, didn't she?" He finishes with a little too much condescension in his voice. I think I'm starting to understand Mayor Altman now.

He reaches in his pocket and pulls out a gold pocket watch. When my eyes fall on it, I can't pull them away. I recognize it instantly. I've seen it countless times.

The hands are both pointed at twelve. Only there's no twelve. Every number has been replaced with a Roman X.

It's the same watch from my recurring dream.

Altman opens it. The watch face looks normal. There are Roman numerals, but they're all correct. There's an inscription on the inside of the cover: *Everything Has Its Time.*

"I've had this watch for a long time, and I love it more than anything." I doubt it; I'm pretty sure he's madly in love with himself. "I love it because no matter what is happening in my day, no matter how I get caught up in the day-to-day business of being mayor, it keeps ticking. Best day of my life or worst, it keeps ticking. And every time it does, I'm one second closer to going home to God." Why did I see this watch already? Why is it important?

"Everything has its time, ladies. And when it's up, it's up." He snaps the lid closed for dramatic effect. I flinch because I was lost in thought, just like he wanted me to. "No ghost or haunted hospital killed Albert Forrester. He was a jackass who fell and hit his head in a condemned building he never should have been in. Pardon my French."

That's enough, and I'm speaking before thinking. "If he was a jackass, it was because of the brain tumor. What's your excuse?" You could hear a pin drop now, as the rest of the diner goes silent. Apparently, we weren't the only ones listening to this conversation. Altman looks furious; I doubt anyone has ever talked to him like that, let alone some complete stranger. I can see the wheels turning in his head, suppressing his rage, and that disarming grin slowly slithers back across his lips.

"Perhaps I spoke out of turn . . ." he says, about to go into some half-assed apology, but I'm done listening.

"Perhaps." I turn my back to Altman and look back to Allison. "I'm going to take a rain check tonight. How much do I owe you for the coffee?"

Allison is smiling ear to ear. "It's on the house," she says, looking directly over my shoulder at Altman. I've still got a teammate.

"Thanks. I'll be in touch." And I walk out without another word, leaving Altman standing awkwardly between the tables and the counter with no one to talk at.

The phone rang, and Carol set down the journal. She stepped through the boxes and boxes of stuff she had hidden away in the closet years ago, things she hadn't thought about since that night, things she wanted never to think of again, things that were buried until some young woman knocked on her door this afternoon. She'd worked through it. She had convinced herself she had to be right. Now, she wasn't so sure.

She picked up the receiver of the corded phone tethered to her wall and nearly instantly regretted it. His voice, his terrible voice.

"Hello, Carrot Cake," said Henry Altman. Her blood went cold. She didn't say anything back, so he continued. "I hear you had a visitor today. Emily something."

"She came by," she said.

"What did she want?"

"Nothing important."

"What did you tell her?"

"There isn't anything to tell her, Henry," Carol said. "She thinks she saw a ghost."

Henry continued, seemingly satisfied with her answer. "Look, if she comes by again, you call me and I'll have Peter come out and arrest her. You don't need some out-of-towner bringing up painful memories." The nerve of this son of a bitch, thought Carol. If Altman didn't want to dust off painful memories, he'd never call her again. She remained quiet. "You just don't worry. OK, honey? Nothing bad is ever going to happen to you while I'm here."

"OK," said Carol, and she hung up. She went back to the journal, holding back happy tears. Her husband's handwriting was so perfect, so beautiful. She read the journal and remembered her own version of the wonderful day he described. They had rented a boat and gone out on the lake all day. They didn't fish, they didn't swim. They just talked all day. They had barely missed the sunrise over the east side of the lake and stayed until it set on the west side to make up for it. That day it was just the two of them. They were the only ones in the world.

As she turned more pages, the handwriting slipped. It got messier and messier. More hectic, more chaotic.

This was the tumor.

Carol wanted to believe he was mugged, but she knows the difficulty he was having. She wanted to believe someone had taken him away—not that his death could have been prevented if she had just taken him to the hospital once he started acting odd. But he couldn't blame her; he knew how much she hated hospitals.

He couldn't blame her because he was dead. Now she could only blame herself.

She got toward the end of the book, the pages now illegible. He had started drawing glyphs, sketches, and utter nonsense. His fractured mind spilled out all over the paper in front of her. *Why didn't I do something?* she thought. *Why didn't I help?* The tears came back as she turned to the last page. She hadn't forced herself to read this book in years, and now, mercifully, she had gotten through it. She wiped the water out of her eyes, and before closing the book, she looked down on the one word pressed into the last page:

CONIR.

NINE

VIDEO ET TACEO

THERE ARE ONLY sounds this time: a laugh, people talking. At first, I think it's outside my door, but it becomes more evident that it's not. The pulsing starts. Boom. Boom. Boom. A locker door closing. "If a tree falls in the woods . . ." A gunshot. More laughter. I hear myself ask, "Can you see me?" And I can't tell if I said it out loud or just heard it. BOOM. BOOM. BOOM. "You did this," I hear Carol Forrester say. BOOMBOOMBOOM.

Then, suddenly, I'm in a long, dark hallway with doors all around me. I can't see it, but I know all the doors are being held shut by terrified people behind them. I'm not supposed to be in this hallway. I should be in my room. I'm exposed. No one will open their door for me. I'm all alone.

No, I'm not.

Something else is in this hallway, moving around the labyrinth, stalking me. I can hear it breathing, faster and faster. It's hungry, and it knows I'm lost.

They let it free. They left us alone with it.

I tap quietly on one of the doors and beg for whomever is inside to let me in. I twist the knob and push on the door, but they push back. They're too strong, and they're screaming. The scream sounds like a pig being slaughtered. And it's very loud.

"Calm down!" I'm saying, but it's not helping. The monster knows where I am.

I look up the hallway, and there it is: the Minotaur. It's almost too big to fit in the hallway, but it moves impossibly quick. I try to run, but my legs feel like they're standing in a swimming pool.

Its hooves pound into the floor. Its horns scrape the ceiling, tearing down what ceiling remains above it. I can't get away.

Boom. Boom. Boom.

It is on me, behind me. I stand still, too terrified to move, as its hands crawl over me. I belong to it.

It doesn't attack, not yet. But I know it will. It always does.

Have I seen this before?

It breathes on my neck, hot putrid breath. I hear the saliva pop on its teeth as it smiles, its mouth dancing over my ear.

Knock knock.

I open my eyes. The comforter I was sleeping under is on the floor. My body feels cold. I don't move because it's not over. Carrot is here.

She's standing at the side of my bed, a foot and a half from my face, and she's talking. I can't hear her, of course. I never hear her. But she's mouthing words to me. A lot of times, I can understand. This time she's talking too fast.

"Slow down," I say, but she doesn't. The knock comes at the door again, and I look up. When I come back to Carrot, she's gone.

"Just a second!" I yell, as I crawl out of bed and grab the same pair of pants I wore yesterday off the floor and put them back on. I get a look at myself in the mirror. I slept hard.

"Morning! Three sugars, right?" says Allison, handing me a warm to-go cup as I open the motel door. The sun seems to punch me in the eyes from behind her. She can tell I have no idea what's happening. "Sorry to show up out of the blue like this, but I was hoping to cash in that rain check."

What is she talking about? What time is it?

"About finding your ghost?" she says, surveying the room. She sees my single red backpack, and I'm sure she realizes this wasn't a well-planned trip.

"Found her, remember? She's not a ghost."

"Well, your whatever-it-is," says Allison.

"So you still believe me?" I say with cautious optimism.

"Wouldn't be here if I didn't. I also wanted to extend an official olive branch on behalf of the lovely village of Blue Water apologizing for our beloved mayor. He can be . . ." She pauses, looking for the most polite word she can think of. "A dickbag."

I laugh. "It's no problem. I've dealt with plenty of power-tripping assholes in"—"Sandy Shores," I almost say—"my time. It's hard to believe a guy like that got elected."

"He's been mayor since before I was born," replies Allison. "Unfortunately, there's nothing in the town charter regarding term limits, and the only way there would be is if the mayor signs off on it."

"Is it true what he said about the hospital releasing its patients when it closed?"

Allison hesitates, like I figured out a dirty little secret. "Yeah. But that was 1984. Most of those people have moved on or—"

"Had kids," I finish.

"Yeah, alright, I get it. We're Crazytown. We hear it at every Lakers away game. Anytime I tell anyone where I'm from, it's all, 'Isn't that where that mental institution is?' It sucks. We have other stuff. The lakefront park is great, and there's a sweet indie records store that sells vinyl across the street."

"It does cast some doubt on the 'haunted hospital' thing though, right?"

"I guess, but I've heard stuff out there too: screams, voices in the woods . . ." I give her a skeptical look, to which she immediately hits me with, "*I* believed *you*." And of course she's right.

"Besides, maybe I can prove it to you, if you're willing. These things you're seeing might have something to do with Riverview. It's at least something. I can't imagine the ghost of a not-dead person is giving you many leads." She's right. It is probably worth looking into, if I'm going to believe it or not. "I'll take you out there tonight. Stone Road runs through the woods right behind the hospital. People have seen some spooky stuff out there. Lights in the woods, shadows, ghosts of little kids—stuff like that. Sounds a lot like what you're seeing, right?"

"Yes, it does." I answer.

"So you're in?"

"I'm in."

"Great!" she exclaims, and I can tell she's really excited to be a part of whatever the hell it is we're doing. "OK, so it looks like I woke you up. I'll leave you alone here, and I'll swing by tonight after work and pick you up, and we'll go check it out."

"Cool. Checking out the haunted hospital. I get to be Daphne," I say with a smile.

"OK," she awkwardly laughs, knowing I hoped she'd get a reference that went over her head. Do twenty-year-olds not know *Scooby-Doo*? "Wear comfy shoes and something warm, if you have it. If not, I can bring something. It gets pretty cold here at night." She's being polite, knowing I couldn't have fit much into my backpack. She's observant, I'll give her that.

Also she's remarkably accurate: it is cold as shit out here.

We sit on the hood of her red 1998 Pontiac Grand Am, a car only a few years younger than her. It was a hand-me-down from her dad to her brother. Her brother Peter works for the BWPD and is also a "car guy." He kept it in pristine condition to give to her when he bought his first new car. Still, it looks and feels like it's moments from death.

We're parked off the edge of Stone Road, a completely unlit dirt road that slices through the middle of a large forest that eventually becomes a state park. I've seen bike paths in woods that are more defined than this. The only light comes from the half-moon and the two flashlights we're holding in our hands. Ghosts or not, this is unsettling to say the least. Our plan is to wait right here to see if something happens. It seems to be as good a plan as any.

"This is right by where Debbie Gomez's dad said he saw the little boy," Allison says, as if it would mean something to me.

"What little boy?"

She chuckles, remembering. "I was best friends with Debbie in third grade. I'd go over to her house sometimes, and her dad would tell us this story of the time he was out here when he blew a tire and he saw a little boy bathed in light."

"Bathed in light? That sounds poetic," I say.

"That's what he'd say: 'bathed in light.' He used to tell the story all the time when I'd come over, usually, just as like a ghost story before we went to bed. I'm not doing it justice though. He'd really get into it, turn off the lights and stuff. I thought he just made it up to try to scare us, and when that didn't work, he just kept telling us to make us laugh. But . . . my mom told me Debbie's dad used to be at the hospital, like admitted. Debbie called me once crying because she said her dad thought he saw Jesus and his dead father fighting over a wishbone at Thanksgiving. He forgot to take his pills sometimes."

"I can relate," I say, without thinking.

"What do you mean?"

Dammit.

"Nothing. Just that, I don't know, seeing things." I stumble through. I'm sure Allison didn't buy that explanation, but she doesn't push. "How far is the hospital from here?" I ask, trying to change the subject.

"It's about a mile and a half west of here."

"That far? So it's more than just the hospital that's supposedly haunted?" Allison gives me a frustrated look, tired of the word "supposedly." Without hesitation, I repeat, "So it's more than the hospital that's haunted?" She nods as if to say thank you.

"Weird things happen all around here. It all really centralizes on the hospital though. But you're not getting me to go up there with nothing but a flashlight. It's creepy enough during the day."

"Maybe it's just coincidence. Maybe the woods are haunted and the hospital just got put there."

"Maybe," she says. It's a pretty weak idea, but Allison looks happy that I'm at least participating.

We sit with nothing but the sound of crickets and the occasional rustling of some animal through the dried leaves littering the ground. The leaves have mostly all fallen off the trees at this point. Where I'm from we'd have two months until we'd start thinking about snow, but Allison told me earlier that they've got three weeks tops. The towns this far north are so remote that people are already buying wood and jugs of water, as well as canned goods. It's a safe bet that at some point every winter the only way to travel is by snowmobile over a good six feet of powder, and during those times, people have to be well stocked up on supplies. It's a far cry from home. Up here, the winters can kill you if you aren't ready for them. Allison tells me that her brother has to be on site to recover a frozen corpse at least once a year. Thankfully, it's never been anyone she knows.

"So about Albert Forrester," I say, and Allison's ears perk up. "At the diner last night, you made it sound like you didn't think it was a mugging, and I'm guessing you aren't buying Altman's theory that he fell and hit his head. So what do you think happened?"

I can't see her face, just the beam of light shining from the flashlight in her hand, casting out and landing on some random tree fifty yards ahead of us. But even in the darkness, I know that she's about to lay something heavy on me and she's wondering if it'll be too much for me to take this seriously anymore. Right before I ask the question again, she inhales quickly, then blurts out, "Have you ever heard of 'Old Lady Abigail?'"

"No," I say. "Should I have?"

"No, of course not. She's a local legend here." She takes a deep breath and holds it, then releases, taking the plunge and trusting me all the way. "There's this woman named Abigail who lives just outside of town. She's a shut-in, kind of creepy. No one I know has ever really seen her more than in passing. She's got to be like a hundred or something at this point. Anyway, she was a patient at the hospital before it closed, and she was always making trouble. She was always in solitary. Well, not solitary—that's prison. Whatever they call it on a psych ward."

"Isolation," I chime in, again without thinking. Allison is observant, and I've dropped way too many hints. There's no way she's not got a clue anymore about where I come from. She again just glances over it after a brief stutter, where I'm sure she put it all together.

"Isolation, right. So, anyway, she was a total mess. They gave her electroshock and stuff. Apparently, nothing helped. And when the hospital shut down, she moved out to an old place past Marsh Road, and no one really hears from her, right? Then one night, she wanders out of the woods right down into the middle of town, and she's laughing. She's delirious, just gone, you know? They had to rush her to St. Mary's because her face had been practically burned off."

"Holy shit." I can feel my pulse pick up. If this isn't true, it's a hell of a good story, especially in the dark woods with flashlights.

"Yeah, apparently it was totally gross. Just burnt face and swelling and yuck, right? So, anyway, the night that happened, the night she got her face burned off, is the same night Albert died. Now, there's no way a little old lady overpowered Albert and crushed his skull, so I think whatever attacked and killed Albert also came after Old Lady Abigail. Only she survived."

"Did they question her? Maybe she could have testified or something."

"She's batshit crazy. Her testimony wouldn't hold up anywhere." She inhales deeply, as if she made a mistake. "Sorry, I didn't mean that."

"Mean what?" I ask, but I know. She's sorry for saying "batshit crazy."

She knows.

"Nothing, just, never mind."

Let it slide, Emily. *She knows, and she's going to laugh at you.*

"No, what did you mean? Is there a problem?"

"No! I don't have a problem, OK? I'm not judging or anything."

"Judging?!" *Kyle is laughing at you with his friends right now. Allison is going to leave you just like Kyle. Just like your dad.*

"I'm sorry," she pleads. "I probably jumped to a conclusion that I shouldn't have."

"What, that I'm batshit crazy?" Jesus, stop. I'm going to ruin this. *You always do.*

"No! That . . . I don't know. Maybe other people thought you were. I seriously don't, Emily. I believe you. You know that, right?"

Breathe, Emily. She's different. *No, she's not.*

I'm trying to calm down and be rational. It's not working too well. "I think I want to go back," I tell her. "It's getting late, and there's nothing going on in your haunted woods anyway." That was juvenile. As soon as I said it, I knew it was low. She still doesn't call me on it. *She wants to leave too—forever.*

"I'm sorry," she says, and it breaks my heart because I know she really means it. I'm burning another bridge for absolutely no reason except that I don't want Allison to burn it first. That's what Dr. Harper would have told me. She's not Kyle or my dad. She knows, and she wants to stay. She wants to help me. As I slide off the hood, I take the breath that, when exhaled, would contain my apology—only it gets caught in my lungs as I look over on the passenger side of the car.

Carrot is here.

She's not looking at me, however. She's looking down the road, and she's pointing. Her breathing is elevated, and her eyes are wide open, unblinking. This is something I've never seen before, and I don't know what to do.

Carrot is terrified.

"EMILY!" Allison yells in a whisper. I look up the road into the woods, and I see what they're both looking at.

A bright white light pierces deep in the woods off the left side of the road and is racing toward the edge of the tree line incredibly fast. I grab Allison's arm and pull her back off the road to the far side of the car, where we both duck down together.

"What is that?" I whisper. She shakes her head, and I barely see it in the moonlight. She has no idea. The light isn't coming at us, but it's headed for Stone Road directly in front of us and it will cut off any escape we have. Our only choice would be to turn back the other way—toward the hospital.

Carrot is frozen in panic, and Allison is subconsciously pinching the hell out of my left thigh, where her hand landed as we ducked behind the passenger door. I poke my head out to see if it's still there.

It's moving faster now. It's almost at the tree line. It knows we're here.

"Emily . . . what do we do?"

I look down the road behind us, and she knows what I'm thinking. "No, fuck that," she says. The look I give her, even in the dark, is easy to interpret. We might not have another choice.

The light makes it out of the woods and has slowed down. It's on the road now. And, in an instant, it turns to two parallel lights that curve toward us.

Goddamn headlights. It's a car turning onto our road.

The pain in my leg releases as Allison lets go. I laugh, a combination of embarrassment and relief, and she joins me. The car moves down the road to us and slows to a stop. And seemingly, just to rub salt in a wound, the window rolls down to reveal Mayor Henry Altman's smirking face.

"Good evening, ladies," he says. "What are we doing out here so late? Oh, don't tell me: ghostbusting?" He's loving this, and I'm feeling my right arm tense up as the desire to punch him in his mouth is getting difficult to resist. We don't laugh, and he forces out one last little chuckle, rewarding himself for being so clever. "How about we pack it up for the night?"

"OK," Allison answers, dejected.

"Attagirl," he says, and now I'm literally clenching my right arm with my left, restraining myself. Altman rolls up his window and pulls out. I take a deep breath. Any anger I had at Allison has now been properly redirected and refocused. I don't make eye contact with her at first, a little ashamed that I got so heated so quickly, when all she was trying to do was spare my feelings.

"It's probably best," I say. "I don't think we were going to see anything. If you want to still help me, that's fine, but if you don't, I totally . . ." It's at this point I notice Allison isn't looking at me. She's looking past me, behind me.

"What?" I ask and turn around.

Oh my God.

Carrot is still here. She isn't scared anymore, she's just standing still watching Altman's taillights fade away. I turn back to Allison, my eyes straining from being so wide open. It's true. I cannot believe it's true.

Allison is staring at Carrot.

Allison can see Carrot.

TEN

DUCUNT VOLENTEM FATA, NOLENTEM TRAHUNT

"CAN YOU SEE her?" Allison asks me, not believing her eyes.

"Can you?!" I ask her back, not believing her eyes either. She nods, not taking her eyes off of Carrot. My heart feels like it's about to jump out of my chest. No single thought is sitting still in my head. Instead, it's like throwing water into a hot frying pan. I don't know whether to laugh or cry, so I do both.

Allison sees my reaction, and instantly she understands. "This is Carrot then?" I nod to her, and she sees it out of the corner of her eye, as she's still not looking away from the little girl in purple pajamas. Then she says the words I've wanted to hear my entire life: "Well . . . you're not crazy."

I'm instantly a complete mess, laughing like the governor called and stayed my execution. My whole life, they told me there was something wrong with me, that I shouldn't be believed, that I was broken. They were wrong. Dr. Harper, Dr. Parker, Mom and Dad, all those sons of bitches at Sandy

Shores, every last one of them were all fucking wrong. I even believed it for a while. But I was wrong too.

I'm just fine. I'm sane. There is nothing wrong with me.

For the first time since I was eight years old, I'm human again.

Allison grabs my shoulders and hugs me, and I lose it. I'm sobbing openly into her chest, and she rubs my back. My hands are shaking, and my knees feel weak, and I have to sit down. Allison helps me to the ground, and I start to regain my composure. Allison looks up to see Carrot is gone, and she looks at me quizzically.

"She does that," I say without her needing to ask.

Allison smiles comfortingly. "I'm sorry about what I said . . ."

"No," I say, "you were right. I'm sorry for jumping down your throat. I'm working on that. As far as Carrot goes, though, we should probably keep it quiet."

Allison reacts as if I just took away a Christmas present. "Seriously? We just saw a ghost . . . or whatever she is. You were right about her, and I can back you up, and you don't want to tell anyone?"

"It's for the best. It's not easy to get people on your side with something like this. Trust me."

She looks at her feet, disappointed, but I can tell she agrees. "So now what?" she asks.

"Now, we find out *why* she's here."

I entered the records hall in the old city hall building at around 11:00 a.m. The building itself is beautiful, a sprawling, old red-brick structure designed with very prestigious-looking architecture, with towers stretching up on the front two corners. The police department, fire department, city hall, and records hall are all housed here, as well as a three-cell jail in the basement and a gymnasium on the second floor, where school dances and formal events have been held since the building was erected in 1912. The kind woman working the counter, Dolores, looks like she's been here since it opened. She gives me a puzzled look over her bifocals when I approach the counter. I've noticed this look a lot in my time in Blue Water. There aren't many new people in this town, and when one shows up, they're greeted with a look that's a perfect blend of welcome and suspicion.

"Can I help you, dear?" she asks with a lovely smile.

"I hope so. I'm looking for records about the old hospital."

"Hospital?" she asks, as if she's never heard the word before. "Ah, Riverview, the old nut house." I'd be offended, but this woman is old and I'm sure anything I point out about political correctness will fall on her possibly literally deaf ears. "Who are you, now?"

"My name is Emily Hunter," I answer, unsure about the relevance of the question.

"And why do you need information on Riverview?" This is also an odd question. Why does this woman care why I need information on the hospital? Isn't her job just to point me in the right direction?

"Research. I'm writing a book about old mental institutions in America," I lie, because I think "there's a ghost of an alive person who brought me to this town and wants to show me something about the woods the hospital is sitting in" seems a little pointless to say out loud.

"Oh, that sounds interesting," she says, because, of course, she's a bookworm. "What type of a story is it? A mystery?"

"It is."

"Oh good. I should like to read that. What's it called?"

Seriously lady? "I don't have a title for it yet, but when I do, I can let you know."

Her smile sits on her face for a moment, before turning to a frown. "That sounds great, dear, but I'm sorry, you need written approval to access the records."

"That's weird. I need written approval to access town records?"

"No, not town records, just records pertaining to the hospital. Unfortunately, there's a lot of red tape because the hospital is either on municipal land or federal land. No one knows. It's just a hassle."

"I've heard," I say. Of course this would be more difficult than it should be. "Who do I need written permission from?"

"I'm sorry, Ms. Hunter, I can't allow you access to the hospital records," Mayor Altman tells me from behind his oversized desk in his oversized office. He's holding a glass of whiskey with two ice cubes, the way I'm sure he's seen powerful people in the movies hold them. His wall is littered with pictures of himself shaking hands with other people. No one I've ever heard of—no presidents, celebrities, or people of note. Again, I'm sure he thinks this is what should be on the walls of important people. The other wall has a large trophy case filled with football trophies, all with his name on them, most from high school and a couple from junior high. Everything about this office is designed to impress whomever unfortunately finds themselves within its walls. I wonder if he knows how hilariously fake it feels.

"May I ask why?" I politely ask. He called me "Ms. Hunter," not "honey" or "darling," so I try to keep it light and professional as well.

"HIPAA for one. There are patient records in there that are strictly confidential."

"I'm only interested in technical information about the building's history. Why would there be patient records in those files?"

"I'm afraid it's all mixed together. The hospital shut down rather quickly. There wasn't a lot of time to sort things out, so it's all kind of thrown together."

"No one sorted through it in the last thirty years?"

"No one knew whose job it was, Blue Water Municipal or the feds, so it just sat there."

I'm understanding at this point that the city/federal excuse was one I was going to run into a lot. I also realize that I really don't buy it. In thirty years, no one filed a petition or official query as to what to do with all the files sitting in that basement? No one ever figured out who owned the hospital? Time to put on a little pressure.

"I'm sorry, Mr. Mayor, I don't believe you."

Altman smiles. This is the game he wants to play, the man dangling the string in front of the cat. "Believe me or not, Ms. Hunter, I really couldn't care less. You can't access the records without my signature, which I am not giving you."

THE FRONT DOOR OPENED, HER SMALL FOOT IN ITS CRUMBLING SHOE STEPPING OVER THE THRESHOLD. SHE WALKED THROUGH THE OPEN HALLWAY, THE SHOCKED LOOKS OF THE PEOPLE IN THE LOBBY NOT GOING UNNOTICED.

And now that he's dropped the professional act and the claws are coming out, I can push even harder. "Is there something in there you don't want me to see, Henry?" Calling him by his first name in his office is a pretty big sign of disrespect, and I'm hoping it gets his blood boiling. I knew coming in here he wouldn't be cooperative, and getting him angry might be the only way to get an advantage on him.

He smirks at me calmly, letting me know he's not taking the bait. "If there's nothing else, honey, I've got important things to do." And he motions toward the door.

"Why was closing the hospital such a hurried event?"

He's done. "I hope you're enjoying your brief stay in Blue Water. Perhaps you could come back in the spring for our Nautical Festival. It's a great time. Pick up a pamphlet on your way out."

OK, time to pull out the stops. "Come on, Henry, it's pretty easy to see no one gets to be mayor for thirty-five years without some skeletons in his closet. You bury them up there?"

He looks up at me impatiently, with something else behind his eyes: anger, incredulousness. That got him.

A shot in the dark and I hit a nerve.

She continued down the hallway, not waiting for permission from the secretary, who was too startled to offer it anyway. Her shuffling feet dragged on the floor, announcing her presence to anyone who could hear over the utter silence that fell when she walked in.

"Are you accusing me of something, sweetheart?"

I lean onto his desk, invading his space. "Right now, I want to investigate the hospital. That's what I'm interested in. I'm a good investigator, Henry, really good. I leave no stone unturned. And I'm excited, Mr. Mayor. Really, I can't sleep at night. I'm that eager to investigate. If I can't investigate that hospital, I'll have to investigate something else."

"Is that a threat?" he asks, knowing the answer.

"Not if you don't have anything to hide, sir. Do you have anything to hide?"

Altman settles back in his chair. His tone changes, his demeanor is now different. He gets quieter, and his eyes cut through me. I don't care about his signature anymore. It's him versus me.

"Listen closely, Ms. Hunter. I would advise you to back down. I am a very powerful man and not only in this town. I know many people, I have a lot of connections, and I could make your life a living . . ." And he stops. He's now looking over my shoulder behind me, and his jaw has dropped. I turn around to see what he's looking at, and my blood runs cold.

An old woman—at least I believe she's an old woman—stands behind me. Her clothes are wrecked, tattered, and dirty. Her hair, gray and strung out, looks like it's gone unwashed for weeks. Those are all the second things I notice. The first is her face.

"Jesus Christ," I hear Altman whisper to himself behind me.

She's wearing an expressionless white facemask, her eyes barely visible in the shadow it creates on her face. Around the outside of the mask, on the side of her face nearest me, horrible scarring is poking out, like her face had been burned.

The mask is the same one I saw in the shower in my apartment.

I hear Altman clear his throat in an attempt to regain his composure; when he speaks, it's obvious he's failed miserably. "Abigail, what can I do for you?" This is Abigail? Allison's description didn't do her justice. I can't keep my eyes off of her mask, and I start to feel nauseous. A ringing begins in my ears. I try to calm myself down by focusing on my breathing.

"You can do nothing for me," she croaks. Her voice sounds like it's buried deep inside her and fighting its way out of her throat. "I'm here for her," she says, pointing to me. My throat dries out, and I stop focusing on my breath because I'm holding it without intending to. It feels like death itself just hunted me down and chose me. I can't move, and the ringing is getting worse.

From behind the mask, a muffled and creaking voice says, "We need to talk, Emily."

ELEVEN

HODIE MIHI, CRAS TIBI

THE HOUSE ITSELF is disgusting. It smells like piss and mold. There is trash everywhere, littering the floors, the counters; any open space is covered. This woman should not have been released because, obviously, she cannot take decent care of herself. Although, looking at her, she's managed for the last thirty-some years to keep herself alive, so I guess she can't be all bad.

The walk here was one of the most unnerving experiences of my life. She never said a single word during the entire half-hour stroll up the road and out of town to her dilapidated old home. She kept ten paces ahead of me, though I had to walk slower than I thought possible to stay there. It was strange, feeling frustrated to be moving so slowly to get somewhere I didn't want to go.

I sit down in a large green felt chair, as a grandfather clock chimes behind me, signaling 8:00 p.m. And in this moment I feel stupid, because it's taken me this long to realize it.

I've been here before.

This is the house from my dream. Although it's buried in garbage, everything is exactly the way I knew it would be. The clock has a shard missing, with masking tape covering the edges of the broken glass. The carpet, in the few places I can see it, is a black-and-red shag. The walk in came through the kitchen, past the stove, and to this room. *Déjà vu* isn't a strong enough word for the feeling I have when all this clicks. This is destiny. I'm supposed to be here; I just don't know why. But there's something else, something I just begin to admit to myself, one big difference, besides the trash, between my dream and this moment. In the dream I'm comfortable, I'm relaxed. Now is different. Now, I feel something else: dread, foreboding. Now, I really don't want to be here at all.

It feels dangerous—necessary, but still somehow wrong in some utilitarian way. My being in this room in real life is a lesser evil than not being here, but an evil nonetheless.

I don't know where any of this emotion is coming from, and I try to remind myself I'm just in some old lady's house. When I turn back from the clock, she's there in front of me. I jump, startled at the mask I'm sure I'll never get used to seeing. Abigail is old, and she shuffled the whole way here, but somehow she just moved like a snake to be in the room with me.

"You know why you're here." I don't know if it's just her voice, which sounds like an old attic door grinding on its hinges, but that sounded like a statement.

"I'm sorry, ma'am, is that a question?" I ask because I genuinely don't know. She had stared at me like she expected an answer, but I still couldn't tell.

"Questions, questions, always questions. So inquisitive, aren't we? Can't just leave well enough alone."

"OK, Ms. Pipkin . . ." I start. That's as far as I got before she came right over on top of me.

"You want my rock, don't you?" she hollered. I believe I know the rock she's talking about. In my dream, I was vaguely aware of a large black rock that sat on her mantle above her fireplace. I look back, and sure enough, there it is. The rock itself looks like nothing I've ever seen before. It's got an odd shimmer to it that manages to show up through what looks like scratches or tick marks all over it. I can't tell if it's a souvenir or if it fell from the sky, but it doesn't look natural.

I turn back to face her, and she's closer, frighteningly close. "You can't have it, not yet. One day, I'll give it to you. After I'm dead, you can inherit it. I'll leave it to you."

"That's really not necessary," I say.

"YOU HAVE NO IDEA WHAT IS NECESSARY!" she screams, and I feel like never speaking again. Every muscle in my body has tightened, and I'm clenching my jaw hard enough to hurt my teeth. "You can have the rock someday, and when you're done, you give it back."

She's all over the place. I talked to people like this all the time at Sandy Shores. I knew not to agitate her and to play along. And then the oddest thing happens: the light bulb in the lamp gets really bright and explodes. I react as anyone would: I let out a tiny startled scream. Abigail, however, completely loses it.

"NO! Not yet!" She starts flailing, her eyes dashing around the room. "Emily!" she screams, as if she can't see me.

"I'm right here. It's OK," I say.

"You don't talk. I talk. You understand?" I just nod, not speaking. "You know why you're here. That's not a question, not yet. No questions yet. No answers yet, not until later, a lot later. You listen now. You were called. The little girl—you followed her here. Tell me now you understand."

"How did you . . ."

"NO QUESTIONS YET! TELL ME YOU UNDERSTAND." There's something wrong. It's getting hotter. The room itself seems to be steaming up. It's making the smell that much worse. I feel a trickle from my hairline over my temple drip to my jaw, and I realize I'm sweating.

"I understand," I say.

She continues: "You want to know about the hospital, about Riverview. I was there. You have to find your own way. It's there, Emily. It's all there. I can't tell you more! I can't!"

"Why can't you—" And in a flash, a plate from the china cabinet comes flying over my head, smashing into the wall she threw it at. I'm out of the chair and standing in a defensive position before I realize what happened.

"NO WHY! NO HOW! NO WHEN! NO QUESTIONS!" Abigail is panicking. Another light flickers from the kitchen, and it's noticeably hotter now. Something is really wrong. My sense of dread has gone through the roof. I don't think we're alone.

"It chose you. It needs you. It called me. I know, I know what it feels like. You have to listen. You have no choice. Listen to the hospital."

"The hospital called me?" And apparently this question was OK because I didn't get anything thrown at me this time.

"It needs you. I don't know why it called you or me. They need you. They all do." She seems scared now, not aggressive anymore, like she's begging. "Save them, Emily. Save us all."

A stack of junk falls over in the middle of the floor, seemingly untouched. Beneath everything, a high-pitched ringing begins, like feedback, and more lights flicker and pop. It's getting darker in here with every breaking light bulb, making the lighting spookier and spookier. Dust unsettles from the ceiling, like someone is walking hard upstairs—only there's no upstairs.

"There isn't time," she says. "They're coming—all of them, the girl, the white sky, everyone, the spirits. They know. You shouldn't be here. You have to go soon—not yet, not yet." She moves close again and makes direct eye contact. Her eyes burn into mine. "Listen: I got close. This happened—my face. Albert died. Oh God . . . it wasn't an accident. He died. He died. He had to. There's a reason. For all of this, there's a reason." There's guilt in her voice now. She knows what happened to Albert Forrester. She sounds like she knows and she had something to do with it. I don't ask; I know I'm not supposed to.

The ceiling cracks, the plaster splitting in a straight line from the north to south wall. Now I hear people talking, voices from everywhere, like there are a dozen radios on but turned down and left all over the house. I can't pinpoint where one is coming from. They might be moving.

"You, Emily, you hold it all. It's up to you now. I can't help anymore. Save us. God save us all." My heart is beating hard enough to break my ribs. The voices around me are getting louder, angrier. There's yelling, screaming, arguing as the lights continue to surge and pop, and more piles of garbage fall. The house. . . Is it shaking? Then I hear it, and I can tell Abigail hears it too.

Boom. Boom. Boom.

"Now!" she says. "Ask. Ask one question, then leave. Hurry."

Twenty-thousand questions flash through my mind as I try to narrow it down to one in what seems like the most chaotic environment I've ever imagined. "What are those voices?"

"NO!" she screams. "Wrong question. Ask again." A pane of glass explodes into the room from the window. She doesn't even flinch. Abigail's hair is beginning to stand up, like she's full of static. I feel mine doing it too.

It's the end of the world in this little goddamn house.

"ASK! ASK!" she yells into my face.

"What is happening?"

"NO!"

"I don't know what you want!" I yell, fully panicking now too. "What killed Albert?"

"NO!"

"What were you close to?"

"NO!"

"Why am I seeing Carol Forrester as a kid?"

"NO!"

The house is definitely shaking now as the pulsing is getting faster and louder.

BOOM. BOOM. BOOM.

"What is CONIR?"

The mask, previously observing the devastation around her, darts back to me. Her eyes are hidden in the dark now that almost every bulb in the house is in pieces on the floor.

"Blades," she says. I feel my breath catch. That's probably one of the creepiest things I could have heard in this moment.

"Blades?" I ask.

"Blades! Look for blades!"

BOOMBOOMBOOMBOOMBOOM.

"Abigail, what the hell does that mean?"

"LEAVE! LEAVE NOW!" she screamed. Telling me the second time wasn't necessary. I'm out of the living room, right turn at the stove, and out the front door before I even made the decision to run.

The sounds subside, the pulsing quiets. Soon all I hear is my breath dashing in and out of my lungs, somehow too quickly and too slowly. The woods surrounding the house are quiet. Crickets chirp out of the darkness. The ringing is still in my ears, but it's farther away.

No, it's not ringing in my ears. It's an emergency horn blowing from the roof of the Blue Water Fire Department. I run back toward town, and I'm there in ten minutes to survey the scene unfolding before me on Lake Street: complete fucking chaos.

Two cars are sitting on the sidewalk, having collided with each other after one of them ripped down a telephone pole holding a power transformer, which is now lying on the roof of the nearest car, sending sparks flying all around the surrounding area. People aren't even looking at it, though, as they run around screaming through the streets in mass hysteria. Other people are pouring out of buildings all up and down the road like they're on fire. It looks as though the zombie apocalypse just began in a small Midwest lake village.

I don't remember this many people being out the night before. Something is off, though, some of them are different: I can see through them.

Now I understand why everyone is terrified. Half the people on the street look like what I can only describe as ghosts; the other half are running, screaming, from the ghosts. They look like Carrot always did: there, but not really there.

And speaking of . . .

In the middle of the road, a little girl in purple pajamas holding a dirty stuffed rabbit watches the insanity. In that moment, everything else gets quiet for me. All I notice is her. The rest seems like it's in slow motion.

Carrot turns around to see me, her bright blue eyes finding me amid the rest of the people pushing and screaming. She calmly walks through it all—sometimes literally, as I see her pass through a few people in her way. The mayhem around us both doesn't intimidate her at all. She comes to me quietly and, standing at my feet, looks up to me with an accusatory look. And for the first time in my life, I hear her speak.

"You did this."

TWELVE

NULLUM MAGNUM INGENIUM SINE MIXTURA DIMENTIAE FUIT

THE STREET LOOKS like the day after Woodstock. Windows are broken, cars are dented, the road is full of trash. It appears Blue Water rioted last night.

People are all over the sidewalk, exchanging accounts of what happened, showing each other photos they took on their cell phones. Some people are still scared, claiming it's the end-time. Others are excited, hoping it happens again tonight.

Allison and I are sitting at the Water Street Café over two omelets that we haven't even touched. She's talking to me about last night as well, but I'm really not listening.

"You did this."

Carrot had spoken to me for the first time in my life. I had heard her scream before, but other than that, I'd never heard her make a sound. Seeing her eyes in the bathroom of my apartment was a huge deal. This was indescribable. Good or bad, I still didn't know.

"Right?" ends Allison. The silence afterward catches my attention. I look up to meet her expectant eyes.

"I'm sorry, what?" I say. She smiles, knowing she was talking to no one the whole time.

"I said it looks like neither one of us is crazy. I mean, Altman or my brother, they can't really make fun of me anymore for believing in this stuff. Oh my God, Emily, that was absolutely ridiculous last night! The whole town just went nuts."

"I saw."

How did I do this? What did I do? Did I somehow cause all that chaos? Did I let something loose at Abigail's? Why now? Why would I hear Carrot now? And how did Abigail know she brought me here? Did Abigail send her?

"She said I did it," I say out loud, not really on purpose.

"Who did?" asks Allison.

I look up from my cold breakfast. "Carrot. She was there last night. She said I did it. I caused what happened last night. People were running around screaming, and she looked at me and said, 'You did this.' I heard her voice. That's never happened before."

Allison is puzzled, almost as much as I am. "Did she say anything else?"

"No. And on top of that cryptic shit, last night Abigail said something about blades."

"Holy shit, what? You saw Old Lady Abigail? You actually talked to her?"

"She came looking for me. She knew my name, she knew about Carrot. What happened at her house last night was . . ."

"Wait, you went in her house? You were actually *in* Old Lady Abigail's house?" I can tell I just won the Blue Water Elementary double-dog dare contest. I'm not sure she heard the part about my name or Carrot; she was too in shock that

I went inside the dilapidated, old house. "What was it like in there?"

"You know, I couldn't even begin to explain it."

"And that's where the Sighting started?"

"The 'Sighting?'"

"That's what people are calling what happened last night."

"What people?" I ask. I can tell she's trying to trademark it.

"People . . . you know, me and . . ." she trails off.

"Yeah," I mercifully begin, "I was there when it started, and it was . . ." I couldn't even try to explain what Abigail's house was like. "If the Sighting was my fault, it was because I was there."

Allison gives a little smile when I say the "Sighting." Now two people call it that.

"All of this started there. I have to go back up," I say, not really excited that the words came out of my mouth. Going back to that house is the last thing I really want to do, but it's the only solid lead I have at this point that I can possibly explore. The records are off limits. Carol won't talk to me. It's Old Lady Abigail or nothing.

"Can I come?"

I'd love it if she did because I don't want to be alone, but I know it isn't safe. "No," I say. "It's too dangerous. Besides, she had enough trouble up there with just me, and I was invited." She looks down at the table. "I promise I'll tell you everything."

I can tell this isn't what Allison wanted to hear, but she looks like she's going to abide by my decision. "Alright." She sighs, then she smiles. "How was breakfast?"

My omelet, my coffee, and my hash browns are still on my plate, completely uneaten. I'm too distracted; I don't feel hungry at all. "Pretty," I answer.

I walk down the road, wondering what to say to Abigail. She screamed at me that I could only ask her one question, that she couldn't help me anymore, but I don't believe that. She knows so much more than she is telling me. I've spent my entire life not knowing, not understanding, not even having an idea where to look. Now some old lady knows what's happening to me. She has answers, and she won't let me ask? Fine, I won't ask. I'll make her tell me.

I pass the city hall building, psyching myself up to do whatever I have to do to figure out my next step, when I notice the old records hall clerk walking out of the building. She's walking with another woman, who, because of the age difference and the fact that she's literally holding her up to go down the stairs, I'm assuming must be her daughter. I slow down to hear their conversation but not slow enough to make it obvious I'm about to listen in. All I catch is that it's one of their birthdays and they're going out to lunch to celebrate. The front of the building has the list of times each of the different municipal offices are open, and the clerk slides Blue Water Records Hall to *CLOSED*. I keep walking, realizing a unique opportunity has just presented itself to me, and wondering if I dare to take it. I need to know what's in that basement, but this whole quest goes belly up if I get arrested. Altman could have me right where he wants me, and I'd have nothing—no leverage, no power, no leg to stand on.

No guts, no glory.

They pass by me and walk down the sidewalk the way I just came. I look up at the building, pretending to admire its architecture, but really looking for a weakness. At the back of the building, facing Lake Huron and what could generously be called a beach, two small, unguarded basement windows greet me. I survey the area: there are a few houses nearby, and if anyone is looking out their windows, I'm exposed. I peer around even more, realizing that there is no conceivable purpose for someone to be standing back here besides breaking in, and if anyone is watching, I'm immediately suspicious looking. The longer I'm here, the more chance I have of getting caught.

I lie down on the grass and pull both windows, and of course they're locked, but they're both surrounded by a rock garden that spans the rear of the building. Not exactly the Pentagon when it comes to security. *One count of breaking and entering on government property, one count of destruction of government property*, I can hear Altman's voice say. Knowing him, he'd try to get me on espionage too.

The sound of the breaking window is like a car crash in the silence, and I clinch up waiting for an alarm of some kind. When none comes, I quickly reach inside and find the old latch, open the window, and manage to only cut myself a couple times as I crawl over the broken glass lying on the windowsill.

I hit the floor and immediately hide under the nearest table, seemingly eating an entire cobweb when my face collides with it. I wait for what seems like an hour, but was really about a minute, to make sure no one came down to investigate the breaking-glass sound. When a reasonable amount of time goes by, I step out.

The basement of the records hall looks like it's been abandoned. There's no light except the sunlight coming in through the windows. The rest of the room is covered in dust and spiderwebs. I think I'm the first person down here in years. The walls are crumbling cinder blocks, the floor just a cement slab. One set of wooden stairs protrudes into the middle of the room from the reception area on the main floor. The east side of the room is a wall of file cabinets, but the rest of the records department appears to just be empty tables and extra storage. There are old Christmas decorations, signage for various city elections, including a couple reading *Re-Elect Mayor Henry Altman: a Candidate you know, a Candidate who knows you.*

Time to move. Who knows how much time I have down here.

I come to the filing cabinets and read the labels. They're all denoting the particular alphabet section contained within, and I search quickly to find *QUA-RUS*. This is where I'll find Riverview Psychiatric.

The drawer sticks, and when I give it enough force, the guide screams from rust and lack of oil, and I'm certain everyone in the building heard it. I freeze, holding my breath. Not moving, not making a sound.

No one comes.

I flip through the various file tabs until I find it: a not-too-thick manila folder labeled *Riverview*. I open it quickly and hold it in the light. Deeds, building plans, bills—it occurs to me at this moment that I don't even know what I'm looking for. There's a small folder labeled *Riverview Face Sheets*, and I grab that. Each of the sheets is contained in a labeled plastic sleeve, probably to keep orderlies from spilling coffee on them. I thumb through them, seeing all the faces of people who at one time or another spent time in Riverview. I find the name I'm looking for: Pipkin, Abigail. It's all I can do to not throw the whole file in frustration. It's just the plastic sleeve; the face sheet has been removed. Flipping through the rest quickly, I see it's the only one missing.

The rest of the papers are various and random. Altman wasn't lying; it seems most of this was just thrown in here, and my access to the patient face sheets was technically illegal. The thought occurs that he might not have been lying. I dismiss that thought. He's hiding something. He didn't want me down here for a reason.

I scan through everything else, and a name keeps coming up: Dr. Gregory Millen. I remember his name from the lighthouse dedicated to him, His signature is all over everything, and I eventually figure out he was the head of psychiatry. Basically, he ran the facility. It's not much, but it might be a new thing to look into—then I reconsider. It's also plastered on the town lighthouse, and I'm sure if I had asked Altman, it's information he would have given up freely. It's nothing.

This is a dead end.

Altman has been mayor since the eighties. He flinched when I mentioned skeletons in his closet. Maybe there's something here.

I creep quietly down the row, being careful not to kick anything in the dark and make noise. I scan the file drawer labels again, and I find *A-BLA* sitting first in line. I open the drawer slowly, trying not to make as much noise as I did the first time, and am happy to find it rolls out much easier than the other one. There sits a manila folder labeled *Altman, Henry*, but all that's inside it is a single piece of paper: an approved recall petition for the current mayoral administration, dated October 14, 1984. I'm batting zero when I hear a table leg slide on the concrete behind me.

I'm not alone down here.

Instinctually and with little subtlety, I duck behind the nearest table. Who knows how long whoever is down here has been watching me. There's no good chance I've actually hidden. I listen for any other clue, but it's quiet. The other person has gone silent too. They know I know they're here.

I quietly crawl under the length of the table toward the north wall by the windows. If I have to, I can make a dash for it. I'm sure I'll cut myself up pretty good trying to quickly get out the window, but I might be able to make it out before they know it was me down here.

Footsteps. They're coming toward me from the row that's now in front of the window. That fast, I'm cut off. I look behind me to the stairs. I could try to get out that way, but I'd be bursting out into an open city hall, which is also the police station. Game over.

I turn back to look at the window from my vantage point and recoil immediately. Someone is standing in the dark directly in front of the window, and they're looking right at me. Do I jump at them? Do I give up? Do I pretend I'm not here?

"Emily?"

I exhale. It's Allison.

"Jesus! What the hell are you doing?" I ask in a whispered yell.

"Me? What the hell are you doing? You said you were leaving to talk to Abigail, and you break into city hall?"

"Altman wouldn't let me come down here; I figured there was a reason. Why did you follow me?"

"I . . . thought you were going to Abigail's."

I sigh in an obvious attempt to convey my frustration. "Allison, I told you to wait, and I'd tell—"

The loud clank of the lock resonates in the room as the door at the top of the stairs opens with a creak. Allison ducks under the table with me. We stop everything else instantly, staring at each other wide eyed, pleading with each other silently to figure out what to do next. A flashlight beam dances over the spiderwebs and dust in the air, and for a moment, I forget everything and realize how disgusting it was that I was breathing all of that in.

"Attention, anyone in the basement," an authoritative male voice booms from the top of the stairs. "This is the Blue

Water Police Department. Make yourself known and come out slowly."

I am so fucked.

"I think it's only the one," says Allison. "You can make it to the window and get out."

"I broke the window," I say. "They're going to know I was here."

"Forget it, just go."

"What about you?"

"I'll take the blame. You're the one seeing things, you're the one who caused the Sighting, you can't get caught here."

It's noble, but there's no way in hell. "No way, I'm not letting you get arrested for me."

"Emily, we don't have time to argue. Go!"

"Allison—"

"Look, they're going to get someone for this. I'm not crawling back through that window. I've still got glass in my arm. So either you go, or we both get caught."

I look at her, not knowing what else to say. The beam is lower now. The cop is in the basement with us.

"I'll be fine. Trust me," she says. I have no choice.

"Thank you," I say. It's all I can come up with.

I move to the end of the table, the wall of cabinets to my right, the window directly in front of me. I start a mental countdown, hoping this isn't a small-town cop with a boner for shooting people. He's in the far corner right now, as far from me as he can get. It's now or never.

One . . .

Two . . .

What the hell?

My eyes fall on the second file cabinet. At first I think, "What a crazy coincidence," until my rational brain kicks in over the fear of being gunned down in an escape attempt.

"Shane, are you out back?" the cop says into his radio.

"Ten-four, no one has come out," the cop's partner radios back. Somewhere in the back of my mind, I make a mental note that I can't leave out the window. It seems unimportant. I'm not leaving anyway. Not until I see what's in that file cabinet.

The one labeled *BLA-DES*.

Allison is trying to get my attention. I see her waving out of the corner of my eye. I feel like she's trying to tell me the first cop is closing in on where I'm crouched down. I wave her off, and she gives me the most incredulous look I've ever seen, like somehow I've forgotten the shit we're both in. Truth is, I have.

The first cop is walking along the north wall now, cutting off my path to the window. Soon he'll round the table, his flashlight falling on me. I'll be carted off to jail, and I'll never know what's in that cabinet. I'll never know. Holy shit, I have to do something. But it's too late, I have no play, nowhere to run.

"I give up!" Allison calls from behind me. "I'm standing up now, don't shoot, Pete."

The beam drops over my head, but the cop holding it isn't looking at the ground. He's looking at his sister.

"Al? Jesus, what the hell are you doing down here?"

"Sorry," she says.

"You find anything?" Shane asks over the radio.

Peter hesitates, but clicks the button. "Just my dumbass sister."

A moment goes by before Shane clicks back, and I can hear him laughing. "Hey, Allison."

"Hey, Shane," she says.

"He didn't hear you. I didn't hit the button. What are you doing in the records hall?"

"I'm looking for evidence to prove the city knows what's going on about the Sighting last night."

"Goddamn it, Allison, you and your stupid conspiracy theories."

"Oh, I'm sorry, Pete, was there not mass fucking panic here last night? Did you sleep through that?"

"If you want a record, just ask Betsy when she gets back from lunch! Don't rob the place."

"Right. 'I'm looking for evidence the city is holding out information. Can I see the proof please?'" I can hear her rolling her eyes without seeing it. "You know Altman would never let that fly. We tried."

"Who is 'we?'" he asks, like he caught her.

"WE! The people of Blue Water, idiot. He's dirty, and you know it."

"Yeah, I do, Al. This"—he gestures to the broken window—"is not the way to prove it."

Shane radios back in: "Hey Peter, what's the plan here?"

Peter takes a moment, playing it out in his head. "Meet me up at the front door, in about five minutes. We're going to come down and check out the disturbance that was reported." He looks at Allison. "You go out that window. I never saw you."

"There's broken glass, Pete."

"Really? Tough shit. Go."

She hugs him and softly guides him back toward the center row leading to the stairs. She's blocking him from seeing me. "I love you. I owe you."

"You bet your ass you do. And Shane," he says.

"Free coffee for life."

"Right. When I come back down here, you better be gone."

She starts climbing on the table toward the window, and he watches her as he makes the stairs. "Pete?" she calls. "Don't tell Dad."

"Yeah," he says as she goes out. He closes the door at the top of the stairs.

I dart across the row. I have to make this quick and quiet.

I slowly pull the *BLA-DES* drawer out, and it's silent. I thumb through the file tabs: *Bridge Road Repairs, Camden Ave., Canal Cleaning and Maintenance Protocol, Canal Dock Regulation, Canal St., City Campground Funds, City Park Maintenance Contracts, City Sewage Maintenance . . .*

Nothing. And then . . .

Oh my God.

A small tab stands out, almost staring back at me, daring me to believe the single nonsense word written on it in old-woman cursive, followed by the most appropriate question mark ever placed:

CONIR?

I grab the file, knowing I have probably seconds until Officer Peter Jacoby opens that door and finds me here. The first thing I notice is that the folder itself isn't empty, but it's not full by any means. It's lighter than I want it to be. I dash for the window, climb on the table, and as I do, I hear the lock unfastening again. The glass cuts little holes in my arms as I wiggle my way out, folder in hand, and run back toward my motel.

PETER STOOD OUTSIDE THE NOW OPEN DOOR. A FEW OTHER COPS MILLED ABOUT, NOT IN ANY RUSH AT ALL WHEN ALTMAN ENTERED THE ROOM, BIG AS LIFE ITSELF.

"SHIT," SAID PETER, AS HE MOTIONED FOR HIS PARTNER SHANE TO CHECK OUT WHO JUST WADDLED THROUGH THE DOOR. SHANE LOOKED BACK TO PETER, ROLLING HIS EYES. PETER STOOD UP AND APPROACHED ALTMAN, TRYING TO REDUCE THE POTENTIAL FALLOUT.

"Jacoby, whadda we got?" said Altman, in the way he'd heard superior officers ask in the movies. Altman was not Peter's superior officer, and often he wished Altman would remember that.

"Well, sir, we have a witness, Mr. Gerhardt, who phoned in a broken basement window he noticed from his house next door. Officer Richards and I were first on scene, made note of the window, and surveyed the premises. There was no one here. Apart from the broken window, there was no sign of intrusion. Nothing appears out of place, nothing else broken, and according to Betsy, nothing appears to be missing. She doesn't recall the last time she came down here but knows it's been at least two weeks. Mr. Gerhardt doesn't recall noticing the window intact in that time, so we think the window may have been broken sometime in that time frame, most likely by kids throwing rocks near the beach. Everything points to that, not at B-and-E. Looks like a false alarm. We've found glass to replace the window. It's already fixed."

Altman looked let down, like he wanted to catch someone for this. That disappointment wasn't lost on Peter. "Well done, Officer. Looks like you got everything covered." A suspicious look came over Altman's face as he looked at Peter. Peter wondered if Altman thought he was lying. He made sure not to blink. After a few moments, Altman smiled. "Mind if I look downstairs?"

Altman walked slowly down the creaky stairs, being careful not to let his cane catch on a loose board. The truth is, he wanted to catch that bitch Emily Hunter down here. He knew denying her access might get her to make a stupid move. As soon as word came across his desk there had possibly been a break-in, he started salivating. Then he gets here and nothing? Altman made note that Jacoby was first on scene. He remembered Jacoby's sister and Emily Hunter embarrassing him at the diner. Maybe her brother was working with them? He'd take them all down, like he does anyone who stands against him. He found the Riverview file, all intact. He didn't bother looking at his own file; he cleared that out years ago. It can't be a coincidence that the window was broken. He looked around, unsatisfied but unable to think of another move. Altman hobbled over to the stairs and looked up them dreadfully. His leg was hurting still from coming down, and now he had to go back up. It ached more now than it did after the hit-and-run that broke it in five places all those years ago. Today, he thought, wasn't the first time people plotted against him, but he'd make an example of them this time. This time, it would be the last.

But first he had to get up these goddamn stairs.

THIRTEEN

MUNDUS VULT DICIPI

THREE DOCUMENTS—THAT'S IT. A pink invoice and two white, paper-clipped stacks. Other than that, the CONIR file is empty. I've been staring them over for hours, reading them, then reading them again. The worst part of all is feeling so close to an answer only to have more questions. "Hey Emily, you know that thing that drove you crazy for years? There's a reason." That's it. That's the only help I get. It's real, and it's maddening.

It was almost less frustrating to believe I was insane.

Allison stops by with another cup of to-go coffee and a jelly donut. I imagine this is what it feels like cramming for a final. I spent my college years under strict supervision and then at Sandy Shores, so I wouldn't know. I'd guess there'd be more study material than three little documents lying on a motel bed.

"Any closer to this making sense?" she asks, and she can tell by my frown the answer is no. "So tell me again, what is CONIR?"

"I have no idea," I reply. "It's this word I keep seeing. I don't know what it is or what it means. I just know it means *something.*"

She lets in and out a deep breath. "Maybe I can take a look? Fresh set of eyes, you know?"

"There's not much to look at, but knock yourself out."

She grabs the pink invoice first, and her eyes widen. "This is an invoice for over two million dollars."

"Right," I answer. "But it doesn't say what it's for, just some coded item." The invoice was for a single line item designated *M12-R8857-A*, then, underneath, the word *Trnspt.*

"Transport?" she asks. I shrug. That was my guess too. She continues reading every single letter on the page. I've done that at least five times by now.

"Hey, sorry if I got you in trouble," I say.

"Nah, don't worry about it. One advantage of having your big brother on the small-town police force. It's not the first time I should have been arrested." She smiles a little, rebellious smile. "I've got to do his laundry for a month. Ever the bachelor."

"It sounds like he doesn't love Altman either."

She shrugs. "Everyone knows he's corrupt, but he's been in charge so long now. People fear change. They tried a recall twice now. Both times, the people spearheading the project suddenly gave up. One said he had a change of heart; the other just disappeared. One day, just poof. Some people think he's on the bottom of the lake."

This is shocking. I knew Altman was a blowhard. I never once considered he'd go that far. "You think he killed someone?"

"Or maybe the guy just left town. It was a while back, you know. Rumors snowball. It's possible the guy just got a new job and moved, but the small-town gossip mill is unstoppable. I guess drama is more fun than staring at the lake all day. People always think I'm making all this ghost stuff up because I'm bored. Pete thinks it's because Mom died. He doesn't say it, but . . ."

I give her a second, then reach out and hold her hand. She smiles at me, looking up from her lap, the edges of her eyes reddening. "It just sucks having no one believe you, you know?" she says.

I give her a knowing smile. She rolls her eyes at herself, embarrassed. "Of course you know," she says.

"Well, it's a good thing we have each other then," I say before taking a moment to realize how true that statement really is. Without Allison, I'd have gotten absolutely nowhere. She believed me, she trusted me, when no one else would. And as excited as I was to have someone on my side that morning in the diner, I know at the time I almost resented her for believing me so quickly. I know what I was saying was madness. I thought her gullible. It turns out, she'd just been wearing my shoes as well. The only difference between us was she wore them with kindness.

"Did you see this?" she asks, holding up the third page of one of the other clipped documents.

"Yeah, it's a little creepy, right?" The page read as follows:

> 11/18/81 – KL CONIR at 42 minutes. GM
>
> 11/19/81 – KL exhibits signs of mental decompensation, consistent with other cases. GM
>
> 11/22/81 – KL sedated, placed in isolation after incident in cafeteria. MS stabbed repeatedly in the neck with a fork before staff could intervene. MS deceased. GM
>
> 12/28/81 – KL readmitted into general pop. Complains of headaches, echoes visible. GM.

"What the hell is 'echoes visible?'" she says.

"It just goes on like that. It sounds like old tests the military did with LSD on prisoners." The page reads like an observation log on a single patient. Due to privacy laws, general patient logging couldn't have full names, just initials. This is about someone named KL.

"GM?"

"Gregory Millen," I answer. It's the first solid lead I've had yet. These tests were done and documented by Gregory Millen, head of psychiatry at Riverview Hospital. Whatever CONIR is, it was definitely at the hospital, and it is seemingly very dangerous.

After a long silent pause, I step back. "I don't get it. This CONIR thing has been bugging me my whole life. None of this helps at all."

"Have you ever been here before?" asks Allison.

The motel phone rings. Odd, as no one has the number. I assume it's the front desk when I answer it.

"Hello, is this Emily Hunter?" a female voice asks.

"Yes, it is. Can I help you?" A silence sits on the line, until finally . . .

"Emily, this is Carol Forrester. We met the other day."

OK, not the front desk. I take a sharp breath and focus. I played this all wrong the first time. This time, I'd get it right.

"Hello, Mrs. Forrester." Allison's ears perk up and her eyes widen. I shake my head to her, acknowledging I have no idea why she's calling either.

"Listen, Ms. Hunter, I would just like to apologize for my rudeness when we first met."

"No apology needed, ma'am. It was entirely my fault. I came into your house and asked a lot of personal questions that I had no business asking. I'm the one who should be apologizing."

There's silence again, as if she's carefully considering what she's going to say next.

"I'd like another opportunity to talk to you. I think I'm ready now."

I find the CONIR file, and Carol wants to talk again in one day. This couldn't be going any better. I contain my excitement dutifully.

"If you're sure," I force myself to say.

"Yes, dear. Yes, I am. Can you come over?"

"Now?" I ask. Seriously?

"Yes, if that's possible."

"Of course, I'm heading over now." Allison's eyes somehow get even wider, and I make another miming gesture, mimicking her excitement and extreme curiosity.

"Alone," she says.

Bitch should have listened.

Mayor Henry Altman perused the sizable stack of paper that had just been faxed to his office. He had friends in high and low places, friends he'd made in his political life and his previous one. Ted was one of the latter. One quick phone call was all it took. Emily Hunter wanted to play with fire. This is what she deserved.

It was an interesting read. Psych notes signed off on by Ted's employee, Dr. Meghan Harper. Schizophrenia, hallucinations, delusions of grandeur, self-harm, and an ATL filed with the Royal Oak Police Department. A suicide attempt, a wrap sheet, a mug shot.

It was like Christmas.

The door opens slowly and the first thing I see is her eyes. The same beautiful striking blue eyes I just found out Carrot has, only older, sadder—especially now, as they're bloodshot from crying.

"Is everything OK, Mrs. Forrester?"

"No, dear. It hasn't been for years—maybe ever." She brings me into her living room again and invites me to sit again and hands me a cup of coffee again. "I'll let you finish this one," she says with a smile not big enough to cut through the melancholy filling the room.

I smile back and take a sip. It's a little cold, but I don't complain. "So, what did you want to talk to me about?"

He knocked on the door of the old shack too loudly, but he knew he was trying to get the attention of an old, crazy woman. Who knows if she could hear or if she was busy pissing herself in a closet. The door creaked open slowly, and there she stood. Something was different, though, even from when she had walked into his office bringing that smell that still lingered there. She seemed taller.

"Well of course," Old Lady Abigail said with disgust. Altman wasn't affected by her grotesque appearance. Abigail wasn't impressed that he was in her doorway.

"Hello, ma'am. I was in the neighborhood, and I thought I'd check in on you."

Abigail turned and walked into the house, leaving Altman on the doorstep to follow her inside.

"Albert believed in this stuff. I never believed him. After last night, there's really no denying it, is there?" I shake my head no, determined not to interrupt her or open my big mouth again. We're going to go at her pace today. "I want to tell you more about Albert."

I nod again. I'm not sure what Albert's death has to do with anything, but I'm guessing it does. The more I ponder over all of this stuff, the more I realize it's all related in some way. I don't know why I'm seeing what I'm seeing. I don't know why I'm seeing Carol as a young girl or why she brought me here, but she did. And Abigail knew about it and led me to the CONIR file, which led me to Millen and the hospital. Abigail's injury and Albert's death were the same night. It's all connected, and somewhere rattling around in Carol Forrester's head, there has to be a bigger piece of the puzzle. I just need to let her hand it over.

"We met when we were little kids. I found him, actually. He was in the woods, lying on the ground, when I happened across him. He didn't remember how he got there. He just recalled seeing a bright light suddenly right in front of his face, like it came out of nowhere." She pauses, studying my face, looking for a reaction. I'm guessing she's probably heard how farfetched this sounds already.

"Maybe it was a seizure? A lot of times, people see lights." I know from experience.

"That's what I thought for years. It accounted for the pain he was in. But there was something else, Ms. Hunter. Something I think I taught myself to ignore." She gets quiet and tentative, like she's about to speak words she's suppressed forever. "He was bruised, Ms. Hunter. Something hurt him." She again stares at me for a reaction. This time it's different. This time it feels like she's expecting something. "I think whatever killed him was the same thing that attacked him the night I found him."

"How old were you?" I ask.

"Eight," she says. "You told me you would see visions of me at that age. Do you . . ." she trails off, and I suddenly get it. After living with uncertainty for all these years, she wants to know if I know what killed her husband. That's why she called.

Why is it so fucking dark?

All the bulbs were broken, lying shattered all over the ground. The living room itself was in shambles. The windows were broken, the ceiling was cracked. The place looked like a warzone. If the house wasn't condemnable before, it would be now. That would probably make things easier.

"Is everything *OK* here, ma'am?" he asked, not really caring.

"Almost. Almost there. Almost," replied Abigail, rocking in place.

"Is there anything I can help you with, Ms. Pipkin?"

"Yes," she replied, not making eye contact, still walking away. She made it clear she couldn't be bothered with him, and it started to get under his skin.

"Come on, we've known each other for a long time . . ." he began.

"I know you're a horrible man." Still she didn't look at him, keeping her back to him. If she thought he was so horrible, why was she not on guard while he stalked around her home, he thought. "Do you think I forgot, Henry? I may be old, but I'm not forgetful. I know you. I know you."

OK, he thought, enough with the polite shit. It was obvious she wasn't buying it, and he was getting sick of doing it anyway.

"You know what, Abby? You're a fucking psycho. You always have been."

She finally made eye contact through her dead face mask—one eye dark, the other pale and blood red, both burning through him. "Doesn't mean I'm wrong."

He couldn't see, but he knew she was smiling.

"Mrs. Forrester, I spoke with Henry Altman, unfortunately." She smirks at that. "He mentioned that at the end, your husband had . . . difficulties."

I see the tears already creep into the bottom of her eyes, not daring to drop out just yet. "Albert . . ." she says, then stops. I can see her pushing the thoughts to the front of her mind and out of her mouth as they clutch and drag and fight to stay hidden. "Albert would have nightmares. He'd sleepwalk. He'd forget who he was, who I was, and he'd get so upset. He'd speak gibberish and get so upset." The tears are coming fast like the dam has broken on her eyes, matching the flood of emotion and words coming from her. She's releasing everything. She couldn't stop now if she wanted to. "Toward the end, 1986, 1987, he became obsessed with the old mental hospital in the woods. He would fall asleep next to me, and I'd wake up and he was gone, and we'd know to look for him up there. He'd be asleep in one of the rooms up there. The police knew exactly why I was calling every time. I knew we were becoming a joke, and I even laughed sometimes, but I hated myself for it. He was such a dignified, beautiful man, and he became a joke. I couldn't do anything. Or shit, maybe I could have. I mean I wanted to get him help, but I was afraid they'd lock him up. But I should have tried. He'd still be alive, and I should have tried." At this point, she's dissolved into the thoughts that ate her alive for all these years, and I leave my seat to hug her. She melts into my arms. Of course she feels guilty, she loved him. She second-guesses everything she did that got her here. This must be how my mom felt.

My mom. I make a quick mental note as I look at my watch behind Carol's back: I never called her after I saw the picture of Carrot. Things just got away from me. I'll call her tomorrow morning. It's too late now. She doesn't deserve the guilt Carol is feeling right now or the stress I'm probably putting her through not knowing where I am. I don't know what she'll think about everything that's happened. I don't know if I should tell her. Maybe I'll get Allison to talk to her, hearing it from another person might be persuasive. Maybe she'll just worry more that someone might be taking advantage of the crazy woman.

"It's not your fault," I say. It's all I can come up with, and I know it's no help.

She turns her nose and stares at the floor. Obviously, she disagrees.

"When they found the tumor in the postmortem, I hated myself. The doctors said it most likely caused all his difficulties.

They said it was unusually aggressive, not treatable by the time we would have noticed it. His dad died a year later—same cancer. Myles and Dawn, his parents, took me in when I was a kid. After Myles got laid off, the man basically raised me. It was too much, losing them both within a year."

"They adopted you?" I ask.

"It was 1971. There weren't public records you could look up on the internet. I was homeless. They told everyone I was a cousin who came to live with them. That raised some eyebrows when Albert and I got married."

"You were homeless when you were eight?" I need to keep the conversation here for as long as she's willing to talk about it. There's a reason for me seeing Carrot all my life—one I will never get to unless I can get Carol to offer up this information willingly.

"My parents died when I was too young to remember them," she says. "My grandmother raised me after that, until I became too difficult for her. She was almost ninety, and I wasn't the easiest kid. She gave me up to the state two months before she died. I bounced around a lot. Then I got tired of bouncing."

"Did something happen? I can't imagine the choice to live on your own at eight made sense unless it was to get away from something much worse."

She stares at me now, recalling memories. There is a question in her eyes, one that I feel like is for me. Altman gave me the same look when he met me.

"I know your face," she says. "You say you've seen me your whole life. I think maybe I've seen you too."

"I heard Emily Hunter came to talk to you," he said. "A couple of crazies having tea together—must've felt like old times. You know she's a nutcase too, right?" Henry decided to start playing dirty. This was more his speed. It was more fun.

"I know much more than you think I do, Henry."

"I'm sure you do," he replied sarcastically.

"I know Emily found the CONIR file."

Altman's blood froze as his mind jumped from conclusion to conclusion. Emily Hunter did break into city hall. He thought she'd look into him or the hospital. Altman didn't even know there was a CONIR file. He'd never even thought to look. Hell, he hadn't thought about it for decades. Dolores must've found documents when she started sorting through the hospital files and just not known where else to put them.

"It doesn't matter. There couldn't have been anything important in there," he said dryly, trying to reassure himself.

"There's enough. Trust me, she's going to figure it out. She has to. She has to. She has no choice."

"Figure out what, Abby? There's nothing to figure out."

"Figure it out, Henry. Figure it out. You know who she is. You know why she's here. You know what she did. It's too late, too late. You know who she is, and you can't stop her."

Altman pinched his nose. Abigail was completely unhinged. All he knew about Emily Hunter was she was an annoying little fly who was about to get what was coming to her—especially now that she had the . . .

No.

She had the CONIR file. She broke in to city hall to get it—a file no one knew existed.

It couldn't be.

"How do you know—"

"I KNOW, I KNOW SO MUCH MORE. I KNOW ABOUT YOUR WATCH. I KNOW HOW YOU GOT IT. I SAW WHAT YOU DID."

HENRY REELED BACK. HIS PULSE QUICKENED. HE WAS SURE SHE WAS BLUFFING. SHE WASN'T THERE. NO ONE ELSE WAS THERE. RIGHT?

TIME TO CHANGE THE SUBJECT. THIS WAS RAPIDLY GETTING OUT OF CONTROL.

"IT CAN'T BE HER, ABBY. ALBERT FORRESTER IS DEAD."

OLD LADY ABIGAIL TURNED TO MAYOR HENRY ALTMAN SLOW ENOUGH TO HEAR HER BONES CREAK.

"I KNOW, HENRY. I KILLED HIM."

The rest of the conversation isn't as enlightening as I had previously hoped. I realize it is more for her, and that's OK. I look at the sketches on the wall, and one stands out to me. There's an X with two dots over top of it, like an umlaut. It's the same symbol I saw in the dream of Altman's watch. I thought they were Roman tens. I ask about it, but she doesn't know. All of Albert Forrester's sketches were bizarre and indecipherable to her. I don't press—not yet at least, not even about her knowing my face. For now, I'm satisfied Carol is back on my side. I've rebuilt the bridge by being a little more tactful. This woman is Carrot or at least she was. If I'm ever going to figure this out, I'm certain I'll need her help.

I finish the coffee, and we small talk for a little while about the town. Then I smile and I kindly leave her at the door with another hug. I tell her to call me anytime, whether it's about my mystery or if she just wants to talk. I do mean it. It's nice to be the stable one, the shoulder someone else leans on.

I walk back toward the motel, breathing in the night air. The stars are incredible over the lake. I take a moment to sit on a bench and reflect. After how well today has gone, I feel like a new person. I'm not the lunatic people made me out to be, especially now that all of Blue Water saw what they saw last night. There's a reason all of this is happening, and it's all tied together. No one can deny that. I smile at the breeze chilling my face coming off Lake Huron. The past is all prologue to what I am at this moment. It's all unimportant detail, stories that I can disempower—and being with Carol Forrester tonight taught me that. I'm free to let it go whenever I want. And looking over the black lake under a hundred thousand watchful stars, I realize now is as good a time as any.

I walk back to my motel room, a tortured lifetime lighter. Tonight feels like the first night of my real life. It all begins now.

Altman slipped on a pair of black gloves while Abigail's back was still to him. She sat in a chair now—green felt, oversized for her frail body. He looked around the room through all the mess, and his eyes fell upon an odd-looking black rock sitting on the mantle, roughly the size of a softball.

It would be perfect.

"We've all done terrible things, Henry," she said, looking at the floor in front of her. "You, me, Dr. Millen. They all needed to be done. They were all . . . important. I said this." She sounded like she was trying to convince herself. Altman didn't need convincing. Important or not, he'd do it all again. He'd do tonight over too. His stomach tightened in anticipation. He loved this part: the Before.

He quietly grabbed the rock and felt its weight in his hand. It was deceptively heavy. Even better.

"I know what you're doing, Henry," she said, still not turning around. He smirked to himself. If you knew what I was doing, he thought, you'd run. "You aren't here to check up on me, are you?" He smiled again. No, not at all, Abby, he thought, I'm here to kill you.

"You're here to kill me," she said.

This stopped him. She did know, and she had let him in. She had let him in alone. She kept her back to him. Her back was still to him, just sitting in the chair, in full striking distance.

It had to be a trap.

He cautiously took a step back and lowered the rock. His eyes darted around the room, looking for anything suspicious. In this house, how would he know? Why isn't she running? Why isn't she afraid?

"Know this, Henry," her voice croaked, "I do not forgive you. I know, to you, that means nothing. I also know you're a slippery shit and you're going to get away with it. There are no witnesses, Henry. Just the way you like it. But just remember, every time you close your eyes to sleep or look at your fat face in a mirror, that you are a coward, Henry. You always have been."

She reached up to her face and slowly pulled off the mask. Altman's pulse raced as she finally turned to look him dead in the eyes. Her face was grotesque, hideous, but not worthy of an entire mask. In fact, the scarring was only on one side. But that one side was awful. The sections of her flesh at her cheekbone and the corner of her forehead in front of her temple were simply burned away to exposed bone. Her cheek above her jaw was separated from the skin underneath, exposing the bottom row of her teeth all the way back. On the flap that remained, there was something scarred into a pattern, like someone or something branded her. It was a perfect X with two dots on the top.

"Well, go on, Henry. This isn't the first time you've done this." Then she laughed, as if she had told a joke.

Half due to the rage he felt and half to stop looking at the mangled mess in front of him, he swung the rock into her skull. He felt it pierce bone and knew, after one shot, she was dead.

Her body hit the floor, and the blood started spreading, mixing in with the already red carpet. The oddest feeling came over him. He expected the release, the adrenaline. This was different, like he forgot something or like déjà vu. He couldn't place it. Her death didn't give him the satisfaction he had hoped for.

But it was about to.

She slept alone, quietly, calmly, with a smile on her face. That was the best part: the smile. So happy, so absolutely fucking clueless.

He was going to make an example of her.

Henry Altman slithered deeper into the room, right up to the foot of her bed. He felt something else now: a stirring, an old friend he hadn't seen in a long time. He took off one of his black gloves and felt her breath, his hand dangerously close to her face. If she smelled the sweat, she'd wake up. He wouldn't mind.

He ran his hand over her, careful to keep it a centimeter away from her body—never touching her, but violating her nonetheless. And still she smiled in her sleep. Of course she did. She wanted it. They always want it.

But not tonight. No evidence he was here tonight.

He reached into his coat pocket and pulled out Abigail's rock, still covered in blood and hair. He looked down on her. He could do it, right here, right now: crush her skull too. It would be more satisfying than the last one. It had to be.

But no, he couldn't kill her, not now. He'd be the first suspect. Better to let her hang herself.

He rolled the rock quietly under the bed, the murder weapon carefully hidden away. She didn't even stir.

On his way out, he noticed the CONIR file on the dresser and grabbed that too. He was relieved by how light it was. It was nothing to worry about after all, but still, no sense in leaving it for the cops. He closed the door quietly and, without a sound, limped down the sidewalk into the night.

Emily kept smiling.

FOURTEEN

IN GIRUM IMUS NOCTE

MY DAVID BOWIE ringtone interrupted the best sleep I've had in years. I reached for my phone and banged my hand against a higher-end table than the one at my apartment. "Rock 'n' Roll Suicide" was now playing from the floor behind the table, where my phone fell. Groggily, I pull the charging cable, careful not to tug too hard and dislodge the cord from the charging port. I must've been thinking about the phone call I was making to my mom this morning, because I just assumed it was her.

"Hello?" I grunt.

"Tell me you didn't do it, and I'll believe you."

"Do what?"

"Kill Old Lady Abigail."

The fuck? My eyes burst open, and I'm sitting up immediately. It's definitely not mom.

"She's dead?"

"Tell me you didn't do it," Allison says, as I finally recognize her voice.

"How did she die?" I ask.

"EMILY!"

"Jesus, no, I didn't fucking kill her, Allison! How did she die?"

"The cops got a tip that you left there last night. Whoever called it in said they heard fighting. They were just up there. She's dead, Emily. Her head was caved in."

"Allison, I was with Carol last night."

"I know that. That's why I think it's bullshit. I told Peter that too, and he believes me. He's cool, Emily. I told him all about you. But Shane and him are on their way to arrest you right now, just on suspicion. They can't hold you without evidence."

The only evidence in my room was of my breaking and entering into a government building. I'll turn myself in right after I hide the . . .

CONIR file—the dresser it was sitting on is bare.

"Allison, the CONIR file, it's gone."

"What?" she answers.

"It's gone, it's fucking gone. He was in my room, Al, he took it."

"Who?"

They can't hold you without evidence.

No. No. No.

"Hold on," I say as I throw the phone onto the bed and tear the room apart.

Closet? No.

Dresser? No.

Bathroom? No.

Under the bed?

Abigail's rock, still sticky with blood. An eternity goes by as I reach back up for the phone without being able to tear my eyes off of the planted evidence in my room.

"I don't have a lot of time, do I?" I manage to whisper through the breath locked in my lungs.

"No, Emily. Just explain to them what is going on."

I just stare at the rock. No one will question why I kept it instead of tossing it in the lake. They'll think they just got lucky and solved a murder case in a few hours. If there was any question, Altman would see it answered the way he wanted.

"I don't think it's going to be that easy, Allison. Listen, don't believe it. This is Altman; he's framing me."

"What can I do?" she asks.

I peek out the window and quickly duck back. Peter and Shane are already here, stepping away from their cruiser toward my front door.

"Stay by your phone." I answer and hang up. I grab the rock, throw it in my red backpack, along with my cell, and I go out the bathroom window in time to hear Peter banging on the door announcing the BWPD.

The best day ever, only to wake up the next day a murder suspect at large. Should've known it wouldn't last.

Altman sat in his old '95 Cadillac Seville in the parking lot of the motel, watching the police come in and out like ants in an anthill. He loved this car. It was his second office, his safe place, his pride and joy. Sure, he could afford a new car. Hell, he could afford ten. This car kept up appearances though; that was important. He'd put a lot of money into keeping it running, but that didn't show through the bright white chassis. Everything under the hood was less than three years old, including the engine, which had a significant upgrade. Plus, the car was as big as a boat. He had the windows tinted to darker than legally allowed, but Sheriff Barkley let it slide. He didn't want people to know who was in the car, just like the president's motorcade—at least that's what he told himself when he got it done. Of course everyone knew it was him. If he thought about it, he knew that. As all the cops poured in and out of that motel room, they knew he was there, watching. The thought made him smile.

He wanted to go in and watch them find the rock, but he knew stepping into an official police investigation, and what would eventually be a crime scene, would be pushing it. He had his fingers in everything in this town, and he had for a long time. He could do it. He could walk in there, "accidentally" peek under the bed and find the rock himself. He'd look Emily Hunter in the eyes at that point and send her a message that no one fucks with Henry Altman.

Appearances, he thought.

A knock came on his window, and he slowly rolled it down to see Sheriff Barkley and Officer Peter Jacoby standing outside.

"Gentlemen," he said, "what's going on here?"

Jacoby smirked, shaking his head. Of course Altman knew what was going on here, thought Peter. This little innocent act wasn't fooling him and hopefully wasn't fooling Barkley either. Who could tell though? Best not to say anything.

"Anonymous tip came in that Old Lady Abigail was in a fight with a Miss Emily Hunter last night. We checked on Abigail this morning, and she's dead," said Barkley. Here, Altman feigned surprise. He's not that great of an actor.

"I'm assuming you've arrested Ms. Hunter then?"

"I'm afraid she wasn't on the premises when our officers arrived," continued Barkley. Shit, that's a tiny setback. She's still out there somewhere.

"Have you found anything inside?" Altman asked.

"A toothbrush, some clothing, nothing significant. It looks like she left quickly, possibly early this morning. Maybe she saw us coming."

Nothing significant? Goddamn it, thought Altman. This was falling apart. Of course they looked under the bed, and of course she did too. How the hell did she know? His eyes met Jacoby's.

"Or she was tipped off," he said.

Both Jacoby and Barkley were furious. How dare this fat piece of shit accuse them of corruption.

"With respect," Barkley said, not letting that respect show in his voice, "we run a tight ship."

"Our number one suspect in a murder case just happens to be buddy-buddy with Officer Jacoby's little sister, and that doesn't seem suspicious to you?" barked Altman.

Peter looked like he was about to come through the window at Altman. As if he knew, Barkley's hand came to rest on his chest, and Peter knew in an instant Barkley wasn't going to honor that speculation with even a thought.

Lucky for Peter. His career was on the line all because he trusted his sister.

Barkley had always acted like a coach to Peter. He taught him how to be a good cop in a bad place. The entire town loved Albin Barkley more than Altman by miles. It didn't matter to Altman; it meant the world to Barkley.

"A lot of this seems suspicious to me, Mr. Mayor," said Barkley. "Like who would call in a tip about a fight they heard in the middle of the night in a house three miles from the nearest neighbor?" he said, not taking his eyes off of Altman. "That person is the only confirmed person to know something had happened at Abigail Pipkin's house last night, and they chose to remain anonymous. And they chose to implicate Ms. Hunter. With no evidence against her, sir, we have to look into people who may have had a problem with Ms. Hunter and would benefit from framing her for murder. Rest assured, sir, Emily Hunter is a suspect in the death of Abigail Pipkin, but she's not our 'number one' suspect." Peter smiled. If Barkley knew what dropping the mic was, he would have done it right then.

Altman's face didn't budge. "Well unless you know and can prove who made that call last night, Ms. Hunter seems to be the only suspect you know by name and, at this moment, seems to be missing, correct?"

Now Barkley's face doesn't budge.

"Thought so," Altman finished. He got out of the car and headed to the small gathering of police officers outside the motel door. "Listen up, everyone, I know you've been working hard, but now I'm going to ask you to work a little harder. You're looking for a woman named Emily Hunter. Five seven, five eight, brunette. She is a paranoid schizophrenic who has been in and out of institutions her whole life."

Peter's eyes closed. Goddamn it, Allison, you probably should have mentioned that part.

"Now that we have her on the run, she is to be considered extremely dangerous. We need to get to her as quickly as possible before she hurts anyone else. I want checkpoints up at all the roads going out of town, as well as a strong presence covering the lake." The lake was most important. If Emily Hunter ditched the rock in the lake, there was nothing left to tie her to the murder except the call, which it seemed obvious Barkley wasn't putting any stock in.

"We have it on good authority she has no transportation, so she is most likely on foot. Get out there, and protect your city."

No one moved. Every cop there knew they didn't take orders from Altman. Barkley had made a special section in new hire orientation specifically to address the mayor's desire to overreach. They all looked to Barkley. With a nod, all of them left the scene. The nod didn't go unnoticed.

Appearances, thought Altman.

"Officer Jacoby," said Altman, "I wonder, if you have permission from your superior officer, if you would accompany me to my home. It isn't a secret Ms. Hunter and I didn't see eye to eye, and I worry for my safety."

Peter rolled his eyes without Altman seeing. He looked to Barkley, who, with his expression, asked if Peter would be OK with it. Peter shrugged. "Absolutely, sir," said Sheriff Barkley. "If she murdered Pipkin, it's possible you'd be her next target. Jacoby will escort you home and make sure you're out of harm's way.

Appearances, thought Barkley.

Peter sat in the passenger seat of Altman's gigantic car. Two minutes into the drive, it became apparent they weren't going to Altman's house.

The car pulled into Peter's driveway. Without a word, Altman stepped out of the car. "Why are we here?" asked Peter, following him up to the front door.

"To talk to your sister. We need to know what she knows," replied Altman.

"Bullshit," said Peter, forgetting his place and not really caring. "She doesn't know anything."

"So sure are we?" asked Altman.

"I can't interrogate my own sister, Mr. Mayor. Anything she says would never be admissible in court. The worst lawyer in the world would get her dismissed before you could blink."

"I guess I'll have to do it then."

"The hell you will. You aren't a cop. You don't have the power or authority to interrogate anyone. And she isn't under arrest, so technically, neither do I. So get back in your car, Henry."

Henry?

"Look, Officer. Maybe I'm just a lowly and powerless mayor, but I do know the phrase 'aiding and abetting.' Did you hear that one? All I'm trying to do is make sure your precious little sister isn't guilty of a major crime. I'd think you'd want to make sure of the same." Peter stopped. He knew that if Emily got caught, the microscope would eventually come to Allison. Maybe making her testimony inadmissible was the best thing for her.

"I talk to her, you understand?"

"Fine by me," answered Altman.

"I haven't seen her since yesterday."

"Did you call her? Let her know we were coming?" asked Altman. Allison didn't answer. She didn't even make eye contact. The little bitch just sat there, arms crossed, like a pissed-off toddler. "Make her answer me."

"She has the right to remain silent," Peter shot back.

"She's not under arrest," said Altman.

"She doesn't have to be." Allison smiled, growing up a cop's sister had its advantages. She knew the rules, and she knew her brother would protect her.

Altman knew it was two against one. Fine. He spotted the iPhone sitting out on the table in front of them, face down. He reached for it quickly.

"Maybe we don't need to ask because I'm going to bet you called her and your call log will show it. Let's take a look at your phone, shall we?"

Peter's hand slammed down on top of the phone, pinning it to the table. "Not without a warrant."

OK, this was getting ridiculous now. Altman's eyes shot daggers through Allison Jacoby. "Listen, girlie, if you helped Ms. Hunter escape, you can be tried as an accessory to murder after the fact. Do I have that right, Peter?"

"Not if she's innocent," said Allison before Peter had a chance to answer, but giving the exact same answer that was on its way out of his mouth. He smiled at his sister proudly.

"What makes you think she's innocent?"

"When you went into her room," asked Allison to Peter, ignoring Altman completely, "did you happen to find a file marked CONIR?"

The color dropped from Altman's face and slowly returned beet red. This was all unraveling. He was too sloppy this time.

"Last night when I was in her room, Emily had a file marked CONIR. Seems like if she were on the run, it's an odd thing to take with her."

"What's CONIR?" Peter asked, but, strangely, he asked Altman. Altman's mind raced as it searched for plausible explanations he could give Sheriff Barkley as to why he had to kill a cop and his little sister. Self-defense? No way he'd buy that. Maybe the house burned down with them inside. But then how would Altman have escaped? Fortunately, he's saved by the bell—or the bang, as the case was.

Outside the window, a loud crash came as a trash can lid hit the ground. All three of them stopped, but only two of them looked toward the window. Allison looked straight ahead, eyes wide open, pretending very poorly that she didn't hear anything. Peter got up and walked toward the window. Allison's eyes followed him. Altman, however, in a quick moment of awareness, grabbed Allison's phone off the table and pocketed it.

And, in an instant, I was running.

I heard Peter yell "It's her!" from behind me as I tore through the backyard and over the fence into the neighborhood behind Allison's house, cursing myself for knocking over the can while trying to hear the conversation. Allison had held her own. I knew she would.

The backpack bounces hard against my spine, punching me with every long step. By the time I hit the woods, I can hear Peter following me. He's yelling to me to stop, but the moment I stop, I'm done.

I still have the rock.

My first instinct was to ditch it in the lake, but then I remembered what Abigail told me: "After I'm dead, you can inherit it. I'll leave it to you." Now she was dead, and I had the rock. That couldn't be coincidence, right?

I look back to see Peter losing paces on me. He's fast, but not as agile as I am. The woods are full of downed trees and long branches, and he's hitting just about all of them. I pop out into a clearing, and I recognize my surroundings. I'm back out on Stone Road, where Allison and I saw Carrot. I start up the hill on the other side of the road. I can hear the sirens now, coming from town. The lights are flickering through the trees, but I've got a good quarter mile on them. At this rate, I'll lose them.

And suddenly I'm not moving anymore, and there's a pain in my leg that is unbearable. I cry out instinctively and realize two things in an instant: one, I hit a tree stump at full speed while looking at police lights, and I can't do anything but limp now, as my thigh is screaming and everything below it is numb; two, I just gave away my position by shouting.

I have to move before Peter sees me, but my leg isn't responding the way I want. I feel like I want to throw up every time I put pressure on it. It's not broken; I've just got the mother of all charlie horses.

I limp toward the edge of a drop-off, and my eyes fall on a cloth lying on the ground. The color is familiar, and as I come up on it, before I can visually confirm it, my mind already knows what it is.

It's a dirty stuffed rabbit.

I pick it up, and it's real. It looks like it's been sitting out here forever. Carrot's rabbit is in my hands. I'm actually holding it. I need to run, I need to hide, but I can't stop staring at the rabbit's only remaining eye. Why is this here?

The sirens are getting louder now, and I'm back. There's a little path in front of me going down the drop-off. It's a thirty-foot drop to the ground, but the path leads to a little hidden indentation in the rock. I wouldn't see it if I wasn't standing right here.

I climb down, some of the feeling coming back to my leg, somehow making this even harder. The indentation is more like a tiny cave, big enough to fit inside. It's perfect.

I slide inside and stop moving. The ground is covered with dead leaves that would crunch and alert everyone to where I am with the slightest flinch. My leg feels like pins and needles right now, but I can feel the pain subsiding. I hear Peter above me: he's stopped too and is looking around for me. His radio comes to life.

"Officer Jac . . ." then he covers the speaker to muffle the sound.

Whatever the other cop said, Peter now answers. "No sir, I think I lost her. She has to be nearby though. I think I'll head up . . ." And he trails off as he runs away, deeper into the woods. I let out a breath and wiggle my leg, trying to get all of the ache out. I don't hear anyone nearby, so I start to relax. I take a look around in the cave, which is actually big enough to fit a small Volkswagen Beetle. The floor is littered with candy wrappers, old candy wrappers, candy I've not seen in years, some I've never even heard of. There's an old weathered winter coat bunched up along the side of the cave. I open it up and see it's child sized. On the inside, over the shoulder blades, written in faded but legible permanent marker are the words *PROPERTY OF RIVERVIEW PSYCHIATRIC HOSPITAL.* I strain to read the words underneath it. When I do, a chill runs up my spine.

Emerson, C.

This coat, this cave, belonged to Carol Emerson, Carol Forrester, Carrot. This was hers as a child, just like I always see her.

Was this why she was so hesitant to get Albert help? She was hospitalized once too?

There's another coat here too, a white one, like a doctor's jacket. I pull it out, only it doesn't come unfurled. It stays in a perfect bunch. I turn it over, and I realize why.

It's covered in a copious amount of dried blood.

I drop it and recoil instantly, still feeling like flakes of blood have stuck to my fingers. Why the hell would Carrot have this?

What did she do?

"We've got Briar Road and Morrow Road covered, as well as the lake. Route 23 north and south out of town are also covered. We've faxed all pertinent information to PD in Ocqueoc, Onaway, and Millersburg."

"Good work, Officer," said Henry Altman. He stepped away from the map on the table and headed back toward his office. He'd be damned if Barkley was going to keep him out of this investigation. At this point, he'd be kidding himself if he believed this would go to his original plan. It's been twelve hours; there's no way she's still got the rock. He'd have to rethink all of this.

The phone in his pocket rang. The ringtone is some boy band—not something a sixty-eight-year-old mayor would have on his phone. It's Allison's phone. He pulled it out and looked at the caller ID, which only displayed one letter: E.

He ducked into his office quickly before the call went to voice mailand put the phone up to his ear. "E—that's got to be Emily, right?"

There was a long pause on the line.

"Where's Allison?" I ask.

"She's fine," he answers, and I can hear his sly smile through the phone. She fucking better be. "She's doing a great job of protecting you. I'll see you get adjoining cells at the women's prison."

"She has nothing to do with this."

"We both know that's not true."

"We both know I didn't kill Abigail Pipkin."

He laughs. "Well, that's interesting. Of course selling that to a jury might be tough."

"If I'm arrested, I'll tell them it was you. I'll tell them all about you. Do you really want an investigation?"

"Oh honey, no one is going to take the word of an insane woman over mine."

Insane? He knows about me. How did he get that information?

"You hungry, Emily? I doubt you are out there with much food or water. And the nights get really cold here." He's right. I grabbed some food at Allison's, but I had to hide before I could stock up. I won't last long. "We'll see you in the morning when you turn yourself in or when we find your body frozen to death. Sleep tight."

I pocket the phone and look up the dirt road leading to the old, decrepit building in front of me. It looks like a castle. Why do they always look like castles?

It's shelter. It will have to do.

Two wings reach out past the main entrance on both sides of me. Ahead, stairs lead up to a covered front door, columns holding up the roof overhead. The three-story, gray stone building has a tower on top over the main entrance, circular with two windows in the front. With the tower and the two wings, the building feels like a distorted version of the sphinx—and I'm walking inside the arms, directly toward its heart, right under the words *Riverview Psychiatric Hospital.*

The hospital is falling apart, all the windows are broken, the walls are covered in graffiti. It looks like the bones left behind. In the moonlight raining down on it, I can't tell if that makes it more or less threatening. I pass two dead trees on either side of the front door, an obviously failed attempt to brighten up the courtyard.

The front door is metal, and it looks like it was added afterward—not to keep people in, but to keep people out. The door is covered in yellow tape and notices all stating the property is condemned and not to be entered under penalty of law. The lock on the door is lying on the ground, and the door is slightly cracked open. I'm guessing the penalty of law wasn't enough to scare kids into leaving the place unmolested if they were brave enough to walk this far.

I reach out to open the door and get a hard static shock from the handle. My hand recoils instinctively as I try to shake it off. I use my foot to slip into the door and push it open. Inside, the hospital is almost pure darkness, with small streaks of light cutting through the broken windows above.

Now or never.

Holding my breath, I feel my legs move before I'm ready as I step into the haunted hospital and close the door behind me.

PART THREE

FIFTEEN

ET CONSUMIMUR IGNI

THIS IS ALL wrong.

The dread I felt at Abigail's is dripping on the walls of this place. Beyond the decrepit state of everything, the peeling paint, the shadows, the broken glass, and generations of dead leaves littering the floor, there's a danger here that I can't describe, like a song you have stuck in your head but don't know the words to.

The floor crunches with every step. I stand in the main lobby, and in front of me sits the remains of a receptionist area. The room itself is gigantic, the ceiling at least thirty feet above me. Large floor-to-ceiling columns brace great wooden beams that hold the second floor up, but given their condition, I'm not sure I trust them. I pull out my phone and turn on the flash to use as a light to see my way around. My phone has one bar and is sitting at 28 percent battery life, so I know I have to find another light somewhere or I'm going to be stumbling around all night.

On the west wall of the lobby sits a custodial closet; inside has been cleared out for the most part, except a few empty bottles of cleaning supplies, a crowbar someone had used to get the door open initially, and a stack of water-soaked pornographic magazines that are only a few years old—no doubt left by teenagers breaking in. There are also two pipes with marijuana resin in the bowl and a crank flashlight. Thank God for rebellious kids.

After a few turns of the crank, the flashlight beam shines brightly enough, so I power my phone off entirely. It all somehow seems even worse in the light. The walls look like they used to be yellow, but now the light casts bizarre shadows over all the paint that's peeled and curled, revealing the black mold underneath. The ceiling above has holes that poke through right into the second floor. It's a damn good thing I found this flashlight or upstairs would be a death trap. I feel like I'm walking through the rotting bones of a Goliath.

Ahead, deep inside the hospital somewhere, I hear voices, and I shut my light off and stand still. Two men, probably Shane and Peter—they're already here. I heard him run off when he lost track of me; of course he got here first. This is the only place I would go.

Every step I take, the sound of dead leaves crunching bounces around every surface in the hospital. I'm not sneaking anywhere. Weighing my options, which I come to realize are very limited, I can either sit here all night, never moving and hoping they don't find me, or I come out and appeal to Peter. Allison said he was on my side.

I step out and slowly creep past reception, down the main hall, the light still off, but my footsteps give away my position anyway. They're talking, but I can't make out what it is they're saying. There are rooms on each side of me that are windowless with open doors, each completely soaked in blackness, and every time I pass one, I'm certain something is coming out to eat me. The voices are coming from this direction, but when the hall ends at a T, forcing me left or right through administration, I can't place which way they're coming from. When I take another step and concentrate, the glass crunching under my feet alerts them, and they go silent. What if it isn't Peter? What if it's some violent delinquents? I suddenly feel very alone and exposed. I make the decision to head back to the janitor closet for the crowbar, and when I do, I freeze like a deer in headlights.

There's someone in the hall behind me.

A large man's silhouette is towering in the hallway, illuminated by the moonlight shining in the lobby. Every muscle in my body locks up, forcing me to stand like an awkward statue. The man has about five inches on Peter Jacoby; it's not him. My way to the exit is blocked. I have no choice but to run deeper into the hospital.

But I'm too scared to move.

The man is looking into the room to his right, like he sees something in there. The more I look at him, the less threatening he looks. He's not in an offensive posture; he's leaning on the doorframe, and it looks like he's talking to someone in the room, but he's not making a sound. He's not even looking at me, and I'm not sure if he even knows I'm here.

"Hello?" I say before realizing I was going to speak.

He doesn't answer. He just stands there as if he didn't even hear me. He's not saying a word. The only sound I can hear is my heart in my neck.

"Sir?" I say. Still nothing. I turn the flashlight on, completely terrified of what I'm about to see. The beam dances over the debris on the floor and slithers its way to the hulking figure in the hallway ahead of me.

There's nothing there.

I close my eyes and exhale a breath I feel like I've been holding for twenty minutes. It was just a shadow, some odd trick of the light. I'm letting the hospital get the best of me.

I lower the beam, and the giant man is back, and now he's coming down the hallway right for me.

Instinctually, I scream and stumble backwards, tripping over a piece of rebar jutting from the wall and falling on my ass. The flashlight falls out of my hands and spins five feet out of my reach. He's on top of me in a quick moment.

Then he steps past me and continues down the hall, turning the corner at admin and leaving my sight.

And deeper in the hospital, in the direction he ran, a blood-curdling woman's scream pierces the silence.

"Emily! No!"

It's Allison.

This time electricity surges through me, and I'm moving immediately. I jump up and chase the shadow around the corner. The screaming is getting louder and louder, more frantic. She's being attacked. My flashlight beam bounces over the walls, even though I'm trying to keep it on the floor so I don't trip again, and I realize I'm entering into a residence hallway. The doors on the wall opposite administration are numbered and heavy, with small sliding windows on each. I thought Sandy Shores was terrible; staying here would have been hell. Although I'm terrified and the adrenaline is pumping through my veins, I notice a small relief in the back of my mind that this place is dead.

"NO! PLEASE! DON'T TOUCH ME! GET AWAY!" The screaming is desperate now, but it's not Allison's voice. I continue tearing down the hallway, heading toward the screaming in front of me, when the oddest thing happens: suddenly, it's behind me.

I stop in my tracks and turn around, no longer running. My flashlight is up now and peering around the empty hallway. I step back toward the screaming. "YOU'RE SNAKES! YOU'RE ALL SNAKES! YOU CAN'T HAVE ME! NO MORE! NO MORE! PLEASE! PLEASE HELP ME!"

Now it's behind me again.

It's coming from the spot I'm standing in. But I'm completely alone.

"Allison! Where are you?" I yell. And the moment I make a noise, it stops. My flashlight zips around all over the place, looking for something, anything, to explain where the screaming came from. But there's nothing but a dusty, empty hallway.

I'm alone.

There's no one here, no Allison, no one to verify whether or not these things are real or in my head. I'm sweating even though the freezing wind seeps through the walls of this building unabated, like water through a colander. A terrifying thought comes over me: just because Allison saw Carrot, I assumed everything was fine in my head. But what if I really am insane? What if I'm still broken? What if I'm hallucinating again?

Then an even more terrifying thought: what if I'm not?

The light lands on a door on the admin side of the hall, and the sign on the door is still intact: *RECORDS: Authorized Personnel Only.*

I'll need a place to hide and keep warm, and I'll be damned if I'm spending the night in one of the patient rooms. This is as good a place as any I'll find. I collect my wits, and I try the doorknob, but it's locked. I push on it, throw my weight into it, hoping it's old enough that it'll just come down. The door is solid, and the frame is metal, but the knob looks old. Maybe if I get something heavy, I can break it off and get inside. I think about the crowbar again back where I started, when I find a large chunk of the cinder block wall lying on the floor. I pick it up, and it's heavier than I anticipated. It'll do nicely. I raise it up over my head to take out the doorknob.

Turning back, I see the door is now wide open.

I swallow hard, but there's no saliva in my mouth. Inside, there's a little moonlight from the exterior windows coming into the main administration area, and it's enough to cast an eerie glow into the back room, where all the records are kept. A few rotted and broken desks still remain in the front room, where various case managers would probably sit to organize their paperwork when they could be bothered to visit their clients. Otherwise the room is empty, scrapped for parts. Wires hang from the ceiling, which has been thoroughly damaged by water. The place looks like a normal office after it's been hit by an 8.5 earthquake and left abandoned for decades. The windows, like all the others in the building, are broken, victims of teenagers with angst and rocks.

My light peeks into the room, and I get a bit of a surprise. There are file cabinets here that, while dented and rusty, appear to still be locked. I leave the room and come back with the crowbar. As I pry open the first drawer, I say a silent thank you that looters never found any value in old files. The drawer is full. Altman was full of shit when he said they moved everything to city hall. I guess I shouldn't be shocked.

One by one, I pop open all the drawers, and most are full. Excitement quickly gives way to exhaustion. If I had a week, I couldn't look through all of this, and I have until the morning, tops, until I go crawling back to Blue Water for food and shelter.

I go through a desk drawer first and come upon a stack of polaroids of patients outside, probably on some group outing. The staff's clothing and hairstyles put this somewhere around the end of the seventies. The patients are all terribly dressed, except for one guy in a full tuxedo. They all look happy to be outside. Flipping through, I find an old, thin woman with a big grin on her face. The photo is labeled *A.P. Black Lake 1978.* I wonder if that's Abigail Pipkin. She looks so happy. I can't help but feel sad.

"I don't know. Do you think I should take him seriously?"

Someone is here—or I'm losing it. I stop moving entirely.

"Is he cute? Does he have money?"

"Of course he does; he's a doctor."

Two women's voices are coming from the main room, muffled sounding, but I can still make out what they're saying. I step toward the door to go back into the main office, and two more dark silhouettes are standing in the reception area to the records section. Again, I put my light on them, and again, they disappear in the beam. They look thicker, deeper somehow, and they block the moonlight reflecting off the glass on the floor. They are definitely not a trick of the light, especially since I can hear them.

"Then give him a shot. It's dinner. You aren't marrying him—not yet anyway."

The shadow on the left grabs something off the desk and walks toward the records door that I'm standing in. This time I don't trip and fall, I don't recoil. I stand there, and let it walk right through me. The feeling I have when it hits me feels like, for a brief second, my entire body falls asleep, and I feel a quick surge of pins and needles followed by pain in my eyes, like staring into a floodlight. The numbness subsides, but my eyes still feel like they're struggling, as if adjusting to brightness. Then I realize they are: all the lights in the building are on. But they don't have to be because the sun is out.

Immediately, I start to panic because I think I've lost time again. If it's morning and I missed my opportunity, it's going to be moments before the police find me carrying the murder weapon that killed Abigail Pipkin. Then my second thought occurs to me: none of the windows the sunlight is poking through are broken. The room is clean and tidy—but not everywhere. There's a border, as if I'm in a large bubble. Inside the bubble, there are people walking, shuffling around, going about their business in an office. Outside of it, the hospital is dark, derelict, destroyed. This can't be in my head, right?

"Shut up," a woman says from behind me. I turn to see a nurse, filing through the cabinets, adding the paperwork she picked up from the front room. She's in the room with me, plain as day, but she doesn't see me. Her hair is feathered, and she can't be more than twenty-five. Her name tag on her white blouse says *Sarah*.

"All I'm saying is, see where he wants to take you and use that as a scale," another woman says from the main room. I'm still standing in the door, and I can see she's another nurse, older with dark, curly hair, also very big. This woman looks to be mid- to late-thirties. "If it's an upscale place, he really likes you. If it's drive-through, he just wants to get some. Not that that's a bad thing."

Sarah laughs. "You're crazy, you know that? I'm pretty sure we have a room available upstairs for you."

"Sweetheart, I'm going to need it if I keep having to work all this overtime."

Sarah has finished filing and walks back through me into the main room. The bubble moves with her, and as she walks further away, the edge comes closer and closer to me.

"No kidding, I haven't been home to . . ." And with that, the threshold crosses me, and I'm outside, back in the old, dirty hospital. My eyes readjust to the darkness. The silhouettes are gone, and I'm alone again.

What the hell just happened?

SIXTEEN

MORTUI VIVOS DOCENT

MY FLASHLIGHT COVERS the main room, until I leave and go back into the hallway I came from. It's empty too. No shadows except the macabre ones my light stretches across the walls. What I just saw, it had to be the eighties sometime, maybe seventies. There was a nurse named Sarah, the hospital was up and running. I go over every detail I can think of and try to sear it into my memory. It seemed random, it seemed useless, and maybe it was, but maybe it wasn't. Maybe there was a reason I had that vision. For the life of me, I can't imagine what it could be.

I decide that I'll look in the file cabinets in the section Sarah was working in. Maybe something was trying to point me in the right direction. I don't make it back into the records office though, because now something even stranger is happening.

Down the hallway, one of the doors to the residential rooms is open. That alone doesn't catch my attention; a lot of them are open—an unsettling amount, as they're all pitch black inside because their windows face the woods. All of them are dark.

All of them except this one.

The light is on and casting into the hallway, interrupted only by the shadow of a person in the room walking in front of the single bulb. Fear takes hold of me again, but only for a split second. Two split seconds later, I'm sprinting down the hallway again toward the room.

Right before I turn the corner to look into the room, the light goes out. By the time I see into the room, all that remains is pieces of a bedframe. I catch my breath leaning on the wall and suddenly know I've ruined my clothes. The wall feels wet, and shining the light on it, I can see my arm has blackened from years of dirt and dust. Wiping it off only spreads the stain to my hand as well. I wonder if I've unknowingly covered myself in muck in the dark. Then out of the corner of my eye, I notice another light has come on further down the hall, and I take off running again. During this mad dash I feel an unsettling nervousness in my stomach. It occurs to me that chasing these lights is drawing me deeper and deeper into the hospital, farther from the way out. I keep running, but now I'm carrying a heavy apprehension: where is the hospital taking me? I couldn't help but think I was running deeper down the throat of some massive beast, running to these lights like a moth to flame.

I turn the corner into the lit room and run right into a group therapy session in a large activity room. Eight people are sitting in a circle, most in robes, along with a doctor in a white jacket. Around the room, other patients are doing puzzles, rocking in chairs, watching TV. Around the outside of the room, the edge of the bubble reveals this room is actually missing most of the east wall in my time.

Something is off here, something I can't place. I can't put my finger on it, but it's lingering in my mind, hanging on like when you know you're forgetting something.

"So last week, Brian and Jonas were talking about their goals for when they leave our care. Brian said he wants to move to Florida. Is that right?"

A middle-aged, unshaven man I assume is Brian is sitting at the eight o-clock position. He shakes his head no with his arms crossed in a stubborn fashion. "No?" continues the doctor. "What would you like to do now?"

"Why should I tell you? I don't even know you," says Brian.

The doctor sighs. "I'm sorry you feel that way, Brian. I know the last few weeks have been difficult, and there have been a lot of new faces around here. That can't be easy, and I know it'll be a while before you trust me and the other staff. Please know, I really do want to get to know you all, and I really want to help."

"China," says Brian.

"You want to move to China? What's in China?"

"Lots of stuff," says Brian, angrily. "Google it."

The doctor frowns. "I mean, what's in China that makes you interested in going there?"

"It's as far away from here as you can get—unless I move to the moon."

"And you want to get away from here. I understand that. It's not easy living here and feeling like you're not in control of your own life."

Brian just frowns like a child. It's obvious he's trying to get a rise out of the doctor and the doctor isn't biting. I know that frustration; I'd felt it plenty of times. I had one doctor who constantly was smiling. No matter what I did, she just . . .

Wait a minute. "Google it?"

Then it falls into place, what was bothering me: the hairstyles, the clothing styles—they're not old. The TVs are flat-screen LCDs. One of the staff is sitting in the corner looking at his iPhone. Riverview Psychiatric Hospital shut down in the early eighties, so what the hell am I looking at?

The woman at the six o'clock position with her back to me suddenly sits up, and she slowly turns around as if she's expecting a killer behind her. Her face meets mine, and we make eye contact. Two things about this shut down all rational thought I have, and I can only stare: First, we make eye contact. She can see me. Second, it's Allison Jacoby.

"Allison?" I say.

"What . . . what are you doing here?" she says.

The others in the circle turn to look at me, but they don't see me. "Allison, who are you talking to?" asks the doctor.

"Can you see me?" I ask.

"I'm sorry! I'm so sorry," she says, and she starts crying. Allison begins a full panic attack, and the doctor motions for the staff to come.

"Allison, what is going on? Are you OK? Do you need help right now?" asks the doctor.

"She's here . . ." she says through gasping breaths.

"Who is here, Allison? Who do you see?"

"Emily Hunter!" she screams. "She's here."

"Allison, you're safe," he says. "There's no one there. I promise."

"She's here for me!" Allison is pulling away, and the staff members hold her arms so she can't run. She struggles against them futilely.

"Calm down, Al, you're fine," says one of the staff. "Let's get her back to her room."

"Leave her alone!" I yell, but no one but Allison seems to hear me.

"Where's that?" asks the second staff member.

"Women's hall, 27," the staff member says to the other, whom, after seeing his apprehension to join the restraint, I can only assume is new.

"No! She's here! I CAN SEE HER!" She pulls harder now as the staff start dragging her toward me. I want to hold her, tell her everything is OK, but my hand passes through her. I can't touch her. After her next five words, I'm sure she wouldn't want me to anyway: "She's going to kill me!"

They pull Allison down the hall, and I watch from the activity room. As she goes out of range, I pass out of the bubble, and the hospital is dead again. My eyes are wet with tears I don't remember crying, and I'm shivering. She was terrified of me, scared for her life. On top of that, Allison was never hospitalized here. She's too young. But what I just saw looked like present day. Now the hospital seemed to be fucking with me. Was it trying to scare me away? Did it know what I was afraid of? I suddenly felt more intimidated than I've ever felt in my life. There was something here, and it knew I was here too.

Maybe the hospital wasn't dead after all.

A younger voice starts screaming, as if she's being set on fire. Allison is fresh in my mind, and I run again. Deeper down the hall, toward the north end of the hospital, another light is on, shining through the small window in the closed door. I'm frazzled, at my wit's end. I haven't been able to stop and wonder why I'm seeing all these things or if I'm really seeing them at all. I want to catch my breath and collect my thoughts and figure out just what the hell is going on, but I have no time. I have to get to the light before it goes out.

The screaming is louder and louder, and by the time I reach the door, it's starting to fade. Not getting quieter, just getting exhausted.

I throw my shoulder into the door, and the latch gives way. I'm inside, and the screaming isn't stopping. The light isn't on because there's no bulb in the dangling cord hanging from the ceiling, but somehow the room is illuminated like it's there.

On the bed frame lying against the wall sits Carrot. She's smiling at me. "Hello," she says, her legs dangling back and forth over the edge.

My nerves are shot, and I don't even question why she's here. "Who is screaming?" I ask, looking around the room frantically.

"Screaming?" asks Carrot.

"You don't hear that?"

She deflects the question. She seems different, less stoic, more alive, like she's home and happy to have company. I don't have the mindset to wonder why. It sounds like someone is being murdered in this room or worse.

"Do you live here?" she asks.

"What? No, I don't live here."

"Why are you here if you don't live here?"

"Carrot! Seriously! Who is screaming?!"

Now she looks scared. "Shh! It's quiet hours. Don't yell, or the bull will come."

"What is the bull? Why are you showing me this?" I look back to the bed. The screaming stops. Carrot is gone.

Now I see myself sitting on the bed where Carrot was. It's my reflection again—at least I think it is. I can't focus enough to make sense of anything I've seen. She is looking out the window toward the woods. She turns and looks at me. She notices me but doesn't seem to care that I'm here.

"Thank you for being a friend," she says dismissively.

The light that was never on goes out. The room is dark again, and once again, I'm alone. And I'm lost in every way imaginable.

SEVENTEEN

FORTUNAE MEAE, MULTORUM FABER

IT'S FOUR IN the morning. Three hours have gone by. I found my way back through the hospital to where I began, in the giant foyer with the columns. The desk I'm sitting on in the lobby isn't at all comfortable, yet I'm trying desperately not to fall asleep. I'm exhausted, both because I haven't slept since Allison's phone call this morning, which seems like a lifetime ago, and because the hospital is full of shadows now. For the last hour, they've been everywhere. They get close to me, I feel the buzz, and I get about ten seconds of some scene before they walk out of range again. There are no less than twenty walking around in front of me at any time. I've given up. I don't know what the point of this is. It's not even shocking anymore. Now, it's just aggravating. None of the things I have seen make sense or are of any use.

Buzz. " . . . today, but if he comes back after Christmas, I'll be back in my office and I . . ."

There's something I'm missing here, but I'm not sure I care.

Buzz. " . . . of it. He just pushes and pushes, and one day I'm going to quit and they . . ."

Dead end after dead end.

Buzz. " . . . view Hospital. Please report to the front desk. Dr. Thompson, please . . ."

I don't want to do this anymore.

Buzz. " . . . broke down about ten miles outside of town, and apparently, no one is . . .

Just quit.

Buzz. " . . . to go ahead with Project CONIR in this location, we're going to ha . . ."

My head is up quickly, trying to find whichever shadow just pulled me in. There are two of them, walking together quickly. I rush to catch up and find myself within the bubble.

A stern-looking military man in dress blues walks down the hallway with a middle-aged doctor in a lab coat. The doctor has a pretty sizable scar on his chin going all the way back to the hinge of his jaw. The military man is mid-sentence when I come back in.

" . . have a breach. Security is our main concern, Dr. Millen, and if your facility cannot provide it, we have no problem pulling out."

Millen—the scarred doctor is Dr. Millen.

"I assure you we can handle this internally without drawing any attention. We're interrogating all our staff. You have absolutely nothing to worry about," says Millen.

"The fuck I don't. I'm sticking my neck out as it is. Now I'm getting intel that we've got a leak, and I have nothing to worry about? Listen to me, Millen . . ." Here, the military man draws in uncomfortably close to Millen's face. "If this isn't contained, it's my ass. If it's my ass, it's your ass. Do we understand each other?"

Millen manages a nod.

The military man walks away. "Plug the leak, Millen."

Dr. Millen manages a quiet "Yes, sir." His eyes are daggers in the military man's back.

When the military man walks out the front entrance, the scene is gone. Now it seems there are even more shadows in the room than before. I look around at all of them, knowing I have nowhere to start, and I see Carrot is standing on the countertop I was previously sitting on. Her arms are at her side, and she's standing still like a statue. This is the Carrot I remember. I walk back and sit next to her, my back to her. This is getting old really fucking quickly.

"Hey," I say. "I suppose you still don't know who I am?"

"I know who you are," she says without moving an inch.

"You didn't before. Why?"

"I didn't before."

That's it. I'm done. I've had enough of this riddle bullshit. Since we're so casual now and can have conversations, it's time to have a heart-to-heart.

"Look, kid, this has been really fun, but I'm pretty sure I'm going to prison for the rest of my life for killing a woman I didn't kill, unless I can figure out what to do next. And at that point, I'm not going to be much help to you from a cell. So how about we skip all the games and you just tell me what the fuck I'm doing here?"

She doesn't move. It just makes me angrier. And then the bigger questions come out, the stuff I've wanted to ask forever:

"Why me? Why have you been following me my whole life? And why did you wait until now to say anything?"

She doesn't move.

"How are you even here? You aren't dead!"

She doesn't move.

"Jesus Christ, Carrot. If you want help, you're going to have to meet me halfway. I got on a fucking plane and came here to the middle of fucking nowhere, and you can't even answer a simple goddamn question? Why are these ghosts here? Why did the hospital shut down? What is 'the bull?'"

Her eyes turn to mine in a flash, and it's enough to shut me up.

"That was you screaming, wasn't it, in your room? Did it hurt you, Carrot? Did it come into your room and hurt you?"

Her eyes look different now, scared.

"Is that why I'm here, kid? You need me to save you?"

Suddenly a vision, like a flicker in front of my eyes:

The long, dark hallway. The Minotaur—I belong to it.

The fear leaves her eyes, and she goes back to the stoneface glare.

"Save us all," she says.

The room is filled with ghosts.

EIGHTEEN

IN CAUDA VENENUM

BACK IN THE records room, I start sifting through more files, but I'm coming up blank. If I wasn't overwhelmed enough, behind the first set of cabinets is another set of drawers built into the wall that were hidden. So now I'm pulling out all the heavy cabinets to get at the drawers behind them, but they're seemingly empty. I'd give up and not check the rest, but I know whatever I need would end up being right there if I did. Something about Project CONIR or Gregory Millen or the military or "the bull" or . . . I don't know what. My fingers are cut up from scraping them across the rusted and jagged metal on the file cabinets, and by the time I crowbar the last one open, it becomes obvious I've wasted the better part of an hour unlocking and opening drawers no one knew were there.

Boom. Boom. Boom.

I throw the crowbar in frustration. I feel like I could eat a cow at this point, and I know if I close my eyes and relax for half a second, I'll be out cold. And though every fiber of my being is trying to convince my mind that sleep is the only rational option at this point, I know I can't. If I give up, I'm done for. I wonder if Michigan has the death penalty.

Boom. Boom. Boom.

It has to be five in the morning. I can hear the birds chirping outside the window now. The hospital itself is freezing cold. I'm not sure I could fall asleep if I tried. I can't stop shivering now, and all I can think about is how great it would be to have a pair of gloves or a large warm bed in Mexico, out of the reach of American authorities.

Boom. Boom. Boom.

Maybe they'll be lenient. I mean, without the rock, they have nothing really pinning me to the crime. Maybe I still have time to throw it in the lake or at least ditch it here and come back for it later. Maybe they already arrested Altman. Maybe he wasn't as good at covering his tracks as he thought he was. Maybe . . .

Boom. Boom. Boom.

What the hell is that noise?

It sounds like a washing machine or something rhythmically pounding a drum. I thought it was just my head pounding from starvation and exhaustion, but it's shaking the floor. It sounds like . . .

Like my dream.

BOOM. BOOM. BOOM.

I step out into the hallway to follow the sound. It's so much louder now and coming so much faster. I focus hard on the sound, trying to place it. It's definitely underneath me, but I don't think the hospital has a basement. If it does, I haven't seen it. Could there be a basement?

BOOMBOOMBOOMBOOMBOOM.

I put my ear to the ground to try to pinpoint it. I can tell it's definitely beneath me. There's a basement, and the thing I heard in my dream over and over again is down there. Finally, a break.

I reach for the flashlight and stand back up, reinvigorated. Only the flashlight isn't there. And apparently, neither am I.

I've stood up into another flashback. One of the shadows must've passed over me. The hallway is filled with nurses, doctors, and patients, all scuttling about. It's the middle of the day, and I'm guessing close to lunch. I've gotten good at this. I immediately start picking the scene apart. I look for familiar faces, listen for familiar words or names. I try to find the person I'm bubbled with, which in this case is tough because the quarters are so close that I can't see the edges of it. There's too many people around me to figure it out anyway.

A man walks by, mumbling to himself nothing coherent. Two nurses talk to a doctor about a patient named Jonas. I feel like I've heard that name before. I stand in the middle of the hallway trying to place it, when a janitor pushing a mop bucket comes from behind me.

"Excuse me," he says with a smile.

I move for him, and I focus on his face. I can't tell if he looks familiar or not, but he looks like he's in a hurry. I realize he's probably a patient here. When I was at Sandy Shores, sometimes the patients could make an extra dollar doing maintenance chores, like mopping or cleaning the dining room tables. Usually they were pretty grouchy about it; a dollar isn't a lot to make for mopping a whole hospital floor. At least this guy seemed polite when he stepped around me—when he saw me.

I look around me slowly, not daring to move, until I see a pen sitting on the edge of a cart in the hall. I reach over and flick it, and it hits the ground.

This isn't a flashback. I'm really here.

I reach out for the doctor, but he walks away. I tap the nurse on the shoulder, but nothing. She acknowledges me, but then quickly ignores me while she continues talking about Jonas.

Alright, I think, the clock is ticking.

"Excuse me, everyone?" I ask loudly and as politely as I can manage. The room slows as a few eyes come up to meet me, complete with a puzzled look as to how I got here. Now that I have their attention, it's time to figure out what the hell I'm going to say.

"Hi. Um . . . You might be wondering what I'm doing here. Frankly, that puts us in the same boat." My bad joke does nothing to ease the tension. "I'm looking for information on something called 'the bull,' and maybe you can help me. You know . . . depending on what year this is."

Blank stares. Not surprising. "Let me start over: My name is . . ."

"Emily Hunter!"

I turn around, not really sure who I'm expecting to see. A large nurse with a terrible haircut comes lumbering over to me, with a bit of an angry look in her eye.

"I'm sorry, have we met?" I ask. It's obvious this question doesn't sit well with the nurse.

"You aren't supposed to be here," she says. I smile at how obvious that statement is.

"You're telling me. Look, maybe you can point me in the direction of . . ."

"You know you can't leave your room. You're on forty-eight-hour restriction. What have we told you about breaking the rules?" Now two orderlies come from her left and walk slowly toward me.

"Wait, what? No, I'm not . . . I don't . . . I'm not a patient here. I just . . ." But I'm too perplexed to get out a coherent thought before the orderlies grab both my arms.

"Stop! Get the fuck off of me!" And I struggle, but I already know it's useless. I've been in restraint before. They're trained for this.

"Take her back to her room," the nurse says. "I can doc this, and you guys just sign off when she's locked up."

They drag me into a room on the corner of the hallway and push me down onto the bed. The smaller, kind-looking orderly is on the door while the larger, scarier-looking one holds me back from getting up before he's safely outside the locked door.

"Wait! Please!" I scream. "I'm not a patient here. You can't just lock me up."

"Good to know," says the large orderly through the window.

"No! This isn't my room. This is . . ." And looking around for the first time, I know exactly where I am. "This is Carrot's room! Carol Emerson—this is her room. I'm not supposed to be here!"

BANG! The orderly pounds his fist into the door. It startles me into silence. "HEY! I've had enough of you, Emily. You got it? Now sit the fuck down and shut up. If we catch you out of your room again, or if I hear another goddamned peep out of this room, I swear to Christ I'm taking you downstairs to isolation, and you and Abigail can hang out in there together until you fucking rot. Do you understand?"

"Abigail? Holy shit! Abigail's alive?"

"Emily . . ." he says, in a tone that makes it abundantly clear he's about to make good on his threat, but I can't help it. Abigail is alive wherever I am right now. I understand now.

"That's why I'm here!" I yell. "I have to tell Abigail. Altman is going to kill her, and I can save her!"

"That's it," he says, in a sickly satisfied voice. "Back away from the door."

"No! No, wait, you can tell her." My mind is racing now. I might have a chance to save her, and then Altman can't frame me for the murder. I'm not stopping to consider how none of this makes a damn bit of sense. They know me here, somehow. Also, I'm a patient here with Abigail. I don't know what year this is supposed to be, I don't know how they know who I am, I don't know why they think this is my room. None of that matters right now if I can just get a message to Abigail Pipkin.

I hear the keys in the door, and I suddenly realize how exposed I am. He's either going to take me to isolation with Abigail in some basement I didn't know existed or he's going to beat the shit out of me. I honestly don't know which to expect.

"Tell her! She's going to die! Please, just tell her! Don't hurt me!"

The door swings open, and there's nothing. As if flipping a switch, it's night again. I'm still somehow in Carrot's room. I didn't wake up in the hallway I started in. I never got through to Abigail.

That one was different. It may be getting too dangerous to stay here.

Outside the window, I hear whispering, hushed but hurried and desperate-sounding. Apprehensively, I peek over the window frame to the woods out back. I don't know if I can take any more questions at this point. I came to the hospital looking for something to implicate Altman; all I've gotten since are snippets, pieces of a story I've never heard and am not even sure is relevant. Carrot told me to save everyone. Is this how I do it? Because, honestly, I can't even save myself at this point.

And speaking of: outside the window and below a story, stands Carrot. She looks terrified again, but she's not looking at me. She's looking underneath me, to whatever is on the floor beneath me. I thought I was on the main floor, and looking out here, I can see the hospital is built over a hill that drops off in the back. There is a basement after all.

A man runs out from underneath my window and grabs her, scooping her up and hastily making his way deeper into the woods, taking her with him. I can't see his face, but he's stealing her, and she looks so scared.

"HEY! STOP!" I scream. He stops and turns back toward the building, looking for the source of the voice. His eyes finally meet mine, and I can tell he knows me.

"Emily, what are y . . ."

And his head fucking explodes.

Carrot screams and hits the ground hard. The man's lifeless and mostly headless body crumbles beneath itself, and Carrot begins scrambling through the dead leaves, trying to regain her footing and get away as quickly as possible.

BLAM, BLAM.

Gunshots.

Carrot runs deeper into the woods as the shots ring out from the window one room over. I've got to protect her—that's the only thought that goes through my mind as I run from my room to the room nextdoor. There, an orderly stands at the window with a large handgun, firing deep into the night and laughing hysterically. He doesn't see me, and I charge him. He's going to go out the fucking window. I raise my shoulder up for impact, hoping that I kill him but knowing that the drop is twenty feet, tops. More than likely, I'm just going to piss him off, but if he stops shooting at Carrot long enough for her to get away, it will be enough.

I brace for the hit, and it never comes.

I go right through the orderly and nearly out the window myself, barely catching the window frame before falling. The pain in my hand is excruciating; I grabbed broken glass still clinging to the window. I can feel warm blood dripping down my hand and over my wrist already.

I pull myself back in and clutch my hand. Looking at it, it's deep, but not nearly as bad as it felt. I brush off the remnants of glass from the rest of my hand and fall onto the floor. The orderly is still shooting, and I'm powerless to stop him.

A second orderly, a taller and stronger-looking man, bursts into the room and surveys the scene, looking barely able to comprehend it either.

"STOP! What the hell are you doing?"

He still doesn't stop shooting, and in my mind, I beg for him to be out of ammo soon.

"Stop, or I'm going to Millen," the second orderly says, pulling the shooter from the window, but in an instant, the shooter spins on him and has him pinned against the wall with the hot gun barrel burning the flesh under his chin.

"I wouldn't," the shooter says with a sick grin. He's a kid, probably nineteen, with horn-rimmed glasses and perfect slicked black hair, and he's enjoying this. He holds the orderly there, staring into his eyes, daring him to move, as if waiting for the big, strong man to cry.

"Fine. Jesus Christ, Bull."

The shooter runs out of the room, presumably after Carrot, leaving the orderly to himself to exhale and rub his burnt neck, and me to finally understand: it's not a monster; it's a kid.

Hello, Bull. Nice to meet you.

NINETEEN

HIC SUNT DRACONES

"Officer Jacoby, come in."

Peter covered his walkie as quick as he could, but it probably wasn't fast enough. If Emily Hunter was nearby, it was a safe bet she knew he was here. He had to get to her first, before Altman, before any other cops. Barkley seemed to think there was something odd going on, but he couldn't speak for anyone else. If he found her first, he could convince her to turn herself in and be a witness against Altman. The son of a bitch could finally go down. There was nothing tying her to Abigail Pipkin's murder except the word of an anonymous call, one that he'd bet his badge came from Henry Altman after he killed the old woman.

In front of him, a dirty stuffed rabbit lay on the ground, probably long forgotten by some local kid. The drop-off in front of him was a dead end.

"I think I lost her," replied Peter over his radio. "She's got to be nearby though. I think I'll make one quick sweep and head up to the hospital. It's the only place she could be going."

Sheriff Albin Barkley sat in his office on the other end of the conversation. "Roger that. Be careful up there, Pete. That place is a death trap."

An enraged Henry Altman burst through the door. His limp looked more pronounced than before. "Where are we at, Albin?" he said. Great, thought Barkley, this is all I need.

"Officer Jacoby is in pursuit right now. He's trying to reestablish a visual on her."

"He lost her? Are you kidding me? I don't buy that for a second," snapped Altman back.

Sheriff Barkley rolled his eyes. This would go so much smoother without this windbag in his office trying to play policeman. Barkley looked up to meet Altman's bloodshot eyes. Altman took that as an invitation to keep talking. It wasn't intended as such.

"Catching Emily Hunter will implicate his sister in this murder case. At the very least, it's a conflict of interest. I want Allison Jacoby arrested for aiding a known fugitive. She was hiding Emily Hunter at her house."

Wait a minute. Barkley pushed back away from his desk and crossed his arms. "How do you know that, Henry?"

"It's where this whole chase started, Albin. Did Peter Jacoby not tell you that? Do you wonder why I'm the one telling you that and not Peter?"

"Frankly, yeah, Henry."

"Obviously, it's something he didn't want you to know. That's why I'm doubting he lost her."

"No, Henry," said Barkley. "Why are you the one telling me that?"

Altman looked into Barkley's face, clearly not understanding the question. Could this guy be a bigger idiot? He reeled back to really lay into Barkley. He'd had enough of this guy's incompetence. His sly little jabs at Altman had gone on too long. But before Altman let the first word pop out of his mouth, he realized what Albin Barkley was really asking.

"I . . . brought Jacoby to talk to his sister, to see if she knew anything. And it turns out I was right because she did."

Barkley couldn't help but shake his head. This man's hubris just killed the entire investigation. Barkley smiled to himself. "You had one of my officers interrogate his own sister without a lawyer present, without the knowledge of his superior officer? You can't make that call, Henry. You don't have the authority to make the police force do your bidding."

"It doesn't matter, Albin. I want Allison Jacoby arrested. The evidence alone is . . ."

"Completely inadmissible in any way. You have to know that. It'll be both our jobs if I go after her. You just gave her a 'get out of jail free' card, Henry. That's why it's best to leave the police work to the police officers."

The rage inside Altman reached dangerous levels. His hands wouldn't stop shaking, even though he was wringing them together. This bastard loved that Altman looked foolish. They were all against him, and no one feared him anymore. Allison Jacoby was going to get away scot-free, and she knew about CONIR. Peter let Emily Hunter go.

Everything was going wrong. All Henry could do was storm out.

Peter reached the hospital and found the large, heavy door cracked open. He pushed on the door to open it further and received a hard static shock for his trouble. Pulling his hand away quickly, he managed to slide through the door without touching it again. The setting sunlight illuminated sections of the main lobby, but parts were covered in darkness. He pulled out his flashlight and lit up the darkness.

"Emily Hunter! This is Officer Peter Jacoby, Blue Water PD. If you are on the premises, please come out slowly and make yourself known." A few birds flew out of the building through a hole in the roof at the sound of his voice. Other than that, there was no movement. Peter unclipped the strap on his holster, but didn't draw his weapon, and went deeper into the hospital.

He turned down a long hallway that ended at a T. He looked either way and determined he'd start on the left. The hallway opened up into a larger space, what he could only assume was a dining hall. From there, three more hallways spread in each direction.

This would take some time. He decided on the farthest hallway.

"Emily! I'm not going to arrest you. I don't think you killed Abigail Pipkin. You and I both know it was Henry Altman. He's doing his damnedest to pin it on you and Al, but if you just come out, I can help you."

"No, you can't."

The voice spun Peter on his heels, both at it's suddenness and it's youth. Behind him stood a little girl with a stuffed rabbit. Her back was to him. In the environment he found himself in, he couldn't recall a creepier moment of his life.

"Little girl, are you OK?"

She didn't answer.

"Little girl, you shouldn't be in here. You could get hurt."

"You shouldn't be in here. You could get hurt," she echoed. It somehow had just gotten creepier. He swallowed hard, collecting himself.

"Sweetheart, you shouldn't be here. There's broken glass all over the place. Do your mommy and daddy know where you are?" He knelt down beside her, seeing her face. Her eyes were closed.

"Honey, are you OK? Look at me." She didn't flinch. He never believed in the haunted hospital his sister was so obsessed with. Maybe he should have listened.

From somewhere in the hospital, a gunshot rang out, and without a moment's hesitation, Peter had his gun pulled and the little girl safely behind him. He checked the immediate area over and, rethinking it, realized the shot was far enough away that he could take care of the kid.

"Listen, sweetie, I need you to step into this room for me, OK?" he said, as he gently but firmly guided her into one of the residential rooms. "I want you to stay in there until I come get you, OK?"

The little girl didn't say a word. She just walked into the room with her rabbit. "Good girl, just stay quiet, OK?" He shut the door. "Like that will be a problem," he said as he reached for his walkie.

"Dispatch, this is Officer Jacoby. Shots fired at Riverview Hospital. Repeat, shots fired at Riverview Hospital. Officer requiring immediate armed assistance." He let go of the transmitter button. Nothing but static.

"Dispatch, please acknowledge! Shots fired at Riverview Hospital. Officer requiring immediate armed assistance. There's a little girl here." Nothing.

"Sheriff Barkley, please respond." Nothing.

"Dammit. OK, little girl, I'm going to go find out what that noise was. You stay here and . . ." he looked through the window into the completely empty room he just put her in. Where the hell did she go?

"Little girl?" he whispered to an empty room.

And he wasn't the only one talking.

From down the hall, he heard voices. His gun drawn, he headed toward the sound of arguing. And there was something else: a pounding sound, like a bass drum. A door in the hallway stood between him and the voices, which had now become full shouts. The door was extremely heavy-duty, solid metal. He put his ear to it.

Boom. Boom. Boom.

The arguing was definitely coming from down there, and it was full-on frantic now. Peter looked for a way through the door and eventually found a latch with a padlock. The lock looked old and only took a few pounds from his club to break off the rusted latch.

The door rolled on a track to his left and took some coaxing to open, but once it did, Peter was faced with a long, narrow stairway going down into darkness. There was a blind corner going left at the end of the staircase. The arguing was much louder now. Gun drawn, he slowly crept downstairs.

BOOM. BOOM. BOOM.

A single bead of sweat dripped over Peter's forehead and luckily over the bridge of his nose, not into his eyes. He'd never had to fire his weapon before, and he'd been proud of that fact. His finger rolled over the safety for what was probably the tenth time, making sure it was off.

BOOMBOOMBOOMBOOMBOOM.

The beat got faster, louder, angrier. And then it was gone. The arguing stopped, the drum beat stopped, there was nothing but silence again. Peter was halfway down the stairs, and it was quiet.

But it was not dark. The stairs and the basement were now fully lit.

He slowly continued down the staircase and made the turn. The room was all white, lit by intense fluorescent bulbs. The room was full of large tables covered in papers and diagrams and sketches of what looked like symbols or glyphs. Two rooms were to his left, smaller rooms with glass walls looking into this one. Those rooms were full of scientific equipment—microscopes and tubes—and tons of equipment Peter had never seen before. The two adjoining rooms were unnaturally immaculate, not a speck of dust anywhere. In the front of the room, however, was the greatest oddity of all: another large metal door, only this one was immense, like a blast door meant to keep out a nuclear explosion. The rest of the room was only protected by the little metal door upstairs. Peter quickly understood that this door wasn't in place to guard the room he was in, but to guard something behind it. It was to keep people on this side of it out or maybe to keep something on the other side of it in.

To the right of the large, ominous door was a keypad with a digital readout, much newer than anything in this hospital should be. None of this made sense, least of all the word embossed on the metal panel above the readout.

"CONIR," Peter read aloud. That's the word Allison had said to ask Altman about. Whatever Altman was hiding was behind this door. Unfortunately, it looked like it would take a fleet of bulldozers to get through it. It didn't matter though; he was sure Barkley would love to see this room. He couldn't wait to see Altman's face when he reported it. Of course he wasn't sure what it was yet, but whatever it was, it was hidden for a reason. Altman would likely know what that reason was.

This was it. The first domino to fall. It would bring Mayor Altman down with it.

"Pete?" a familiar voice asked from behind him. He turned his head without turning his gun. He knew it was Allison. Of course it was Allison. She stood a few steps into the room away from the stairs. She had followed him down here.

"Al, what are you doing?"

"Me? What are you doing?" The smile she gave him didn't feel right.

"I heard gunshots, and there was a little girl . . ." he suddenly realized he didn't need to explain any of this to her. "Why did you follow me? You shouldn't be here."

"Did you come to stop them?" That smile again. She was happy to see him, elated. It hadn't even been an hour since they were at the kitchen table together, but she looked different, tired, exhausted. Something wasn't right.

"Come to . . . no. What are you talking about? I'm looking for Emily. Are you OK?" he asked, walking toward her.

"Who's Emily?" she asked.

Peter stopped in his tracks. Something was very wrong.

"Officer Jacoby?" a man's voice asked from the staircase behind her. Peter raised the gun again and aimed it behind Allison, motioning for her to come toward him. She hesitated, and in that moment, a man in a medical lab coat entered the room from the stairway. The man's hands instantly went up to show he was unarmed and not a threat. Peter didn't recognize his face. He'd remember the massive chin scar if he'd seen it before. He lowered the gun, but still kept it drawn.

"Who are you?" he asked. "What is this place?"

The old man smiled and lowered his hands. "You shouldn't be down here."

A half a second later, all hell broke loose.

Two men in full black ops military gear opened the metal door by the staircase with poised M16 assault rifles and instantly fired flanking left and right. The doctor ducked down, dragging Allison with him, and Peter raised his weapon but was hit in the shoulder before he could get a shot off. The bullet spun him around and dropped him to the ground behind a table, but he managed to hold onto his weapon. Allison screamed. A third black ops soldier came through the door, and Peter heard the doctor tell him his instructions before forcefully dragging his frantic sister out of the room.

"He doesn't leave here alive."

Peter's shoulder burned so hot his eyes began to water. He quickly wiped the tears away. He needed to be able to see. "HOLD YOUR FIRE!" he yelled. "I'm a police officer!"

It didn't seem to matter. The wall suddenly started raining down dust and cinder as the bullets sprayed over his head. He was in cover, but he knew he wasn't going to be for long. This was suppression fire. They were trying to keep him in place.

Peter's vision started to narrow as the blood seeped from his body through the hole in his left shoulder. He still wasn't aware of the exit wound in his back that was bleeding even heavier. The arm underneath felt dead and couldn't hold his gun, so that job belonged to his right hand, leaving his shoulder uncovered to bleed out freely. The noise from the rifle was unbearable, especially in such a confined room. Louder still were the shots hitting the large CONIR door and ricocheting without even denting the steel.

Peter dragged himself to the right side of the table, his weapon drawn and waiting for the soldier that would inevitably be coming that way for him. Peter swallowed, waiting to see his covered face, and when he did, he tasted blood. In this moment, Peter realized he didn't have a strategy. Even if he could shoot his way out of this room, he'd bleed to death in minutes. His only hope was to make it out into the woods and radio for help and hope they could get to him in time. That left Allison alone here with the doctor and any other soldiers that might be in the facility. His only option wasn't a good one.

In front of him, around another table, the soldier's head finally poked out. Peter started firing, but his vision was going. He heard breaking glass as he hit the windows sealing the sterile laboratories. It seemed to be enough, as the soldier ducked back behind the table again. Peter tried to keep track of his shots, but he lost count almost instantly. He took a breath and tried to gather himself. The only way out was the small staircase or the room, if it were unlocked. If he could get to the doctor, free Allison, hold him hostage to get released, maybe that—

Peter's chest exploded in front of him before he fell face down onto the floor.

The soldier from behind Peter's vantage point stood up, calling a ceasefire, and the noise stopped. Boots crunched broken glass and cinder as three men walked up to surround Peter. But Peter felt nothing anymore. The pain in his shoulder was gone. His back felt like someone was sitting on him; it was uncomfortable at best. He wasn't scared anymore. In fact, he felt comfortable. The floor was the most comfortable place he'd ever lain, and all he wanted to do was close his eyes and go to sleep. He felt hands on him, and they were hands like his, five fingers on each one—hands like his, like his sister's, like his mother's. He wondered who the soldiers were, the one who shot him most of all—not why he was here, but how he got to this point: who his parents were, whether or not he had a wife or kids, if he had ever been loved, what different paths they each had taken to end up on opposite ends of that final bullet. He wasn't angry. In fact, he wished the man well. As the soldiers rolled him over, he was smiling at how funny last thoughts could be.

The man who shot him looked at that smile. It wasn't the strangest reaction to dying he'd ever seen, he thought to himself as he pulled out his handgun and fired two shots into the cop's skull.

TWENTY

POLLICE VERSO

THIS IS A longshot, but it might be all I have left. I walk down the hallway, my flashlight on the door numbers. I'm kidding myself. The sun is coming up and shining directly through a hole in the ceiling. I don't need the light anymore, but I'm still using it, pretending that it's still night, pretending that time isn't up.

Twenty-three, twenty-five . . . and here we are: room twenty-seven. This is the room the orderlies took Allison to after she saw me in group therapy. I can only hope she is still here, but when I see the door, my stomach sinks. It's wide open and, other than a single chair, is completely empty. I sit in the chair and open my phone to see it's 6:20 a.m. The cops will be here any minute, I'm sure of it. This is the only place I could be. I rest my head against the wall, and I give in. I can't keep my eyes open anymore. I tell myself I'm just resting for a moment, that I'll get up after about five minutes and keep searching. It's a lie. I know it. I'm done.

The hospital is surrounded by police. Helicopters hover overhead. They wake me up and drag me out in handcuffs. Outside, Henry Altman is there, and he's laughing. "I told you that you wouldn't find anything, psycho," he says. Beyond him, two cops talk to my mom and Dr. Harper. They're both crying, even Harper. That's odd. Allison is there too. She's being held down on the hood of a car, being handcuffed, and she's talking to me. "Why are you here?" she says. I came like a plague into her life, ruining everything. "Why are you here? Why are you here?"

My eyes open. I'm in room twenty-seven and so is Allison.

"Why are you here?" she asks from the bed across the room that wasn't there when I fell asleep. She's not happy to see me. Instead, she looks terrified, panicked.

"Allison, calm down," I say. "Why are you here? You told me you never were a resident here."

She closes her eyes hard and rocks on her bed, her hands in fists pressing on her temples. "It's not real, it's not real, it's not real," she chants to herself.

"Al . . . please," I say reaching out my hand to her. She instantly recoils before I touch her.

"NO! Don't hurt me!" She's so scared of me, and I can feel the tears coming back.

"I'd never hurt you, you know that. We're friends, right?"

She begins bawling. "I'm sorry! I'm so, so sorry!"

"Why are you sorry?"

"It's my fault. I'm so sorry. I told, I told on you, about Tony and the rabbit's foot keys. You left me. You said you wouldn't leave me, and you left me. I was so mad, so I told. It's my fault you're dead."

What. The. Hell.

"What do you mean 'I'm dead?'"

"The accident."

"What accident, Al? I'm not dead. I'm right here."

"The explosion or the earthquake or whatever the hell that was. Two weeks ago—you don't remember that?"

I'm starting to get upset. "Allison, look at me. I'm not dead."

"The cops all came and interviewed us. My brother was here. The FBI came too. At least they said they were the FBI. You can't always tell."

"Allison, listen . . ."

"You were right though," she says finally starting to relax, "about the stuff in the basement."

"The basement?"

"Yeah, the CONIR project. They got everyone."

Holy shit. "CONIR? It's in the basement?"

"Sure is."

"How do I get to the basement?"

"There's a metal door in the west wing by the dining hall. It's down there."

"What is it?"

Allison gives me a quizzical look. "How the hell should I know?"

"Well, how do you know everything else?"

"You told me."

I thought I was lost before. I'm starting to regret ever coming to this town. I decide to switch gears.

"Do you know anything about an orderly here they call 'Bull?'"

Allison thinks a moment. "Yeah, Jonas talks about him. Apparently, he was the worst. He terrorized the people here, did some awful stuff. Jonas said he killed a patient."

"Yeah, I think I saw that happen."

There's that quizzical look again. "How? He died a long time before you got here."

Wait. "He's dead?"

She studies my face. "Bull died a year or two after Jonas was admitted to the hospital, and that guy's been in the same room since like the seventies. Jonas said he pushed a resident too far, and they killed him on an overnight shift. They found his body the next morning with his throat bitten out. It's kind of a legendary story here."

I cover my eyes in frustration. So, finding Bull is out.

"Jonas said the resident that killed him was just a little girl."

I look up quickly, but she's gone. The room is empty again.

The west wing hallway is full of metal doors, each with a small window the size of an envelope. This is the isolation wing, where the worst patients were put. The selling point was that it was to keep the other residents safe, but it was really to make the orderlies' and nurses' lives easier. Locking up the psychopaths as punishment for being mentally ill and not having to doc the trouble they may have gotten into made their shift go by faster. Peeking into one of the windows, I realize I've seen closets larger than these rooms. This was torture. It was inhuman. But it was easy when you didn't regard your patients as people.

There's one door on the west wall that has no window. It's the only one. I walk up to the door to see a padlock lying on the floor, broken off of a rusty latch. The door is cracked slightly. This has to be it.

I roll the door to the left, and in front of me lies a narrow staircase with a blind left turn at the bottom. The smell of burnt gunpowder reaches my nose. There's been no power in the rest of the hospital, but somehow the lights are on down there. There are people talking. I focus on keeping my breathing quiet, and I step onto the stairs. Beneath my foot, I step on a loose piece of rebar. I pick it up and brandish it like a club as I continue down the staircase.

Creeeeeak.

A step under my foot alerts seemingly everyone in the world to my presence. The voices in the basement stop. They know I'm here. I'm frozen on the stairs.

The light goes out.

Shit. Shit, shit, shit.

No movement. No sound. Nothing. Up or down? Up or down?

I wait for way too long until I make the decision to keep moving. I get to the corner, and I slowly peek my head around.

The large room is full of tables. To the left, large solid windows seal off two other rooms. In the front of the room, a large intimidating steel door seals off whatever is behind it. Everything is covered in dust and cobwebs.

No one has been down here in years.

I find a light switch and flip it on. Nothing happens, the room is still dark. I pop my flashlight back on as I wonder where that light had come from. Maybe from behind the giant door?

I approach the door cautiously, and I find a keypad to the right. The readout is off; the keypad is dead. When I try to force it open, the door doesn't budge. Pushing harder, I feel as if I'm about to blow a blood vessel in my head, and my flashlight shines on a metal plate about the keypad. On it is a single word: *CONIR*.

Holy shit, I found it.

I look around the room, and I find a binder near where I came in. The cover reads C*ONIR Project: Section 2 of 3*. I open the binder and see nothing but sketches of glyphs. They look exactly like the ones Carol Forrester had framed on her wall, the ones Albert Forrester drew before he died. Each glyph has a code number and a short description: *Water, Mother, Food, Hands.*

The next glyph is an *X* with two dots. The description reads: *Move.*

From the corner of my eye, I see movement. I look up instinctively, and I see my reflected self again, staring back at me from in front of the CONIR door.

"Not now," I beg her. But this is different again, like the hospital room. She's facing me, and she's out of breath. I set the binder down, and she doesn't make the same movement. Instead, she just stares at me, as if trying to figure me out. She points at the farthest sterile room.

"Look," she says.

I turn to look at the room, and I see nothing. I turn back, and the other me turns and runs—right through the giant steel door.

I can't follow her, so I walk back to the sterile room, wondering what she pointed at. In the room is a single silhouette of a man, just like I've seen all over the hospital. He's looking around like he doesn't want to be discovered doing whatever he's doing. I reach out to touch him, and I feel that familiar buzz again.

Then, everything goes black.

TWENTY-ONE

NEC TAMEN CONSUMEBATUR

He hated Christmas Eve. Every holiday was rough, but this one especially. The shift always went wrong. All the inmates were crazy enough already, but day shift got everyone hopped up on cookies and candy, and night shift always paid for it.

Bull walked down the hallway, and silence followed him. This was the respect he earned. His scowl was enough to earn it from most of them. Some of them needed further lessons, lessons he enjoyed teaching.

From the sound of crying behind the door in front of him, he'd get to teach it that night.

Nurse Amy Brown leaned on the desk down the hall and watched Bull walk up the hallway. She knew him, mostly by reputation, but she'd never talked to him. She'd never wanted to. He was a horrible kid, just out of high school, who had managed to keep himself out of Vietnam so far. She felt terrible for thinking it, but she wished his number would get drawn. Maybe that would knock him down a few pegs.

Bull pulled out his club and banged it on the door. The crying inside got worse, as if being startled exacerbated whatever was going on in that room. He looked at the piece of paper crudely taped to the wall beside the door, reading the name of the resident. He hadn't met this one before. He must be new.

"Jonas, shut up and go to sleep!"

The crying got worse. Bull smiled. He hoped it would.

"HEY! Are you going to lie down and shut up, or am I going to open this door and knock you out?"

"Bull, that's enough!" Amy said, finally speaking up. "He's transitioning to our care."

Bull looked up to meet Amy's death stare. He hadn't even noticed she was there, nor did he really care.

"Oh, well then, let me help him."

Bull opened the door to find Jonas, his face stained with tears. He was older than the crying made him sound, probably close to thirty. He sat on the edge of his bed, with his standard-issue comforter pulled up to his shoulder for protection. His hospital pajamas were soaked. The room smelled like piss.

"I wet my bed," Jonas managed to say through the sniffles.

Bull took a moment to make a face specifically to let Jonas know how disgusting he was, then he pulled his club from the clip on his belt.

"You shouldn't have done that," said Bull through the sick grin on his face as he locked the door behind him.

"Do you know why you're here?" asked Dr. Gregory Millen from behind his large oak desk. Bull always admired this office. Everything in it, from the furniture to the frames on the wall, looked solid, heavy, angular. It exuded authority.

"I'm assuming we're going to talk about my application for the staff coordinator position?" said Bull, honestly believing it. Millen was a rough man, but he could keep himself in check. He knew when to turn it on and when to turn it off. This kid with his silly-looking glasses was a different animal altogether. He seemed to be oblivious to himself. Millen didn't know what was worse, the idea that Bull was trying to miss the point or the idea that he was actually missing the point.

"You aren't getting the job, Bull."

"Sir, I've been here since I was seventeen. I've got seniority here, but in the last five years I've seen everyone promoted around me. It's my time now."

"Your time . . ." Millen said, shaking his head. It was the latter. This kid was so detached from reality, he really didn't get the point. "It'll never be your time, Bull, not when I keep hearing about you. Nurses come to me about your interactions with patients. Therapists are reporting their clients have bruises."

"Tell them to come do my job," Bull interrupted.

"Excuse me?"

In for a penny, thought Bull. "I'll trade anytime. I'll go sit in a comfy chair while these psychopaths are comfortably sedated, and I'll ask them why they think they're fucking nuts. Those therapists see these guys for an hour a week. I'm out there every night—"

"*OK*," interrupted Millen, holding his hand up. Bull wasn't the first staff member he'd had tell him how hard their job was compared to the therapists'. It always astounded Dr. Millen how everyone forgot he was a licensed psychiatrist, but then again, they didn't hire kids right out of high school because they were brilliant.

Millen opened a drawer and pulled out a manila envelope. Inside was a documented incident report and some polaroid photos. He took the photos and set them in front of Bull.

"You could have killed him. You're goddamn lucky you didn't."

Bull looked at the pictures of Jonas. His face was purple and swollen, a tooth was missing. His right eye was completely bloodshot, no white remaining. Bull didn't care. He couldn't believe he wasn't getting promoted, again.

"Did he attack you when you entered his room?"

Bull didn't look up. "No," he said quietly.

"I'm sorry, I didn't hear you."

Bull gritted his teeth. He respected Millen, but he hated when Millen talked down to him. He remembered every single time it happened. One day would be the last day.

"No," Bull said, louder this time.

"I'm sorry, I still didn't hear you."

Bull looked up to see Millen squinting at him over his desk. He definitely heard him, so what was Millen getting at?

" . . .Yes?" said Bull.

"Good. Then at least you were defending yourself."

Bull smiled. Millen wasn't so bad. He understood.

"Look, Bull, I understand. I know what these patients are capable of. I know that a little discipline, or fear of it, can go a long way to keeping everyone safe. The therapists, the nurses, they don't want to hear that, so just tone it down in front of them."

"Yes, sir," said Bull. Millen waved his hand, dismissing Bull. Bull stood up and made it to the door before he just had to ask: "Only in front of them?"

Millen didn't even look up. "If a tree falls in the woods . . ."

That was all Bull needed to hear. Keeping it secret could actually be fun, like a little game. He opened the door to leave and almost walked directly into a man in full military garb waiting outside the door.

From behind him, Millen spoke up. "That's all, Bull. Thank you." The military man pushed past him into the room, shutting the door behind him. Bull lingered outside the door a moment, wondering who the man was before walking away.

The locker room smelled horrible, like mold and sweat weeks old. It was odd because it was for the male hospital staff. It's not like they were running marathons, yet the odor seemed to be baked into the walls, never able to be scrubbed out.

As Bull was changing back into his street clothes, Reese was getting ready to go on shift. Reese had been hired about a year after Bull was, and because of that, he shadowed Bull, informally acting as a student to the way Bull did things. He'd never seen Reese hit a patient, but he'd never known Reese to object to Bull doing it either. He was one of the only staff Bull talked to because he was one of the only staff who tolerated Bull. That left him pretty far from being called "friend," but it was as close as Bull had. They'd gone to high school together, Reese a year behind Bull, but Bull had noticed him. It was hard not to notice the only colored kid in the entire high school. Bull had left him alone, not something he could say about the rest of the kids. Bull never saw the point of making an enemy just for the sake of making an enemy. All his enemies were there for a reason.

"Let me ask you something," said Bull. "You see these army guys around here?"

Reese laughed. "I haven't seen shit I ain't supposed to see."

Bull moved in closer and whispered, "You have seen them though, right? You got any idea what that's about?"

"All I know is they keep coming in and out of the isolation wing. Tony said he seen them going downstairs."

Bull looked intrigued. He'd heard a rumor there was a basement to the hospital, where they did weird experiments on patients. He was pretty sure it was just something they said to keep the residents in line. He didn't even remember where he had heard it. It was just always a story roaming around the halls.

"Look man, don't go all Sherlock Holmes. It don't concern us. Just keep your head down and do your job."

"Yeah . . ." is what Bull said, but in his head, he was a million miles away.

New Year's Day, 1970—finally, all the goddamn holidays were over.

Bull walked down the east hallway quietly. His overnight shift was halfway finished. Two on-call nurses were sleepers tonight, camped out in their quarters. The other three orderlies on tonight were sitting in the lobby, playing cards. They'd be there all night. Bull had the hospital to himself. He'd been thinking about it for hours, before he'd even gotten on shift. He was going to make a visit tonight.

He came to the corner and knocked on the door. There was no answer.

"Carol, honey. Are you in there?"

Nothing. He knocked louder.

"Carol, come open the door for me."

Nothing. He knew she wasn't sleeping. She'd gotten to know the schedule just as well as he had. It was Monday night, Bull's night.

"Carrot cake, if you make me open the door, I promise one of us isn't going to have any fun," he said in a sweet voice. A few seconds later, the door clicked, and eight-year-old Carol Emerson stood there, eyes already welling up with tears. She turned around and went back into the room and sat on the bed without making eye contact with him. Bull walked into the room and began removing his belt slowly. "That's a good girl," he said.

Carrot held her breath and watched him enter her room, blocking her only way out. She thought about jumping out the window. She was pretty sure the fall would kill her. That used to matter.

From somewhere in the hospital, a gunshot rang out. Bull turned to look out the door and quickly refastened his belt. "Stay here, close the door and stay quiet," he said, as if he were heroic. Carrot shut the door quickly and locked it.

He ran out of the hallway and toward the sound of a commotion. None of the other orderlies heard it, apparently, because he was the only one walking the halls with his flashlight. He came into the isolation wing and saw a door rolled open. Behind it, a light was on and a staircase led downward.

There was a basement after all.

Of course it was Lewis. Who else could it have been?

Dr. Millen and two other scientists were locked in the sterile room, trying to reason with the madman waving a gun in the next room—at least, they pretended he was a madman. The truth is, they did this to him. Apparently, they didn't do a good enough job.

On the floor laid a third scientist; on the floor next to him lay his brains. Standing over both was Kevin Lewis, holding a 9 mm Beretta he somehow managed to smuggle down here.

"You don't have to do this. We can make a deal," said Millen with no intention of making a deal.

"Yeah? Here's the deal: I go to the cops, you go to prison for the rest of your life. How's that deal?"

"They'll never believe you, son. Just put down the gun and let us out."

"They'll believe me, Millen," he said with a knowing smile. "I've been sneaking shit about the CONIR project out of here for months. There's only been two times you put me in that fucking room that I didn't come out with something."

There it is: confirmation. Kevin Lewis is the leak. And not only that, he's got them all dead to rights. Who knows what information he's gotten his hands on? And who knows where it's gotten to? Maybe he was bluffing, maybe he wasn't.

"You aren't torturing any more people, doc. You're all going down. You, Forrester . . ."

"Think this through, Kevin. We can make you a rich man."

Kevin smiled. "So can the book rights." He turned and walked toward the stairs, about to expose the entire organization.

Instead, he felt a club swing around the corner and smash his nose to pieces.

Kevin hit the floor hard and instantly clutched at his already bleeding nose. The tears started in his eyes so heavily he couldn't see. He thrashed around on the ground, searching for the gun that came out of his grasp when he hit the floor.

Click.

Too late.

He wiped out his eyes to see Bull standing over him, his gun in his hand. No one moved—not Kevin, not Millen, not the other two scientists in the room—just Bull with a new skip in his step, astounded at the scene he just added himself to.

"Kevin Lewis?" he said, with feigned surprise. "I thought you got transferred last July, man. How've you been?" Bull didn't point the gun anywhere. He didn't have to. Kevin was unarmed, his boss was trapped. He took a moment to observe his surroundings: the scientific equipment, the massive steel door. He had everyone over a barrel, and he was going to enjoy every second of it.

His eyes met Millen's. Millen knew what type of man Bull was. This had the potential to go very wrong. Bull acted for himself, always for himself and only for himself. Millen could try to bribe him, but exposing them would inevitably play better. Once it got out what Millen was doing here, everyone would know the face of whoever brought it to the national spotlight. But there was something else going on with Bull. His eyes weren't calculating anything, he wasn't thinking that far ahead. He was just staring at Millen before he cracked a smile.

"If a tree falls in the woods," said Bull, then he fired. Kevin fell limp next to the other dead body on the floor.

Something came over Bull in that instant. He'd always coveted power, and he just tasted the ultimate. He took a life, just like that. He squeezed a trigger, and Kevin Lewis no longer existed. His whole body buzzed with excitement. He immediately started coming down. The gunshot only lasted an instant, so he fired again two more times into the corpse. It didn't even flinch. He looked up from the body, back to Millen and the scientists. The scientists looked horrified. Millen looked pleased.

Bull buried the body of Kevin Lewis between two old pine trees in the woods behind the hospital, dusted himself off, and got back to the hospital before the next shift arrived. At 7:15 a.m. on Tuesday, January 2, 1970, Bull walked out of the hospital and went home. No one but Amy, who had for the first time received a smile and a wave from him, even noticed.

The next Monday, Bull began his new position as senior staff coordinator. He entered the locker room that morning to somber looks from everyone except Reese.

"Congratulations, Bull," he said with a smile. "Couldn't have happened to a nicer guy."

"Thanks, man," he said, opening his locker. Inside was a box wrapped in purple paper. He gave it a moment's notice before a thought occurred to him. "Hey, maybe no more 'Bull' though. I gotta sound respectable."

"No problem, boss," replied Reese. Bull grinned from ear to ear.

The room cleared out without another word. Bull stayed behind and read the note attached to the gift.

"For going above and beyond the call of duty. Congratulations.—G. Millen"

He beamed. Opening the box, he found a gold pocket watch. Inscribed on the outside were the words: Everything has its time.

He closed the locker door. The nameplate on the locker read H. Altman.

I got you now, motherfucker.

I step out of the bubble, away from the silhouette, and the old dead hospital is back. It's still morning. I got what I came for. Altman is a killer, and Kevin Lewis's body is behind the hospital. Time to go to the cops.

The walk back to Blue Water is a long one. It's still cold out, and I am starving and a little nauseous. A few times I have to stop in the woods to hold on to a tree to keep myself upright. I'm exhausted, and I keep getting dizzy spells. It's been a long time since I've pulled an all-nighter.

I step into the police station, fully expecting to be tackled by cops, but thankfully they show more restraint. As I pass a large, darkened window I catch my reflection for the first time: I look like I've slept in a hole. I'm dirty, my clothes are torn, probably from rusty nails sticking out of the walls. My eyes are strung out too, bloodshot from being forced open. Needless to say, I've looked better.

The officers see me and stop what they're doing. I'm guessing they didn't expect me to just walk in here. I put my hands up and announce that I'm there to turn myself in. Two officers come to me, and instead of cuffing me, they sit me down on a chair. A third stands in front of me, hand on his belt.

"I also want it known I have evidence implicating Mayor Henry Altman in the death of Riverview patient Kevin Lewis. He is also responsible for the murder of Abigail Pipkin—not me."

The cop in front of me begins the questioning. "Who are you saying the murderer is?"

"Altman. Mayor Henry Altman," I say. I hadn't stuttered.

The cops all look to each other, and my stomach tightens. Something is wrong.

"Ma'am, the mayor's name is Michael Bronson," the cop continues.

"No . . . Blue Water's mayor, Henry Altman. He's been mayor since the eighties."

"Well, Bronson is mayor now. Before that was Amy Brown. Before that was . . . honestly I can't remember."

What the fuck was this guy talking about? "Look, I just came from Riverview. I saw the mayor kill a man—Henry fucking Altman, mayor of Blue Water."

A fourth cop now comes from behind me, probably because I'm swearing. "Ma'am, please remain calm, and we can figure this out. First, let's start with your name."

"Emily Hunter, I'm Emily Hunter. You've been looking for me." I turn now to see him.

"Emily," he says, "it's nice to meet you. My name is Officer Peter Jacoby."

PART FOUR

TWENTY-TWO

TEMPORA MUTANTUR ET NOS MUTAMUR IN ILLIS

"THREE SUGARS, RIGHT?"

Peter Jacoby walks into the interrogation room with an extremely small Styrofoam cup of coffee. "Sorry, all we have is decaf."

I've already eaten three donuts, and someone made a run to the Lake Street Cafe to grab me a short stack of pancakes, which I devoured in what had to be record time.

"What's today?" I ask.

"Friday," he answers.

"No, I mean the date."

"September 18." Shit, that's what I thought.

"What year is it?" I ask. Maybe I'm still in a vision? Maybe I'm still at the hospital? Peter Jacoby doesn't remember me despite chasing me through the woods not eighteen hours ago.

"It's 2015," he answers, not exactly shocked at my question. It's the right day, it's the right year, it's the right town. So what the hell has gone wrong?

"Am I being charged with anything?" I ask. If they don't remember me, it's possible I've beaten a murder charge in the most insane way ever.

"Not at all," he answers. "We just want to ask you some questions if that's OK with you. About this Abigail . . ."

"Pipkin," I answer. This is odd to me too. It's strange that they don't know who I am. It's even stranger that they don't know who Old Lady Abigail is. None of this makes an ounce of sense.

"Pipkin, right. So tell me again what happened?"

I sigh. This is the third time I've been through this. "I was being framed for her murder by the mayor."

"Not Mr. Bronson, a man named . . ."

"Henry Altman." They haven't heard of him either. I suddenly realize this all feels like a *Twilight Zone* episode. I chuckle to myself because for some reason this particular moment, not the hundreds of strange ones before it, was the first time I thought of that. "Altman bludgeoned her with a rock, then hid it in my hotel room so I'd take the fall." The rock is still in my backpack, which is hanging off the back of my chair. I don't feel that part is necessary to tell.

"And why did he want to frame you?"

My teeth are on edge. He's talking to me in *that* tone, the one that would pat you on the head gently if it had arms. I heard it at Sandy Shores, I heard it from doctors and therapists, I heard it from my parents. It's the tone that says, "I don't believe a thing you're saying, but I'm going to keep you talking." It's the tone you give a kindergartener when you ask them about their day. I breathe through it, but if he doesn't stop, I'm going to have a hard time resisting punching him in the mouth.

"I found out information on him. Abigail pointed me in the right direction, and he killed her for that, and he killed at least two other people. A patient named Kevin Lewis, and . . . another man." I don't know who the man was that Bull shot from the window as he was trying to carry Carrot away through the woods, but I bet his body is buried between the same two pine trees. "He's also guilty of assault against many of the residents and sexual assault of a minor, Carol Forrester. If you ask her, she can probably tell you."

"And who is she?" replied Peter. What the fuck? Now they don't know her either?

"Carol Forrester? She was Carol Emerson back then."

Peter shakes his head. "Sorry. But that's OK. What else?"

"They would run secret experiments on patients in the basement of the hospital. The government was in on it in some capacity."

"Really?" he asks, and I hear it too: I sound batshit insane. And looking at the state of myself, my ragged clothes and my lack of sleep, I probably look batshit insane to match. So it's time to change tactics.

"So, you have no idea who I am?"

"I'm sorry, ma'am, I do not."

"Then how do you explain that I know you live on Bell River Lane? In a brown house with a cracked sidewalk leading to a small porch? Your backyard butts up against the woods."

That got his attention.

"How do you explain that I know you have a sister named Allison?"

"You know Allison?" he asks, interest piqued.

"Yeah, I do. She was helping me investigate Altman. If you talk to her, she can confirm everything."

He pauses a moment, like he's considering it.

"OK, I'll give her a call," he says. "Maybe we can clear all of this up. Sound good?"

"Or just take me up to the hospital. I can prove it all. I'll show you the lab and everything."

"We're working on that," he says. "We're just trying to arrange transport, and I'll go up there with you myself. OK?"

I nod.

"In the meantime, I'll call Al and see what she can tell me about Henry Altman."

I nod again, and he gets up and leaves the room, and I'm alone.

Or . . . no. I'm not.

BARKLEY STOOD OUTSIDE THE INTERROGATION ROOM WHEN PETER JACOBY APPROACHED HIM. "WHAT HAVE WE GOT?" HE ASKED.

PETER TOOK A DEEP BREATH. "CAUCASIAN FEMALE NAMED EMILY HUNTER. SHE WANDERED OUT OF THE WOODS THIS MORNING, SAYING SHE'S BEING FRAMED FOR THE MURDER OF A WOMAN WE'VE NEVER HEARD OF BY A MAN WE'VE NEVER HEARD OF. THIS MAN IS THE MAYOR AND ALSO WAS AN ORDERLY AT RPH WHO KILLED A BUNCH OF PATIENTS AND RAN SECRET GOVERNMENT EXPERIMENTS OUT OF THE BASEMENT."

BARKLEY'S FACE SAID IT ALL. WHAT A WAY TO END THE WEEK.

"APART FROM THAT, SHE SAYS SHE KNOWS MY SISTER AND THAT SHE CAN PROVE IT ALL IF WE TAKE HER BACK UP TO RIVERVIEW."

"FINE BY ME. TAKE MIKE WITH YOU," BARKLEY REPLIED. THE WEEKEND COULDN'T COME FAST ENOUGH.

SHE STARED AT THEM THROUGH THE GLASS. HER HANDS MOVED UP AND DOWN LIKE SHE WAS AWKWARDLY WAVING TO SOMEONE IN THE MIRROR. BARKLEY LEFT WITHOUT ANOTHER WORD.

I stare at my reflection in the interrogation room mirror, and it's somehow wrong. When I move my left hand, my reflection moves its left hand—only it shouldn't work like that. It's like I'm watching myself on a TV, not in a mirror. There's something else: My reflection's eyes are closed.

Peter opens the door too quickly, and I jump. "Alright, grab your bag, Ms. Hunter. My partner and I are going to head up to the hospital with you. You can show us what you're talking about, OK?"

I check the mirror again. Everything has gone back to normal. "Fine," I say. "You think I'm crazy, don't you?"

"No, ma'am," he lies. "We just want to help you understand what's going on."

"Did you get ahold of Allison?"

"Not yet," he answers. "I will." A second officer shows up in the doorway, and they escort me to a police car. I sit in the back on the drive through the woods. The solid plastic seat is extremely uncomfortable, especially since I just want to lie down and close my eyes for ten minutes. I settle for leaning my head on the window and watching the trees go by. The officers in the front seat don't say a word the entire trip, no doubt not looking forward to drudging through the old, condemned building.

The old . . .

Oh my God.

"Here we are," says Peter from the front seat as we pull up the long driveway to the hospital. The hospital looms larger in the day than it did last night. I left it not two hours ago, when the sun was just starting to creep over the trees. Now, in full direct sunlight, it looks quite different—not because I can see it any better, but because the windows aren't broken, the graffiti is gone, the staff is waiting for our police cruiser in the driveway.

The hospital is operational.

"No! No, wait, what the hell is going on?" I manage to stutter out.

The other cop in the front seat looks over to Peter with a knowing smile.

"Here we go," he says, as if he knew this would be my reaction. I understand why. If the hospital was operational and I wandered out of the woods dirty and strung out, talking about evil orderlies and secret government projects, of course they thought I escaped and they were bringing me back. But this doesn't make sense: I was literally just here, and the building was condemned.

Wasn't it?

A thought creeps into my mind, and I immediately kick it back out. I can't even acknowledge it.

A nurse opens the back door to let me out as the car comes to a stop. "Wait, wait," I beg. "There's a mistake, I'm not supposed to be here."

The second cop laughs. "Lady, if anyone is supposed to be here, it's you."

"This is her," Peter says to the nurse. "She says her name is Emily Hunter."

"She appears to be in crisis. We have an emergency service center set up. We could bring her there until we figure out what to do next." She motions to the orderlies, and they come for me.

This is all wrong. I push myself deeper into the car, but it doesn't stop them. They reach in and pull me out, kicking and screaming. "This isn't real! None of this is real!" I yell. I feel a quick pinch on my arm, and suddenly my arm feels heavy. My toes start tingling, and my lips feel too big. Everything slows down, and I realize I've been sedated. My screams become slurred, and my eyes get heavy.

A tall male doctor walks out to meet us as my squirming becomes sluggish. Peter hands a file over to him and says, "This is all we have on her."

My vision is getting blurry, but before I go under, I see his face. It's him, I swear it's him. He's older than he was the last time I saw him, a few short hours ago.

"You did the right thing. We'll take good care of her, Officer Jacoby," says Doctor Gregory Millen.

TWENTY-THREE

OMNIA MUTANTUR, NIHIL INTERIT

THE CEILING LOOKS perfect, except for the one tile. It's straight and the lines running along it fit beautifully, but the one tile is missing and I can't stop looking at it. There's nothing there. It's just empty, flawed. Such a shame.

The bed is comfortable. My bed at Sandy Shores was hard as a rock. This one feels like it's mine. This is my bed. I like my bed.

My red backpack is on the floor. All the stuff that was in it is all over the floor—my clothes, my toothbrush, my cell phone, my rock. Pretty rude that they just threw it all over the place. Or maybe I did it. I don't remember.

The clothes I'm wearing are standard-issue gray, boring, property of Riverview Psychiatric Hospital. This is my least favorite part, these pajamas. I forgot how much I hate them. Of course I forgot. I'm not sure I remember now.

I'm standing at the door now. I don't remember getting up, but I remember my feet feeling colder. I'm barefoot on the tile floor. That must be why. I think I heard a pounding sound a few seconds or minutes ago. Maybe I knocked on the door?

The air feels like molasses. I feel it oozing through my nose slowly. I can't feel my cheeks.

The door opens, and two or three nurses come in. They're really tall, towering over me. My back feels cold now too, and the back of my head is starting to ache. I'm looking at the ceiling again. I must've fallen over. I wish they'd put a tile in that hole.

"Going in to farmer inlet," says the first nurse—or something like that.

"Half inside. Only. Call them over some inwardly," the other replies.

My eyes are getting heavy again. I miss my bed. The pain in my head is in my skin. If I pretend it's not there, it goes away—until the nurse reaches behind me and touches it, then it hurts again. She looks at my face sadly. She looks like Rue McClanahan, or whatever her name is from *The Golden Girls*.

"Any darling? Hover high into it all. OK?" she says.

Thank you for being a friend. Travel down the road and back again . . .

"Do you have anything to add, Emily?" says Dr. Franklin. I like this guy, which is odd because I usually don't like the doctors here. I didn't realize my hand was raised, but everyone in the circle was waiting for me to contribute. Group therapy wasn't my thing, it never was, so I smile and sing.

"If you threw a party and invited everyone you knew . . ."

He frowns. "Give me your muffin."

This bitch always took my muffin, but she was really big and I sat alone at lunch, so no one would back me up. It was a coffee cake muffin today, my favorite. They made them really well here, at least that's what I heard. No matter how many times I've tried to eat a coffee cake muffin, this woman always took it. I hand it over, and she stumbles back to her lunch table. That girl is a total dick. I look out the window to the woods. What a beautiful day. And I love sitting on my bed. It's so comfortable, not like the rock I slept on at Sandy Shores. This one is mine, my bed. I look away from the window, and I see myself standing in my room with me, except I'm dirty, ragged, exhausted looking. The other me looks surprised to see me. I'm not. I've seen this over and over and over and over.

Time to lie down in my bed. Before my eyes close, I look at the ceiling again. The tile has been replaced. My ceiling is perfect.

Someone is yelling in the hallway.

I have to pee.

The nurse walks into my room and hands me a small cup. Two blue pills, three yellow tablets, and one round white one. The white one looks smaller than usual. Maybe they're changing my dosage. I spill the water on my Property of Riverview Psychiatric pajamas, and she gets me another cup. I lie back down with a wet shirt, and I want to just take it off. The room is hot, and the shirt itches. But any orderly can unlock my door and walk in at any time, so I keep my shirt on and close my eyes.

It's Thursday morning. It's October, not sure of the date. My head aches this morning because I'm so thirsty. The meds I'm taking dry me out terribly.

I wander out into the hallway. My feet feel heavy, like I'm wearing brick shoes—only I'm wearing slippers. I'm making a conscious effort to not twist my ankle as I make my way to the activity room.

Everyone is milling about in mismatched clothing. The TVs are on, one playing some daytime judge show; on the other, Maury is telling someone they are the father of a kid CPS is going to take away anyway. This is the room exactly as I saw it when Allison saw me and had to be carried out. I scan over the room, and I see a little blonde girl facing the wall away from me, and I instantly know: it's her.

I sit down at the table with her, and I know right away I'm not going to get any answers. She's not blinking. She's drooling on her shirt. She's medicated to the point of catatonia. I can't help it, I just start crying. It's all way too much. I don't know why she's here. I don't know why I'm here. I don't know why the hospital is here. And the thought creeps back in again. This time I can't push it out.

Maybe I've always been here.

It's real, I know now it's real. I'm not dreaming, I'm not in a vision from some ghost walking around the decayed version of the very real building I'm standing in. Maybe all that was the dream. It certainly feels that way now. I made it all up. There's no Carrot, there's no CONIR, there's no Altman, there's no Abigail. It's all in my head, it has to be.

But the rock, Abigail's rock—I have it. It proves I didn't make it up, right? Unless I just found a pretty rock and I made up some shit about that too. Who knows?

It's getting too hard to care.

"Hey Al," I say, rubbing her back. I doubt she can hear me. "Do you remember me? Emily? We met at the diner you work at. We were trying to figure out why I kept seeing a little girl. Remember?" Jesus, this all had to be a delusion. A little girl? It sounds so ridiculous. "I wish you were awake. Maybe you could tell me what's going on. I thought I had uncovered the truth about Altman, but then I got to town and no one knew who he was, so I guess none of it matters. Next thing I know, your brother drives me up here and drops me off." Telling Peter I knew his sister was the nail in my coffin. It was probably all he needed to convince himself I belonged up here.

He was probably right. I do belong up here.

"Pee," says Allison. Her voice is weak, slurring, but what she said is pretty clear.

"OK, Al, I'll find someone to help you to the bathroom." I look around for an orderly, but she quickly moves and grabs my arm. I turn back, and she's looking right at me, her eyes straining. They'd pop out of her head if she pushed a little harder. "Pee. Ded."

"What? What are you trying to say?"

"Pee. Tay. Drggd. Ded." She's looking frustrated now. She takes a deep breath and focuses.

"Peedr. Deadd. Tey dragged mm."

"Allison . . . can you hear me right now?" I say. She's trying so hard. "Go slow."

"Peter. Dead. They dragged him out. They killed him."

"Who killed him? Allison. Who killed Peter?"

She looks behind me and goes silent. I turn to follow her gaze, and behind me stands an older-looking Dr. Millen. He smiles at me politely. I don't know if he heard our conversation, but I can't imagine he didn't.

"YOU KILLED MY BROTHER!" screams Allison.

"Allison, dear, we've been over this," he says with a comforting grin. "Your brother is fine. I saw him a few weeks ago when he dropped off Ms. Hunter. Isn't that right, Emily?"

I'm skeptical of agreeing with Millen, but I also know he's right. Peter is fine—at least he was a few weeks ago. "Yeah, that's right, Al. Peter dropped me off here."

"There, see?" he says. "You can call him if you like, just to make sure. Would that make you happy?"

She nods. Millen motions for one of the orderlies to come over. "OK, I'll have Robert here help you with the phone."

Robert and Allison walk over to the phone together, leaving Millen and I together. "I don't believe I've properly introduced myself. My name is Dr. Greg Millen. I'm the facilitator of the hospital."

I play dumb. "Hello. What's wrong with Allison?"

"I can't really go into it, confidentiality after all."

"She thinks you killed Peter?"

"Amongst other things. She believes she saw me bring his body out of the hospital with some soldiers." He says this looking at my face, studying it for a reaction. "It's odd, Ms. Hunter. When you were admitted here, you said you knew Ms. Jacoby. The police assumed it was because you were a resident here, but not only do we have no record of you ever being a patient here, but you seem shocked at Allison's condition, even though she's been a patient here for years."

He stops, and I know it's my turn to talk. "I was confused. I've been confused a lot lately. I'm sure you don't hear this a lot, Dr. Millen, but I'm glad to be here. It may give me an opportunity to get a few things straightened out." Now I'm studying his face.

He nods. "Well, Emily, I hope we can work together to get those answers," he replies, his eyes again lingering a little too long. He turns around and joins Allison by the phone. When he gets there, he turns back to me and smiles. I smile back, not to be friendly, but to myself because I feel so much better.

I didn't make up anything. I know it.

He knows it too.

TWENTY-FOUR

DECENSUS IN CUNICULL CAVUM

The hallways were dark as nurse Lori Novak looked over her paperwork. The night shifts were killer. Thankfully, she was only on them another two weeks. It felt like a lifetime. The extra money was nice, but you had to be awake and able to see your friends to spend it. Still, the hospital was pretty peaceful at night, at least it was in her wing. It could be worse. She could be on nights and overseeing isolation. For now, she was done for the night. All the documentation was in order, the patients were asleep. Unless there was a crisis, which there never was, she could spend the rest of the night binge watching Doctor Who on her phone.

"Sweetheart, you shouldn't be here. There's broken glass all over the place." She looked up to see the hallways completely empty. The man's voice had seemed to come from right in front of her, but there was nothing.

"Do your mommy and daddy know where you are?"

She turned around to see a little girl, her eyes closed tightly, her purple pajamas and stuffed rabbit barely visible in the single light in the hallway.

"It's almost over now," said the little girl.

It was the last thing Lori remembered before staff found her the next morning, cowering under her desk. By that time, all the damage had been done.

The phone rings. I reach for it without waking up entirely. There's no table. I'm in the hospital. As my eyes open up, it all comes back to me.

I find the phone in my backpack, vaguely aware that it's one in the morning. No caller ID. Also, somehow, the phone's battery is fully charged, which is quite odd as it died a week ago and I haven't had a plug to charge it with.

"Hello?"

A long pause before a woman's voice comes over the line. "Hi, um . . . I seem to have lost my phone. Who is this?"

"This is Emily Hunter. Who is this?"

A bang at my door, and I turn to see two eyes peering in the window at me. It's Tony, the night shift orderly. He's an asshole. Nowhere near as bad as Altman, but still an asshole.

"Emily, where the hell did you get a phone?"

"It's mine," I answer. "They let me keep it."

"Bullshit," he says as he starts to open the door. He sees my red bag. "You can't have any of this stuff. You know that. Give it up, and you can get it back later."

He grabs the phone out of my hand after a struggle and goes for the bag. I push back, and he wraps his arms around me in a common restraint that I'm sure he's been taught and never used. I know, because he's doing it wrong.

"Give me my phone, Tony."

"Emily, if you don't stop struggling, I'm putting you in isolation tonight."

He isn't supporting my shoulders, so I throw my head back, crushing his nose. He hits the ground hard and blood starts pouring out of his face. I think I may have actually knocked out a tooth too, but I can't tell in the dark. His head hit my bedframe on the way down, and he's not moving. This is going to cost me.

I bend down to try to shake him awake, excuses flying through my head as to how I didn't mean to hit him that hard. He's breathing, but he's definitely concussed. I roll him onto his side, so the blood from his nose doesn't get breathed in, and I reach for his radio to call for help from one of the other orderlies. Maybe if I report it, they'll see I wasn't trying to be aggressive. Something fuzzy touches my hand near his pocket, and I pull back instinctively. It felt like a rat. I grab his flashlight and try to see what it could have been. Hanging off his belt is his keychain attached to a recoiling cord and a rabbit's foot.

Rabbit's foot keys—that sounds so familiar.

Allison had said something about Tony and the rabbit's foot keys when I saw her in room twenty-seven back when the hospital was destroyed, back when she told me I had died.

It dawns on me right then: she's in room twenty-seven, and I have the keys.

I take the keys off of Tony, as well as his flashlight and radio, and I lock the door behind me. The hospital is obviously where I'm supposed to be, but I can't do anything locked in a tiny room. I'm going to get out of here, and I'm bringing Allison with me. Once we're out, we regroup and we find a new approach—that is, if she's not actually crazy.

As I go down the hallway, I realize the night nurse will be at her station, right where I need to be. I wrack my brain for a way to get past her, but I keep moving without a strategy. When I get to Allison's hallway, the nurse is not there. I can't believe my luck.

I am as quiet as possible sliding the key into the lock on Allison's room, but in the silence, each tumbler sounds like a car crash. I open her door, and she's dead asleep. I creep into the room quickly and close the door, leaving it open only a tiny crack so as to not have to worry about the doorknob again. Allison is snoring heavily, much louder than a tiny, little girl like her should be capable of. I try to wake her, but she's out cold, medicated. Eventually I get her eyes open, but she's still not awake.

"Allison, wake up!"

Her eyes fall on me, and a blink slowly rolls over her face from left to right. This might be tougher than I imagined.

"Who are you . . ." she slurs.

"It's Emily. I'm going to get you out of here, OK?"

She's asleep.

"Shit, Al. We're going to see your brother. Come on."

"Peter's dead," she says.

"Peter's alive, Al. We're going to his house right now, but we gotta go quick. Get your shoes on."

This is never going to work.

"We're gonna go see him?" she says.

"Yeah, right now. We're gonna go see him. Then, we're going to get him to get off his ass and come up here and see whatever CONIR is. Then, he's going to arrest Millen and you'll get to go home for good. How's that sound?"

"Who's Connor?"

"Put your shoes on," I say. "I'll tell you all about it."

We go out the door quietly, or as quietly as possible. Allison is in no condition for an escape attempt, but we're out of options. It took me tying her shoes to get us out into the hallway. The nurse's station is still empty, thank God, so we make our way around the corner and into the north hallway.

"Can we rest a minute?" asks Allison from behind me. I turn to see she isn't waiting for an answer. She's leaning hard on the wall, her eyes closed. We've been out of her room for barely thirty seconds. I go back and grab her shoulder to pull her along.

"There's a spot in the woods, Al. It's a little cave. It's perfect. We'll get there, and you can sleep for hours. Right now, we have to move."

She's out again. I slap her across the face. She'll either be really pissed or it'll wake her up. Either way, I doubt she'll remember it in the morning.

Her eyes light up. "Talk to me, OK?" I say, trying to cut off any anger she feels about the slap. I step forward to look around the corner. It looks clear. Allison lunges for me.

"Don't leave me!"

"I'm not leaving you," I say. "I'm not going to leave you. We're going to get out of here together. I promise."

She forces what I imagine was supposed to be a smile. "Why did you come get me?" she asks as we start down the hallway toward the west wing. There's an exit there, off the back of the dining hall. Beyond that is a fence and then the woods.

"Believe it or not, you told me to. You told me about Tony's keys. Remember that? With the rabbit's foot?"

"No."

"Yeah, you thought I was mad at you."

"Why?"

Why . . . because I left her. That's what she had said, I left her.

That's not going to happen.

"I don't remember. It's not important. Listen to me, you're not crazy. I know that. They did something to you. This hospital is the only thing different, and without it, you're totally fine and working in a diner." I probably shouldn't have told her that, but it was more for me. Like I said, she probably won't remember it anyway.

"My parents own a diner," she says. Her pace has started to improve, but it's nowhere near where it needs to be if we're going to make it through the woods to Carrot's old cave.

"Your parents own it? The place on Water Street? That's great," I say, trying to keep her engaged. "Tell you what, we'll go there in the morning and you can buy me a cup of coffee. After you sleep this off, we'll go there together."

"Good," she says, "I don't think I could make it on my own."

There's an understatement.

We skitter along the hallway in the shadows toward the west wing exit. There's a cross hallway in front of us leading to the west wing and the dining hall, and an orderly's flashlight beam bounces out of it. That hallway is where we need to be. If he turns the corner our way, we're done.

"Who is Connor?" she whispers.

"CONIR isn't a person. It's a project or an experiment or something that Millen is running in the basement. I don't know what it is, but there's a big door and . . ."

She stops. "There's a big door and hallways and a big white room at the end."

Now I stop. "You've been through the door?"

"It's where you have to go when they call you. They make you touch that thing, and it hurts you."

"Touch what thing?"

Wrong question. Allison starts breathing heavily. Her eyes are darting from left to right, up and down. She's either having a flashback or a panic attack. I grab her face and force her to look into my eyes.

"It's OK, we don't have to talk about it. We just have to leave."

She's hyperventilating now. It's obvious she's somewhere else, remembering something horrible.

"Allison, listen to me," I say very deliberately. "If we leave, you never have to go in there again."

She slowly catches her breath and nods to me.

I watch as the orderly's flashlight comes closer and closer to the end of the hall. Suddenly, his radio sparks to life.

"Dex, you there?"

He picks it up. "Go ahead."

"You seen Tony?"

"He's probably out having a smoke or something."

"Janet is going to have his ass. He's not answering his radio. I'm sick of covering for him. Can I get you to come to the cafeteria? We need help."

"On my way." He turns around, and I can't believe our luck. It's like someone is running interference for us.

"Come on, we're going that way too." I grab Allison's hand, and we follow far behind the orderly in the dark.

By the time we get to the dining hall, there's a hell of a commotion. Some patient has gotten loose, and there are five orderlies and a nurse standing around her. She's screaming and yelling, swinging a broken broomstick. The door is across the room, behind them. It's perfect.

"Come on, now's our chance," I say. We slide along the wall quietly, although we could probably be playing trombones on our way out and no one would hear it over this woman losing her shit.

"Put it down!" yells one of them. "No one has to get hurt."

We keep moving. Allison creeps slowly behind me, and we pass an open but barred window. The draft from the window hits the exposed part of my lower back, and I shudder. It's freezing out there. We don't have warm clothes. By the time we make the door, I start thinking about how building a fire in the woods might give our position away. Maybe we cuddle all night to keep warm? It might be awkward, but without it, we might not make it. Maybe this is all a terrible idea.

It's too late to turn back. I stick the key in the lock and turn it, praying there's no alarm. There isn't, but the blast of cold air from the cracked door is enough to make me reconsider this entire thing yet again. With Allison being this medicated, she won't be able to tell how cold she is. This might be too dangerous.

Unless . . . Maybe I can get to some warmer clothes in the locker room. Everyone had to have brought coats. I look at Allison. She barely made it here. If she can stay put, I can be there and back in two minutes.

You left me. You said you wouldn't leave me and you left me.

I don't think I have a choice. That's when the end of that conversation comes into my mind, freezing every muscle in my body.

It's my fault you're dead.

Whatever she was alluding to, it happened in the hospital. She said there was an earthquake or an explosion. Since we're in Northern Michigan, I'm betting on the latter. But if we get out of the hospital, we're safe—and we don't get out of the hospital without those coats.

"Listen, Allison . . . it's really cold out there. We need to stay warm or . . ."

"Put down the broomstick, Abigail!" screams the orderly from the middle of the dining hall.

The rest of my words stick in my mouth. I turn to look, really look, at the commotion going on. The six hospital staff are surrounding one old woman.

She's here. She's alive. She hasn't even been burned. Her face is ancient looking, but it's unscarred.

"DEMONS! You're all snakes! You can't have me!" she screams, swinging wildly. An orderly takes a shot on the cheek, but amazingly maintains his composure.

I turn back to Allison, who is now awake enough to wonder what the hold-up is. Sadness comes over me. She was right after all.

"I'm sorry, Al. I have to go back."

Her face is a mix of shock and anger, combined with sleepiness. "What?"

"That woman is Abigail Pipkin. She has something to do with why I'm here. I need her to tell me how to put things back to normal. She died, and I can save her. I think I have to."

"OK, then give me the keys." I know she means it, and I know I can't.

"Allison, you could get killed out there. It's freezing, and you can barely stand. You'd never make it back to town alive."

"You *are* leaving me," she says. Her eyes would strangle me if they could.

"I'm so sorry. I know you don't understand now, but I might be able to fix everything."

"Fuck you," she says.

"Al . . ."

"FUCK YOU," she screams and pushes me with all her strength, which isn't much at all. I can't let her go in this condition, and her weak push just reaffirmed it. It doesn't take the sting away. I've let her down. I'm leaving her.

She crumbles down into the wall and begins sobbing. I'm crying too, but I have to do this.

"HEY!" I scream.

Three of the orderlies turn to see me, as does the old woman in the middle.

"Go back to your room," says the nurse. I've seen her face before. She commanded me back to my room from the hallway when I knocked the pen down, the first time this place felt real.

"Abigail Pipkin? Are you Abigail Pipkin?"

"Emily?" she says, and a chill runs down my spine. In her moment of confusion, the orderlies spring on her.

"Leave her alone!" I jump into the fray, upgrading it to full mayhem. My elbow goes into one of the orderly's guts, my nails dig deep into another's collarbone. One of the orderlies lies down on top of Abigail to hold her in place while the nurse sedates her. I reach for her, and one of the other four grab my arm, putting me in a makeshift arm bar while another holds me around the neck. The nurse is on me next, and I feel the prick in my thigh. My vision goes narrow, and they slowly guide me to the floor. The last thing I see is Abigail's face being forced to the ground inches from me, her eyes piercing mine.

TWENTY-FIVE

ORDO AB CHAO

THE LIGHTS HURT. They physically hurt.

The floor is surprisingly comfortable.

It smells like bleach.

I taste copper.

I hear crying, screaming, laughing, pounding.

Everything comes back gradually, and I wake up in a very small padded cell behind a locked steel door with a tiny eyehole window. I'm in isolation. I was a bad girl.

I slowly gain use of my feet back and manage to get standing. My neck is stiff, my arm is asleep, and I wonder how long I've been lying awkwardly on the floor. I shuffle over to the window and peek out: more doors, more little windows, not much else. The people behind each door seem to be protesting their current position—each door except one. From that door, a pair of striking eyes is staring at me.

"Did you see them too?" asks the old voice from that room.

"See who?" I ask.

"The demons—did you see them?"

"Are you talking about the ghosts? Yeah, Abigail, I saw them."

She still stares at me. I don't think she's blinked the entire time.

"Abigail, I have to ask you something very important, OK?"

Still nothing.

"Do you remember me? You said my name upstairs when you saw me. What's my name, Abigail?"

A long pause, and I think the woman must've died standing up staring. Finally, "Emily Hunter."

"That's right! I'm Emily Hunter. Do you remember me coming to your house? You came into town to try to find me. You had a mask then. Do you remember that?"

Nothing.

"Do you remember your rock, the one from the mantle? You gave it to me and told me to give it back when I was done. I have it, I brought it with me. One of the orderlies took it, but I can get it back and I can get it to you. You need it, don't you? Will that help us put things back?"

Nothing.

"Do you remember Altman?"

Nothing.

I've lost her. She's not even moving now. I sink down beneath the door. If I couldn't do much from my room before, being stuck in isolation was going to be even harder. I can hear Allison crying in my head. I can't stop hearing it. I promised she'd see her brother, then I left her. Who knows what they did with her. Hopefully, they think I took her against her will, sedated. She was a victim of my escape attempt, not a conspirator.

I was mad, and I told.

It's my fault you're dead.

"He was the mayor."

My eyes widen. I stand up like I was shot out of a canon, and I'm back at the window.

"Yes! That's right, Abigail. He was the mayor. You remember that?"

Her eyes are closed now. "They told me. The demons, they told me he was the mayor. You told me. You're one of them, aren't you? You want me to die."

"No! Just the opposite. I'm trying to save you. What is the rock for, Abigail?"

"You want them to kill me. You want the demons to take me, like they took him downstairs."

"Downstairs? You mean CONIR? What is it, Abigail? Who did they take?"

"Three snakes, a bird, a tall man, and a short man. The Devil, the Devil is downstairs. He touched the Devil and he was gone. They took him." She opens her eyes and silences me.

"Don't go downstairs," she says.

Corporal Focault entered Millen's office. He hated being here. The office, the hospital, Blue Water, Michigan—he hated all of it. He signed up for Special Forces for Afghanistan, Russia, Cambodia—not the fucking Midwest. Yet here he was, answering to Staff Sergeant Gregory Millen in some flyover state while all his buddies made a real difference.

"It's done, sir," he said. Millen didn't look up from the file he was staring at so intently his glare could burn a hole in it.

"And you made sure he'll stay buried?"

"Yes, sir. Not that it would make sense if anyone found him."

"No one will find him, correct?"

Focault rolled his eyes in his mind. "No, sir, no one will find him."

What followed was a long awkward silence. He wasn't dismissed; S.Sgt. Millen was too engrossed in the file to remember he was in the room, so he decided to speak up.

"Sir, do you mind explaining . . ."

"Above your pay-grade son," interrupted Millen, who had honestly forgotten this little bastard was in his office. What the hell made him think he would volunteer that information? Focault was a little too friendly for his own good. Millen waved him away, and the nuisance was gone. He continued poring over the file. He reached into his desk drawer and pulled out the wallet that was hidden under a stack of paperwork he'd never looked at. Opening it, he stared at the golden badge of Officer Peter Jacoby, the man he'd had killed three weeks ago in the basement, the man who a week later showed up and dropped off that Emily woman at his doorstep with no apparent knowledge of being dead. It could only mean one thing: CONIR was working.

TWENTY-SIX

IN REGIONE CAECORUM REX EST LUSCUS

THEY CAME FOR Abigail at two in the morning. It had woken me up—her terrified screaming, the orderlies yelling back. Tony was one of them, his nose bandaged and swollen. I yelled too, but it didn't make a difference. As abruptly as it had started, it was over. They had taken her through the door into the basement.

That was an hour ago, and she hasn't come back up yet. It's too quiet to sleep now. Instead, I just pace back and forth in my tiny room. I feel short of breath. I try to ignore it, but it's getting worse now. I'm too worked up. I need to calm down. I close my eyes, bracing myself against the wall, but it's not helping. Now I'm getting upset because I'm already upset. Maybe that's how it started? I hadn't noticed the walls before—the color, the tears in the fabric. How had I not noticed that? Maybe I did and I don't remember? How long have I been in this room? Did I lock myself in here? No one will ever find me. I'm going to die here, locked in this torn-down hospital. No one knew I was here. Or did they? Did I tell anyone? Did I tell Allison? Is the hospital running again or not? My mind is flying at a mile a minute, and I can't breathe. I can't relax. I start sweating. I know what's coming.

The ringing in my ears starts almost on cue.

"Abigail . . ." I manage before the sick feeling takes over, and I can't hold myself up.

I fall to the ground, landing on my ass, and I brace myself with my arms behind me, sitting like a kid in kindergarten. In front of me, once again, is me, except the reflected me is standing, still facing away from me.

From in front of her, by her legs, out steps Carrot. She's beaming, so extremely happy. But there's something horrifying about it. Her eyes, bright blue as always, now look maddened, crazed. Her mouth, her hands, and her pajamas are all covered in blood.

"Look what I did!" she says, excited and proud as a kid who drew a picture of a house for the first time. I look behind me, and my hands are sitting in a puddle of blood. I jump to my feet. Suddenly, I'm not in my isolation room anymore. I'm in Carrot's room, my room, in the middle of the night. The blood is all over the floor, pouring out the neck of an orderly on the floor. His horn-rimmed glasses broken, his perfect hair messed and sweaty, his pants around his ankles. He clutches at his neck, but there's no stopping it. She bit him good and deep. Then, it looks like she beat the shit out of him with his club.

Bull died on the floor in front of me, slowly, painfully, perfectly.

"What happened, Carrot? How did you kill him if he was alive to kill Abigail? None of this makes . . ." And this is when I turn back around to see I'm back in my apartment, alone.

The place is destroyed, just as I had left it. I'm in the living room in the middle of the day. The mural I had drawn on the wall is still fresh, and now I'm seeing things that make more sense. Parts of it before that seemed like gibberish now fall into place. I had written the letters *K* and *L*, which are for Kevin Lewis, the patient who Altman shot in the basement. I had written the word *blades*, the phrases *plug the leak* and, beneath it, *you did this*, the first words Carrot had ever spoken to me. How did I know this would happen? Without thinking about it too hard, I scan the wall for anything else that might help me. If the mural was designed to guide me, I need to study it. There's *CONIR* written a few times, the word *basement*, and I see some symbols that look like the ones Albert Forrester had drawn. I try to commit them to memory: an *M* stretched vertically, the number *8* missing the top quarter, a set of three backward *S*'s, two female symbols, one with a longer stem. I do my best to remember them mnemonically. There's the *X* with the two dots. Why do I keep seeing that one?

Behind me, something falls over. I turn to see what, and the reflected me is back, convulsing again, struggling.

And, for the first time, I notice I'm doing it too.

I can't stop shaking. I clench my teeth. My vision narrows. I'm having a seizure. I've had them before, but not often. With my last bit of control, I fall toward my couch to try to give myself somewhere safer to be—but I don't hit the couch. I hit dried leaves and dirt.

The seizure comes to an end, and I'm in extreme pain. It feels like a full-body cramp, and all I want to do is sleep, but I can't, it hurts too much. My vision returns, and I'm in the woods behind the hospital. I sit up, unable to stand just yet, and I see two pine trees. At their base is a hole.

This is where Altman buried Kevin Lewis.

I crawl over to the hole to look inside, and there's Kevin lying in the bottom of the hole. He's smiling, like he just woke up from a nap.

"Hi, Emily," he says.

I have no idea how to answer that, so I just go with, "Hi, Kevin," as I lie down next to his grave, trying to regain my strength.

"Thanks for trying to save me," he says.

"Emily, is that you?" another voice calls out. I raise my head and see another open hole. I roll my way to that one, and inside lies Peter Jacoby.

"Peter? Are you really dead too?"

"CONIR," he says. "You have to kill it."

"Abigail told me to stay out of the basement."

"Who's Abigail?" he says.

"She's the old w . . ." And I see something that catches my eye.

The ground is full of dozens and dozens of open holes.

I turn back, but I'm not in the woods anymore. I'm on Stone Road, where Allison and I saw Carrot, where I found out I wasn't crazy—a fact that I'm having the most difficult time remembering now.

Through the dark, a little boy comes walking down the road. He doesn't see me. He's crying to himself. Someone has hurt him. A light begins to shine on his face, and I feel like it's coming from me. He looks up to see me. He actually sees me. The light gets brighter and brighter, and I remember Allison's friend's dad's story about the boy consumed by light. And suddenly Carol Forrester's story comes back to me:

We met when we were little kids. I found him, actually. He was in the woods, lying on the ground, when I happened across him. He didn't remember how he got there. He just recalled seeing a bright light, suddenly, right in front of his face, like it came out of nowhere.

"Albert?" I say, taking a guess.

He stares at me, terrified. The light gets brighter and brighter.

"What time is it?" a voice asks.

And somehow I'm in my dream again, the one where I'm in the green felt chair. Only this time I know I'm in Abigail's house, and this time I'm not in the chair. I'm watching the dream from another place. I see my reflected me and my original me. I'm a third party.

And this time, I know it's Abigail on the floor, her skull crushed.

"Everything has its time," says the original me. That's different. I look up from the dead body to see the original me staring me down.

"Everything has its time," says the reflected me, and she's doing the same thing.

I back up slowly into another me in the room. "Everything has its time," she says. And when I back away from her, I see the room is full of me's, all of them reaching for me, all of them sad looking, each of them repeating "Everything has its time." Abigail's dead body stands up, and it's not Abigail. She's me too, but her head is caved in. One of her eyes is smashed, the other is looking dead into mine. "Everything has its time," she says, walking toward me. And right before she grabs me, I wake up in my isolation cell, sweating through my clothes. I successfully suppress the urge to vomit, before closing my eyes and falling asleep from exhaustion.

The sun poked through the window almost directly into her eyes. Millen could have closed the curtains, but he liked it better this way. Anyone who sat across from him in the morning was instantly on edge and couldn't see his face. It made him loom large in the office, more a presence than a person.

Tony was still in the room. Millen dismissed him. Tony objected. Millen dismissed him again, this time more sternly, just like they had rehearsed.

"Do you mind if I record this?" asked Millen.

She shook her head. She didn't care, and she didn't mind ratting out the bitch who dragged her to the cafeteria and left her.

"I'm sorry, dear, I need you to say it out loud so it's on the tape."

"No, I don't mind," said Allison.

"We know Emily Hunter took you out of your room after assaulting a staff member and stealing his keys. Then, she proceeded to attack another group of staff members who were trying to sedate a patient. Does all that sound right so far?"

She nodded again and then remembered. "Yes, it does," she said aloud.

"OK," said Millen, smiling. "You aren't in any trouble. It's important that you know that. Is there anything you want to add to our account? Did she threaten you in any way?"

"No."

"Did she put her hands on you?"

"She tied my shoes," said Allison, smiling to herself.

Millen smiled too. This was pretty standard. Patient tries to escape, interview witnesses, document everything, drop them in iso for a week, go about your day. Something about Emily stood out to him though, something about the first time they met. He had placed a mental bookmark on her and promised he'd think about her later. Now it looked like that bookmark was front and center.

"Any idea why she came for you?"

"What do you mean?"

"Well," continued Millen, "when we admitted her, she seemed to know you. She at least knew your name. Had you met her before?"

"No."

"Well, here's what I don't get," he said, getting up and sitting on the desk in front of her. "She breaks Tony's nose, steals his keys, and instead of just making a break for it, she comes for you. And when she finds you heavily sedated, she still brings you. You had to be a tremendous burden to an escape attempt, but that didn't stop her. So, why you?"

"Maybe because my brother's a cop? I don't know."

That struck Millen as odd. "Why would your brother being a cop mean anything?" If Allison's brother had anything to do with it, it piqued his interest, especially given the circumstances of the last few weeks. Thankfully he had the foresight to let Allison talk to Peter on the phone before this little interview. Officer Jacoby had been very kind and asked Allison to cooperate with Dr. Millen in anyway she could—awfully nice for a dead cop.

"She said she was going to talk to Peter and have you arrested."

Ah yes, this was pretty standard too. Over the years he'd collected his favorite reasons for his impending arrest and lengthy prison sentence. He was a lizard alien, he'd killed President Abraham Lincoln, the chicken they served at lunch tasted terrible. They made fun stories.

"What was I going to be arrested for?"

"Something in the basement called CONIR."

The smile and color raced off of Millen's face.

"I'm sure I don't know what she's talking about," lied Millen. "Do you?"

Allison doesn't answer. Her silence is deafening.

"Allison?" asks Millen, his heart pounding.

"I remember a big door. She mentioned that. And a white room with something big in the middle. A rock?"

Shit.

"Allison, remember your therapy with Dr. Hausen? Those things aren't real," he lied.

"Then how did Emily know about it?"

"I don't know," he didn't lie. "At any rate, how about you go back to your room and get some rest."

She nodded and got up. Tony came into the office and gently guided her by the arm back to her room.

Millen sat alone in his office, staring blankly at the wall for what felt like forever before he uttered two words: "Emily Hunter."

He stopped the tape and ejected it from the cassette player. Then, reaching into his desk, he pulled out a cigarette lighter and burned the magnetic tape inside the cassette.

TWENTY-SEVEN

OMNE IGNOTUM PRO MAGNIFICO

BANG BANG.

I'm up.

The orderly outside begins opening the door. The keys click in the latch and turn. My eyes are struggling to focus, but I recognize his face.

It's Bull.

He smiles at me and reaches for his belt as he steps into the room. I crawl backwards into the wall, but I can't go any farther. He slithers into the room. I push away, closing my eyes, but I feel his hot breath on my neck.

"Told you no one would believe you," he says. "Now look where you are, you crazy bitch. Right where I said you'd be."

"Emily! Let's go."

I open my eyes to see no one is in the room with me. Tony is standing at the door, removing me from the isolation room. His bandaged nose and split lip look painful. I'd apologize, but he wouldn't hear it.

"Where? I've got three more days in here."

"Millen's apparently ending your sentence. He wants to talk to you."

I suddenly want to stay in isolation.

He leads me up to the second floor and to Millen's office. The curtains are closed. An empty tape recorder sits on his desk. The room itself looks just how I remember it when he was talking to Bull years ago—or days ago, depending on how I look at it.

"Have a seat, Ms. Hunter," he says. "That'll be all, Tony."

Tony leaves without objection, looking pissed off. Millen gives a quizzical look to him as he walks out, but then turns his attention to me. "Coffee?" he asks.

I don't answer. I just look back at him. My apprehension of being in his office mixed with my contempt for him isn't lost on Millen. He sits down and begins to speak.

"I can tell you want to get to the point. I respect that, and I'll accommodate. I've been looking over your file, and it has some omissions. Maybe you can help me fill in some blanks?"

Tony said Millen was removing me from isolation. This can't be why I'm here.

"OK," I say.

"Great," he continues, looking at the file. "According to this, you were a resident at Sandy Beach Psychiatric Care starting in 2002."

"Shores," I correct.

He looks back at the file. "Yes, Sandy Shores. And it was 2002?"

"Yes."

"And your reason for admittance? Apart from your diagnosis, of course."

I struggle to say "attempted suicide." He looks at the file but doesn't write anything. "Are you going to write that down?" I ask.

"One more thing," he says. "When were you discharged from Sandy Shores?"

"June 4, 2008."

He smiles again. Something about that one made him smile. "Why aren't you writing this down? You know all of this already, don't you?"

"No, not all of it." He closes the file. Now it's just him and me. "Your file is incomplete, Emily. There is no discharge date on this file. However, you aren't the first person I asked when I noticed the omission this morning. I called Sandy Shores. June 4, 2008 is not the date they have on file."

He leans in closer. "I have confirmation from Sandy Shores Psychiatric Care that as of two hours ago, Emily Hunter is still a resident at their facility."

Fucking what?

"So my next question is: who are you?"

What the hell is going on? How am I still a patient at Sandy Shores? I was released seven years ago. Allison is hospitalized, and so am I? I mean, I obviously am, but I'm in two different facilities at the same time? That's got to be a record for insanity.

"Have we caught you in a lie?" he says, narrowing his eyes. "Did you spend time at Sandy Shores with Emily Hunter and just told us her name when you were admitted? What is your real name?" He's standing now, trying to scare me into the truth.

"Emily Hunter," I say.

"Bullshit! Then can you explain how you're in two places at the same time?" he yells.

"You wouldn't believe me if I told you."

And something about that answer must've been correct. He smiles, his posture relaxes, and he goes back to his chair.

"Oh, Miss Hunter. You'd be surprised what I'd believe."

He knows. In that instant, I get it: he knows.

"Let me get you started: a few weeks ago, you stumbled out of the woods claiming a man named Henry Altman murdered a patient named Kevin Lewis and a woman named Abigail Pipkin. Here's what stood out about that: I knew Henry Altman, and he did kill Kevin Lewis. I was there. But you no doubt have seen that Abigail Pipkin is alive and well—well, as well as can be expected anyway. I hadn't thought about Altman in years. He died here in the hospital when a patient killed him, bit his throat out. Between you and me, he had it coming. We planted a tree for him and everything after they buried him, but you seem to think he's alive and well and mayor of Blue Water. Now Altman—'Bull' as I recall they used to call him—died when you were two years old, so you obviously never met him, at least not here."

"Not here?" I ask.

"I have no doubt that you're Emily Hunter. You're just not *our* Emily Hunter."

He pauses, letting that sink in. He could pause for weeks, it still wouldn't.

"I'm sure you're wondering which one of us is crazier, right?" he says with a laugh. I'm still trying to wrap my mind around still being at Sandy Shores. It's going to take me some time to catch up. "Might I ask where you heard the word 'CONIR?' "

OK, I can put all that weird shit on the backburner for a second and stick to what I know. "It's that thing you're hiding in the basement," I say with as much defiance as I can manage.

"You're mistaken, Ms. Hunter."

"Yeah? I've seen it: huge metal door, a bunch of labs . . ."

"No ,you misunderstand," he interrupts. "You aren't mistaken that it's there. You're mistaken that we're hiding it." He leans in again, taking a deep breath in through his nostrils. "Would you like to know what it is?"

I'm stunned. Hell yes, I want to know what it is. I've wanted to know for as long as I remember, and this guy is just going to offer up the information in this seemingly friendly conversation we're having in his office? All I manage is a nod.

"It's a long story, Emily, so get comfortable." He leans back into his chair and begins.

"Almost fifty years ago now, maybe a little over, a group of archaeologists found a large barrel-shaped stone in Palenque, a Mayan city in what is now Chiapas, Mexico. It was covered in symbols, some Mayan, some not. They believed it to be a codex, something to translate a language. The other words on the stone were something they'd never seen before, no known language, just a series of symbols. They sent it to Harvard University to be studied, and that's when things got strange." He stands up now and walks to the wall, looking at a photograph of himself and another two men. "The stone was stopped at the border for giving off medium-grade levels of radiation, despite all evidence of it being just a large piece of limestone and quartz. This was at the height of the Cold War, and the military was notified immediately. Upon finding it was just a big rock, not a nuclear weapon, we took possession of it and have had it ever since."

Of course. "'We'—you're military."

"Experimental Weapons Tech. It sounds more dastardly than it is. We're basically just military science."

"Still sounds dastardly," I say.

"Weeks later," he continued, ignoring my comment, "the archaeologists who found the artifact began getting sick—not with radiation poisoning, but with dementia. The ones who had very limited exposure to it described a feeling of what they called "unshakable *déjà vu*." They claimed the feeling wouldn't go away for up to . . . five days, I think was the longest case.

Once we took possession of it, our people started experiencing the same thing."

I shift in my chair. I know the feeling he's talking about. "Unshakeable *déjà vu*" is a better way to describe it than I could ever come up with in the twenty-some years I'd been feeling it.

"We shielded the artifact, codenamed it CONIR after the last names of the five archaeologists who found it, and brought it to a military facility in Texas. Then we noticed an odd side effect: We all started seeing these . . . ghosts, for lack of a better descriptive term. 'Visual echoes' is what we called them. No matter where we took the artifact—Texas, Montana, Groom Lake—these things eventually started showing up, so one of our top researchers, a man named Myles Forrester, had the idea of bringing the artifact to an obscure place, somewhere with a local folklore about supernatural encounters, somewhere no one would think it odd if someone came into a room saying they saw a ghost in the woods. Once we also found out Blue Water had a psych hospital, it was a lock."

"Because it gave you people to expose to CONIR. No one would notice dementia in someone who already had it," I say, holding back my urge to strangle this horrible man to death.

"Exactly," he answers. Then the pieces fall into place, and I want to kill him even more.

"You son of a bitch. You ran out of people, didn't you? Patients—you had to bring in others, expose them to the rock, and then admit them. That's why Allison is here. She's not insane, you made her this way. You took away her life."

He smiles at me. The motherfucker smiles at me, and he touches his nose to tell me I'm right. "The mind can only take so much before it breaks and destroys itself. We burned through patients a lot quicker than we had anticipated, especially since they were already cracked to begin with. Fortunately, these woods give us plenty of places to bury things. So Allison is sane on your side?"

"What the fuck do you mean, 'my side?'" He just admitted to killing off nearly an entire hospital full of people, and his tone hasn't changed. This still sounds like a pleasant conversation.

He sits back down. "I'm sorry, Emily. I'm getting ahead of myself. I was talking about Myles. We started working on CONIR together up here and for years got nowhere. People who were exposed to the artifact just became confused, irate, and eventually dead. We had no idea what it was used for—not until Myles' son decided to join us. A young man named . . ."

"Albert Forrester," I say. And for the first time, I can tell I said something that surprised Millen.

"Yes, that's right, Albert Forrester. He was just a little boy when Myles moved to Blue Water, but he eventually grew up and joined the project. And thank God he did. He was brilliant, thought outside the box—like, way outside the box. But it turns out it's what we needed. He theorized that the Mayan Calendar wasn't a countdown to doomsday as so many people before 2012 thought it was. It was a guide for using CONIR. Mayan culture wasn't so incredibly advanced because of aliens or UFOs; it was because, when used correctly, CONIR could show them the future, perhaps even allow them to travel through time."

He sees the skepticism on my face—but even as I put it there, I feel like I know it makes just as much sense as anything else has. The mural I had drawn on my wall had clues about the future, the visions I had all my life were mostly things I would eventually experience when I got to Blue Water, none more so than the word CONIR.

"Albert figured that bringing the artifact to the 'haunted woods' was why the woods were haunted in the first place. If this object acted outside of time, it would affect the future, but also affect the past. Bringing it there could have been why, for the previous hundreds of years, people had been experiencing ghost-sightings. He called it an 'ontological paradox.' We brought the artifact to the woods because of the ghost sightings, but there were only ghost sightings because we eventually would bring the artifact to the woods. What created what? It's very trippy, and when he drew it on the chalkboard, it blew all of our minds. We knew we had the right guy."

It's obvious I don't follow. "The rock causes ghosts?"

"According to Albert, they aren't ghosts, at least not in the sense you think they are. We called them 'visual echoes' because that's what they are: echoes of the past or the future caused by some destabilization of the space-time continuum, some kind of imperfection. I don't get it either. It made sense when he pointed something out though. If ghosts were spirits of our bodies, our souls escaped and roaming the Earth or whatever nonsense you believe, why would we see them wearing clothes?"

"So Albert saved the project," I say, not really caring about fashion choices of ghosts, "and you kept plugging away at the citizens of Blue Water like human guinea pigs, throwing them out in the woods when you used them up. You're fucking disgusting."

Millen frowns. "Apparently Albert agreed with you." He reaches down into his desk and pops a latch that opens a hidden drawer above it. Inside is a single VHS tape. He removes it and puts it into a TV/VCR combo. "It may seem archaic, but all our security tapes are still VHS. You can't download it to a flash drive. The old things are still most secure, it would seem." The tape starts with static and opens to a soundless black-and-white shot of a large octagonal white room. At the top left of the picture, three men work feverishly behind an observation window. Near the bottom of the frame, alone inside the room, stands a man and an older woman. The man is speaking into a voice recorder, but we can't hear what he's saying. The woman is unprotected.

In the center of the octagon, on top of a pedestal is a large gray barrel-shaped rock covered in symbols. The woman looks terrified to be in the room with it and is clinging to the man's shirt.

The date on the recording is 9/16/1987.

The man pockets the recorder and begins talking to the woman, but their backs are to the camera. She reluctantly moves toward the stone, each step looking like her last walk down death row. He then stops her. She turns back to him, and there seems to be confusion in the room. The people in the observation room seem to be trying to get the man's attention, but he isn't listening. He's just staring at the wall for what the counter on the tape confirms to be thirty-three seconds. He then sets down the clipboard in his hand, takes off his lead apron, and swiftly approaches the stone. The observation room lights up as they start banging on the glass. He touches the stone in a very specific manner, his fingers landing on specific symbols.

A bright light flares from the stone, and a wave blasts out of the center of the room, knocking down the woman and temporarily interrupting the video feed. When the static ends, the picture comes back. The old woman is on the floor, the door on the left side of the room is open, and one of the people in the observation room is already entering, looking around frantically for the man who touched the rock because he is no longer in the room.

"That was the last we ever saw of Albert Forrester."

I turn wide-eyed to Millen, who looks sad now. What the hell did I just watch? He clicks off the TV.

"Since he's been gone, our research has kind of hit a wall. The money is still coming in, based on previous results. But it's been almost thirty years now with nothing new to show for it. The money will dry up soon enough, and we'll be forced to shut the hospital down."

I want to give him some sarcastic shot about how awful it would be if suddenly they couldn't run this place anymore, but so many other questions are pressing at me right now. "Who was the woman?" I ask.

"That was Abigail Pipkin. Albert apparently had moral obligations to forcing a ninety-five-year old woman to touch the stone."

"Ninety-five? Wait . . . if she was ninety-five in 1987, that makes her . . ."

"One hundred twenty-four this November. And still pretty fucking strong, right? You saw her with those orderlies the other night."

Holy shit. Everyone always said she was ancient, but that's unbelievable. Millen reads the shock on my face.

"We can only guess either her prolonged exposure to the artifact or her being in the room for this incident is what has caused her unnaturally long life. We can only guess because our lead scientist went and got a conscience, disappeared off the face of the fucking Earth and left us with jack-squat in terms of understanding how to make CONIR work. Fortunately, that's where you come in."

"Me? You just explained to me what it is. How the hell should I know how it works?"

"You still don't know, do you?" He rubs his chin and bites his lip before resting his head on his hand, propping himself up with his desk. "OK, all cards on the table: CONIR has been a paperweight for years. Apart from scrambling crazy people's brains even further, it really doesn't do anything. Then, about four weeks ago, Officer Peter Jacoby was down there wandering around, trespassing on a top secret military facility." He opens a drawer and pulls out Peter's badge, tossing it on the desk in front of me. "That's all that's left of him."

"Allison was right: you did kill him," I say. I've never hated a man more than this.

"Seemingly not. Three days later, he brought you up here to the hospital with absolutely no memory of the incident. That's when I realized the Jacoby we killed came through CONIR. I kicked myself for the last few weeks. The first proof that CONIR worked, and I fucking shot it." He takes a deep breath. He's still pissed about it. Then, he smiles and looks at me. "Then there was you. I believe you came through CONIR too. You activated it somehow. I want you to do it again."

"OK, one big problem with your entire theory here, Millen," I say. And there is the thing that makes absolutely no sense. "If this is all about time travel, why am I in the same time? The day is right for me, it's just everything else is wrong. The hospital wasn't working where I came from. Allison was fine. You were dead."

Millen's brow furrows at that last one. Then he shakes it off. "That I cannot answer. These were Albert Forrester's ideas, not mine."

"What if I go to the police? The FBI? Tell them you killed a cop?"

"First of all," he says, "this is a military operation. We'll circumvent any authority that comes our way. Secondly, what police officer? Jacoby? He looked fine last time I saw him."

"That still won't stop a full investigation if it slips to the media to look for all the dead bodies by the two pine trees behind the hospital."

And, for the first time, Millen looks angry. He knows that I know they killed people; he didn't know that I know where they are buried. Now I'm an actual threat. In that moment, I realize that might not be the best position to be in.

"It's irrelevant, Ms. Hunter. You won't have a chance to tell anyone."

"Because you'll kill me." Of course they'd kill me. They had no problem doing it to the dozens of patients they'd done it to so far.

"No, not at all. Emily Hunter is alive and well at Sandy Shores Psychiatric Care. No one is even looking for you. You're not even supposed to be here. You won't have a chance to tell anyone, because, God willing, you'll be home by tomorrow. If you get CONIR to work, none of this will matter. You'll go back to your own little universe where I'm dead, you and Allison are best friends, and you're free to go."

"Failing that," he says, "yes, plan B is to kill you."

TWENTY-EIGHT

NEMO DAT QUOD NON HABET

THE NEXT HOUR was a blur as I tried to wrap my mind around what was going on. All I had were pieces of memories.

Millen's cologne smelled good. His grip on my arm was strong.

No one was in isolation.

The basement was full of bullet holes, the glass in the observation windows broken.

The code on the keypad was nine, two, six, and then four more numbers I didn't see.

The massive CONIR door opened to the left, and behind it was a long hallway with multiple passages and doors. No way to memorize it on the way through. Halls spread out like spiderwebs, like whoever designed it made it intentionally confusing. It worked.

There were black ops soldiers all over the place, each with an assault rifle and secondary weapons. Apart from them, there were scientists in lab coats. There was no way out of here alive. All of these realizations lead me to this room.

The hospital bed I'm lying in is much more comfortable than my bed upstairs. Three doctors, as well as Millen and two soldiers guarding the door, are here with me. The doctors look giddy, like they've found a unicorn. One draws my blood, the others hold their breath.

"Do you have all you need?" asks Millen.

"Yeah, that should be enough," the doctor answers, and they walk out of the room together, carefully carrying my blood like they're holding the Holy Grail.

Millen smiles comfortingly, even though he's threatened my life if I can't make his rock time machine work. "Did you get a chance to look at the files?"

About twenty minutes ago, they had dropped off a large file box. In it was the collected works of Albert Forrester. The binder I had seen last time I was down here, the one marked *2 of 3,* was in there, except now it was *2 of 42*. The rest of the 42 were in the box as well. It all may as well have been in Latin.

"Nothing jumped out at me," I say. "I don't know what you want me to say. Right now, this is as close as I've ever been. I didn't even get through the door on my side."

He pats my shoulder. "I understand it's a long shot, Emily." He motions to the two guards holding rifles at the door. "That's why they're here."

No pressure.

Another doctor comes into the room, carrying my red backpack and my clothes. "Oh good," says Millen. He hands it over to me. "We want to recreate all the variables that happened when you came through, so here's what you were wearing and here's your bag."

"And everything is back in it?" I ask, checking for myself—my phone, my clothes, a toothbrush, my charger, the rock that killed Abigail.

"Everything," he says. "The walls down here are lead lined, so you have no reception on that phone." He takes a breath and slaps his leg. "Well then, ready to go?"

"No."

He smiles.

"Well tough shit, we're out of time."

I grab the bag and follow him out of the room. The guards follow us.

Dead woman walking.

Peter Jacoby crawled into bed quietly. His mind wasn't ready for sleep, but the clock on the wall said it was bedtime. His shift began early tomorrow. Thoughts kept racing through his head, peeling his eyes open. Dr. Millen had reported to him that his sister had tried to escape with the help of the woman he brought up to the hospital, the woman who claimed she knew Allison. Al had never tried anything like that before. Was this woman dangerous? Was she right? Was something going on that put Allison in danger? She was his sister, he loved her more than anything. The thought of her being in trouble was too much to let him fall asleep. He reached over to his nightstand where his walkie-talkie sat and opened the drawer. He reached in and grabbed a bottle of melatonin and swallowed two pills dry.

Tomorrow, he thought, or maybe Friday, he'd check it out.

"Oh my God!" I say. Millen stops. The soldiers stop behind us. He turns around to look at me, about to give me shit for stalling, but the look on my face stops him.

I know what to do.

I rummage through the backpack laughing. "I get it. Jesus, I fucking get it!"

There it is, the rock.

"This is it. This is the key!" He stares at me eagerly. "It didn't make sense before, I couldn't see it. But . . . holy shit."

Millen obviously wants me to get to the point. I want to get there too.

"I had this rock when I came through. I got it from Abigail, my Abigail, in my time. Your Abigail was in the room when Forrester disappeared, right?"

"Yeah," says Millen.

"She told me, before I got the rock, that I had to give it back to her. When I was finished with it, she said those words: 'Give it back when you're finished with it.' " The look on my face is pure excitement. I look like I'm getting it, like I have all the answers.

I hope I'm not overselling it.

"I need to talk to Abigail, now!" I say. Millen is grinning like a kid on Christmas.

"Go get Abigail Pipkin. Bring her down here," he says to one of the soldiers.

"Yes, sir," the soldier says, and he runs back down the hallway.

One left.

I look at the rock and at the light overhead, and turn my back to Millen, making it look like I need more light. "Look at this." I say, and Millen follows. He's now standing between the soldier and me. So far, so good.

"See these scratches? They aren't natural, Abigail put them there. They're also not random. See this one on the top? The longer one?"

He squints and leans in to stare at it, nodding.

"If you follow where it points all the way around," I say, twisting the rock until my hand is underneath it. "See that?"

He squints harder. "See what?" he asks.

"Right there," I say.

And I smash the rock into his face.

He staggers back, clutching his already bloody face, and I drop my shoulder, pushing him into the soldier behind him. Both hit the ground, and I sprint over them, around the corner. My only shot is to get through this corridor, unarmed, through the giant door, which I can only hope is still open, back out of the hospital, which I've not been able to escape from yet, all while being pursued by special ops soldiers.

This is a horrible fucking plan, but I'm dead either way.

I turn the third corner, and surprisingly, there's the door. And even more surprisingly, it is still open. That feeling that someone is running interference returns. There's no way I could be this lucky.

I burst out of the giant doorframe into the lobby. The three doctors that took my blood stand in the nearer room, their mouths agape at the fact that I'm free. I only barely notice them. My eyes fall on the other person in the room: me.

In front of me stands another me, semi-transparent. This all feels familiar, and I suddenly realize why: I've seen this before, only I was that other me. I point to the far observation room, just like I had seen myself do before. I have to give myself this clue, just like I did before.

"Look," I say.

The other me turns around to look at the far room, but now I'm not paying attention to her anymore. Now I'm looking at the two new soldiers who are coming down the stairs to reinforce the ones who are trying to catch me. I see her look back just in time to see me turn and run into the CONIR hallway. I have nowhere to go but deeper in, and I can feel how naked my back is right now, almost like the laser sights are tickling my ribs. The moment one of them pulls a trigger I'm dead, unless I can make the corner first. I baseball slide into the far wall and roll into the corridor just as the bullets explode into the wall over my head. Suddenly sirens are going off, and emergency lighting comes on. The facility is on alert. I'm going to run out of time any second. I get up and start sprinting again. A four-way cross section of hallway opens in front of me, and I turn left, into three armed guards about twenty yards down the corridor. My hand catches the wall and pulls me back into the original hallway I was in, and I keep going. Now five of them know where I am. I hear their boots in the hall, and once again I'm quite aware the only thing between their M16s and me is the red backpack pounding against my spine.

The hallway I'm running down ends at a solid metal door. There are no turns, no twists, nowhere else to go. I've run into a dead end. I'm still sprinting at it, when about ten feet away, it opens a crack. I drop my shoulder and hit it full force, instantly knocking the soldier who was opening it back into the room. We both hit the ground hard, but I was ready for it and I didn't just get a big metal door in the mouth. He's stunned, and I take that moment to grab his rifle and shut the door behind us. He struggles to shake the cobwebs out of his head, when he turns to see me standing over him, rifle pointing directly at his face. He makes a motion for the handgun on his waist, but stops when I fire shots above his head. He then puts his hands up, surrendering.

"Slowly," I say, "strip."

"I'm going alone," said Sheriff Barkley. The other officers stared at him in disbelief. He looked at all their faces, one by one, for dramatic affect. Then he set it down: right bower, left bower, ace, king, queen of diamonds. Perfect loner.

"Game, kids," he said, moving the five of clubs to show he cleared ten points. He was cheating. He had to be. No one ever beat him at euchre.

The dispatch radio sparked to life: "Dispatch, this is Officer Jacoby. Shots fired at Riverview Hospital. Repeat, shots fired at Riverview Hospital. Officer requiring immediate assistance."

Immediately, all the officers were up and moving toward their car, the fastest of which was Barkley, who briefly noted that Peter was off tonight. He took his radio into his hand. "Jacoby, officers en route to your location. Can you tell us the situation?"

Peter's voice crackled over the radio again. "Dispatch, please acknowledge! Shots fired at Riverview Hospital. Officer requiring immediate armed assistance. There's a little girl here."

"Jacoby, please repeat. There's a little girl?" Riverview closed their children's services decades ago—something about abuse, resulting in the death of an orderly.

"Sheriff Barkley, please respond," said Peter. Barkley's heart sank. Peter's radio must be broken. One of his kids was in trouble, and he couldn't hear help was on the way.

"Mandy," Barkley said to the dispatch officer. "Wake everyone up, and get them to Riverview, weapons drawn. Now."

The cars screeched out of the station, while Mandy Gibson got on the radio.

The melatonin wasn't working. Peter was still just staring at the ceiling when his radio blared, nearly blowing his left eardrum. "All available units, all available officers, officer requires immediate assistance at Riverview Hospital. Repeat, shots fired at Riverview Hospital, officer on scene requires assistance. Available units report to the scene."

Looks like he was getting up to the hospital earlier than he thought.

The banging is startling, and the door sounds like it will come off the hinges at any moment. They've started hitting it with a battering ram. The soldier in the room with me is naked. All his clothes in one pile, the other pile has all his gear, as well as two handguns, two concussion grenades, a bowie knife, and a pair of handcuffs. The rifle is still in my hands pointed directly at him.

"What's your name?" I ask.

"Shane," he answers with some reluctance.

"Shane," I point the rifle at the pipe protruding from the wall over his head, and I toss him the handcuffs, "handcuff yourself to that pipe. Both hands around the pipe."

He smiles at me. “You’re not the first woman to handcuff me naked.”

“Want me to be the last?” I say.

He does it. I pinch both cuffs tighter than he did them, until they hurt.

“Emily?” a voice says from behind me, coming over Shane’s walkie.

It’s Millen.

I grab the 9 mm, trading in the much more intimidating but heavier rifle, and I point it at Shane. I pick up the radio and, for the first time, get a good look at my surroundings. There’s a desk, a table really, with a few computer monitors. There’s another door, but it’s keypad locked. There’s a big window, but there’s nothing but black to see through it.

BANG. The door is starting to bend. I look up to see a security camera. He’s watching me. That’s how he knew I had a walkie.

I get on the radio. “Tell them to stop hitting the door or I kill this guy.”

After a brief second. “Do it.”

I didn’t expect that. From the look on his face, neither did Shane.

“You kill him, and we get in and kill you. You don’t kill him, we still get in and kill you. So, either way.”

BANG. The top lip of the door is coming away. A few more shots and it will be wide enough to drop tear gas into.

“Of course, Emily, that’s still all plan B.” I hear how hard it is for him to say “plan B,” and I smile. It sounded more like “plan me.” I hit him good. “Do you see that light switch on the wall to your left? Flip it.”

BANG.

I cautiously reach over to the switch and flip it. Now, illuminated through the window, I see an octagonal white room with a large rock on a pedestal in the direct center.

I ran right where he wanted me to run. Those soldiers didn't miss me, they guided me right here.

"There's always plan A," says Millen.

BANG.

I take a deep breath, and I lower the weapon. I am out of options. I raise the radio to my mouth.

"What's the door combination?"

Three police cruisers pulled up to Riverview Hospital. All the officers jumped out immediately and had their weapons ready. The rest of the officers were on their way, but they couldn't wait. Peter Jacoby was in trouble. They hadn't heard from him since his distress call. They ran up to the hospital entrance, guns trained on every window along the way.

The radio is on my belt, the gun is in my hand, and the door opens with a whoosh. The room smells metallic, like right before a rainstorm but mixed with burnt plastic. I feel dizzy as soon as I breathe it in.

The stone is in the middle of the room, and even without walking toward it, it's intimidating. It's surprisingly immense;

without the pedestal, it would still come up to my shoulders. As it stands, I can barely see over the top. As I get closer to it, I start feeling nauseous. The symbols cover the stone, and altogether there have to be two hundred, if not more. They look like the ones Albert drew. I'm sure they're the same. I start scanning for the ones I drew on my wall, but I've already forgotten what they looked like. I saw them in the middle of a seizure; it's a wonder I remember I saw anything at all.

BANG.

They're still trying to get in. The radio clicks on. "Tick tock, Emily. I hope you work well under pressure."

BANG.

Think. Think.

BANG.

Think.

BANG.

To hell with this.

I walk out of the room and back into the observation room. From the pile of weapons, I grab one of Shane's grenades. I tuck the gun into my jeans and walk back into the CONIR room. With one hand I grab the radio, the other holds the grenade, and I stand in front of CONIR. I find the camera in the room, the same one that recorded Albert Forrester disappearing, and I stare directly into it.

"Can you see me?" I say.

A moment goes by, then, "Yes."

BANG.

I pull the pin but hold the clip down. The grenade is now live. If I let go, it goes off in eight seconds. My insides turn to jelly, and suddenly my hand feels too small, but I have to keep a bad ass exterior. "Tell them to back off or I break your fucking rock."

BANG.

"If I'm dead anyway, I'd rather go out this way. Shut down your hospital, make sure no one ever has to come in this room again." Even I am shocked to realize I'm not bluffing.

The banging stops.

The officers crowded the lobby, much to the shock of the receptionist who was just about to go home for the night. Sheriff Barkley, her neighbor, came in next, gun drawn.

"Betty, we've got a report of gunshots here at the hospital."

"What?" she said, confused. She thought up until now, it had been a pretty quiet night.

One of the other officers stepped in. "Ma'am, I'm going to need you to come out from behind the desk and follow me out of the hospital." She did, without another word. Barkley was about to give the order for his team to split up and search the grounds when Peter Jacoby entered the building.

"Peter! Thank God, son. What's the situation?" exclaimed Barkley.

Peter looked around to all the other officer's faces, who all stared at him expectantly. "Um . . . I don't know, sir. I just got here."

"What the hell do you mean? You radioed in a call of shots fired."

"I was at home in bed when Mandy called in all officers. I didn't radio in anything."

Peter's stunned confusion and the calm lobby convinced Barkley. "Fucking hell. Pack it in, everyone. False alarm, someone radioed in a false alarm." It took a second

FOR HIM TO REALIZE THIS WAS THE BEST POSSIBLE OUTCOME TO A SHOTS-FIRED CALL.

THE OFFICERS ALL STOWED THEIR WEAPONS AND WALKED OUT OF THE BUILDING BACK TOWARD THEIR CARS. THE RECEPTIONIST DIDN'T GO BACK INSIDE. HER SHIFT WAS DONE ANYWAY. SHE GOT IN HER CAR AND DROVE AWAY MINUTES BEFORE THE EXPLOSION.

The dizzy spell comes back again. This one is bad, not just because I can't see straight, but because I'm holding a live grenade. I breathe through it, and it passes. Something about being this close to the rock is setting me off.

From behind me steps Carrot. Her hands are behind her back, her demeanor is childlike. She has a different expression. She's smiling, but she's not happy.

She looks proud of me but sad, like someone holding it together at a funeral.

"Hey kid," I say, my nose tingling signaling the tears that were on their way. "I think I've painted myself into a corner here. Any advice?"

"Don't let him look," she says.

Everything slows down and gets quiet. The banging sounds distant, almost muffled. I very carefully switch the grenade to my left hand, and I pull out the handgun. I take aim and shoot the camera. I get it on my second shot.

A moment later, the banging starts again. This time harder, faster. They were pretending before. Now they're coming in. I put the gun back and hold the grenade with my right hand again. It feels safer in my stronger hand.

"Don't you look either," she says sadly. I look down to Carrot, this little girl who has been with me all my life. I'm still not sure why, but I'm glad she's here now, at the end. She closes her eyes again, and I accept it: I am going to die very soon.

Questions float through my mind: Why this? Why here? What was the point of any of it? Was I here just to destroy the rock? If so, I'm OK with it. Millen's CONIR project dies with me; that's not a bad thing. It's noble. My mom would be proud of me. That thought finally starts the tears.

I never called her back.

BANG.

I wonder what she thinks happened to me.

BANG.

I wonder if she'll ever find Blue Water.

BANG.

I wonder if she'll find Allison, my Allison, my friend.

BANG.

Three snakes.

BANG.

My eyes flash open.

Three snakes, Abigail had said three snakes. I look around the rock quickly, and I find it: three backward *S*'s, just like I had drawn on my wall.

She was telling me what to touch. She was in the room, she saw Albert touch them, and he was gone.

I touch the three snakes with my left index finger, and I feel heat. But beyond that, I faintly hear something very familiar.

Boom. Boom. Boom.

I look at Carrot. Her eyes are open again, and she's smiling at me. This is right. What else was there?

A bird, the stretched *M*. Left pinky.

BOOM. BOOM. BOOM.

BANG.

My left hand is starting to feel hot, like a current is going between the two fingers touching the stone. What else was there? The short man and the tall man, which I drew as two female symbols, one with a longer stem, and the devil, a figure eight missing the top quarter. I look over the stone, and I find them. Both symbols are on the right side of the stone, and I could touch them both with the other hand—If only the other hand wasn't holding the lever down on a live grenade.

Peter Jacoby and Albin Barkley stood next to their cars. The rest of the officers had just finished pulling away. Albin knew how much it killed Peter that his sister was here, but Peter rarely talked about it. Tonight, though, something prompted him to ask. And tonight something persuaded Peter to answer. Peter told him about the escape attempt, about the phone calls making sure he was still alive. The last few weeks had been harder than usual on him, Albin could see it. Now seemed like as good a time as any to check in.

The conversation was about to be cut short.

BANG.

OK, OK, OK . . .

BANG.

Shit shit shit shit shit.

The pain in my left hand is getting worse. My right hand is starting to cramp from squeezing the grenade. The two symbols I need are right there. The soldiers are almost through the door. One last play.

Deep breath. Hold it.

I set the grenade down on top of the stone.

It's armed and eighteen inches from my face.

Eight seconds.

My hand drops instantly and finds the short man and the tall man. I touch it with my right index finger.

BOOMBOOMBOOMBOOM. CONIR gets louder and faster.

Seven seconds.

My right thumb stretches to the devil. As soon as I touch it, I feel the current coursing through my right hand and up around through each arm and my chest, looping back to the stone.

And nothing else happens.

Six seconds.

Fuck fuck fuck . . .

Five seconds.

BOOMBOOMBOOMBOOMBOOMBOOMBOOM.

Four seconds.

The X, with the two dots.

Three seconds.

I look all over the right side. It's not there.

Two seconds.

I look at the left side.

One second.

There it is, I can reach it with my thumb.

The soldiers breached and entered the observation room, guns drawn. Shane was naked, handcuffed to a pipe, screaming to be let go. The girl was in the other room seemingly hugging a big rock. She looked at them briefly through the window, then the room fucking exploded.

From outside, the hospital shuddered while Sheriff Barkley and Officer Peter Jacoby leaned on their cars. In one instant, their conversation ended; in the next, Barkley was radioing for the cops to come back while Peter ran inside.

Allison sat in her room crying, feeling terrible about telling on the girl who tried to save her, especially to Millen, who she was sure had killed her brother. Her room shook and dust fell from the ceiling as she sat up in bed.

Millen heard the boom from his office, and he knew it was over. The rock was destroyed, his work was for nothing. One of the other security monitors showed two cops running into the building. There was no hiding this. He was at the end of the line anyway. The military was about to cut him loose; now they'd have no choice but to disavow him. They'd let him take the fall for everything. The dead bodies in the woods, the torture of patients—he'd go down for all of it. He took a drink of whiskey, then he took three more. Then, he reached into his desk and pulled out the Smith and Wesson model 625. He always thought there was something romantic about a revolver.

The full moon shone on the hospital, a tiny oasis in a sea of trees. There was a loud boom. Moments later there was a quieter bang.

Then there was silence again.

PART FIVE

TWENTY-NINE

PROGREDI EST REGREDI

BOOM.

Silence.

Darkness.

Silence.

Darkness.

Wind.

Darkness.

Crickets.

Darkness.

Leaves.

Darkness.

Breath.

Darkness.

Moonlight.

I think I'm alive. Maybe.

It's so peaceful, quiet. I like that it's quiet. Not like before; before was noisy. I think. I don't remember.

I yawn deeply. I must've fallen asleep out here on this hillside. The half-moon lights up the woods around me in a tranquil glow. An owl hoots somewhere. Am I camping? No, not this time, next time.

There was banging, loud banging, and my hands used to hurt. They feel fine now.

I sit up, and twigs stick in my hair, and I realize for the first time that I'm really cold. I wonder how long I've been lying here without a blanket. I wonder why I'm only wearing a T-shirt and jeans. I wonder who that guy lying next to me is.

The white room.

There was a white room. There was something in it, and a little girl. Who was the little girl?

"Carol?" asks the man. He's starting to stir now, and he's noticed me. Carol, is that my name? I'm not sure. It sounds familiar. No, that's not right.

"Hold on," I say, helping him up. He's about my age, maybe younger.

Hospital.

Things are starting to come back now, just fragments, bits and pieces.

"My name is Emily . . . Hunter," I say after remembering my last name too.

"Albert Forrester," he says. That sounds familiar too. He gets to his feet and stretches out the stiffness in his back.

Carrot.

I feel like I just woke up from the best sleep of my life. I take in my surroundings, and there's not much to look at: trees, stars.

Blue Water.

Save us all.

Mayor Henry Altman.

"How did we get up here?" he asks.

"I don't think I know where here is," I answer. Or maybe I do?

"It looks familiar. I'm having really bad *déjà vu*."

What they came to describe as "unshakable déjà vu."

"Me too," I say.

"I think I've been here before."

What year is it? It's 2015.

"What year is it?" I ask, without really meaning to.

"1987?" he says.

Millen.

Abigail Pipkin.

Room twenty-seven.

X with two dots.

CONIR.

He touched the devil and he was gone.

I remember everything.

"I saw you," I say. "Millen showed me the video. You were in the room with Abigail Pipkin. You disappeared."

"Disappeared?" he asks.

"Do you remember CONIR?"

His eyes widen. "CONIR, the big stone with the markings—I touched it. There was a bright light, the big night."

"Then you were here."

"Then I was here," he says.

"Me too. So where is here?"

"Oh, we're only a mile or so from town."

"From town? From Blue Water?" I ask.

He nods. It didn't even occur to me that we were still on Earth. I pick up my red backpack.

"Let's go then," I say.

The wind blows through the leaves on the trees and kicks up dust from the ground into my eyes. I feel like I could use two showers. “Are you remembering anything else?” I say as I try desperately to wipe the sand out of my face.

Albert sighs. “The hospital. The stone. Symbols, lots of symbols. Not much else. Why?”

“Because,” I say, “you’re supposed to be the expert on CONIR. I apparently got it to work by being near it or touching it or something.”

“How did you do that?”

“I was hoping you’d tell me.” I reach into the bag and grab the cell phone. Apparently Millen had charged it, knowing that it was charged when I had come through. He didn’t miss a detail.

“What is that?” he asks as I flip it open.

“I’m calling Allison. I need to see if she remembers me.” I flip through the contact list to Allison and hit send. Nothing happens. I check the bars and find I have none. I’ll have to wait until I get closer to town. Luckily for Albert, he’s lived here his whole life. I’m not sure of the way back to town. All I can think of is Allison. Is she OK? Is she still in the hospital? The thought of her still being there physically hurts. If I did my job, the stone is gone at least. But I don’t know anything about grenades. Maybe I didn’t even dent it.

If all of this was for nothing, if they’re still torturing her . . . I want so much to believe I’m on my side again, but Albert Forrester was just sent here too.

“Hey Albert, when we get to town, I have to make a stop.” Finding Allison is all that’s important.

About a half hour later we walk into the Water Street Café.

My eyes dart around the room looking for her face, hoping to see it smiling at me, see her wave, see her recognize me. I sit at the counter, and my eyes pass over a newspaper. Weather report, BWHS baseball scores, another school shooting somewhere—at least I know I'm in the right time.

The waitress pours me a cup of water. She asks if I need anything else, but I'm fine for now. She looks to be about 16.

"Wait," I say. "Is Allison working tonight?" The look on her face is like a punch in the stomach.

"Sorry, ma'am. No one works here by that name. How about your fella here?"

I didn't even notice Albert had sat down next to me. "Pork chops and an ice water, please, Annie."

She gives him a puzzled look as if trying to place his face. "Do I know you, dude?" she asks.

"Not yet," he answers with a smile. She looks at me, wondering if I'm OK with his flirting. It dawns on me then she thinks he's my boyfriend. I roll my eyes, as if to say he does it all the time, and she walks away.

"Not yet?" I ask in a hushed tone. But Albert is beaming, grinning from ear to ear. He nods his head toward the newspaper I already looked at. I glance at it and look back up to him, making sure that's what he wanted me to see.

"Look at it," he says.

Weather, sports scores, school shooting at Kent State University.

Wait a minute.

Kent State?

I grab the paper like my life depends on it. My eyes dart to the top line, to the date: May 5, 1970.

"Happy Cinco de Mayo," says Albert with a grin.

THIRTY

QUOD EST NECESSARIUM EST LICITUM

WHAT. THE. FUCK.

He's smiling still. He's happy with himself.

"It's . . .1970?" I ask. He nods excitedly. "Why aren't you upset?"

"Because it worked."

"What . . ." I stop. Annie has brought our food: two big pork chops for Albert, a burger and fries for me. She smiles at us both. "Thanks," I say.

"This looks perfect," says Albert.

He tears into it pretty quickly, and I have to admit, my burger is calling me. I've had nothing but terrible hospital food for weeks now. "What worked?"

He waits until he's finished chewing. "The stone, CONIR, it brought me back here. You too, apparently. You touched the symbols, right? I'd been seeing them my whole life, trying to draw them so I could understand them. Then I got to the stone, and there they were. It was so surreal."

"What do you mean you got . . ." And it hits me. And when it does, I know I'm completely screwed.

He called me Carol. When he woke up, the first thing he did was call me Carol.

"You're the wrong Albert Forrester."

He looks at me, squinting his eyes, not following. Oh my God, how could I be so stupid?

"You weren't working with Millen, you didn't work on CONIR. You don't know any more about it than I do."

"I'm not sure I understand," he says.

"Where I just came from, Albert Forrester was the leading scientist working with Dr. Millen on the CONIR project. He knew everything about it. You're not that guy. You're the Albert Forrester who . . ." went crazy and died in the woods with your head beaten in, I almost finished. " . . . is from my time."

"Your time?" he asks.

"When is the present for you?"

"September 1987."

"Yeah," I say, "October 2015."

His eyes widen. "You're from the future?"

I point to the newspaper. "Technically we both are."

"And you know my wife? Carol, you know her?"

"Yes—I mean, I've met her."

He pauses a moment, and the tears well up in his eyes. "Is she OK? Is she happy?"

Something about this question seems more desperate than it should be. He didn't ask about himself, he didn't ask about flying cars or who won the World Series. He asks about his wife being happy, as if she shouldn't be.

"She's fine. Look, I don't know how much I should tell you. I've seen science fiction movies where this kind of thing screws up the universe, so let's focus on something else. If you're not the Albert Forrester I was expecting, how did you know about CONIR?"

He pushes away from the counter a little and takes a deep breath. "When I was a kid," he begins, "my dad used to work at the hospital. He was in the military. We moved around a lot. I didn't get to see him that often, not as often as a little boy wants to see his father. He was a short-tempered man. Even when he was around, he wasn't really around, you know?"

I nod.

"Anyway, one day, his birthday or Father's Day or something, I buy him this horrible blue-and-gold tie. It wasn't much, but I was really proud because I bought it with my own money." He smiles at the memory. "I brought it up to the hospital, snuck past the front desk because I wanted to surprise him. I didn't want them to tell him I was there. I see him, and I sneak up behind him, and I yell 'SURPRISE!' " His growing smile suddenly fades. "He jumps, you know, and turns around, and there's this stupid little kid holding an awful-looking tie, big grin on his face. He grabbed me by the arm so hard if I think about it, I can still feel it. He pulled me into an empty room and tore me apart, screaming at me about how important his work was and how he shouldn't be interrupted. I threw the tie at him, and I left." His eyes are wet again now. This memory still hurts.

"I started to walk home, through the woods. That's all I really remember. There was a bright light. It just came out of nowhere. Then I woke up in Dr. Ford's office in town, this pretty girl with me."

I saw this happen. The light, it came from me, somehow. I don't want to interrupt his story, especially with something that probably isn't helpful, so I keep my mouth shut.

"Since that moment," he continues, "I started having visions, dreams, sometimes while I was awake. I'd see things. I'd see this big white room with a giant stone in the middle of it. I'd see the word CONIR. I'd see the symbols, and I'd understand them, somehow. I knew what they meant. I'd have these visions of the woods and the hospital, and I'd black out. Then I'd wake up in different places."

This sounds frighteningly familiar.

"Carol . . . she suggested I get medication. It worked for a while, but I'd feel these urges, like I had to stop taking them. The pills silenced the visions, and that started to feel like a bad thing. I felt like I was supposed to see them."

This sounds way too frighteningly familiar.

"I guess that sounds crazy," he finishes.

"No, not at all," I manage to say through my dry throat. I take a drink of water.

"Anyway, I stopped taking the medication. I made my way up to the hospital, found the stone, and here I am."

He can see I'm replaying the entire story in my head, so he gives me a minute while he eats more pork chops. I follow suit and finish my burger, when he asks, "How about you?"

"It's a much longer and crazier story," I answer with a smile.

"Well, I really want to hear it. But first, I'm going to use the bathroom. Then, you tell me everything. OK?"

"OK," I answer, and he sets his napkin on the counter and steps away. I start poring through my story in my mind, trying to figure out where to start. If I start at being on the other side at Riverview, with Millen and Abigail, I have to tell him about being on our side first and then Abigail dying and Altman and coming to Blue Water in the first place because of Carrot, who just happens to be his wife. There really isn't a great spot to begin.

Annie drops off the check, and I go into my bag and grab my card out of my wallet. I'm about to hand it over, when it occurs to me the bank account it's tied to won't exist for another forty years. Then a bit of dread comes over me, as I look into my wallet: the bill for both meals is $4.12; I have seven dollars, but the design of the five-dollar bill isn't the same as it would be in 1970 and both my singles say *Series 2006*. Essentially, I'm carrying counterfeit money.

Annie notices my sudden discomfort, and she approaches me suspiciously.

"Problem, Miss?" she asks, probably having dealt with her share of dine-and-dashers. I smile to her with as much fake sincerity as I can muster.

"Albert . . . my uh, boyfriend. He's got the cash. He'll be right back."

She's not buying it. This is how it goes. One dasher leaves first, the other shortly behind.

"You know what, let me go get him," I say, and I get up. Annie positions herself between me and the front door as I walk back to the restrooms.

I crack open the men's room door and call inside. "Hey Albert, I sure hope you have some cash issued in the sixties, or else we're washing dishes."

Nothing.

"Albert, you OK in there?"

Nothing.

I crack the door a little more and peek inside to see a wide-open frosted window. Other than that, the bathroom stall doors are open and no one is in them.

He's gone.

THIRTY-ONE

PEDE POENA CLAUDO

I HAVE TO make a run for it. He can't have gotten too far yet. I haven't dined-and-dashed since I was in high school. I go for the front door as fast as I can.

"Hey!" yells Annie, but she's too slow to stop me. The door is right in front of me. Once I hit it, I'll have to keep going. I'll figure out where I'm going later. I go through the front door, and I hear Annie yelling behind me. I look both ways as soon as I get out the door. Left, no Albert. Right—

A police officer, and he's already grabbed my arm.

The cop brings me back into the restaurant and forcibly sits me down in a booth. He and Annie stand in front of the seat, blocking my exit. Albert is getting farther away. All kinds of thoughts go through my head. The cop is probably nineteen years old. I could barrel through both of them, but then the cops would be chasing me while I was chasing Albert.

The gun—before I touched the stone and got sent to the seventies, I tucked a gun into the waistband of my jeans. I forgot it was there. It's odd that I didn't feel it. Slowly, I reach my hand back to grab it. I'm not going to shoot anyone, I'm just going to use it to slow down everything, explain my situation, then get them to let me go.

My hand hits nothing, and I understand why I didn't feel it. The gun is gone.

"How come you didn't pay your bill, ma'am?" asks the cop.

"Listen, officer . . ." I look at his nameplate. I have to look twice. " . . . Jacoby. The guy with the money, he just jumped out the men's room window." Now that I look, I see Peter in his face. This must be Allison and Peter's dad.

"Well, that's unfortunate," he says. "Still leaves us with the problem of an unpaid bill."

"I'm sorry. I don't have any money on me. Please, you have to let me go. I need to find the guy I came in here with."

"No," he says. "You *need* to pay this lovely girl for the wonderful meal she just made for you." He smiles at her. She smiles back. Jesus, he's flirting. I'm not getting out of here, not unless I can make him look good. Maybe give her something? I think about the contents of my backpack: some clothes, some toiletries, a rock. My cell phone—the technology that's in it is probably worth billions in 1970. I'm sure that would cause some kind of universe-ending paradox or something.

"Wait!" I say. "Annie, right? How's this?" I take off my watch, and I hand it over. "Look, it runs great, it's gold. It'll cover my bill."

She looks at it stunned. "Your bill is four bucks, this is a forty-dollar watch." In 1970s money, I think. It was three times that when I got it for Christmas.

"Is it enough?" I say.

She looks at me for a long moment, then looks to Jacoby. He shrugs to her. She puts the watch on.

"I don't want to see you in here again," she says.

No promises, I think, as I run out the door.

The night air feels warm on my skin, and I hear the waves from Lake Huron washing up over the shore. There is nothing else moving but the fish flies swarming over the street lamps.

Where could he be?

He was happy, even excited. He meant to get here. He was aiming for 1970, and he made it. Why?

And it hits me like a ton of bricks: I know where he's going, and I know where the gun went.

THE DOOR OPENED QUIETLY, AND THE STRANGE MAN IN THE STRANGE CLOTHES APPROACHED THE DESK. VISITING HOURS WERE OVER, AND REBECCA WAS ALREADY PREPARING HER SPEECH TO TURN HIM AWAY. HIS SMILE WAS DISARMING, AND SHE LET HIM TALK FIRST.

"HI, MY NAME IS ALBERT. I'M A FRIEND OF HENRY ALTMAN'S. IS HE WORKING TONIGHT?"

THIRTY-TWO

PROPTER VITAM VIVENDO PERDEDE CAUSAS

I HAD HOPED I had seen the last of this place when I was holding a live hand grenade while soldiers tried to break down the door to kill me. That was an hour ago—or forty-five years from now. Again, it depends on how you look at it.

But here I am, standing in front of Riverview Psychiatric Hospital, and once again, I'm not sure what to expect. I've wandered around this place when it was dead and full of ghosts. I've been locked in it when it was alive and full of patients. Now I'm walking into it for the third time. This time I'm ready. This time I go in on my terms.

I know it's late. They won't have visitors anymore tonight. I look around the newly paved driveway headed up to the front door and see a large mud puddle. It'll do nicely. After a few good stomps in the puddle, my shoes are dirty, the legs of my jeans are good and muddy. I mess my hair up just a little bit, and I walk toward the entrance.

The receptionist gives me an odd glance as I step into the lobby. I smile kindly and shake my head as if I've just had the worst night of my life.

"Are you OK?" she asks.

"It's been a hell of a night," I reply, rubbing my face.

"It looks like it. What can I help you with?"

I lean on the desk she's sitting behind, as if to give my feet a rest. "I'm Dr. Meghan Harper. I'm a caseworker for a resident here, little girl named Carol Emerson."

"We don't usually get workers this late," she says.

"Yeah, I was trying to get here by dinner time, but my car broke down about ten miles outside of town and apparently no one is out on the roads tonight to help, so I had to walk. Is there anyway I can see her before she goes to bed?"

"Don't you want to use the phone? Call about your car?"

"Not yet," I say. "I'll see her first, then if you don't mind, I'll call a cab or something, see if I can stay at a hotel in town."

She gives me a suspicious glance. I'm not dressed like a doctor at all. She hands me the clipboard anyway. "Sign in here."

I sign *Dr. Meghan Harper LMHC* without trying to overthink it.

"You know where you're going?" she asks.

I nod and head toward Carrot's room. This has to be where Albert is going.

"Ma'am?" the receptionist calls from behind me. Shit, what did I do wrong? I turn back to her to see her holding out a visitor sticker. I roll my eyes, as if to say I'd forget my head if it weren't attached, and I graciously take the sticker, attaching it to my shirt.

I feel like I should be in trouble, walking these halls at night alone. When a kid grows up to be a teacher and they work at their old school, this is what they must feel like. I was a patient here for a few weeks, and in that short time, I came to fear these halls, fear the staff.

"Hey!" a voice yells from behind me.

Fear that voice.

I turn around slowly, and there he is. He's racing up the hall toward me, and even in the low light, I can see his perfect hair, his horn-rimmed glasses, his club.

I stand face to face with Henry Altman, with Bull.

His face is contorted in a mix of anger and joy as he slowly reaches for the club at his waist. I tense up, putting myself in a defensive position. My eyes dart around the hallway, looking for anything to use as a weapon. Nothing. He'll be on me in three seconds. I clench my fists. He isn't expecting an attack to come first. If I spring him, I might be able to get the club. Two seconds. He's grinning now. Now or never. I pull my arm back, readying it to throw into his face. One second.

"Oh sorry, ma'am," he says, and his posture drops. My adrenaline has kicked in, and my hands are shaking. "I thought you were one of the residents out of their room. We have to keep everyone accounted for, for safety." He saw the visitor sticker, and now he's talking like a perfect gentleman. He's oozing charm, like the politician he'll grow up to be.

"Of course," I say. I need to keep up appearances and not rip his face off right here.

"Visiting hours are over though. Are you lost?"

"No, I'm a case manager for Carol Emerson."

His face—the look on it I'm sure I'll treasure forever.

"You're here to talk to Carrot?"

"Carol, yes."

"She . . . uh . . . I've never seen you here before. I actually haven't seen anyone here for Carrot . . . Carol before." He's sweating. I love it. I look right into his eyes with a confidence I thought these walls had stolen from me.

"I've been working with her for quite some time. What did you say your name was?"

"H-Henry, ma'am."

"Henry . . . Altman?" I ask. It looks like he's trying his damnedest not to piss his pants. "They call you 'Bull,' right?"

"Uh, yes, ma'am. It's more just a silly nickname . . . why?"

"I've heard about you," I say, and I let it sit there in the air for an uncomfortable amount of time, until I follow up with, "I've heard a lot about you. I've written a lot about you down."

He knows I know. I don't take my eyes off of him. I crush him with my stare. He's suddenly so small, so insignificant, so weak and powerless.

"So are you going to show me to her room or what?" I say.

"Uh . . . of course," he manages to croak out of his dried throat.

He walks ahead of me, and I follow closely behind through the hallway. I know exactly where I'm going, but this has the feeling of walking a condemned man to the gallows and I want him to regret every step of the way. I want him to cry.

We get to the door, and he unlocks it slowly.

"Look," he says, "sometimes the residents find a staff member they don't like and they single him out, you know? Make stuff up."

"Henry, shut your mouth," I say. After a brief thought of protest, he shuts his mouth.

The door opens without a sound, and there's a young Carol Emerson, looking exactly like Carrot, pushing herself into the corner of the room. She sees Bull only, so I step in front of him and into the room.

"Carol, honey, it's OK. I'm here to help you, OK?" She doesn't look at me, she just looks at Bull. I touch her shoulder, and she squirms away. Her breathing is so elevated, I'm worried she's going to pass out. "Carol! Look at me," I say, guiding her face to look directly into mine. She slowly recognizes I'm in the room with her. "I'm here right now. You're safe. He's not going to hurt you. He's never going to hurt you again."

A sniffle comes from behind me. It's the best sound I've ever heard. Bull is dead to rights. He's got no play. He can't hurt me, he can't hurt her. He's done.

"Who are you?" asks Carrot, and my bluff dies right then and there.

Bull suddenly has new life. "Wait, you said you're her doctor. She doesn't know you. Who the hell are you?"

OK, time to double down. "Henry, I'm the person who has amassed proof that you've been sexually assaulting this little girl, lots and lots of proof. And I'm here to stop it. Do you know what they do to kiddie rapists in prison?" He silently shakes his head.

"Do you want to find out?" I finish. Henry Altman has been defeated.

I turn back to Carrot. "Honey, I need to talk to you, OK?" She doesn't answer. "Do you want him to leave?" She nods her head. Without breaking eye contact, "Henry, you need to leave now." She needs to feel safe. She deserves to feel safe after what this inhuman monster has done to her. But right now, I also need to find Albert, and I'm sure this is where he's coming.

Altman hasn't left. "Henry, I swear to God . . ." I say as I turn back to the scene that's unfolded behind my back.

I found Albert.

I found my gun.

Albert has found Henry Altman.

"He's not going anywhere," says Albert Forrester as he presses the barrel of a 9 mm Beretta hard enough against Bull's head to leave a mark.

THIRTY-THREE

QUI TOTEM VULT TOTUM PERDIT

ALBERT FORRESTER STANDS in the hallway, pointing a gun to the head of Henry Altman. Altman is standing in the doorway in front of me. I'm crouching on the floor in front of Carol Emerson. Carol is sitting on her bed.

No one is moving. No one is even breathing.

Finally, after what feels like years, "I'm gonna kill you, Altman," says Albert.

"Albert . . ." I say. He needs to calm down. He needs to think about this.

"I'm going to kill you," he says again. This time it's not a threat. This time it's excitement. He said he was going to kill Altman in the same manner someone says they're going to Disney World. He's wished this his whole life, and now it's possible.

"I don't know you, man," says Bull.

"Don't," I say.

"This is why we're here, Emily. The *X* with the two dots. This is where it brings us. We're here to kill him."

"We don't have to kill anyone."

"Yeah, listen to her, man. You don't have to kill anyone."

"Shut up! I'm going to shoot you. I'm going to shoot you in the fucking face, you piece of shit. Shut the fuck up." Bull shuts the fuck up.

"Albert, listen . . ." I say, but I don't know how to finish that sentence. Albert interrupts anyway.

"He raped my wife, Emily. Over and over again, he raped my wife."

"Whoa, man! I never raped anyone's wife! You got the wrong guy! I just . . ." And Bull stops talking when the hammer on the Beretta gets pulled back. That sound silences all of us, even Albert. But now Altman's eyes are different. He's thinking. He's solving a puzzle.

"He deserves this," he whispers to all of us. He's trying not to lose his nerve.

"Yeah, he does," I say. "Putting a bullet in his head is going to save us all a lot of trouble, believe me. But you're better than this."

Albert takes a short breath, and I can see the tears start rolling down his cheeks. He never takes his eyes off of Bull. "You didn't hear her, Emily. You never heard her waking up in the middle of the night screaming. The kind of screaming that rips your stomach out of your body, for years."

"You're right, I didn't. And I can't say that, given the opportunity, I wouldn't be doing the exact same thing. But this is going to be traumatizing too, Albert. You can't shoot someone in the head in front of an eight-year-old girl."

I know I'll never unhear the next three words spoken. The beautiful, innocent voice of a child from the bed behind me, a cute little girl with bright blue eyes: "Yes, he can."

You could hear a pin drop a mile away. All three of us look at little Carol, sitting on the bed. She's watching all of this with a dark, vengeful smile. She wants to see this. After a brief moment of shock at how easily that smile sits on her lips, Albert smiles almost identically.

"That's all the permission I need."

Bull starts to beg. "Wait . . . don't, please. Come on, you don't mean that, Carrot Cake."

Albert explodes: "Don't you call her that! Don't you ever fucking call her that."

A second later, all hell breaks loose.

Bull swipes his hand up and grabs the barrel of the gun. Albert, totally not expecting it, manages to maintain his grip on the handle, barely, and the two start wrestling over the weapon. Albert lowers his shoulder and pushes Bull into the door to try to knock him off balance. Bull counters perfectly and tries to roll Albert over his shoulder and into the room. I don't care about any of this. I grab Carrot, and I run past them out the open door.

Outside the door, about thirty yards down the hallway, I find the nurses' station. I set Carrot down behind the desk, and I hold her shoulders again. She looks into my eyes for help. I do my best.

"Stay here, OK? I'm going to go try to find help. Don't get up until I come get you. Do you understand?" She nods, and I step out into the hallway. The hospital is practically empty of staff. The overnight shift has started. There may be two or three people here who can help.

A gunshot rings out from Carrot's room.

A moment later, out stumbles Bull. He's got blood all over his shirt. He's dazed, trying to grab the doorframe to brace himself. He trips over himself and falls to the ground, catching himself at the last minute with his right hand. He looks confused when he sees the blood soaking his shirt. His other hand comes back around to help get him to his feet.

He's holding the Beretta.

It's not his blood.

Blood has sprayed into his face, Albert's blood. His eyes find me in the middle of the hallway alone, unarmed, unprotected.

"Shit," I mutter to myself. I'm next.

I turn the corner as quickly as I can, and I can hear him chasing me. Instantly, this feels familiar. I just did this an hour ago, only this time I'm running through the halls above ground. This time there's only one gunman.

This time he's not herding me. He's going to do his best to kill me.

Carol watched two sets of legs go tearing past, followed by complete silence. That man was going to kill Bull. The woman said she was her case manager, but Carol had never seen her before.

Wait . . . that's not true. She remembered that woman from somewhere. She had thought it was a dream. She got those, sometimes. Sometimes, they predicted things. That woman was in her room once, a while ago. She was asking who was screaming. Carol couldn't hear anything. The man, she knew she hadn't seen, but he felt familiar, somehow. Albert, his name was. She heard the woman call him Albert.

The coast looked clear, so Carol stepped out. She walked back to her room to see if Albert was dead. She peeked her head around the doorframe as quiet as she could. The blood was all over the floor. All her stuff was broken in the fight that had gone on. Albert sat against her bed, holding his stomach, breathing heavily, and staring at the wall. He was shot, he was bleeding, but he was alive. The color had drained from his face everywhere but the red circles around his eyes, which slowly came to find Carol. He swallowed gingerly and smiled at her, trying to be comforting amid the horror show in front of her.

"Hi, sweetheart," he said.

"Hello," Carol said back.

With new determination, Albert forced himself to stand, wincing through the pain in his guts. Everything beneath his chest felt like it was on fire, but this little girl, his eventual wife, needed him.

He knew how this was going to end. He got up anyway.

"Come on, Carol. We have to go now."

They made it around the bend in the hallway right before the nurses, hearing the commotion, found the bloodbath in Carol Emerson's room.

THIRTY-FOUR

CONSUMMATUM EST

MY HEART IS beating so hard it might give out on me, but I can't slow down. If I stop sprinting, I die. Bull is right behind me, but he's running too fast to get an accurate shot off, and he's in the middle of a populated hospital. If he's going to fire that gun again, he's going to have to make it count.

My legs are about to give, and I can't breathe. Bull doesn't even seem winded. I need a new strategy.

"FIRE!" I scream, and I start banging on doors as I run past them. "Fire! Everyone up! Get out of the building!"

Slowly, the doors behind me begin opening and people come out into the hallway. Bull tucks the gun but continues running, bumping into resident after resident. I've slowed him down, but he's still coming strong. The back of my throat tastes like metal, and my thighs are on fire. Ahead of me is an exit, and I go through it, directly into a parking lot. There are only a few hospital staff working right now, but the lot is nearly full. Everyone must be in the basement laboratories. I slide feet first to the ground and around the side of a red Chevy Bel Air, and

I try to slow my breathing down. Bull comes through the door behind me. The flood of residents I had hoped would follow him never comes. He must have told them it was a false alarm and to go back to bed. With the blood all over him, I doubt anyone argued. He has to know I'm close by. He opened the door only moments after I did.

"Come out, come out wherever you are!" he calls. The Bel Air is locked, so I crawl to the front of it, in front of the grill, before Bull's flashlight illuminates the area I was just in. My breathing has slowed, but not enough. I try holding it, but it's only making it worse. I have no control over my lungs, and the thought that they might give me away isn't helping.

"You're from CONIR, aren't you?" he yells. Before I wonder how the hell he'd know that, he answers. "Millen told me all about it. Why else would that guy think my little Carrot Cake is his wife?"

My little Carrot Cake—I should have just let Albert kill him. So what if it might unmake existence? Consequences be damned.

"I killed someone already to protect the project and I killed that guy in Carrot's room, so what's one more?"

The station wagon I'm crouched by now is old and rusty, but it's unlocked. I pop the door open slowly and get inside without closing the door all the way. I look on top of the visor, praying that movies haven't lied to me and that's the spot where the keys always wait for the person needing to make a getaway. Of course no such luck. Bull's flashlight beam flows through the rear window. He's behind the car, but he doesn't see me. I slide down the seat, trying to fit on the floor, which, because the front seat is the old bench style, is actually not difficult. My hand lands on the floor mat by the accelerator, and I feel a pointy lump underneath. There's the keys.

I take them out and from the floor slide them into the ignition. The car is a stick shift. I've driven a stick before; my dad was one of those dads who insisted that his daughter know how to drive a manual transmission. It's one of my only good memories of him.

I've never driven one with my hands before. I'm going to have to learn quickly.

I turn the key, drop the car into reverse, and hit the gas as hard as I can. The car jerks back, and I roll forward, unable to brace myself as both my hands are on pedals. It only pushes my hand down on the accelerator harder. In an instant I hit the car behind me, but not before hearing the sound I needed to hear.

Bull screams. I hit him.

Gunshots ring out, and glass shatters and falls all around me.

"SHIT! YOU BITCH! PULL UP!" More gunshots. The rearview mirror breaks off, the leather seats pop with holes, and stuffing fills the air. I push the accelerator harder, and he screams more. He drops the gun and uses both hands to futilely but instinctively push against the station wagon. I must have pinned him between the rear of this car and the front of the Bel Air.

I climb up and look out the back of the car. I barely caught him by his leg, but I got him good. He's not moving until I move the car. I shift into first and peel out of the parking lot, and Bull drops to the ground, clutching his mangled leg.

CARROT ENTERED THE CAFETERIA FOLLOWED SLOWLY BY A BLEEDING ALBERT FORRESTER. ON THE FAR SIDE OF THE ROOM WAS AN EXIT. IF HE COULD GET HER TO THAT DOOR, SHE WOULD BE home free. There was a cave in the side of a rock hill that Carol had told him about. When she stayed at the hospital, she would dream of escaping. A few times, she had gotten out and found this cave. It was her safe place, her home. But, inevitably and tragically, every night she'd get there, she'd be forced to choose between going back to the hospital or starving to death. A few times, she'd managed to sneak food out, candy bars mostly, and those were the times she'd believe she could make it. It never happened though—not until the day she had found Albert on the edge of the woods, bruised and unconscious, babbling about a light that attacked him. That's when all the CONIR visions started. That was the night Carol escaped, the night of that incident.

That was tonight.

Whatever made him blackout that night was out there now. He vaguely remembered a transparent woman standing in the road. She said his name. She became bright light and . . .

Dr. Ford's office. Pain.

Carol.

Whatever was out there, he was going to see it, if he could manage to not bleed to death. First thing's first: he had to get her to that door.

They walked toward the exit together when Albert's equilibrium checked out, and he hit the ground. Carol came back for him and tried her best to help him up. This poor girl, she never deserved this life. He only hoped in those moments they were together, in those moments they were married, that she was really as happy as she said she was. He can't imagine ever smiling again after what she had been through. Yet here she was, strong as ever.

Here she was.

And there she was too.

Carol must have understood the confused look on Albert's face because she stopped trying to lift him and turned around.

There behind her is . . . her.

The other Carol was standing stoically with her eyes closed. They were wearing the same purple pajamas, but this other version of her was carrying the stuffed rabbit she had lost the last time she went to the cave.

The other Carol stood like a statue, until finally reaching out her hand. Albert and Carol didn't move, still not believing what they were seeing. She wanted something. She was reaching for something. Carol stepped away from Albert slowly.

"No," he said, but he couldn't keep himself off the floor and definitely couldn't stop her.

"It's OK," said Carol, not really believing it herself.

Carol approached the other Carol slowly, carefully. Her eyes still weren't open, but her hand was still outstretched. She didn't move otherwise. Carol reached out her hand as well and grasped the other's hand. Instantly, the other's eyes opened. That wasn't the most startling thing to happen.

The room lit up.

The room was full of people.

The people were all from different times, from different timelines. Some of them were eating food, some were smoking pot with flashlights, some were building the room they were standing in, some were tearing it down, some were hunting for food in the woods before the hospital was built, some were hunting for food in the woods long after it was gone. If they knew what they were looking for, they would have seen Emily and Allison crouched by the door they were heading toward.

As quickly as it began, it was over. Carol had let go, and all that remained was the other Carol, with her eyes now open.

"OK," said Carol to the other Carol. The other Carol nodded and disappeared slowly.

She turned back to Albert, who had just gotten to his knees. She smiled at him sadly.

"Not that way," she said, as she helped him up. Together they went back into the hospital.

Bull screamed in rage and pain as he regained his feet. Blind fury had taken over. He didn't give a shit about anything but killing that bitch and then killing Carrot and killing anyone who tried to stop him. He reached down, trying to keep all the pressure on his good leg, and grabbed the gun off the ground. He stood back up and hobbled to the rear door of the hospital. His leg was broken.

He didn't care.

The rooms were empty. Nurses must've heard the crash and the gunshots. They probably evacuated everyone. Good, less people to get in the way. Adrenaline was lessening the pain, but his leg wasn't working the way he was used to. He limped down the hallway, covered in blood, and got back to Carol's room, craving the sound of her begging for her life. Carol Emerson was gone, and a trail of blood went out of the room. The dead body he was expecting was decidedly missing.

Good, he thought, I get to kill him again.

Carol led Albert to the east fire door that emptied out of the back of the hospital and into the woods. The night air was cooler than she had anticipated. Albert shivered, probably because he was going into shock, but otherwise he seemed to have a second wind. Carol knew now what was coming. She knew this next part. She was going to hate this next part very much.

She ran out the back of the hospital into the woods. The hill sloped down and curved east toward the road. Once she got there, she'd be home free.

Albert caught his breath and watched Carol run toward the woods. "Wait for me!" he cried, and she stopped. He knew he was holding her up, and he couldn't stand it. He took a deep breath, and he promised to hurt later.

Albert ran as fast as he could to get to Carol and picked her up. They'd make the road together.

"HEY, STOP!" a woman yelled from behind them.

Albert turned to see Emily Hunter standing in a window above them, in what looked like Carol's room. She must've lost Bull and was trying to get them to regroup. He couldn't wait for her long. He stared at her, and he couldn't tell whether it was the loss of blood or not, but she didn't look right. She looked . . . transparent.

Bull was about to begin the long limp back to the parking lot when he heard the voice too. He thought it came from Carol's room, but he literally just walked out of it and it was empty. He tried the room next door. It was empty too, but out of the window, he saw something move.

He opened the window as quietly as he could, and in the moonlight, he saw a figure holding a little girl. It was the man he thought he killed. From the amount of blood all over him, it was obvious he barely failed.

He wouldn't this time.

The man was looking up at the window next to him with Carol in his arms. Carol wasn't; she was looking directly at Bull. She knew he was there, and she didn't say a word.

"Emily, what are y—"

Bull fired; direct hit. Blood and skull and brain burst out of his head, and Albert hit the ground. Carol screamed and hit the ground as well, falling from the dead man's arms. Bull laughed and kept firing, as Carol got up and ran as fast as she could deeper into the woods.

Reese burst into the room to see Bull covered in blood and laughing as he shot a gun at someone or something in the forest. Since his promotion, Bull had gotten worse. He was tolerable before, now he was a one-man wrecking ball. The scene in front of Reese was pure insanity.

"STOP! What the hell are you doing?" screamed Reese.

He still didn't stop shooting.

"Stop, or I'm going to Millen," Reese said, pulling Bull from the window, but in an instant, Bull spun on him and had him pinned against the wall with the hot gun barrel burning the flesh under his chin.

"I wouldn't," Bull said with a sick grin. He held the orderly there, staring into his eyes, daring him to move, as if waiting for the big, strong man to cry.

"Fine. Jesus Christ, Bull," said Reese.

Bull lowered the weapon and limped toward the fire exit.

I can finally breathe again. I make the turn from the hospital to Stone Road and head east. I need to get back to town, to the police. I can't take Altman alone. That's when I hear the gunshots. They sound like they're coming from up at the hospital, and my heart sinks. If Albert was dead, who was Bull shooting at? It had to be Carol. I start to cry, a mix of coming down from the adrenaline and the raw emotion of the man I just dined-and-dashed with being shot to death. If Bull got Carol, then who knows what Albert and I coming back to 1970 had screwed up? I'm sure the universe will probably collapse before I make it back to Blue Water. I squint through the hole that used to be the windshield of the station wagon. For the first time, I realize I'm not squinting because of the wind blowing in my eyes, but because the headlights aren't on and the moonlight is the only thing lighting the road. Cars in 2015 turn them on automatically; back here in 1970, you have to turn them on manually. I reach to the left of the steering wheel and pull the light switch—just in time to see a young, crying boy in the road, just in time to hear the sickening thud.

I slam on the brakes, and all the adrenaline rushes back, along with a fresh wave of nausea—and something else: *déjà vu*. I just hit a little kid with a car. I'm not sure why I feel *déjà vu*. I've definitely never done this before.

I jump out of the car and rush behind me. The red glow of the taillights don't make anything look any better. He's not moving.

"Oh Jesus, oh Jesus" is all I can manage to say. I feel for a pulse, and he's got one, so that means no CPR, right? I can't remember the rules. I can't remember what I'm supposed to do. Don't move him, I know that one, don't move him. Every first aid class I've ever had to sit through blurs together. Check if he's breathing; he is. OK, now what? Call for help—but there won't be a cell phone tower up here for another thirty years, and I don't want to attract too much attention out here. What the fuck do I do? What the fuck do I do?

I feel a hand on my shoulder, and I instantly spin and jump away from it, falling onto the road.

It's Carrot.

More accurately, it's Carol Emerson.

"I'll stay with him," she says. "Someone at the hospital heard gunshots and called the police. They're on their way. They're bringing two ambulances. They'll take us to Dr. Ford, and he'll be OK."

She's so sure and confident that I almost just believe her without question. "How do you know all that?"

"She showed me everything," she answers. "Albert is dead, but he knew he would be. You can't be here when the police get here."

"But what do I do? How do I get home from here?"

The sirens—I can hear them now, and they're close.

"Go. Now," she says.

And so I do.

He started shaking, but she held his hand and wiped the hair out of his face. She could see the older man's face in this young boy. The older man had been . . . kind. He was . . .

The sirens got louder.

He was . . . dead, right?

Flashing lights turned the corner from Morrow Road to Stone. They came closer, and Carol waved down one of the ambulances.

Who was the older man? And who was this poor kid?

How did she get here? She remembered Bull opening her door. After that . . .

The EMT jumped out of the front seat, followed shortly by another who opened the back of the ambulance.

What day was it?

"What happened?" Carol had no idea. She had lost time again.

"I don't know, I just found him here," she answered, not exactly sure where "here" was.

The EMT's carefully put young Albert Forrester on the stretcher and placed him in the back of the ambulance. They kindly offered to let his little friend ride along.

THIRTY-FIVE

GUTTA CAVAT LAPIDEM, NON VISED SAEPE CANENDO

Albert Forrester raised the small black tape recorder to his mouth: "September the 16, 1987. Subject designated AP trial number twenty-four." He stood in the white room, and in the center, CONIR stood, already pulsing.

Boom. Boom. Boom.

He noticed Abigail's face. She looked terrified, as well she should be. Every time they've done this, Abigail has needed a week in isolation just to calm back down. The old woman smelled like piss. She always smelled like piss. It always took a day for that smell to dissipate from this room. He hated when Abigail was up, but he knew she showed the most promise. And for some reason, she was chosen by . . .

Her.

He saw himself shaving.

He saw the hospital in ruins.

He saw the Water Street Café.

He saw Emily.

"Albert?"

And it was over. Dr. Millen stood in the room with him. "Are you OK, kid?"

He hated when Millen called him "kid." He was a few years away from thirty now. It felt like disrespect, but he knew it was Millen's way of being assertive. He knew Millen was usually in charge, usually the big dog, but in this room, Albert Forrester was king. Millen was usually struggling to just keep up. The fact that Millen felt threatened at all by Forrester was respect enough.

"I'm fine," Forrester replied. The visions had stopped.

It wasn't the first time this had happened.

Millen patted him hard on the shoulder, not really convinced, and made his way to the observation room. Forrester blinked hard, cleared his throat, and then continued into his recorder: "CONIR pulsating at an iteration of approximately 1.5 bps . . ."

"Please don't," said Abigail.

Forrester sighed. She interrupted his train of thought. He took another second to collect his thoughts and shot her a hard stare. She didn't speak again.

"Subject AP will make contact with symbols Alpha eighteen, K nine, Charlie fourteen, J seven . . ." He looked over the clipboard in his hand. "The fifth symbol will act as the variable. Today's test will be . . . M five." He stopped the recorder and put it into his pocket and then turned to Abigail. "Ready?"

"I don't want to do this," she said.

Why was this always a fight? "Would you rather go back to isolation for three weeks?" he said. She started to cry.

It wasn't the first time this had happened.

"Look, Abigail, the quicker you do this the quicker . . ."

She was here again.

Across the room, Forrester saw Emily. She stood there like a statue, her eyes closed. They were always closed.

It wasn't the first time this had happened.

Emily pointed to the rock. "Your turn now," she said.

Abigail stared at Forrester, not seeing what he saw. The observation room came to life as Millen and the other scientists came over the loudspeaker, asking what the hold up was. Forrester heard none of it. He took off his lead apron, set down his clipboard, walked up to the rock, and touched it very specifically.

Bright white light. Pain.

And Albert woke up screaming.

Carol woke up next to him and grabbed his arm. "You OK?" she managed to mumble. He smiled. It seemed it was his turn to have the nightmare tonight. Her grip on his arm was tight. She was trying to come across as comforting, but he knew she was making sure he didn't run off.

"Just a dream. I'm here, I promise." In the years he'd been having his "episodes," they had come up with that: "I'm here, I promise." He made sure to say it if he knew where he was. If he didn't say it, she knew he wasn't aware and was in a fugue state. It was like their safe word.

"Go back to sleep then," she said, but he was up. It was five in the morning, might as well get started.

He walked into the bathroom and took a shower. The nightmares always made him sweat. He took a few extra minutes to let the water run off his head and breathe in the steam. He felt his body relax.

He wiped off the mirror and lathered his face, turning the water on low so he wouldn't wake up Carol. He dragged the blade across his cheek.

He saw himself shaving.

He stopped; he's seen this before. Then he shook it off. Of course he had seen it before, he's been shaving since he was sixteen.

He got dressed, combed his hair, and kissed his wife goodbye. She stirred slowly.

"Have a good day," she said without opening her eyes.

"You too."

"What do you think about pork chops tonight?" she asked. Nothing sounded better.

"I love it," he replied.

"I love you," she said, still motionless.

He smiled. "I love you too. Go back to sleep."

He didn't have to tell her twice.

The bell rung over the door as Albert stepped into the Water Street Café. Annie looked up to see him sit down at the counter. He was surprised to still see her there. She was due any second.

"Same as always?" she asked. He nodded as if the question was even necessary. Two pancakes, eggs scrambled hard, a side of bacon, and a black coffee—it wasn't officially morning without them. He picked up the Sunday paper to the large headline Reagan Criticizes Central American Peace Plan, and he flipped to the back. No one had touched the crossword yet. It was going to be a good day after all.

Annie dropped off the coffee first, and Albert looked up to see her glowing face. "You got a spare pen?" he asked. She handed one over from behind her ear. He nodded toward her painfully large-looking stomach. "You and Walt pick out a name yet?"

She grinned. Only the fiftieth time she's answered that question. "Leah," she said.

Albert nodded approvingly. "I like it. What if it's a boy?"

"It's not," she said.

"You're so sure?" he asked.

"Absolutely."

"But what if?"

She sighed. "If it is a boy, and she isn't . . . we'll probably name him after my dad, Peter."

Perfect, he thought. "He would have liked that."

She smiled sadly. "I think so too. But it's not going to happen."

Albert laughs before going back to his crossword, and Annie poured a cup for the middle-aged woman sitting down the counter. His breakfast came out shortly afterward, and his day began. He looked outside the front window to the street while taking the first bite of his pancake. It looked like it would be a sunny day today, and thankfully it hadn't started getting cold out yet. It felt like it was only a week or so away before they'd have to bundle themselves up, and the tops of the trees were already starting to turn orange. But today was going to be beautiful.

The older woman at the counter was smiling at him. He hadn't noticed that he was grinning so much, and his smile must have been infectious.

"Morning," she said.

"Morning," he replied. He knew her from somewhere, church or something. Everyone in this town knew everyone else, but he was having a hard time placing her name. That bothered him. He used to be so good at names, then he took the medication and he felt slow. Everything had dragged.

He hadn't taken it in three weeks. Most everything had come back: the dreams, the visions, everything, seemingly but this poor woman's name.

"I'm sorry, ma'am, I know you, don't I?" he asked.

"Maybe," I say. "I'm not sure." This is the first time I've seen Albert in seventeen years. The strange part is that he's technically younger than he was that day, and now I'm almost fifty-five.

"You look very familiar," he says. I'm not sure how that's possible, but he told me all those years ago that he had visions. I saw his wife as a kid; maybe he saw me? Thinking about that night reminds me, and I look at Annie. She's still wearing my watch.

Looks like she forgot about banning me.

"Well, if you think of it, let me know," I say, getting up.

"I will," he says.

"Seriously, Albert, try to remember," I say. I let it hang there a moment, and I leave. I need him tonight. Tonight's the big night.

He watched her walk out the door and turn the corner past the window. Then she was gone.

"Who was that?" asked Annie.

Albert thought a moment. "No idea." He wasn't being entirely honest.

He turned his attention back to the crossword. His hand was clutching the pen hard. All over the crossword and the surrounding area he had unknowingly written one word over and over: CONIR.

It wasn't the first time this had happened.

Albert's shift was almost over. He had waited to stock the shelves until the very end of the day. It seemed to make the time go by quicker. The cans lined up nicely. He liked that, like everything had its time.

Place, everything had its place.

The ringing had started. He quickly looked around to find the store was empty. He'd long since learned the warning signs of having these visions. He also learned to try to keep them quiet and to try to make sure he was alone. It was hard enough to explain to Carol, he didn't want to have to . . .

Carol, she was here—only she was different than she was this morning. Now she was eight years old, but her eyes were still closed.

"Save me," Carrot said.

"I'm trying," replied Albert. "The symbols, tell me what they mean."

"You'll know tonight."

"Tonight? What's tonight?"

Carrot smiled. "Tonight's the big night."

The bell at the counter rang, ending the ringing in Albert's ears and bringing him back to reality. Carrot was gone. He felt cold, like he had never been warm in his life. She had told him about Bull. She told him everything. Albert wanted nothing more than to kill Altman, but the son of a bitch was mayor now. Besides, the damage had been done. But if what Carrot had been showing him all these years was true, then maybe the damage could be undone?

He wanted to tell his wife. He wanted to be as honest with her as she was with him. He wanted to tell her what he thought he was being told by his visions, but she'd been through enough without him bringing it all back up. Besides, he was insane enough as it was.

The bell at the counter rang again, and Albert made his way to the front of the store, apologizing the entire way there: "Sorry, it's just me today. The other two clerks are out with the flu. Although, between you and me, I think they're out with each other." He laughed. Albert tended to try to diffuse situations before they escalated.

Standing at the counter was the woman from the diner. She had a package of hot dogs and buns.

"Hey, it's you again," she said. "You remember me yet?"

"No, but you know me. Why don't you tell me how?" Albert wasn't in a mood for games, and this woman was very familiar. He knew he'd seen her in dreams, but she was older now than she appeared then. He didn't know why.

The woman smiled. "What makes you think I know you?"

"You said my name at breakfast. I never introduced myself."

"No. No, you didn't," she said. "But you don't remember me?" He started to feel the anger rise in him.

"If I said the word 'CONIR' to you, would that mean anything?" I ask. The surprised look on his face tells me everything. "I'll take that as a yes," I say.

"How . . .?" he mumbles.

"How, I don't know. I'm hoping to find out tonight."

"What's tonight?"

I've waited seventeen years for tonight. Ever since I hit this poor guy with my car out on Stone Road. I could never get back into the CONIR room until the hospital eventually shut down from lack of funding about five years ago. Once that happened, I had managed to get inside, but the giant metal door was in my way. With no power to the facility, I was at a dead end. But it was finally September 16, 1987. This was the day that I had been waiting for. I pray I didn't wait for nothing.

"Tonight, Albert," I say, "is the big night."

He grabs my arm hard, painfully hard. I was not expecting that.

"What did you say? 'The big night,' why did you say that?"

"What do you mean?" I say trying to pull away. I can't; he's too strong.

"Why did you say 'the big night'?!" He's mad, desperate, furious.

"I don't know. Why? Does that mean something?"

"Why did you say it?" he yells.

"Why does it matter?" I ask.

"Tell me why you said it!"

"You're hurting me, Albert." My hand is starting to go numb.

"You know what I have to do, don't you? To save Carol, you know what I have to do!"

"Let me go!" I scream.

"Tell me what I have to do!" His fingertips have gone pale, he's squeezing so hard.

"Calm down!"

"Tell me, Emily!"

I heard it. He heard it too. He lets go and catches his breath while I rub the feeling back into my arm.

"Emily Hunter," he says, still in the process of steadying himself. "How do I know your name?"

"I don't know," I say. "You and me, we know lots of things we shouldn't know."

His eyes well up with tears, and I instantly understand. I've been in his exact same position. The visions are overwhelming enough, but paired with the fact that everyone thinks you're insane and continuously getting small clues that you're not, it's too much. He leans down on the countertop and drops his head.

"Can you help me? Can you help me save Carol? I need to stop him from hurting her. I just don't know how."

I put my hand on his shoulder. "I can," I say. "But first I need you to help me."

"What do you need me to do?" he asks.

I smile. "I need you to ring up these hot dogs."

She thought about calling at six, when he didn't come home, but she let herself believe he was just running late. She waited until seven to put the pork chops in the refrigerator. At eight, she called.

"Blue Water Police Department," the voice answered over the phone.

"Hey Walt, it's Carol."

A momentary pause over the phone. He doesn't need to ask; she doesn't need to answer.

"We'll start looking," he says sadly.

I haven't done this since I was a kid. The fire glows under the stars. It's such a peaceful night. Inside though, my stomach is full of butterflies. This should be right. I hope this is right.

I take a bite of the hot dog, and it burns the inside of my mouth. I breathe through it, wishing I had remembered to bring a beer. Suddenly a small flash of light goes off to my left, and I close my eyes and breathe. I was right. Finally, some answers.

"There you are," I say to myself.

He lies on the ground, not moving. I blow on the hot dog and take another bite. That one was better. My eyes were still watering a little from the last bite when he suddenly jumps. He flips over, trying to focus but obviously completely disoriented. He's trying to get to his feet long before his feet are ready to listen to his brain.

"Easy," I say. "Take your time."

He sees me for the first time and falls back to his side. He rubs his eyes and looks around himself: nothing but night and woods.

"Now what?" he asks.

"What do you mean?"

"You said it was my turn, so now what?"

I'm definitely not following. "Who do you think I am?" I ask.

He looks at me harder now. "Sorry, I thought you were someone . . . younger."

I feign offense. "Thanks," I say.

He tries to get to his feet again, and this time I rest my hand on him. He's not strong enough to get it off yet. "Wait until you're ready. Just relax."

"Do you know me?" he asks.

"That's kind of a loaded question," I answer. Apparently, from the scowl he gives me, that answer isn't good enough. So strange that I saw that exact same scowl hours ago, only on a different face.

"Your name is Albert Forrester. You're the lead on the CONIR Project at Riverview Psychiatric."

His expression goes from shock to confusion as he tries to cover himself. "I don't know what you're talking about," he says.

"I was hoping we could just skip this part," I say. I reach for his pocket and pull out the tape recorder from his pocket, tap rewind, and then hit play:

" . . .bject AP will make contact with symbols Alpha eighteen, *K* nine, Charlie fourteen, *J* seven . . .The fifth symbol will act as the vari—" I stop the tape.

"AP, that's Abigail Pipkin. She was in the room when you touched the stone." The shocked look is back, and Forrester must know there's no point in lying.

"How did you know about that?"

"The recorder? I saw you put it in your pocket in a security tape of your disappearance."

"My disappearance? That just happened."

"Well I saw the tape seventeen years ago—or twenty-eight years from now. It's a matter of perspective, I guess."

He gets it now. "You touched the stone too. You travelled through time." I nod. "OK, where did I end up?"

"It's September 16, 1987."

He frowns. "That's the same day I left. Something went wrong. I need to get back to the project and look at my notes."

"It's gone," I say. "All of it shut down with the hospital in 1982."

That stopped him. "Wait, how is that possible?"

"Forrester," I say, "after waiting here for seventeen years, I was hoping you could tell me."

THE HOSPITAL WAS DARK AND COVERED IN WEEDS. A FEW OF THE WINDOWS WERE BROKEN OUT. ALBERT HAD BEEN UP HERE A FEW TIMES—AND A FEW TIMES MORE THAN HE REMEMBERED. IN ALL THE TIMES HE'D HAD DREAMS OF THIS PLACE, HE KNEW THERE WAS A BASEMENT, HE KNEW THERE WAS A GIANT STEEL DOOR, HE KNEW ABOUT THE LATCH, AND HE KNEW ABOUT THE WHITE ROOM. HE JUST NEVER FOUND THE STAIRCASE DOWNSTAIRS. THE PAPER EMILY GAVE HIM SOLVED THAT PROBLEM. NOW HE KNEW EXACTLY WHERE HE WAS GOING. HE FOLDED THE PAPER BACK UP AND WALKED THROUGH THE FRONT DOOR.

"So," Forrester says, pinching the bridge of his nose, "you and me—the other me, the one from here—met back in time, in 1970. The other me dies saving some little girl—"

"Carol Emerson, you ended up marrying her," I interrupt.

"*He* ended up marrying her. Somehow I never end up working on CONIR, the project loses funding, the hospital shuts down, and here we are in an alternate timeline. You both somehow changed the future into this."

"Well, for me, yours is the alternate timeline and everything here is correct. But, essentially, yes."

He sits still, thinking for a solid minute. "No, we're missing something because that doesn't make any sense."

"You're telling me," I say.

"Have you heard of the Grandfather Paradox?"

I had. I hadn't been sitting still for seventeen years. I'd tried researching time travel theories and concepts. Unfortunately, it was a lot slower without Google, and no one but this man knew anything about CONIR.

"Yeah, basically, you can't go back and kill your grandfather in the past because then he never has kids, and you're never born, and you never go back and kill him."

"Right, you can't unmake your own existence," he says. "Only it works the other way too: you can't go back and cause yourself to exist. And the only reason your Albert exists is because he went back in time from this timeline and subsequently created the timeline he left from. If he hadn't gone back in time and gotten the little girl out of the hospital, he wouldn't even exist. So there's something else we're missing." He pauses again, and this time he's silent for at least two minutes. Then: "What happened the minute the timeline split?"

I furrow my brow. "How would I know that?"

"You'd feel it. Anyone affected by it would feel it. The timeline would go out of sync, and people splitting off on different branches of the timeline would be experiencing both timelines nearly simultaneously until they were far enough apart that each version of yourself only felt one timeline. It would only last a few seconds, but for those few seconds, you'd be living in the current time as well as a fraction of a second in the past or future. So everything you were experiencing would feel as if you were also remembering."

"You're describing *déjà vu*?" I ask.

He nods. "We all experience it, usually when we make some insignificantly small yet terribly important decision: left turn or right turn, red tie or blue tie. Something about that moment changes our lives forever and starts us down one of a series of different timelines. Red tie gets you noticed by the boss in a crowd, who picks you for a job that you fail at, getting you fired, you find a new job in another state and meet your spouse. Blue tie gets you looked over, and you go about your day and die single after getting hit by a bus in your hometown."

I suddenly think about my life and imagine how many times I've had that feeling. One instance pops into mind, and it also had to do with neckties.

"You told me . . . well, *other* you told me about a time you brought a tie to your dad at the hospital. He got really mad, and you stormed off into the woods. It was the night you met Carol, you saw a light. . . Any of that sound familiar?"

He squints his eyes. "I remember the tie. I brought it to him, he yelled at me. I went home, and he came home that night after work and woke me up to apologize. He told me he was under a lot of stress at work and that he shouldn't have taken it out on me," he says. "No little girl, no light."

"That's because in this timeline, I hit you with a car on the road behind the hospital. I felt it then, that feeling, *déjà vu*."

He rubs his chin knowingly. "Then that's something. The other Albert didn't cause this timeline at all," he says. "You did this."

He held the map in his hand and studied the symbols crudely sketched on the bottom of the paper: three wavy lines; two circled, different-sized pluses on the bottom; an M; a circle with two curved lines coming off the top. He'd seen them all before. He'd drawn them in notebooks over and over. The fifth one was different. He didn't recognize it. It looked like a capital X with an umlaut. Emily had told him that was the most important one.

He stepped into the isolation wing and found the windowless door. So much easier when you know what you're looking for.

"What does it matter if it's him or me? It's still impossible according to you."

Forrester shakes his head in frustration. "There must be something you're doing. Somehow this timeline isn't collapsing in on itself, which means there's something you're doing to keep it open. The other Albert is dead. Even if he's alive right now, we know where his part ends. His loop is set in stone."

Stone.

"He's there now, at the stone, at CONIR?" Forrester asks.

"Tonight's the night he goes back," I say. Albert had said he thought it was 1987 when he met me all those years ago. It only made sense he went back tonight.

"We have to get there. There's something you need to tell him before he goes back," says Forrester.

I can't imagine what that could possibly be. "Sure," I say, but I'm not convinced. Forrester is not Albert, even though they wear the same face. This man worked with Millen. He had become cruel and malicious, and exposed people to CONIR for years without a care for their well-being.

I don't trust him. I never trusted him. I just need to know what he knows.

When we make it to the hospital, Forrester goes pale, as if now was the first time he could let himself believe what I had told him. There was no denying it: the hospital was in advanced stages of decay. It wasn't the one he showed up to work at this morning. I could see it all sink in for him.

"I can't believe Millen would let this happen."

"Millen's dead," I say, with no small satisfaction in my voice. "Not exactly sure how it happened, but right about the same time he died, the hospital shut down and a man named Henry Altman got really rich."

"Who's Henry Altman?" he asks. I wave his question away. It's way too long of a story.

The plan had been to vet Forrester; to see what he knows. Albert, to be safe, was to go to the hospital and wait in the basement. All of this hinged on me getting Forrester to come to the hospital with me because no matter how much we did know, no matter how hard I had tried, there was still the not-so-small matter of the large steel door blocking our way to CONIR. Because Albert had shown up in the past, I knew there was a way through it, but in all the years since the hospital had gone down, I had never figured it out. If anyone knew, it was Forrester. He had to be the way through, which is how I knew tonight was the night all of this was going to happen. This was the big night.

Which is why I couldn't believe it when Forrester and I turned the blind corner at the end of the staircase to see the CONIR door completely open and Albert nowhere in sight.

"How did he get it open? It's been sealed for years."

"There's a mechanical latch hidden at the back of a cabinet in one of the sterile rooms that unlocks the door. It's there in case of power failure."

"How the hell did he know that?" I ask, completely frustrated. If he knew that, I wouldn't have had to bring Forrester.

"He knew that because I know that," he says. "I think because we're so close to this thing, that somehow our existences cross over, almost like feedback. It explains why people thought you and Albert were insane."

"So, did you ever see visions?" I ask. His silence is all the answer I need.

"This way," he says, leading me through the CONIR door, into the dark hallways beyond. There's emergency lighting that must've been triggered somehow when Albert opened the door, but it's barely candlelight. Some of the bulbs aren't working at all. The air in here is stale, full of dust. There's no spray paint on the walls or broken glass though. The vandals never got to the basement, and even if they had, they wouldn't have gotten through the door.

"OK," I say. "If I'm really the one keeping the loop open, how am I doing it? What could I possibly be doing to keep the universe from falling apart?"

Forrester scratches the back of his head. "I don't know, but whatever it is, you're doing it now." He pauses to look around the darkened hallways, then turns to me. "When paradoxes occur in thought problems, they operate under the assumption that all our choices are locked. The Grandfather Paradox, for example, only works that way because when the loop occurs, if you go back and kill your grandfather the first time, you'll do it on every iteration of the loop. The reason is because everything only happens, in actuality, once. Everything about the timeline he dies in and everything about the timeline he lives in is completely identical on every pass of the loop, down to the position of every single atom in the entire universe. If somehow that weren't the case, that might be enough."

He stops now, and I can tell he's in his own head, patting his own back for his brilliance. "So say I took an infant and I went back in time five years. I hand that kid to myself in 1982, and I say, 'In 1987, when you get in the time machine, bring this kid with you.' But say my young self misunderstands and doesn't bring back the infant to his younger self, but brings the same kid, the same literal kid, who is now five. Then, instead of handing off an infant, he hands off a five-year-old. The same five years pass, and now he brings back a ten-year-old, a fifteen-year-old, etcetera. See? The loop would be just different enough every time. Do you understand?"

"No," I say. He frowns. I guess I'm not his usual audience.

"It doesn't matter, we're here."

I look ahead to see the door to the observation room to CONIR. It's open. We both walk inside quietly. The lights barely illuminate the stone in the center of the room and the man standing next to it searching for symbols.

"Thank God, we're not too late," he says.

"OK," I say. "What do I need to tell him?"

Forrester lets the question roll across his face before remembering that he had told me Albert was missing a key piece of information. In that moment, I know I was right not to trust him. There wasn't anything Albert needed to be told.

"Don't touch the stone!" Forrester yells out. Albert jumps at the sound of a voice down here with him and backs away from CONIR.

"If he doesn't, our whole timeline doesn't exist," I say. Forrester doesn't even flinch, and I suddenly wish more than anything I had known about the secret latch. "What are we doing here?" I say, all my mistrust pouring out in my tone.

He obviously picks up on it and turns to meet my glare. "What has to be done," he says, before entering the chamber. I tear in right behind him.

"Forrester, stop!" I yell.

A perplexed Albert stands in the dingy white room, watching himself and me walk through the door from the observation room. "I did," he says.

"Not you," I say to him. I can tell this is going to get confusing really quick.

"What are you trying to do, Albert?" says Forrester.

"Who are you?" he asks.

"I'm you, Albert. I'm the correct you."

"If you're me," says Albert, "then you know what I'm trying to do."

"You can't," says Forrester. "This timeline, everything in it, shouldn't exist. It's all wrong. It's too dangerous to the universe. Emily has found a way to keep it open somehow, but it has to stop. It has to close."

"What do you mean 'close?'" I ask, suddenly aware that all the hair on my arm is standing up. There's a ringing in my ears and, behind it . . . voices.

Forrester ignores me. "Step away from the artifact, Albert."

More people are talking, and the shadows in the room feel like they're moving. I've seen this before, when the hospital was full of ghosts. They're waking up now.

"What is that?" a frightened Albert cries.

"That's us, Albert. We're too close. We create a problem for reality. The same person in the same place twice. You need to leave this room and get far away. I'll use the stone to get back to my universe, and everything will be fine."

CONIR begins vibrating almost too fast to see, but loud enough to hear. The room starts shaking too. More voices are in the room now as the ghosts start moving everywhere. I see scientists walking in and out of the observation room. I see hospital patients being forced to touch the stone. I see them haul the damn thing in. Everything is falling apart and unraveling.

I've seen this before too.

"Emily?" Albert asks. It's obvious he doesn't trust this other version of himself either. I look to Forrester and back to Albert.

"Touch the stone, Albert. Go."

"No!" screams Forrester, and the floor cracks. CONIR starts pulsing again without being touched.

Boom. Boom. Boom.

"Don't listen to him, Albert," I say. Then I turn to the same eyes on Forrester: "You're going to kill us. All six billion people in this timeline die if he doesn't go back."

"You won't die, Emily. You won't have existed in this timeline. You'll still be alive in mine. The universe is unstable as long as this timeline is allowed to persist. It needs to end!"

"Touch the stone, Albert." And he's just about to, until Forrester opens his mouth again.

"You're going to die back there," he says.

Albert looks up in shock at his doppelganger, then to me with pain in his eyes. He trusted me, I know that. Goddammit.

"She didn't tell you that, did she?" Forrester says with a grin. "In the past, you die saving that little girl."

The glass begins to split in the observation window. Dust is falling down from the ceiling, and the screaming of patients forced on the stone is unnerving. None of that registers with us. "I die?" asks Albert, directly to me.

I want to tell him something, anything to be comforting. But the sheer disappointment in his eyes is too much for me to look at. I turn my head away.

"She knew," continues Forrester, gloating, "that she was sending you to your death. That's why she didn't tell you. She thought if she told you that you were a dead man, you wouldn't go."

Albert stares at me, but I'm too ashamed to look back. Then he says another three words I know I'll never unhear: "She was wrong."

Albert reaches up to touch the stone.

The three snakes.

The short man and the tall man.

The bird.

The devil.

And Forrester tackles him.

And instantly all hell breaks loose.

Every silhouette in the room grabs their head and screams as if they were in extreme pain. The walls and roof of the white room start rippling with electricity and sparks as if someone had thrown a fork in the microwave. A furious wind tears through the room cycling around CONIR, which is vibrating so violently that it starts to glow with heat. And two men with the same face are beating the hell out of each other.

If it was bad when they were too close, they definitely weren't supposed to touch.

Albert throws a punch directly into Forrester's mouth, dropping him back, but not loosening his grip. Forrester then pulls Albert toward him with that momentum and wraps his arms around his chest, squeezing while Albert squirms. The wind picks up even more, and the screaming gets even louder. Albert reverses pressure and forces Forrester back into the observation window that finishes shattering upon impact.

The walls of the white room start warping inward, and the pipes in the ceiling burst out. The cinder block walls of the exterior of the observation room crumble through the now open window into the room with us. The big parts hit the ground, but the dust gets swept up into the air current, blinding me right before the pebbles hit my skin like they were shot out of a BB gun. It feels like getting stung by wasps over and over.

"Stop touching!" I scream over all the chaos, but I can barely hear myself. Forrester rolls over on top of Albert and starts choking him. His back is to me. Now is my chance.

I jump on Forrester's back and wrap my arms around his jaw. I squeeze harder than I think is possible. Forrester is now worried about me and lets go of Albert. The instant he does, the screaming stops and the wind dies down. But the ghosts are still here, the stone is still shaking, though it's not glowing anymore. It's still not OK in the white room.

Forrester shakes and twists trying to get me off, but I wrap my legs around him and lock them together. He's not getting away. He starts moving quickly, as if he's going to try to crush me into the wall, but he trips on the cinder block chunks that litter the floor, and he drops on top of me. The impact knocks the wind out of me, but I don't let go. He tries throwing an elbow into my ribs. It hurts, but not as much as it would if he had all his strength. He's starting to fade. Within a minute, he stops moving and I roll out from under him. Albert is sitting up against the far wall, trying to stay as far away as he can.

"Thanks," he says with a raspy voice. He rubs his throat, trying to make it feel normal again. I help him up.

"I'm sorry. I'm so sorry I didn't tell you."

He shakes his head. "I wouldn't have told me either."

"You're still going to go?" I ask, not really believing it.

"I have to stop him. Altman, I have to stop him from hurting Carol. If I don't make it back, then . . ." He doesn't finish his sentence. He doesn't have to. I'm face to face with the bravest, most selfless man I've ever met. "What about you?" he asks, trying to break the tension.

"Me? I just have to figure out how to stop the universe from collapsing."

He smirks. "Good luck with that." He reaches for the stone and instantly pulls away, shaking his finger. "Shit! It's still hot."

"Do them all at once," I say. "It'll only burn for a second."

He takes a deep breath and lets it out, rubbing all his fingers into his palms, mentally preparing to burn himself, mentally preparing to travel through time, mentally preparing to die.

"Wait," I say. "When you get there, I'll be there too. I'll be younger. I won't be awake. I have a gun tucked into my waistband behind my backpack. Make sure you get it from me before I fully know what's going on. I'll be in a daze for a while. You'll have plenty of time."

"Got it," he says. "I guess I'll see you later then."

"Yeah," I smile. "Or earlier."

He quickly touches the stone at all five points. I see his face wince in pain, and then he's gone. The room silences and is still.

It's done.

"You stupid bitch," says Forrester from behind me. He's standing again, regaining his composure, and his face is wincing in pain too, making the same expression I just saw Albert make. His is from the massive headache he has to be feeling.

"It's over," I say. "He's gone."

Forrester leans against the crumbled wall, shaking loose the cobwebs. He rubs his face hard, and when his hand comes off, he's got the most wicked smirk I've ever seen.

"Nothing is over, Emily," he says. "I've got twenty-eight years to stop you from using the artifact. I could destroy it right here. I could wait around and stop you when you get to town. Stopping Albert from using CONIR was the most humane way to end this timeline. Hell, I could find you and kill you as a kid."

"You'd kill a little kid?" I ask, as I move into a defensive posture. He doesn't look like he's going to attack me, and from what he's saying, he doesn't really have to.

"It wouldn't be killing a little kid if she's never going to have existed. Why don't you understand that? You aren't supposed to be here."

"No," I say. "I've seen the other side of this coin, the one where your involvement in the CONIR Project leads to the torture and death of dozens of innocent people, where my friend Allison has been broken by your goddamn stone . . ."

Stone.

" . . .Where a little girl is assaulted repeatedly by a terrible man before she kills him. Trust me Forrester, *you* aren't supposed to be here."

"Well then," he says, "it looks like we have a stalemate." He moves quickly, and suddenly I can't see. I'm breathing in dust, the dust he threw in my face from the cinder wall he was leaning on. I start coughing as I try to clear my eyes when I feel the first punch across my left cheekbone. I've been in fights before, a few at Sandy Shores. That is the hardest I've ever been hit in my life—that is, until I feel the second punch in the right side of my rib cage.

I hit the ground hard as I still try to wipe the debris out of my eyes. I can finally see out of my right eye, and I could probably see out of my left if my cheek weren't already swelling over it. He's on me fast.

"Don't struggle, just give up. I'll make it quick and painless, I promise. It's the only way." My hand lands on a large shard of glass from the broken window. It's not the only way.

I'm up quickly, and I swing at him, catching him with the glass across his left shoulder. He falls back and clutches at himself, but already I can see the blood start to trickle down his white coat. He looks at me cautiously, but with a burning fury.

"Stay back!" I scream. I swing it at him again, but even as my arm is moving forward, I regret how much I telegraphed this move. I'm off balance, and he can see it plainly. I feel his grip around my wrist, and I drop to one knee as he twists my arm behind my back.

"Drop it!" he yells, but I can't. If I do, this is all over. He's got an arm free and could just take it from me if I stopped wiggling my hand back and forth to cut his fingers every time he tried. If I let go of the glass, he cuts my throat with it. But it's a matter of time; he'll break my arm or dislocate my shoulder. I've still got one foot down, and I press back hard enough to get my other one under me again. I twist against him, and I feel the point of the glass stick him in the bicep. He lets out a shout and loosens his grip enough for me to turn around to face him. I manage to throw my forehead into his nose, and I hear it break. The noise makes me queasy. He reels back, but manages to hold on to my wrist still. The tears have filled his eyes. Now he can't see. I reach down to grab the shard of glass, to switch it to my open hand, and I mentally prepare myself for what I'm about to do. His neck is completely exposed. I get my hand over the glass and pull it free. I'm about to stab him directly in the throat, and I hesitate.

It was all the time he needed.

He kicks my legs out from underneath me, and I hit the ground, his grip still on my wrist. He spins me around, and with his free hand, he grabs a handful of my hair and forces my face into CONIR.

It's still extremely hot, and I didn't know I had the capacity for so much pain.

I scream from a depth I was unaware of. I can feel my skin burning. I can feel it melting. I can feel the flesh burn away to nothing.

"Drop it!" he screams, and I do. I want him to cut my throat to end this. He lets go of my hair to grab the glass, and in that moment I pull forward, toward the stone. He falls off balance, trying not to touch it, and when I pull my face away,

I feel part of it stick and come off of me. I throw my entire weight back into him, and I land on top of him hard.

I flip around toward him. The look on his face as he sees what's left of mine is the last vivid memory I have. The rest is a blur. I know I picked up the cinder block chunk he had tripped over. I know I hit him right between the eyes with it. I know I did it again and again and again, until he finally stopped moving. I wasn't in control in that moment. The pain took over.

And when I finally regain possession of my senses, Forrester is dead.

And I can't stop laughing.

I get it now, and it's hilarious.

I wrap Forrester's head . . . what's left of it, in his lab coat, and I drag him upstairs to the cafeteria.

I ditch the coat in Carrot's secret cave, where no one will find it—no one but me, in twenty-eight years.

Walt Jacoby's shift had just ended nearly two hours late. It was a wild one tonight. People all over town had flooded the station with calls about intruders in their houses or ghosts in their gardens. It was odd, he thought, as he looked up at the sky. The full moon was last week.

He walked up Lake Street alone, on his way to see Annie. She would have something made up for him quickly, and he needed it. He hadn't eaten since before noon, and it was just about ten. He could feel how empty his stomach was. He smiled, wondering if his beautiful and expectant wife remembered that feeling. He tried to think up a joke with that premise. Nothing was coming to him. It was too long of a night for jokes.

Down the road, someone screamed. He wanted to pretend he didn't hear it, but he couldn't. This night would seemingly never end.

He ran down the road wondering if it was another ghost sighting. What he saw when he got there would give him nightmares for years.

Three people were gathered around a fourth: a woman whose clothes were covered in blood, whose face was half swollen beyond recognition and half burned clean off. The woman had fallen to the ground, babbling incoherently and easily in shock. The other people didn't know whether to help or to run.

Jacoby radioed for an ambulance and cleared the bystanders away. When he got close enough to her, he saw just how grotesque the scene was. He forced himself through it.

"Ma'am," he said, "Can you hear me?" She mumbled. "Ma'am, an ambulance in on its way. They'll take you to a hospital." More mumbling. "I need you to focus for me, OK? Do you know what happened? Do you know where you are?" Mumbles. "Can you tell me your name?"

"Abigail," I say. "My name is Abigail Pipkin."

THIRTY-SIX

EPILOGUE

THEY DID ALL they could.

I look into the mirror to see how badly I was scarred. It was pretty brutal. Plastic surgery is going to grow by leaps and bounds by 2015. They basically just staved off infection. I can still see the symbols from CONIR on what's left of my face. They'll be there forever.

The mask they gave me is not great. I'll buy another one someday. It's odd that I already know exactly what it will look like.

I already know a lot that I shouldn't.

I know being in this timeline twice, all the bending of reality I've done, is going to drive me insane. I saw who I thought was Abigail Pipkin before I entered the hospital the very first time. I saw how deteriorated both physically and mentally she was. The last few decades, while I've been living here alone, I've seen Carrot almost every day. I've seen the mask I'm holding in my hands, I've seen all the words I used to, had the same nightmares, the same hallucinations, the same breaks with the world around me. Only now there's context. The solitude is eerily familiar, like being back at Sandy Shores, unable to talk to anyone. I've even started crocheting again and jewelry making, and I continued learning Latin. Now I'll do anything to not have a roaming thought, to not have to face the inevitable: I know where this road ends, and it's going to get a lot worse before Henry Altman eventually puts me out of my misery.

Albert Forrester made a leap he knew he wouldn't come back from, and he did it for one woman. I need to keep this loop going to save the world. Who am I to back out now?

Two days later, I break into the record department at city hall. I know the layout this time, and I am patient. I steal the facesheet for the real Abigail Pipkin, who, without being tortured by CONIR for years, died peacefully in her sleep at Riverview Psychiatric Hospital in 1981. The facesheet lists no next of kin. She was cremated.

I open my closet. Inside on the floor, I find the old red backpack with a thick layer of dust covering it. Inside it are all the things I brought with me: clothes, a toothbrush, my cell phone, the stone.

Stone.

I take it out and look it over. I give myself a minute to really admire it. It's a beautiful piece of black quartz, and it's covered in tiny scratches. I estimate about two hundred of them, like tally marks.

I can't change any more than this. I can't tell my mom, who is 28 right now, that I'm going to be OK. I lived a full life, or at least I will have before I go completely insane and am murdered. The last she heard, the last she will ever know, is that I jumped on a plane and flew off chasing an imaginary friend. The guilt of that is almost unbearable, but it's my burden. There's too much at stake to risk telling her the truth. Like she'd believe it anyway.

I take the tiny chisel I bought on my way home from city hall, and I scratch one more tally before placing the rock on my mantle, where it will sit and wait for Emily Hunter to take it through the loop again and again, making the loop just a little different every time, just different enough.

It's going to kill me, and yet it's the only thing keeping us all alive.

The turntable spins a 45 of Beethoven's *Moonlight Sonata*. I finally know the name of the piece. I sit in the large olive chair and close my eyes while the impatient grandfather clock with the shard missing counts the moments left. And I breathe. And I breathe.

I've been here before.

GRAND PATRONS

Nick Cook
Meghan Strader
Brian Hosler
RJ Naugle
Scott Galeski
Kristen Stotts
Tom Wadlow
Erin Parcell
Nancy Kohlman
Jean Parcell

ABOUT THE AUTHOR

Joseph Parcell was born in Port Huron, Michigan and grew up harboring an obsession with storytelling. He is a graduate of the New York Film Academy, and still makes movies as often as he can. His first novel, Blue Water, was originally designed as a substantial film project, when he came to the realization it would work much better as a book. Hopefully you agree. He is the husband of a beautiful wife, and the father of a beautiful daughter.

He currently lives in East Lansing, Michigan.

INKSHARES

INKSHARES is a reader-driven publisher and producer based in Oakland, California. Our books are selected not by a group of editors, but by readers worldwide.

While we've published books by established writers like *Big Fish* author Daniel Wallace and *Star Wars: Rogue One* scribe Gary Whitta, our aim remains surfacing and developing the new author voices of tomorrow.

Previously unknown Inkshares authors have received starred reviews and been featured in the *New York Times*. Their books are on the front tables of Barnes & Noble and hundreds of independents nationwide, and many have been licensed by publishers in other major markets. They are also being adapted by Oscar-winning screenwriters at the biggest studios and networks.

Interested in making your own story a reality? Visit Inkshares.com to start your own project or find other great books.

Printed in the USA
CPSIA information can be obtained
at www.ICGtesting.com
JSHW022206140824
68134JS00018B/887

9 781947 848566